THE FLOATING WORLD

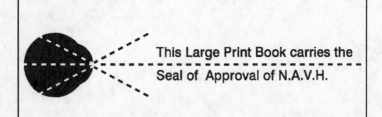

THE FLOATING WORLD

C. MORGAN BABST

THORNDIKE PRESS
A part of Gale, a Cengage Company

GALE
A Cengage Company

Farmington Hills, Mich • San Francisco • New York • Waterville, Maine
Meriden, Conn • Mason, Ohio • Chicago

GALE
A Cengage Company

Thorndike Press® Large Print Bill's Bookshelf.
The text of this Large Print edition is unabridged.
Other aspects of the book may vary from the original edition.
Set in 16 pt. Plantin.

LIBRARY OF CONGRESS CIP DATA ON FILE.
CATALOGUING IN PUBLICATION FOR THIS BOOK
IS AVAILABLE FROM THE LIBRARY OF CONGRESS

ISBN-13: 978-1-4328-4892-7 (hardcover)

Published in 2018 by arrangement with Algonquin Books of Chapel Hill, a division of Workman Publishing for New Orleans

. . .
When the sun refuse to shine
. . .
When the moon turns red with blood
. . .
When the winds begin to howl
. . .
On that Hallelujah day
. . .
When the revolution comes
. . .
When our leaders learn to cry
. . .
When the saints go marching in
Oh, when the saints go marching in
How I want to be in that number
When the saints go marching in.
— TRADITIONAL

Each must be his own hope.
— VIRGIL, *The Aeneid,* Book XI

■ ■ ■ ■

PART ONE:
THE SORROWING
HOUSES

■ ■ ■ ■

FORTY-SEVEN DAYS
AFTER LANDFALL
OCTOBER 15

The house bobbed in a dark lake. The flood was gone, but Cora still felt it wrapped around her waist, its head nestled on her hip. She laid her hands out, palms on its surface, and the drifting hem of her night-shirt fingered her thighs. Under her feet, lake bed slipped: pebbles and grit, mud broken into scales that curled up at their edges. Her legs dragged as she moved under the tilting crosses of the electrical poles, keeping her head tipped up, her mouth open. Her fingers trailed behind her, shirr-ing the water that was air.

Troy's bloated house reeked of flood. Dirt, mildew, algae, the smell of the dead. On the dusty siding, she traced the line of sediment that circled the house, high up where the water had come. Beside the door was the mark of the storm:

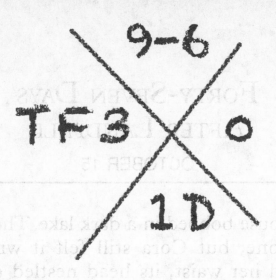

The broken concrete of the driveway seesawed, and the kitchen window was still open as she and Troy had left it when they came for the children, the shutters banged flat against the weatherboard. The little boy had jumped at her from the windowsill, naked except for a pair of water wings, a frenzy of brown and orange. She closed her eyes — *Blot it out* — but even in the dark, she could feel his head cupped in her hand. She could hear Reyna screaming. She saw herself rocking in the pirogue in the thick air, the little boy nestled against her chest. The flood had floated them high.

Now, she got up and put one foot against the siding, two hands on the sill. She strained, scrambled, jumped. She hauled her body up and perched in the window, her muscles trembling.

The moon cast Cora's shadow, long and black, across the kitchen floor, where a woman lay, her face no longer a face, only a mess of blackened blood. She shut her eyes. *Blot it out.* But when she looked again Reyna's body still lay curled, as if in sleep, around the shotgun that was missing from the house on Esplanade, her arm trailing awkwardly behind her like something ripped apart by a strong wind.

Blot it out, Mrs. Randsell had told her. So she had been sleeping. Drugs like a dark river to drown in. But now she felt again the gun recoil against her shoulder. Saw again the light of the blast in the high hall. *Blot it out,* but she could see as clear as if it were happening again in front of her now: Troy standing above her at the top of the stairs, the little boy reaching out to stroke his mother's smooth, unmaddened brow. She saw Reyna press her face against the window, her eyes plucked out by birds. Cora looked down from the window, and the pool of blood whirled through the woman's face, through the kitchen floor, pulling her under. The storm threw a barge against the floodwall. The surge dug out handfuls of sand. The Gulf bent its head and rammed into the breach until it had tunneled through to air. *The lowest pressure ever recorded,* the radio voices said, and the vacuum pulled at her, her nightdress snapping against her body like a flag.

Night poured in through the window. Stars streaked down through the sky. She would fall. She was falling. The flood's reek rose.

THURSDAY

OCTOBER 20

Joe saw it only for an instant, the hawk perched on a peak of the Mississippi River Bridge. He had never seen a hawk before in the city, but now that the animals had returned, he saw them everywhere. Above all the little creatures that scuffled and twittered, reestablishing their territories among the fallen pines, raptors floated in an emptied sky.

Joe looked in the rearview to be sure it was a hawk he'd seen and not a vulture or a crow; the mirror reflected only the X's of the steel arch. He might paint it anyway, he thought — the predator with her hooked beak, silhouetted against the river and the illusory sea.

At the end of the bridge, he merged onto General DeGaulle, towards his father's nursing home. He had always hated this drive, the elevated highway over the big-box stores and the Vietnamese places and the *nothing,* Tess would say. (*No,* he should have corrected her, *not the nothing. The houses.*) Now that the roofs below him were covered in the Crayola-blue FEMA tarps as if the city was drowning in a cartoon ocean, he hated it even more. But this was the final trip — the West Bank had seen the last of Joseph Boisdoré. He made his mouth smile. *The physical state affects the mental, and vice versa,* Tess had said, dragging Cora out of bed for a walk in the suburban sunshine of Houston. *If you smile, you'll find yourself happier.* Smile, and, given time, even this knob of guilt might melt away.

In the parking lot at the Little Sisters', Sister Cecilia was waiting for him. She was the picture of a nun: short gray hair, a hank of keys clipped to her elastic waistband. *Mother Superior,* Tess liked to call her, though she was not.

"Sister, how good to see you." He stuck out his hand, and she took it in both of hers.

"A rare pleasure, Mr. Boisdoré. How is your father?"

He nodded, maintained his smile, didn't say, *So much better, now that he's back home.* "He's puttering."

They had all been opposed when he suggested moving Vincent out to the cabin, but his father was better off alone with Joe,

16

somewhere Tess couldn't interfere. Since they'd been home, Vincent had put a French polish on all the good furniture and oiled the rest. He'd been walking around in the felled trees. *So much old-growth pine. You'll let me buy it off you? Ten dollars a cord —* Okay, it wasn't perfect, but the old man mostly knew where he was. *People don't buy good things nowadays,* he'd said, last night over red beans. *Particle board crap. Comes flat in a box and you put it together yourself, with plastic pegs.* He was so well this morning, Joe had left him there alone.

"That's good to hear. We've had a lot of bad news." Sister Cecilia led him in towards the emergency stairs. BROKEN was written big on masking tape across the elevator doors. "Many who couldn't make the transition."

Joe nodded as she crumpled her skirt in her fingers — trouser sock above tennis shoe — and began to climb.

"I'm sure he's grateful to be getting Tess's cooking more often. He used to really go on about it — so much crab she put in the gumbo, how crispy was the chicken."

"Actually, it's just us boys at the cabin, Sister. For the time being." Confession was a long habit. "Tess's in the city, looking after our daughter Cora. She's not doing well."

17

Sister Cecelia's hand stopped on the railing, gripped it the way you grip a tool.

"I'm sorry to hear that." She took another step. "This has been hard on many married people. Hard on everyone. I hope you will find a way to reconcile."

"Yes, Sister." He paused on the landing to catch his breath and looked up at her. It was amazing how much they understood, nuns, considering how little they had experienced, but "hard" was an understatement. "I think we will. Tess just needs time. To take it in."

"And you do not need time?"

Rembrandt could have painted her: the judgmental patience in her face.

"Pop grew up in that cabin, you know," Joe said. "Been in the family since 1815. I do think the familiarity's doing him good."

She nodded. "I will pray for you."

They walked up the remaining floors in silence. He was breathing hard; otherwise he would have felt odd, being with somebody now without going over all of it. *How did you make out?* and *I guess we always knew those levees weren't worth shit.* and *Happen to know a tree man who can do a job quick?* If it was late, if there'd been drinking, or even in the day, in a dimly lit hardware store with the door's jingle bells gone quiet, if it was just you and him, if there was trust, you might talk of other things. *Did you hear about the shooting on the Danziger?* It was not an act of God. *They pulled AKs on me in my own goddamned house.* It was not a natural disaster. *You think they might have blown the levees, like they did in '27?* It was manmade. *You think a one of them is going to be called to account?* An act of man.

The battery-lit stairwell was a column of heat, and sweat ran down his chest, but Joe reminded himself to smile: otherwise, his chest might start burning. Smile if you want to feel happy. Move if you need to feel strength.

On the ninth floor, Sister Cecilia waited. She was breathing lightly through her nose.

"You're in great shape, Sister," he said as he huffed up the last steps.

"Last spring, some of us gave up the elevators for Lent." A smile flickered on her mouth. "I kept it up for the sake of my heart, but now I wonder if the Lord was not preparing us."

When they came out onto the floor where his father had lived for five years, wheelchairs were stalled at odd angles in the hallway, and a humid murk of urine, mildew, and microwaved food hung in the air. Sister Cecelia's Reeboks squeaked on the linoleum. They turned beside the nurses' station, where a beach scene in paper ribbon still hung above the filing cabinets: construction paper sun, corrugated sea. The door to the room across from it was open. Inside, Joe saw the usual plastic-wrapped mattress, the vacant stare of a television screen. Now, though, a pane of the window was cracked, the glass split but still together, as though someone had tried, and failed, to escape.

At the end of the hall, Sister Cecelia was weighing the two ends of her keychain in her hands, her straight form in bloomy cotton backlit by the window.

"Sorry." As he lifted his hand from the arm of a wheelchair, blue imitation leather flaked off in his palm.

Somehow he hadn't expected that the room would be just the same. Laundry overflowing the hamper, slippers stepped out of beside the bed. Damage was normal now: The bathtub ring around the city, the misplaced houses and overturned cars. Their home on Esplanade wallpapered in mold, a magnolia tree in the kitchen, his unfinished sculptures of dogs and children hanging in the dying branches. Their furniture all crammed into the Dobies' house, their boxes in the storage barn. He and Tess were not speaking to each other, and Cora was not speaking at all. The thoroughness of the destruction almost kept you from remembering what had been destroyed. But here, the remote was hidden in the Barca-Lounger. The ceramic pheasants, dull with dust, roosted on the windowsill. A photograph of his mother in her wedding dress stood on the bedside table, her dress gone as sepia as her skin.

Smile, he told himself. He breathed through his teeth.

In his pocket, his phone rang. It was Sol, the overseer of the farm behind them. He looked at Sister Cecelia, stationed in the corner, and took the call.

"Hey, Joe?"

"Yeah?"

"You aware your dad's out walking along Lee Road? I pulled over to see if y'all was in trouble, if he need any help, but he just waved me on."

The muscles between Joe's ribs seized up, and he bent over as if just to grab his father's pajamas from the foot of the bed. *You're in over your head,* Tess had said.

"He seemed alright, to be fair. Said he was out looking for the dog got loose."

"We don't have a dog."

"Well, shit. I couldn't recollect if you did or you didn't."

"Can you try again?"

"Would if I could, Joe, but I've been twenty minutes driving before I could get any signal, and now I'm at the feed store. You ain't off somewhere, are you? Tess at the house, maybe?"

"No."

"Well, damn. If I'd've known you had errands to run. Hell, I coulda —"

Joe bowed his head down over the folded red blanket his mother had crocheted. He pressed the end button with his thumb, and held his breath, his feet still on the floor.

"Are you all right, Mr. Boisdoré?"

Sister Cecelia laid her hand on his back, but he only pressed his cheek against the blanket's weave, breathing in the wet sheep and Woolite, trying not to see his father standing on the shoulder, waiting for a break in the traffic. People sped on Lee Road, roaring around the blind corners — he could hear the whip of the wind against the gateposts and the trees. He shook his head against the blanket, dug his nails into the wool. He tried to remember his mother's hands. Index finger wrapping the yarn around the hook, the hook pulling through the chain. If only life followed that regular,

22

smooth rhythm, time falling into your lap in a well-knotted braid. But instead there were always snags, holes, cut strands of yarn that, if pulled, could unravel the whole thing. There was no pattern for peace. His chest still burned.

Today, Tess told herself, they would make it to the hedge.

The confederate jasmine that Laura Dobie had trained along her iron fence had begun to insinuate itself into the boxwoods, and ripping it out was the least they could do. *The least we can do,* Tess told Cora, *considering the Dobies are lending us their house.* The main objective, of course, was just to get Cora out of bed, but Dan Dobie really had been so sweet — the way he'd just thrown his house keys at her through the car window as he and Laura headed out of town.

"Keeping their house from falling down in their absence is really the very least we can do," Tess said, petting her daughter's arm, and Cora slid her skeletal legs off the mattress of her childhood bed, let her feet fall on the padded floor of Dan's home gym. Cora then stood up under her own power and walked, her bony knees trembling, all the way to the hall door.

Cora's nightgown was half-tucked into the seat of her underpants, but Tess had not made a move to fix it, worried that that would break the spell. Her daughter was on her arm now. They were descending the stairs. Tess held onto the banister, feeling a bit unsteady herself.

She saw how one might think neurosis could be catching. They used to joke about it in the office — *I think you've caught Verlander's kleptomania, Alice* — but emotional contagion was a real thing, at least according to Hatfield. Since moving alone with Cora into the Dobies' house, Tess had had to fight not only against the ubiquitous grief but against the urge to sink into the mattress and disappear, as Cora was trying so desperately to do. Tess had to remind herself that Cora had experienced a direct trauma — had seen the storm with her own eyes, had been out in the flood in a pirogue, and to top it off had had the tremendous bad luck to rescue Mrs. Randsell, only to watch her die of a stroke just one week after they'd finally made it to Houston. Still, when Tess tried to be happy that Del was coming today — that in a few hours her healthy daughter would be here with her feet up on the Dobies' coffee table, helping her drink a bottle of chardonnay — she only felt exhausted.

For now, though, she and Cora were going down the stairs. They took one at a time, Cora staring hard at her toes. Her feet were dirty again, God knew why. Again, her dinner tray had not been touched. Again, she smelled oddly of river mud. But they reached the bottom of the stairs without incident — Tess told herself that this was progress.

When she tugged her daughter's nightgown free so that it fell over her legs in a muslin cloud, however, Cora stopped short in the middle of the foyer and, as Tess had feared, refused to budge. Yesterday, though, they'd gotten as far as the front porch; today they would make it to the hedge.

"Cora, come on now," Tess said, her hand calm in her daughter's hand. "Your sister's coming today. We need to make things pretty for her."

Cora didn't move.

"We can't let Del see how we've been letting ourselves go, can we?" she asked, offering Cora a chance to agree. "Won't it be nice to just work a little while in the fresh air?"

"Fresh," Cora said, her face full of stubborn sleep, like the face of an awakened child. She shook her head slowly. "No."

Tess could admit that she would have

liked to stay in bed. The world outside was hot and sour, and it was nice to take refuge in the air-conditioning, among the old mahogany furniture she and Joe had rescued from their house on Esplanade. The curtained rooms were quiet, and Laura's ugly high pile carpets were so soft beneath your feet. But you couldn't just sleep. Already, Tess had cleaned the Dobies' kitchen cabinets with Murphy's Oil, washed the mustiness out of all of the sheets, polished the Marleybone silver that had traveled with her to Houston and back again. You couldn't sleep. She had been telling Cora this since Houston, even as she handed over the Ambien. You couldn't just sleep until it was over, even if you were drained beyond your last drop, reamed out like a lemon down to the pith. You couldn't just sleep, even if that was the only thing that felt good. Even if, alone on the Dobies' nice pillow-topped mattress, Joe not in it, Tess slept like a baby. Every morning now, she woke up clutching her pillow, sprawled out and drooling. But she got herself out of bed.

"Come on now —" she reached out her two hands, remained upright, cheerful. *Project the effect you would like to see echoed in the patient.* "It's like cold storage in here."

Tess turned and opened the front door,

26

let a rectangle of yellow sun swoon across the barge boards, but Cora backed away.

"Cora," Tess said, in the same calm, conspiring voice.

Cora's eyes, ringed in dark circles like the city's flooded houses, were blank.

"Cora," she said again, more forcefully now.

But Cora just stared straight ahead as though she knew no one by that name.

"Sheba!" Vincent put his foot down between the logs. Hollered. "Sheba, goddamn it, you come!"

Heat dripped down the insides of his thighs like urine, and a smell of waste rose up out of the knocked-down trees. A hamster-cage, rot-wood smell. Not like the sharp, clear smell of sanding and saws — like trash. Like a bedpan tipped over, soiling the sheets. Like the dog dead, flies clustered on her eyelids.

"Sheba!"

Out over the forest, something had come. He licked his finger, held it into the air. No wind. But something had come and knocked it all down. Must have been how the dog got loose. Didn't like thunder, that dog. Went to ground if you didn't let her in the bathtub. He marched out into the forest. A few steps was all it took to put him out of breath, but still, he couldn't hear the road behind him anymore. He looked over his shoulder. Couldn't see the road.

Mr. Vincent, where you headed? Some old redneck, pulled up off the shoulder in his dualie, thinks he's a big man. *You sure you should be out here by yourself?* Like he was some pickaninny needed scolding. Damn him if the Boisdorés hadn't owned this tract for almost as long back as there'd been men here of that name. The name had belonged first to white men, of course — Frenchmen you didn't call bigamists, even if that's what they were — who passed it on to the children of colored women who were neither wives nor whores. *Adelaide* was the only name she had, but then her grandson was Boisdoré — or so it was written on the deed to these 180 acres when it was given to him in exchange for his service in the 1812 war, though landowning in even so great a parcel did not convey the rest of what it should have: "Personhood." A vote. And now even the trees had been knocked down.

Vincent squinted to see how far this all went. Whether tornado or hurricane. Far. Out in the distance, scavengers circled in the air.

They had found her near to the edge of

the property, Sheba. Flies encrusted in the grayed fur around her eyes. A shameful thing to have forgotten, and then for him to go calling in the woods for a dead dog like a fool — *Pop, they say it's dementia. Nothing to be ashamed of.* Damn them if it was nothing to be ashamed of, a grown man wetting his pants. And the dog was under the soil these twenty-five years. Under a stone angel Sylvia had bought her — had her name carved in it, and those narrow dates like a tragic child, except she'd been an old dog when she died. He'd picked her up in his arms and felt all those lumps the veterinarian said were benign, brushed her face clean, almost laughed at the dirt on her. Paws clay-red from digging. Dug 'til her heart had stopped. She must've been hunting. Moles, maybe it was, though in all his life he'd never seen a mole. But that dog always went out with a purpose, her nose to the ground, flung back the mud with quick claws. Shovel-foot. You wanted her to dig postholes for you, but she had her own ideas.

They all had their own ideas, comes down to it. Your purposes were never good enough for them. Build a business and watch them turn up their noses. Build a home and watch them run away. To Texas. To Esplanade

Avenue, with some white girl's money. Nothing you ever did was good enough, not even the cabin, which his father, said by most to be the finest cabinetmaker in the South since the Butterfly Man, had built by hand — each board cut to notch into the next, so that there wasn't a nail in the whole house they hadn't hung a picture on. But it wasn't good enough, not for Joe under Tess's thumb. Not even the sleeping porch, the pleasantest place to spend a night, a little breeze and the fireflies blinking, was good enough. No, they'd torn it off and built a two-story camelback addition that looked like it had fallen from the sky, like one of those L-shaped bricks on the kids' Nintendo game. He wanted sometimes to turn off the water and lead them by candle to the outhouse, show them what, for centuries, had been just fine.

Vincent covered the sun with his hand and looked out again to where the vultures or buzzards or what have you were wheeling around the dead pecan, like they were tied to it by strings. The scavengers liked the dead tree was why they'd left it up. He contended it was edifying, to remember what we built ourselves out of, what we went to. Not dust so much as flesh. Flesh to flesh. Sylvia hadn't liked hearing it. She believed in transcendence, the way Joe did with his art, his *higher purpose* as he'd shouted once, mad as hell. According to them, there was something surpassed the material. A soul, some swishy stuff that wormed around in the air. He didn't have much talent for religious feeling, though he went to church regular, even now that Sylvia was gone. *What's an hour every Sunday and a few fish dinners compared to even the slimmest possibility of an eternity in Paradise?* she'd say. He'd never had a problem with her fish dinners, no matter what day it was, but transcendence was not something he had much truck with. He liked making things you could sleep on, sit in. Things that had function. And it comforted him, to know he would be recycled, as the kids would put it, become a buzzard, even a little worm. He could blink and be there and hardly know the difference, the way his mind was going. Blink, and you're tunneling through the darkness, the mud cool and soft on your sides. Blink, and you're afloat on a cushion of air, scanning for death on the weather-beaten ground.

The plane tilted low over Kenner, too low, so that Del could read the names on the buildings, see the dogs, boxes, lumber riding in the beds of trucks. The white guy in the middle seat leaned over her and peered out — he'd been gone since the storm, probably, like a lot of the rest of them who had congregated around the podium at La-Guardia, introducing themselves, talking like it was some kind of family reunion. Del looked away. She'd chosen the window seat as she had ever since she'd gone away to college eight years ago; she'd liked looking out of the plane window at the bridges over the lake, the highway over the swamp, the sun flashing off the hotel towers and glowing on the gray roof of the Superdome. All of it was always still waiting for her, always exactly the same. But now she couldn't bear to watch the city coming in, to see for herself where the brown lake ended or did not end.

Above the beat in her headphones, she could hear the captain saying they'd take one more low turn, and she dropped her head into her lap, her hands hard against the buds in her ears. The plane was banking, it shuddered. Maybe when they landed, she could go to the podium and ask to fly standby back to New York, take a temp job, prostrate herself at Fran's feet, at Zack's: abandon your roommate — *atta girl, Del* — and fuck your best friend while you're at it.

She looked down at the steel roof of Bryan Chevrolet, bleak and shining in the heat. She didn't want this; it made no sense. It was obligation and obligation only: *go be with them, go help.* But what help, really, could she be? Her father would pick her up, bring her downtown, and they would sit awkwardly in the Dobies' living room not saying anything useful to one another, until her father slapped his knees and rose to go.

"Miss? Miss —" She heard him over Master P, but she didn't look up until the middle seat tapped her shoulder.

"I'm afraid you need to turn that off. We're landing," said the flight attendant, his soft face full of pity. She took her earphones out but left the music running — tinny, tiny, metal forks on strings.

At baggage claim, the people from her flight stood around, sifting the change in their pockets, looking anxiously towards the rubber curtains where the bags would emerge. She thought she could tell the New Orleanians without even hearing them talk. They were the tired ones. The bloodshot. The ones who looked uncomfortable standing up straight, like they felt guilty for being unable to relax. Others, earnest kids, her age and younger, had come to help clean. MAKE GOOD, said a T-shirt one boy was wearing. MAKE GOOD, as if any good could be made out of what was, essentially, a hate crime of municipal proportion. Put on your waders, boys, and grab your hammers, your jars of rusty nails. As if the centuries-old institutions of racism and poverty could be torn down by installing plastic soffits on a couple of 501(c)(3) houses. She looked towards the sign stanchioned by the escalators, NO RE-ENTRY BEYOND THIS POINT. The belt began to move, rubber mats interlocking. Her duffel came out first — her lucky day! — and she dragged it to the curb.

Outside, the air was hot, almost oily, the way it glommed onto her skin. In New York, it was already fall. They had taken off from LaGuardia through a veil of cold fog and landed back in summer. In the eight years she'd been away, she had become a person of seasons. She liked them, the way they divided time, gave each day a sense of urgency, of possibility. Here, in the eternal heat and wetness, everything was slow, nothing ever changed. She settled her bag on the pavement and looked down the tunnel. Older, squeaking cars and the kind whose lights clicked on automatically in the dark came towards her. They'd all been getaway cars, probably. Standing still on the highways or plunging upstream in the contra-

34

flow. Her father had tried to laugh when he called from the five-mile bridge: *The storm's gaining on us, at this rate.*

She dug in her purse for her BlackBerry, turned it on, and stared down at the screen, expecting the little red message light to flash. Around her, people were kissing each other, throwing bags into trunks, driving away. The light stayed dark. She thumbed down through her recent calls to her dad's cell number and dialed it, got a busy signal. She hung up and dialed again. The aggressive bleating of downed phone lines. She called Zack — *I'm home,* she was going to say, laughing a little, but she hung up before the call went through.

I'll call you when I get home, she had told him the morning after they'd fucked, that predawn morning when he had stood above her on the stairs to his apartment — sweet old Zack in bare feet and boxers, his face behind his glasses puffy with sleep.

She hadn't called him then, though, and so she shouldn't be calling now.

Zack, on the other hand, had left dozens of messages on her machine, apologizing for "taking advantage" of her when she was the one who was in the wrong. She should have been on her knees — fuck your best friend and drop him, Del — but she couldn't even get up the courage to let the phone ring.

Why can't you go home again? he'd asked. It had been all downhill from there. It was three days after the storm, and there was a bowl of rocky road with a spoon stuck in it on his coffee table and the room was spinning. She had left her purse in some bar on Avenue A, and Fran hadn't answered the buzzer, and so here she was on Zack's couch, and she hadn't understood what he meant when he said *Why can't you go home again?*

She was so drunk. She kept seeing herself pulling at the door of her tenement building on 6th Street, shouting, and she could smell the stale piss and grime on the concrete steps, which was the same smell — mingled with beer — that came up from the gutters on Bourbon Street when the police rode down it on Mardi Gras at midnight, their horses flank to flank. And then she remembered that New Orleans was on lockdown, remembered that her sister was trapped inside.

Zack was sitting beside her on the couch in his boxers and bathrobe, his brown ringlets tangled, smelling of sleep. *Just go back,* he was saying. *Of course you can go back.*

36

No, I can't, she said. *I left. I just* — She waved a hand in the air. *Everything's locked up.*

You can't or you don't want to? The couch was small, and Zack's thigh was pressed against hers, and she could feel the tickle of his breath in the tiny curls on the back of her neck. *I doubt Fran meant to lock you out. You sure you don't just want to call her?*

No, she said, remembering how she had slammed her bedroom door in Fran's face that afternoon, when Fran had just wanted to comfort her. *I deserve it. I was a bitch.*

Zack patted her knee and she let him. She was half-glad she'd been locked out, half-glad she'd wound up here. Zack was the only one she could always count on to understand. They'd become friends during a sophomore seminar at U of C when she'd gone on offense over Serena Williams's treatment at Indian Wells and he'd piped up to support her. He believed in the reality she lived in. He'd never made her feel insane.

You saw what they did. She slapped her chest, drank her water. *Couldn't be bothered. All the school buses, just sitting in the water? And Cora's there* — *And thank God she's lighter than me, but you saw how the Gretna police closed the bridge. You saw the Conven-*

tion Center — *did you see one white face?*

Zack took her mug and went to the kitchen with it. *Two or three.*

My parents left her! If I'd just been there, I could have made her come, thrown her in the fucking car.

Zack took the Brita from the fridge, filled her cup. The water seemed to slow, twisting in the air. He put the foggy pitcher back on its shelf, closed the door.

This isn't your fault, he said.

She shook her head. *I should have done something.* She stared at the water, at a warped crumb of chocolate lying at the bottom of the mug. *I should have done something. But I was here.*

He'd sat back down, and she could feel the heat of him through the terry cloth. He put his hand on her shoulder, and she leaned against him, into his smell of Tide and sleep. He had always taken care of her — held her hair back, brought her pad thai when she was sad, listened and listened, unlike Fran who talked and talked. It was stupid, the way she was with him. Say one thing and do another, her body a dumb little homing pigeon. His hand had worked up the back of her neck through her hair, his fingers splayed against her scalp.

Come on, Del. Your sister isn't your respon-

sibility. That city isn't your responsibility. You know why you're here: To make a life for yourself. To escape all that, he said. *Say it with me: "This is not my responsibility."*

She shook her head, folded down over her lap, and his hand moved, heavy, over the hilled muscles of her back, the canal of her spine. Water was captured between the levees, the pumps were down. The flood had washed out the roads, it had picked up sections of the bridges off their pilings and carried them away. She imagined subway gates locked across the entrances to the I-10, police horses standing flank to flank across River Road. Her chest was tight with crying and bourbon, and she sat up, closed her eyes. In Zack's bedroom, Hendrix rattled from the speakers as Zack brought his arm down and wrapped it around her rib cage, his hand at the cusp of her breast.

I love you, he said. He had said it before, a couple of times. But he had always been the drunk one, and she had always pretended not to hear.

I know, she said, with this feeling in her chest like water straining against a door. He bent and kissed the bone at the base of her neck — wet mouth inside his beard — and she started to cry.

I'm sorry, he said, beginning to draw his

39

hand away, but she reached up and took it in her hand, brought it under her shirt, under her bra.

The next morning, she had tried to leave before he caught up with her, but the knob on the street door was loose, and she didn't make it in time.

Del, I'm so sorry. You were drunk. I — He brushed his hand across his mouth, his toes curled around the step, his glasses on. Sweet old Zack.

She should have said no then, that she was the one in the wrong: she had used him like a security blanket, and now she was throwing him away. But she'd said nothing. Hadn't even called when she got home.

Behind the airport parking lot, the sky was the color of cement. She looked at Zack's name on her phone, tried to press the green button again, but that wasn't the sort of conversation you could have here — in the anonymous throngs of New York, sure, but not here, never here. *Those Boisdoré girls are fast,* she could hear the Buckner mothers clucking, pink tongues flicking inside their collagen-plump lips. *Oh, but it's hard to be of mixed parentage, Leslie. I worry about them. They're both so pretty, but who will they find to marry?*

She pulled her long-sleeved tee off over

her head, sat down again on her bag and hunched over to watch the headlights as they went around and around. She rubbed the sweat into her biceps. She called Fran again, for the fifth time that day, but it just rang once and went to voice mail.

"Hey, Fran," she said to the machine. "I just wanted to say — again — how sorry I am for treating you the way I did. You were just trying to help, I know, and I treated you like shit. I'm having a hard time. I just got to New Orleans. Going to see what I can try and do —"

A long beep cut her off. She stared for a second at the screen, her thumb over the send button, then tried to get through to her father again, then her mother. Nothing. Even when she dialed the house line, she got the fail-tone.

She picked up her bag and went across the traffic to the taxi line. She'd been forgotten.

The truck's wheels thumped over the seams in the bridge, and the Tiffany lamp and the laundry basket with his mother's crocheted blanket in it knocked against the flatbed. Sister Cecelia would donate whatever he'd left behind to the poor. Sol wasn't picking up the phone, and the cabin line just rang.

Twenty-four miles of this, and then Joe knew he was likely to get caught in traffic on the 190 through Covington, and then he would have to drive slow down the length of Lee Road, looking in the scrub for his father, stopping at the shops to ask, praying to God someone had found him and brought him home.

The lake was placid today — no whitecaps, no waterspouts spinning up towards a darkening sky — but trauma had a tendency to repeat itself, as Tess would say. He had left his father, just as he had left Cora, not realizing he shouldn't have until it was too late.

It wasn't until they were stalled in the bumper-to-bumper evacuation traffic on the five-mile bridge, brake lights blinking as hopeful as Christmas lights over the water that Joe had known — the dread manifest as pain in his gut — that they had to go back for their daughter right away. But they weren't allowed to exit the highway until they reached Mississippi, and there, all the roads went north, the DO NOT ENTER signs skimming past at 50 mph in the contraflow. By the next day, the bridges were washed out. When he'd finally managed to leave Houston three days later — Tess incandescent with rage in the porch light, her nightgown glowing blue — he'd sped back down along the highways, empty now except for the convoys of Humvees, and found the National Guard blocking the entrance to the twelve-mile bridge.

Nothing you can do, brother, said a corn-fed black boy from Illinois. *Brother,* when he'd never laid eyes on the man in his life.

But my daughter's in there, Joe said.

She's not safe. You have to have faith, sir.

Faith? He'd laughed, before looking harder: The uniform starched and shiny. The cross tattooed on the side of his neck. *You tell me what you have faith in. You believe in God? You trust in the goddamned government?*

The boy just blinked.

They'd shoot you as soon as look at you, son, Joe said, and that was when the other soldier shouldered his rifle and he realized he had Vin's 9mm in his belt — all among the Humvees, the click-clack of rifles brought to ready.

Back upriver and then down through the spillway, past its flooded clay pits and the graveyards of defunct sugar plantations, he picked his way. He saw what the storm had left: A gator flipped on its back, showing its pale belly. A wild boar with a shredded coat, hung by its tusks from a tree. Shards of bridges, whole houses floating on the water. He crept downriver along the levee, through the dark fabric of the night, his headlights out, his windows open.

The moon was no more than a fingernail clipping, and the shadows of things identified themselves only by their sounds. Wind whipped through the batture trees, while generators roared beside the whisper of clapboard shacks and revenant dovecotes. Warehouses lumbered towards him and then retreated until their noise merged with the river's sibilant hush. Every now and then a bird cried out, and he fingered the safety of the pistol in his lap. As the stench of the rotting city rolled up towards him, overtaking the sharper smells of swamp and sulfur, he thought of the sentries, what he'd do if they stopped him again. *My daughter's still in the city. You have to let me in.* He saw himself pounding on a huge steel door.

No cars passed, no helicopters, and he imagined he heard breathing — people hunkered down behind their barricades of fallen trees and locked doors, tossing in their sweaty beds. They were waiting for someone to come up from the city and drive them at gunpoint from their homes. The pickups and old sedans they'd parked nose to nose across the gates of their suburbs eyed him as he passed.

When finally, up ahead, he saw a Humvee hunched on the shoulder, its lights off, he steered the truck slightly left and shifted it into neutral. The sound of tires rushing across asphalt was like the surge of a river. He fingered the pistol's safety and glided, waiting, but the Humvee didn't move. Beyond the levee, flashlight beams played in the mossed canopies of the trees.

Frogs shrilled like sirens as he shifted the truck back into drive and pressed the pedal to the ground, feeling the cold sweat prick up on the back of his neck as speed threw him against the seat. He was on the inside again, one of them, and as the humid stench of the city grew denser, he felt fear like a huge black bird descend upon his shoulders and dig its talons in.

He followed the river through its bend, over the train tracks at Magazine and into the wet heart of the park, where he had to inch the truck around limbs fallen from the big oaks. He veered back out to rejoin the river at Tchoupitoulas, where the warehouses and gray wharfs lengthened into the night, wharf upon wharf upon wharf, and the shotgun shacks of long-dead longshoremen crouched, their chimneys strangled by alligator vines that laughed in yellow bursts of flower. His eyes began to close. He opened them with a start to see only the endless gray wall that protected the river from the city, protected the city from the river so well that even the sound of the water could no longer reach him. He knew the river was there, though; he felt its flow like the moored ships must feel it, their heads bent like beasts of burden against the current, their bodies brushing against the endless walls as they slept.

When his bumper scraped against the port's wall, his eyes flew open. He'd fallen asleep. His foot was off the gas, thank God, but he would have to pull over and rest. To the left was a sea of asphalt. He pulled the truck in and parked. He could not see the light-spangled bridge either in front or behind him. He could see nothing. He could not stay awake. He was home. He had no idea where he was.

When Joe thought of his father's forgetting, he imagined it was like falling asleep at the wheel, like a blinding rain that fell hard and with no warning. Sometimes a wind would push through, parting the rain for long enough that his father could see figures, Tess and the girls swimming in the pool in Folsom, Sylvia walking the dog along the levee. Sometimes the sun was hot enough to burn the clouds off for a day, maybe two, but often the forgetting came down so hard that there was nothing to see but water.

There were snakes in the roadside ditches. Speeding cars on the road. He should have put a collar on his father, like a cat, complete with jingle bells and an address-stamped tag. But even if Vincent never left the cabin, there were still dangers — a fireplace, a stove, stairs, bottles of bleach and drain cleaner. He should have gotten the child-locks out of the attic, the gates you had to drill into the wall. No matter how well he'd been doing, it was neglect, plain and simple, to have left his father alone.

As the truck mounted the bridge over the Bogue Falaya, he looked across the railing at the stream, the trees shaking their shadows down into the rock-strewn water, and prayed. That his father was not in the river. That he was not wandering among the for-sale motorcycle trailers or inside the abandoned church. He scanned the weedy ditches, his neighbors' tree-strewn driveways. He rolled off the road onto their property and squinted up the shell drive, his foot on the brake. Now that the trees were down, he could see all the way to the cabin. The front door was open.

He threw the truck in park, left the keys in the ignition. He wished he'd gotten farther clearing the trees, but he'd been waiting on cooler weather. As it was, he had to pick his way over a thicket of fallen pines — the small broken branches, the needles spiking his legs — to get to the clearing in front of the house. Even from the driveway, he could feel the air-conditioning pumping out of the open door.

"Pop?" Dead wood absorbed the sound.

In the great room, the TV was still on, playing a black-and-white episode of *Lassie*. His father's bowl of Grape-Nuts sat untouched on the kitchen counter.

"Pop!"

From around the house, he thought he heard the creak of hinges, but it could have been nothing, just another door left open in the wind. He didn't want to run. His father's voice was feeble now, and if he'd come back of his own accord, come back to himself, Joe didn't want to look frightened, though the swath of grass between the house and the studio seemed infinite.

"Pop?" He stuffed his fists in his pockets. A shadow moved inside the workshed. "You in the workshed?" He made it into an everyday question: his mother just setting dinner on the table.

"— for the third time." His father, blinking, emerged from the door.

Joe pushed his fists higher, into his belly, to stop the burn. "Hi."

"Hello." His father nodded his head.

"Working on something?"

"Ach —" Vincent flapped a hand. "I'm not tinkering with your arts and crafts, you don't have to worry about me. I'm just doing some thinking."

"Sol, from over at the Harricks' —"

"I know who Sol is."

"— he said he saw you out walking." Joe pressed his hands together in front of his heart. "You went out to run some errands?"

His father shook his head, jutted his chin out. "Where is she?"

"Who?" Joe prayed he didn't mean the dog, or worse, his mother. Whenever he forgot she was dead, whenever they had to remind him, it hit him like a Mack Truck that's jumped the divider.

"The girl —" His father's hand flapped, bad, as always, with everybody's name. "Adelaide. Del."

The shades were drawn, and the room was crowded with the dense, shadowy shapes of furniture. Del knew half of their things had gone into a storage unit in Folsom, but it

49

still looked like every last one of their beds and chests of drawers, every single side table and upholstered chair was here, leaning against and upon one another on the bouncy floor of the Dobies' home gym. Across the hall, her mother's things were scattered around Laura and Dan's master bedroom — her Chinatown kimono deflated on the unmade bed, worn-once clothes piled in the lounge chair by the defunct fireplace, her reading glasses abandoned on the book left open on the nightstand: Jung's *Answer to Job*. She'd thought her mother had given up Jung over a decade ago.

Getting out of the taxi, Del had found the Dobies' driveway empty, the kitchen door unlocked, and she had wandered into the strange house, hallooing. She couldn't make herself loud enough. The thick velvet drapes and deep upholstery conspired to absorb sound. She'd only ever been here before for Mardi Gras parties and the couple of times when Laura and Dan had needed her to feed the cat, and the house felt conjured, as if she were remembering it out loud — Crate and Barrel farm table, Noguchi lanterns hung from original plaster medallions, flea market chairs.

Peering into Dan's home gym, she thought she saw a NordicTrack balanced upright in a far corner, but the room was so cluttered with the furniture Del had grown up with that the hall light struggled to enter, getting caught in the tilted mirrors on the vanity and the doors of the chifferobes. Del thought of the firetraps she'd visited with Phillip when she was still an assistant at the auction house — apartments of wealthy Manhattan hoarders whose contents they would be called in to consign. Phillip would dandle the Edwardian hardware, while he had her climbing under tables through drifts of trash, turning drawers upside down, the flashlight glancing off old paper labels and branded wood. *Five hundred K for the lot,* she heard Phillip pronounce over her family's things, *considering condition.* Without the water damage, it would have been much more, depending on the market for early Louisiana furniture: four times that, maybe five. Back in the day, Papie could have fixed it all up again, restored it to very near its original condition. But that was all over, now. He hadn't trained a single person — not that it would have to have been Del — to replace him.

She took a hesitant step into the room, balancing herself on a wobbly demilune. Between the two dim squares of windows, Cora's tall tester bed gathered itself together out of the darkness. The silver ghost of Del's face flew from her mother's vanity mirror, and only then did she see Cora's body under the sheets.

Del jumped. "Holy God, you scared me." She pressed a hand to her chest for effect. "Where's the damn light switch?"

Cora didn't answer, and Del had to drop her bag and fumble along the wall and behind the NordicTrack to find it. Under the canopy of her bed, Cora's face flashed into focus. She looked terrible, at least a decade older than her twenty-eight years. She had always been thin, a sycamore tree of a person with eerie blue eyes set deep in the smooth bark of her face, but she was hollowed out now, storm felled. She had to be forced to eat, their mother said. Her eyes closed, and Cora waved a thin hand as if she could brush away the light.

"I didn't know you were home," Del said. "You didn't hear me calling?"

"It's too bright."

Del looked up at the ceiling fan, the single bulb cocooned inside a globe of frosted glass. "Well, no. Not really."

"Out there —" Cora cocked her head at one of the blinded windows.

"Okay."

Del threw her bag onto a made-up sleeper

sofa, and the springs creaked. Her own bed was dismantled, its pieces leaning in a corner by the window that overlooked the Dobies' courtyard. The tester and the mattress were gone — rain had come through the hole the tree had made in the roof and flooded the attic, dripping down into her childhood bedroom to destroy the finish on every piece of furniture, as well as the bed's silk canopy, her books, the macramé box that held her prom corsage. Her mother had delivered this news in caressing tones, as if she'd expected Del to cry.

"How did your stuff make out?" Del asked, though she already knew: Cora's flat-on-the-ground cottage near the track had flooded to the windowsills — it was a total loss.

"I don't want to talk about it. I didn't want to talk about it. I won't ever want to talk about it," Cora repeated as if it were a conjugation drill. *Je déprime. Tu déprimes. Nous déprimons. Qui? Nous-memes.*

Del finished unpacking her bags into the armoire — the one from her parents' room, with the monogrammed patera and the lovely holly stringing — and when she turned back around, Cora had vanished into the mattress again. Del climbed up into the bed beside her and reached under the covers to pet her sister's glossy head.

"You know what this reminds me of?" she said. "Back when we used to play hide-and-go-seek in Papie's workshop."

While Del counted, Cora would close herself silently in the empty case of a grand-father clock or shut the lid of a cedar trunk over her head. It could take a half hour to find her — sometimes so long that Del would get scared, start yelling, and Papie would turn from the workbench with his hands on his hips, and say if they didn't quit their ruckus he'd call Mamie away from the books to drive them home. She could still hear the dozens of clocks ticking, the whisk of sandpaper across the spindle in Papie's hand. Cora never said a word, and when Del found her, sometimes it would take her a while to move — her eyes closed, her face pressed against the wood. When Cora was the seeker, though, she was some-thing else: miraculously aware, not methodi-cal so much as inspired. Del was rarely in her hiding spot (under the drop cloths maybe or behind the shutters and peeking through the chinks) for a count of twenty after Cora had opened her eyes.

"You were really good at it," she said, find-ing Cora's hand, interweaving their fingers. "Remember?"

"I don't want to remember anything."

Del peeled back the covers from her sister's face. "Why not? We used to have so much fun." She took Cora's shoulders, shook her once for each word. "Didn't. We. Used. To. Have. So. Much. Fun?"

"Stop!" Cora jerked herself away, turning her face to the pillow. "Stop!"

"You're being ridiculous!" Del sat up and stripped the sheets from the bed. Her sister's stick legs lay still on the white cotton. They were covered in pink patches like peeled-back bark. Scars, where chemical burns from the floodwaters had healed.

"I'm sorry," she said. "Jesus." She picked up the sheets and pulled them slowly back up over her sister's body. "I'm so sorry. I don't know why I did that. I —"

She could feel her heart beating in her neck. Cora turned over and, facedown now, lay still. On the TV at Odessa, her regular bar on Avenue A, she had seen the clothes of a drowned woman ballooning on the brown water. She had seen the men and women and children teeming on the bridges and on the concrete skirt of the Dome. She had looked among them for her sister's face.

You know there's a train station a block from there, she had said to Yuri, the bartender, pushing her glass across to him for another shot. *Don't you think maybe you put your people on a train instead of in a motherfucking football stadium in the path of the storm?*

She'd drunk the whiskey, put it back down on the far side of the bar. *Built that thing in the same spot where they used to make slaves fight to the death, you know. Superdome, Thunderdome. Twenty thousand men enter, no man leaves.*

Yuri didn't laugh. Just filled her glass, licked his lips. *They should have left on their own, no? You cannot expect — you cannot rely on the government to take care of you.*

She rolled her eyes. *This isn't Ukraine, Yuri. This is supposed to be America. America!* she shouted at the TV, feeling the old Polish men in the booths look up from their herring. *America!*

Calm yourself, he'd said as he laid a hand on her arm, rubbing his thumb along the inside of her wrist. *Calm down, or I'll have to take you home.*

"You should have left with them, Cora," Del said.

Tess had been circling the terminal for a half hour now, hitting redial each time she left the dusk of Arrivals for the outer light. She had looked for Del in every young girl

56

sitting wide-legged on her duffel, in every light-skinned woman leaning against the aggregate columns. To the rescue again, she kept thinking. Tess to the rescue. No matter what had been agreed upon or how often Joe was reminded or what responsibilities she had besides, it was always Tess to the rescue. Except, today, it seemed that it was not.

She made another circuit — stopped at all the crosswalks, jolted at five miles per hour over the speed bumps, kept expecting to see those amber eyes flash as Del caught sight of her, to see the blank, disappointed look on her daughter's face change to a put-on smile, the way it always had when she was a little girl, forgotten by her father at school. Adelaide could be hunched over her knees in one of the short plastic chairs with their backs up against the wall, a vacuum roaring in a far-off classroom, the receptionist tapping the desk with her purple fingernails, but as soon she noticed Tess, it was always *Mommy, Mommy!* and the big hug and the beaten dog's eyes. But Adelaide was a grown woman now. She was not waiting. She must have taken a cab.

Tess stopped the car at terminal's edge and looked back at the taxi stand, but there was no one in line. From the edge of the overhang, the fumes wavered like a lace curtain. She drove through it and out onto Airline Drive.

The drainage canal streamed by beside her, and behind it, across the littered brown no-man's-land that had once been grass, the houses flaunted their waist-high flood lines. It made her ill, to think that Del had had to see this for the first time, alone. She wanted to call Joe back and scream at him. Before, she'd only hung up the phone. He knew as well as she did what it was like, seeing this for the first time; you could watch all the TV news you wanted — out in Houston, they had been glued to Vin's leather couch for days — but there was no way to adequately prepare. The flood itself had been straight out of an apocalypse movie, but the aftermath was something else. The innards of sofas strewn across lawns. Cars belly up in the streets. An inch-thick crust of sewage on every goddamned thing. You almost wanted the water to come back. On TV, the flood had shimmered, glinting with sun as the news helicopters ruffled the surface. The water had hidden the mess, lifted everything up, given the city a sense of buoyancy. It had kept you from having to really believe it, and if she could have stayed there, safe in her dream of

58

disbelief, in the gin-smogged Twilight Zone of Vin and Zizi's suburb, that Purgatory of vacuums and air-conditioning and chain restaurants, she might have. If they had all gotten away, maybe they could have stayed away. If the second hurricane had swerved just a little east and destroyed New Orleans once and for all. If they hadn't left Cora there. If she hadn't, in the end, been found.

Tess couldn't say this out loud, of course. Not to anyone, but certainly not to the girls. Once upon a time, both of them had come to her for advice, snuggled up into the big bed in the early morning, let Tess stroke their lamb-soft heads. Once upon a time, they had let Tess see them cry, had come running even, a red gash on a little brown knee or a cruel word lodged in an ear. Tess would cradle a heavy head against her chest and whisper reassurances. She would hold a pink palm in her hand and carefully draw out the splinter, hold the outrage down until she could make the necessary cutting phone calls behind closed doors, just hold on until her little girl stopped crying. But that had ended some time ago. Now she wasn't allowed to help. Wasn't allowed to see the tears. Wasn't allowed to touch the hair, God forbid. Cora just barricaded herself away in her house, in her room, in her body — that refuge of last resort. And the last time she could remember Adelaide asking her a serious question was her senior year in high school when she'd taken it into her head to skip college and stay home to apprentice in Vincent's workshop instead. Tess had told her no, and Adelaide hadn't liked that answer, and that had been the end of it — of everything, apparently.

She would admit she'd been glad when Joe had phoned to say he'd pick her up from the airport. Del was Daddy's girl, despite everything. She was still open with him, whereas with Tess she was shut watertight, her shoulders hunched, bra straps showing. But he hadn't come, had he.

I just forgot, Tess, I had a crisis with Dad, I'm sorry. Sorry, he sure was. That was at least true. He'd had enough of "being governed," was ready to be "in control of his own life." So he'd set up housekeeping with an eighty-six-year-old man in the terminal phases of a degenerative disease. She used to find it cute, the way he played at cooking, played house like a little boy. *Honey, I'm home,* she'd shout as she walked in the door after work when she'd left him in charge, and he'd scoop Kraft macaroni onto the plate and they'd tuck their napkins into their shirtfronts. But while he was playing at life, he'd forgotten his daughters — abandoned Del to the aftermath, just as he'd abandoned Cora to the storm.

And instead of waiting for her mother, for rescue, Del had taken a goddamned cab.

Beyond the far lane, Tess caught sight of the Coca-Cola façade of the roller rink where the Velcro skates and cookie cakes of all those childhood birthdays must have bobbed against the disco-ball ceiling in the flood. She could still hear the sound of the wheels, the DJ in his tinseled booth, Adelaide skating all sweaty through the break in the wall and into her arms, could still feel the impact of a head on her ribs, just over the heart.

She made a U-turn and pulled into the rink's parking lot, where the blue box of a payphone hung from a pole, and stood up out of the car into the flat desert heat of asphalt. Leaving the engine on to pump air-conditioning at her through the open door, she rummaged in her skirt pocket for change.

There was not another soul out here — no one as far as she could see along the frontage of strip mall and fast-food and warehouse — and when she dropped the quarter on the pavement, she broke out in a cold sweat. Something had gone terribly wrong, as wrong as carpools crashed on highways, children kidnapped from among the wax-cold pizzas and Skee-Ball lanes. Behind the swinging doors of the skate center, there would be nothing but dirty red carpet and warped wood floor and the plexiglass boxes where a claw was always reaching, never holding, like a palsied hand.

She put the quarter into the slot, dialed the Dobies' landline. The phone, miraculously, rang.

"Hello? This is the Dobie residence," Del said, formal as she'd been trained.

"Oh, thank God, honey, you're there," Tess said. "Are you alright, did you take a cab? I've just been to the airport, driving around and around."

"Yeah. United. It's okay," Del said, and she was chewing something already, she seemed so unperturbed. "I had cash."

"I can't believe — I just can't believe your father! You shouldn't have had to see this alone, honey. It is so hard. So hard to see. I should have been there for you. He should have been there."

"I'm a grown woman, Mom. I can handle it." Del laughed, dismissive. Tess should have expected that. "Anyway —" It was Triscuits she was chewing on. Triscuits and that crummy Popeye dip she'd bought.

"*Grief is the loneliest emotion* — isn't that what you always say, Dr. Eshleman?"

"Well —" Tess pulled herself up and back, the silver cord going tight against the pole. "Well, I'm sorry anyway. I should never have left it to him. I should have come for you in the first place"

"Please stop apologizing, Mom. It's okay. I'm alright. Everything's fine."

"No," Tess said, shaking her head against the heavy receiver, that she only now realized smelled of vomit. "No, it's not."

"Well, Cora does look like hell," Del said, crunching Triscuits.

Tess laughed. "Ain't that the truth."

"And you've got me sleeping on a shitty sofa bed in a firetrap."

Tess laughed again.

"And of course the city is a fucking bombed-out wasteland —"

She didn't know why she was laughing, but she couldn't stop. Reflected on the hood of her car, her face looked like a fun house freak's, her mascara running, her dyed hair standing up like a clown's wig, her features warped.

"But everything's fine, sure," Del was saying as Tess laughed, bent over her legs. "Everything is completely fine."

The water, Tess had heard, had come up

through the manhole covers once the drainage canals were overwhelmed. It had not, as she'd always imagined, come as a great wave rising above the river levee the way unladen ships did in spring. No, it had been more active and more sinister. It had broken what was built to keep it back. It had snuck in along channels dug to lead it away. It had acted as if with the intent to swallow, to smother, to ruin, to uproot, but most of all, to lift. It had raised sewage, dirt, poisons, furniture, cars, homes, families high above the ground as if to allow God to get a better look, and the things He rejected it had dropped, left them strewn in ruined piles.

So, then, Joe was on the Northshore with his father, she and Cora silent in the Dobies' borrowed house. But now here was Del munching crackers and telling jokes, sarcastic as she'd been when she left them after Jazz Fest. She was like the glass orb on the highest shelf in Tess's office that hadn't, unlike the file cabinets, the picture frames, the desk chair, the stapler, moved an inch. It hadn't even, like the books, grown mold. No, it was clean, blank, crystal clear as ever, and as Tess turned towards the ravaged city, she realized why she hadn't, deep down, wanted Adelaide to come home.

Del hesitated on the corner of Esplanade and Royal, looking up at the house she'd grown up in. It towered above her, the long, wrought-iron railing of the upper gallery reaching back until it was lost in the branches of the fallen magnolia. The pinkish-brown paint was peeling off the scored plaster in hand-sized flakes, and the shutters were still lashed shut. In the urns on either side of the portico, the impatiens had shriveled to skeletons during their long abandonment.

The night the storm hit, she had dreamed of the house's rooms exposed to the city like an elaborate diorama, the wallpaper coming unglued from the cardboard, the furniture standing on toothpick legs. She almost believed she had felt the thump of the tree as it fell through the back of the house, but when she'd awoken with her heart racing, it was 3:00 a.m., and a garbage truck shifted into first gear on Avenue A then stopped with a *thunk,* grinding its steel jaws.

She went up into the portico where the National Guard or whoever had spray-painted an X with a date in its arms and a zero in its crotch to say they hadn't found anything in their inspection — no people, no dogs, no cats alive or dead, nothing drowned or starved, no one in the attic, nothing trapped under the porches. This had happened between her father's solo attempt to rescue Cora and her parents' joint second try. Her mother had called her panicked from the bridge after dark: *Even the patrols couldn't find her, baby. Where in hell do you think she could be?* The front door had been kicked open, and now a chain was looped through the vestibule shutters and held shut with a padlock. Del fished the tiny key from her pocket.

In the dim light that seeped through the shutter slats, the house felt like a tomb. All of their furniture was gone, but it still smelled like mildew and humid wood. Scraps of tape and cellophane littered the floor, and the sticky dust was printed with boot tracks.

Her footsteps ricocheted off the high ceiling. Inside the walls, mold had taken root, and huge varicolored blooms spread over the plaster. The movers had left the doors of the built-in bookcase in the library open, and she went into the room to close them before the hardware started to fail. The wood was swollen, and she had to muscle the doors shut. As she turned away, she noticed bare footprints coming in through the far door of the library. They moved around the perimeter of the room, skirting the bookcase and then exiting through the door into the living room, where they moved around the walls again — a short foot, with a long second toe — and stopped in front of the pier mirror that still stood between the two front windows. The person had moved up close to the mirror and stayed there for some time, shuffling. Del went to stand where the person had stood — not her sister, who had triangular size nines like her own, but not a looter either, not when the silver trays had still been on their tables when her parents had returned, and the television on its console, her mother's fur coats hanging slack in the cedar closet. They'd thought her maternal grandfather's shotgun was missing when they'd found it gone from the safe — they'd thought maybe Cora had just forgotten she'd taken it to Augie's house when she and Mrs. Randsell had evacuated there — but they'd found it again when they'd unpacked at the Dobies' a week or so ago, dismantled inside a laundry basket.

The mirror's silvering had begun to oxidize, and little tarnished dots marked the side of her face like the dark freckles that showed up on her skin every spring like daffodils. She was surprised by how anxious she looked. Her forehead was creased, and when she tried to relax her brow, her whole face fell, becoming the jowly Boisdoré mask she wore whenever she was tired or a couple of pounds too heavy.

Del wrapped her arms around her chest, feeling her heart clench like a fist. Everything her father had done to restore this place — two decades of patching, of sanding the plaster, rewelding the wrought iron, reglazing the arched windows of the stairwell with stained glass, retiling the gallery floor — had been ruined in a single month. Water and evacuation had finished what the tree started. It had been the project of a lifetime, and maybe it had been too big. Maybe, as her father sometimes said, they would have been better off in a little center hall cottage they could have paid for themselves. Then they could have used her mother's inheritance to send Cora to one of those special schools that were all outdoor living and therapeutic cows, and her father wouldn't have had to spend his life on a ladder being mistaken for the help by every UPS driver or florist who stopped by. Maybe then, their whole lives wouldn't have been able to collapse in a single night.

Regardless, it was over now. Her parents were over, and anyway there wouldn't be enough money, even if the insurance paid out, to put their home back the way it was. She had to say good-bye.

The smell of mildew and wet wool got stronger as she climbed the stairs. The oculus was cracked, and from the landing, she could see the water condensed like sweat between the stained glass window and the sheet of plywood that protected it, and there was one more bare footprint, the round heel almost wedged into the corner beside the banister. The stair treads groaned as she put her weight on them. From the ceiling of the upstairs hall, brown blisters half-filled with rain hung from the ceiling, and the carpet was stained worse than she would have expected, the boot tracks making a pattern over the dirty water stains. On the floor between her parents' and Cora's bedrooms at the front of the house, a dark puddle had seeped into the wool — something spilled and left to soak.

Her room was farther back, just before the dividing door between the front and back of the house. Her door was closed, and someone had jammed towels in along the threshold. Del took a deep breath and turned the knob.

Her chandelier lay in a heap on the floor, one wire still attached to the box in the middle of the ceiling, which had been skinned down to the lath. Chunks of plaster, held together by dozens of layers of paint, had been swept into a corner beside the curtains that still hung from the windows, so mildewed now that even from this distance, Del could see fuzz on the folds where the light hit. She had had nightmares like this when she was a child: her parents would have vanished, and she would crouch behind a tattered curtain or inside a piece of furniture in an otherwise empty house, hiding so that no one could take her away. She had thought that she would cry, but she just felt numb. It wasn't her room anymore, nor her house. If she was honest, it hadn't been for a long time, and she couldn't blame that on anyone but herself.

Cora was piled up in her sweats in one of Alice's vast armchairs — Dr. Luce's armchairs, Tess reminded herself. She would have to remember to call her Dr. Luce.

As they had discussed on the phone, Tess would go in first, in the interest of expediency, but Alice was blinking at Cora, in her condescending way.

"You don't mind, honey," Dr. Luce said, "if your mom speaks to me first?"

Cora shook her ragged, bed-ruffled hair. Clear assent, but Alice kept standing squarely in front of her in her chic professional slacks, her blonde hair newly bobbed. *If she was talking, Alice, we wouldn't have to have a preliminary chat, now would we?*

"You're sure?"

Cora nodded, a finger in her mouth.

"Sure sure?"

Tess had always avoided sending Cora to someone in her own practice, but Nemetz was off in Phoenix and Dr. Boudreaux was in Atlanta and Letitia Hull's service was saying she wouldn't be returning until the new year. She trusted Alice, otherwise she would never have hired her oh those many years ago; she reminded herself that this was why.

Alice put a hand on the pickled cypress door that led to her study, opened it, then craned her still-lovely neck back into the parlor.

"If you need anything, honey, you know

71

where the kitchen is, yeah? Gerry's thumping around somewhere."

Cora looked up briefly from her cuticles, and the door closed with an elegant click.

"Smells wonderful in here." Everything on the bookshelves — the brown leather volumes, alphabetized paperbacks, stereo equipment, knickknacks — were all dusted and in their proper places.

Alice smiled, pink lips gapping over whitened teeth. "Gerry, bless his heart, fought tooth and nail until I agreed to put the whole, practically brand-new Sub-Zero on the curb."

"I saw that. I'm sorry."

"Maggots, but you know. Anyway, we've had an exorcism. Baking soda, a box of super-expensive scented candles, and I've been baking. Have one." She picked up a chocolate chip cookie from a plate on her desk and held it out. "I've made dozens and dozens. I sort of feel like a real estate agent."

"You need the house to be a haven, if you're going to be practicing here." Tess nodded, though she wasn't sure every patient would find the right-side-upness so comforting. Personally, she had a fondness for oases, but Cora — when they'd finally gotten her back to Houston, she had kept turning off Vin's air-conditioning. Had

72

refused, for a few days, to shower. Tess took a bite out of the cookie, and the sugar — or maybe the Tollhouse perfection of it — brought tears to her eyes.

"Well, yes, that's the essence, isn't it. A house should be a safe, warm place."

"Protective. Maternal," Tess said.

"Right, right — the origin, the center, the place to which you return."

"Or the place you mean to build —" One of Alice's faults was that she always interpreted in retrospect. Always dug into the roots of a thing, and so missed out on what it anticipated. Tess's archetypal "home," as an example, was not the house she'd grown up in, where her mother locked herself in the bedroom and her father loomed over the bar, calling her boyfriend a "coon." No, home had always been a place she longed towards: the family she would build, the house she'd restore, fill. The house that now had a tree in its kitchen.

"It's anticipatory too, remember," Tess said, then swatted that little criticism out of the air.

"Mm-hm." Alice was drifting back towards her desk, the pleats of her slacks so very very straight, to gather a pad, a pen.

"Anyway, I'd say onset was the morning we moved from our house into the Dobies'."

Alice's face was settling into a benignly patient smile. "Laura and Dan's. Such nice people. You might have met them at New Year's —"

Alice folded back the orange cover of the notepad, uncapped her pen. "That was when, exactly? Two weeks ago?"

"Last Sunday, I think?"

"The sixteenth?"

"I have no idea, Alice. It was a couple of days after we came back from Houston. Dan and Laura had come back in pre-Rita, and Dan — they really are nice people — just threw me the house keys as they were leaving." Tess cleared her throat. "It wasn't as though Cora had been well-well. I mean, I'm not sure anybody could have been, after what she went through."

Hell, Mrs. Randsell had called it, though it had looked at first like the opposite.

Tess and Augie Randsell had imagined so many horrors on the drive out from Houston — his mother drowned, Cora raped or murdered or imprisoned or all three — that they had stopped short at the gate to his garden, half-disbelieving their eyes. It seemed impossible that they had found them both immediately, first place they looked, sitting in the garden, drinking coffee.

74

They looked like a painting — a Sargent tableau — their feet hidden in the high grass, their skirts occluded by the overgrown rose bushes. Cora was wearing one of Madge's linen shirt dresses, and even from across the lawn, Tess could smell her friend's old gardenia perfume. Despite her eternal mourning weeds, Mrs. Randsell glittered. She had on all the jewelry — her engagement ring, an emerald solitaire, her late husband's signet on her thumb. Around her neck were three strands of large pearls, and her dress was pinned with a gold narcissus, blooming diamonds. When Augie pushed the groaning gate open, his mother turned, pacifically, and twiddled her fingers. Cora lifted her hooded eyes to her mother's face.

We were expecting you, Mrs. Randsell said, grinning, but she'd probably been waiting her whole life for this, Tess thought: a flood or a nuclear attack, a new Civil War.

On the table, a camp percolator burbled, and beside it sat three bone china cups. *Cora, darling, would you run into the kitchen and fetch a cup for your mother,* Mrs. Randsell said, and Tess watched her daughter stand, watched her waft, obediently, across the lawn and into the tall white house, her hair long and shining like raven's wings folded along her back.

Augie walked across the lawn in long strides. *How on earth?*

Mrs. Randsell raised her eyebrows, closing a book of Hesiod around her thumb.

How were you expecting us, Mother? Augie said, and Tess thought she could hear his racing heart.

Mrs. Randsell patted the top of a wind-up radio with her jeweled hand. *I figured once the gates of Hell were opened, you'd come rushing in.*

Hell, she'd said, though it looked like heaven. Hell, though, it must have been.

"Not that we'd know anything about it," Tess told Alice. She realized she'd been plucking at her cuticles and quit it, sat on her hands. "After Augie and I finally found Cora, when we'd gotten her safely to Houston, she was pretty uncommunicative, but we could get her to dress, she was eating. I gave her a few Ambien, at first, to help her sleep. Of course, she doesn't need it now!" Tess tried to laugh. "But that morning we moved to Laura and Dan's — Sunday — the lights just wouldn't go on." She snapped her fingers. "I went in to wake her — she wouldn't get up. This is the first time I've gotten her out of the house. Did you have a chance to look at the chart?"

Alice nodded. "She had a depressive

76

episode in '95, I saw. Please go on — but if you'd like to take a seat —" Alice waved her hand at the various chairs — reading, desk, wing — that had been dislocated from their normal positions to make a circle at the center of the room.

"You're starting groups already?" Tess settled herself in the Eames, spreading her long skirt out over her legs as she marveled at how comfortable the chair was — more comfortable, in fact, than any piece of furniture she owned. Alice's was a different sort of life, full of new things. Or not new — this chair was fifty years old — but different. Sentimental Tess, she chose chairs that broke, antiques with original hardware, original finishes you were supposed to look after to the tune of thousands of dollars a year. She could just as easily have had this: A comfortable chair. Simple, gleaming things. Disposable things.

"Kids' groups, grown-ups' groups, couples' groups, and singles' groups," Alice was saying, her mouth full of cookie. "The city's desperate for them. As soon as you're up for it you should take on a few. They — we all — need grief counseling. There's PTSD, depression, anxiety everywhere, just everywhere."

"The Katrina Crazies."

"Oh, like Katrina Cough?" Alice didn't laugh. "If you need space, by the way, to see your people —" She took another tactful bite of cookie. "Joyce Perret called yesterday wondering if you were back. The service doesn't know how to reach you?"

Tess looked at her feet, then up into Alice's face. "I've had a lot on my plate, Alice. I'm not sure —" She shook her head, shut her mouth. "We were talking about Cora, though. She's — We should have stayed in Houston until everything was cleaned up again. Especially not brought her back to Esplanade while it was still a shambles. She feels guilty, I think, that all this happened on her watch." She pressed a hand against her chest to stop herself. "I'm sorry. I'm getting ahead of us."

Alice rushed to swallow. "No, no." She choked a little, cleared her throat. "Why did she stay, anyway? You couldn't reach her, or —"

Tess closed her eyes, and her eyelids glowed orange with the afternoon sun. "She refused to leave." She took a deep breath. "Said we were being alarmist."

"Alarmist?"

"Ask her —" Tess heard the exasperation in her voice and fought against it. "Anyway, Joe and I discussed it. Argued about it.

She'd been doing so well."

"How long was she here?" Alice said quietly.

"Um —" Tess counted on her fingers, partially to avoid looking in Alice's eyes. It was only three days after the storm hit that Joe had tried to go back into New Orleans for her, leaving Tess in Houston like a troublesome dog — *Go back to bed, Tess. Go. Back. To. Bed.* Four days by the time he came back, having failed to even cross the parish line. Ten days before the mayor had reopened the city, and she and Joe had tried again and been unable to find her. Twenty-five days before Tess had hitched a ride back in with Augie Randsell as Hurricane Rita approached the Louisiana coast, and they had discovered Cora having coffee with Mrs. Randsell on Augie's lawn.

"Just over three weeks. Joe went back right after the storm and couldn't get into the city. He said the National Guard stopped him at the bridge?" She sighed; you were not supposed to criticize your spouse in front of others. "Anyway, by the time he and I came back together, she was nowhere to be found. The front door to the house had been kicked open, there was mold on all the food. I thought she'd been evacuated. Was in one of those shelters in Ohio or something with no way to reach us, since all the cellphones were down. But she was here. She was here the whole time. God knows what she saw, what happened to her. She won't tell us. We know that for a while she was out in a boat with this friend of hers, Troy, rescuing people. She saved Ida Randsell from her little house in Metairie, then stayed uptown with her —"

"Augie's mother? I saw the obit."

"A stroke, the week after we got them to Houston."

I figured once the gates of Hell were opened —

"You and Joe are separated for the time being, you told me?" Alice said.

"He took his father out of the Little Sisters'. They're playing house out at the cabin."

Tess turned her face to the window, ran her fingers through her graying hair. She needed a professional coloring, but Shelly had not yet come back to town. Beyond her reflection, she saw that a limb was missing from the big oak in the side yard. It had been ripped off at the first crotch, and a stake of warm yellow wood jutted up like a bone.

"Your poor tree," Tess said, shutting her

eyes just long enough to make the tears go away.

"Terrible, isn't it?" Alice said. "Though Gerry had some good fun hacking it apart with his new chainsaw. Joe's father has Lewy Body, right?"

"Vincent. Yes," she said. "I think we're approaching end-stage, unfortunately — no thanks to the Valiums Joe was sneaking him in Houston. He tried to tear up one of his earliest pieces, even. Went after it with an oyster knife. I had to stop him."

"I'm sorry to hear that."

Go. Back. To. Bed. Joe had said with so much bile as he stuffed the duffel with clothes. She had grabbed Vincent a bit harder than she would have liked, but she had only been trying to save what was salvageable. For that, he left without her to rescue their daughter. And because he went alone, he failed.

Alice looked up from her pad with curtained eyes. "Were they — Joe, I mean — already living across the lake the morning Cora —"

"— wouldn't get out of bed." Tess shook her head violently, like shaking off flies. *Now,* she reminded herself. *Be here now.* She looked straight at Alice. "That's how I've been putting it, so you know. We don't use

81

the word 'depression.' It just turns her negative."

"So Joe was at the Dobies' with you?"

"What difference does that make?" Tess said.

Alice bit her lip. "Really?"

That tone was a problem of Alice's, a chink in her clinical armor through which one spied condescension, even a little bit of mockery.

"She's not one of your mini-neurotics, Alice. She's nearly thirty. She knows her father's and my relationship has nothing to do with her."

Alice let loose a snort. "Ah thank *you* might be the one who's off her rocka, Dr. Eshlemun," she said in a Yankee's best Mississippi drawl. It was an old, stupid joke bestowed on the office by a patient whom Tess had never been able to convince to come out of the closet: Tess's own joke. She didn't find it particularly funny anymore.

"You're right. I know." Tess sighed. "I know you're right. I just don't feel like talking about Joe." Even saying his name hurt, as if her lungs were being wrung out like wet clothes. "Of course you should ask Cora about it."

"I will," Alice said, and they sat in silence

as a breeze tossed the oak's remaining leaves.

"But that's not it. I know that's not it. It's what happened here, after the storm. Whatever she won't talk about. And it's the city." She threw her hand around. "She's grieving."

"Honey, you and I both know grief and depression are different." Alice laughed.

"No. I know," she said, her eyes closed. "I know."

"Okay." Alice's pen hovered as she read over the chart. "I see that Cora's had other difficulties. 'Delusional,' 'Possibly hypomanic'?"

Tess shook her head. "No." She pointed at the file in Alice's lap. "Is that Boudreaux? That was a long time ago. When she was just out of DePaul. They had her on drugs. I mean, she's an artistic person, imaginative, very sensitive, but nothing I'd call delusions. Flights of fancy."

"This is Letitia."

"Oh, Letitia. Loves her DSM!" Tess sighed. "Listen, Alice, I don't even know anymore. She's my child. I know her as a person, not a diagnosis. And, after all, what can any of us know? The problem of the black box, and all of that." Tess made like to zip her lip. "What am I talking to you for? You're the doctor here, I'm the mother, and I'm just telling you she's missing. It's like my child has fallen down a well."

Suddenly, she remembered a dream she'd had the night before, while she was blacked out in the middle of the Dobies' mattress: a rope hung taut in a column of water, air bubbles clinging to the twisted fibers. Just a slip of a dream.

Alice leaned towards her desk to grab the file, opened it, thumbed through a few pages. "She's not on medication now?"

"No. No more Ambien. Nemetz was doing some cognitive behavioral with her."

Alice nodded.

"She had been improving so much. Functioning so well."

Alice nodded again, but she didn't look up from her notepad.

"It's not bipolar: she scores in the teens. Little m, definitely little m. Her 'problem' if it is one is just that she's too emotive, too empathetic. Gets so upset over dead squirrels, that sort of thing, it interferes with her life. Out there, in that boat, I can't even imagine what she must have seen."

"I'm not arguing," Alice said.

Tess closed her mouth.

Alice glanced at her watch. "Anything else you need to tell me before I invite her in?"

Her mind had gone blank. She looked at the bright green, very expensive new carpet under the feet of the circling chairs. Alice had done well. Alice would continue to do well.

"Weight loss?" Alice suggested.

"Yes, though not terrible. She eats in the middle of the night."

"Oh?"

Tess shook her head. "It's bad, Alice. Without Joe snoring in the bed next to me, I sleep so soundly, I don't hear her get up. But she does get up. I don't know if she's sleepwalking or has just reversed night and day the way she did when she was a baby —"

"I'll find out. So she wakes up and just, like, makes a sandwich? Or —"

"I think she maybe goes and sits in the garden. I don't know. Her feet are always dirty in the mornings."

"Photosensitivity?"

"Oh," Tess said, looking towards the study door as if she could see Cora's pupils through it. "I don't know. That hadn't occurred to me. She had her eyes closed all the way over here. She keeps her blinds drawn. But why?"

"Could she be taking something you don't know about? That didn't get put in her chart? St. John's Wort? Thorazine?"

"Thorazine?" Tess laughed.

Alice shrugged her shoulders. "I've got to ask."

"Thorazine!" Tess gesticulated wildly as she stood from her chair. "That explains everything!"

"Oh, don't." Alice went for the plate of cookies, took another one for herself. "Don't you want me to cover all your bases?"

"It would be so easy, if we could just get them all off the Thorazine!"

Alice stared at her, Alice of the Concerned Brow.

"Sorry, I shouldn't joke."

Cookie still in her hand, Alice opened her arms wide and folded Tess into them. Tess laid her head on Alice's cashmere shoulder, and then Alice released her and opened the door. In the crewel armchair, Cora was asleep, hugging herself, her bare feet on the embroidery, arms wrapped around her folded knees. Slender bones of arms, her daughter's arms.

Joe revved the chainsaw. Back in the day, it would have excited him: all this raw material, the blades spinning in his hands. Only two months ago, he'd already be seeing things in the felled tree — a stag totem, a hieroglyph hawk — but nothing was going to come of this forest except sawdust and fire.

Heat loomed in the clouded day. Been hot since he'd opened the door at six. Didn't even try to sneak up. Didn't even bide its time. It was ten now, and he was sweating as he guided the chainsaw down through the big pine lying like a bridge over the shell drive. Ostensibly the first day of fall had been weeks ago, the day Tess and Augie had found Cora, two days before Rita made landfall, but the only change he could sense was this very negligible softening in the sky. They should call the seasons by their right names, he thought, and Louisiana had only two: a hurricane season and a season of calm.

He wrestled the hauling chain down through the limbs, under a section of trunk, and up again, thrusting his arms deep in the spiny branches, while the needles crept like spiders into his nose. When Joe came up for air, the dusty, menthol scent of the pines filled his lungs. He reminded himself, as he often had lately, of slaves crouching in the cotton fields, sick with smallpox in the cane. There was much that was endurable that didn't look it, and it was a privilege, not a burden, to do labor on your own account. The forest shrieked, and he sat back on the trunk for a moment and listened. A sound like a teakettle boiling. Tree frogs. Crickets. He'd read somewhere that the Northshore wasn't alluvial like New Orleans, but Pleistocene uplands; though he didn't know what that meant, the words came to him sometimes, particularly when he heard that sound, like the call of a raptor. It was the scream of melting glaciers, the sound of heat.

Out on the road, Sol's rig slowed, then pulled up across the entrance to the property. A woman's arm extended out of the passenger window, but she was turned away so that he only saw the thick chestnut hair knotted at the nape of her neck. Sol helloed, lifting his sweat-stained John Deere hat from his bald sunburned head, and Joe brushed his sleeve across his brow.

"Y'all doing alright?" Sol yelled.

"Yeah." Joe trotted towards him up the drive.

"You caught him?"

"Yeah. Big net." Joe laughed, shook his head. "Came back on his own."

"What'd we lose?" The woman sat up into the window — Monica Selvaggio, a woman he knew a little from church. She lifted a long hand off the door, let him shake it, though his forearms were flecked with sawdust. "Cow?" she asked. "Dog? Pony?"

"My dad."

She clucked, let his hand go. "I'm sorry."

"He's all right."

"Good to hear it," Sol said. "Somebody's keeping an eye on him now? He's at the house?"

From the back of the rig came the thumping of hooves against rubber. A dun face, a black eye bobbed in the window.

"Whose horses?" Joe asked.

Monica craned her long, tanned neck from the window and looked back at the trailer. "Mine. Sol is helping me out, keeping them for me while I get my fences mended. Lost a good half of it, which we could ill afford."

"But all the animals are okay?"

"The horses —" Monica sighed upwards into her bangs. "Well, they're stressed out now with this back and forth, but they're funny. The storm itself hardly phased them. They just turn their tails to the wind, put their heads down."

"Yeah," Sol said. "It's just us human-folk can't deal with this all."

"Just us." Monica nodded. "They don't have mortgages."

"True that."

Sol gathered tobacco juice in his mouth and spat into the ditch.

"Listen, Joe," Sol said, leaning over the center console. "You ever need anything, help with them trees or just someone to sit with Mr. Vincent, you just holler, hear? I don't mind doing it. A night in 1957 might just be what the doctor ordered."

Joe nodded. "I thank you, but we're doing all right. Yesterday was a fluke. By the time I saw him, he was just fine, and he's good today."

Monica, a tight smile on her face, reached out her hand again, and he took it, a rough but slender paw.

"Whatever you say, son," Sol said. "Whatever you say. But listen, y'all want to get out of the house Sunday you come on over to mine, alright? We're going to have us a barbeque to welcome our new barnguests." He turned and winked at Monica. "Ain't that right."

Joe could see himself there, beside the grill, the light coming down over the clover fields, pretending everything was fine. "Oh, I'm not sure," he said.

"Being around the horses always helped my mom," Monica said, looking at him from between her heavy lashes. "It was like

90

— they didn't care what year it was, so why should she worry about it."

"I'll think about it," he said, backing away from the rig as Sol pulled down on the gearshift and hauled the huge machinery back onto the road. Above the trailer's double doors, the horses' tails swished, and their rumps rolled and tensed as they readied themselves for the ride.

A man and a woman were walking up the front steps from Esplanade just as Del stepped out of the door. She had barely taken them in — sweat-stained T-shirts, the man's wide cornrows, the green backpack slung over the woman's left shoulder — when she realized that the Jeep parked at the curb was Cora's.

In classic Cora fashion, she had given the car to Troy, the man she'd ridden out the storm with, so that he could use it to abandon her. Del glared at the man coming up the steps. She figured that someone who would allow himself to take a woman's only means of transportation — Well, she had been fairly certain none of them would ever see the Jeep again, yet somehow here it was. Through the tinted glass, she could see that a child was sitting in the backseat. For a second, her face appeared then dropped back down again.

The couple had stopped halfway up the steps. She'd met Troy, apparently, that summer she worked at Eleusis, but the face didn't ring any bells. The woman looked at her, then at the house number, looked back.

"He said straight hair, skinny," she said to the man, who shook his head.

"Are you Cora?" he asked her. "Cora Boisdoré?"

She shook her head, feeling her curls spring around her face. "She's my sister. You're not Troy?"

"Cousin." The man nodded, his upper lip held in his bottom teeth.

"She here?" the woman asked.

Del stepped out into the portico, letting the vestibule door slam, and put out her hand.

"I'm Adelaide."

The women shook hands. She smelled like sweat and ketchup, long driving.

"I'm Kea, and this's —"

"Anthony." He grasped Del's hand in both of his. "Cora's here or no?"

Del shook her head.

Anthony nodded. "Her car —" He pointed. "We're supposed to deliver it back."

"To her," Kea cut in. "Troy said, specific, ask for her. Make sure you see how she's doing, he said."

It was kind of Troy to be so concerned now, Del thought. She liked this suspicion too, the two of them looking at her like she was a thief.

"You're his cousin, you said?"

Anthony nodded.

"You left the city with him?" Del asked.

"No," Kea said. "We were up in St. Louis, and he came and got us from the Red Cross, offered us the Jeep to drive down in."

Del nodded. On TV, she'd seen pictures of the shelters — cots lined up on concrete floors, people playing cards, being interviewed, eating salad out of tinfoil lasagna pans.

"Well, thank you," she said, "for bringing it back. Cora will be happy to know the car was put to good use in getting you home safe."

"Right," Anthony said to himself, looking up, looking away.

"She's here, then?" Kea asked.

Del shook her head and looked behind her at the broken door of her home. "Not here. Nobody's here." She put her hand on the fluted column at the corner of the portico and pushed against it, as if she expected it to fall over. "She's out at the doctor. I was just going to pick her up."

"She's not doing well?"

Del pursed her lips.

"I'm sorry." Kea nodded. "I can't imagine
— saving all of those people in the flood,
and then what she did for those kids —"

Kea stopped abruptly. The back door to
Cora's Jeep had opened, and the little girl
was running towards them, skipping on
every third step.

"What kids?" Del asked.

"Tyrone and Willy?" Kea said, watching
the little girl wrap her arms around one of
Anthony's legs. "Reyna's little boys? You
know Reyna — Troy's batshit sister."

Anthony placed a hand on the back of her
neck.

"I'm sorry." Kea peeled his hand from her,
not sounding sorry. "I'm not going to not
say it. You've got to acknowledge. It's not
like she don't know, we know, everybody
knows."

"I'm sorry — what?" Del asked.

"Those kids were stranded out there in
that water, and she and Troy saved them.
Had to paddle them out in a goddamned
boat."

"Hush, Kea." Anthony shook his head,
looking down at the child.

"It's the facts of life, Anthony, and no

shame in it," Kea said. "If you don't think Neesa knows about it, after what we've been through — she's the same age as Willy, you know."

"Oof," Del said. "I had no idea."

"We're going to see Tyrone and Willy?" Neesa said.

Anthony rolled his eyes.

"No, honey." Kea reached down and scooped the little girl up into her arms. "They're in Illinois with your Uncle Troy like you know. We're going to see about staying by your granny's."

Del nodded at her. It was like how her mother taught her to deal with Cora and her anxieties — you didn't dwell on them, you helped her move away from them to some new idea. No talking about the flood, then. Best not mention children stranded in the flood.

"You're going to go see your granny?" Del asked the little girl.

"No," Anthony said. "She's in Georgia."

Kea had started to tap her foot, the webbed jelly sandal making wet sounds as it hit the tile. "We've just got to go see about the house. See if we can stay there, because ours —"

Anthony was shaking his head. "There wasn't any point even looking."

95

"I'm sorry." Del looked down at the mosaic on the floor of the portico. One brown tile had been dislodged from its place in the eye of a whale, and she ran the toe of her shoe over it, kicked it into the garden. "Bad?"

"It's just not there," Kea shrugged, and picked the little girl up in her arms. "I mean, there's a house there, but it's not a house for us anymore. The whole neighborhood's just —"

Del nodded at her; even up here on high ground the neighborhood was empty, gone. The few who had come back ghosted around like dead Greeks who'd gotten on the wrong side of the gods, repairing windows so that they could be blown out again, draining basements so that they could flood again. She looked at Kea with what she hoped was compassion, but Kea had stopped talking.

"Bought it last year," Anthony said. "Lots of third shifts in that deposit."

"I'm so sorry."

Kea nodded. Neesa's chin cupped her shoulder, her nose nestled into the stretched blue neck of her mother's tee.

"Do you want me to drive you to your mom's house?" Del said, as gently as she could. "I've got to pick up Cora from the doctor first, but it would be no problem."

Kea looked behind her at the car. "We've been on the road a long time now."

"We'd appreciate it," Anthony said.

As Del turned to pull the chain through the ripped screen, Anthony held out the keys on Cora's pelican ring. She must have handed them over to Troy as he left, just reached out and put them in a clump in his palm — her own house key, the key to Esplanade, the key to the restaurant. Even as a child, she'd been like that — giving her tuna sandwich to a stray cat on the way to school, standing aside so the other, pushier children could take her turn on the slide at the playground. She always rushed to help, gave away what she needed without thinking, kept nothing for herself.

Vincent knelt at the front window of the cabin. His knees ached, but he couldn't go to sit on the furniture behind him. Strange furniture except for the rocking chair with the needlepoint seat that tasted of something — the sound of rocking, the smell of a wood fire, his mother humming as she held him tight to her deflated bosom. The tune she hummed was always the same but always different, because she made it up as she went along, pushing her toe into the carpet, holding his head against her with her large, rough hand. The light on the shell road was too bright, and there was a smell of oil burning with the wood. A motor kicked on again. To calm himself, Vincent tried to hum his mother's song.

His humming seemed to splinter the cold air. The outside of the windowpane was beaded with condensate. He had to think: dew formed on the outside of a glass of ice tea, which meant water condensed on a surface colder than the air it was suspended in, and so the window must be colder than the air beyond it, which meant the whole house was like an icebox, this house that was familiar and yet unfamiliar, like a place visited in a dream.

He turned his head from the clouded window. His mother's rocking chair stood still, like a captive, surrounded by the other, unfamiliar furniture he felt he should know, like the men at his father's funeral who had reached out to shake his hand, like his own father laid out in the living room — this room — with his mother in her rocking chair beside him where it was warm from the heat of the fire and cold outside, where the wind blew the boughs of the tall pines. The pines should be shading the room, and yet it was sunlit. He scraped at the dew on the window, but it would not come off. Beside the shell road, the trees had been felled. Something terrible had happened. Something terrible — his father had died. He would have to go to work. That explained the trees; his mother was selling them for money. She said she wanted him to finish his schooling, as she held his head against her bosom, but he would have to go to work instead, though he was only fourteen. She had sent letters, and he would make things like his father had, and before that his father and his father's father, and his father's father's father. He would press a chisel into pine and tap the handle with his mallet, so that the wood curled up like cold butter. That explained the smell of sawdust floating above the shell road, but it didn't explain the strange furniture, the way the weather had been reversed — condensate on the outside of the glass.

He pressed himself to the wall, hair up on the back of his neck. They said a place goes cold when a spirit passes through, though he felt ashamed thinking that. Belief in ghosts wasn't educated, his mama would say, wasn't Christian neither, for we know unready souls wait patiently in Limbo until the gates are opened, but his mama would also say to trust your instincts, and his instincts told him something was wrong.

He imagined his papa coming home down the shell road, back the same way he'd gone after crouching to kiss him where he sat in his mama's lap in front of the fire that was just getting going in the hearth. *Catch me a nice big one, Louis,* his mama said, and his papa had nodded out the door. But something was wrong about the day. He'd felt it the same way a dog does, getting his hair up before he sees the moccasin in the water. He'd woken before sunup, his father crouched at the grate to light the fire, and the sound of the match had been a paper-doll sound, vivid but thin. He fed the chickens, helped to put wax on a new-built table, did his school work. They sat down to supper, his father's place empty at the head. His mama said grace in a voice thin as paper, but her words blew out of the open end of the day.

Something terrible had happened. She took him on her lap in the rocking chair though he was too old for it, his legs reaching almost to the floor. She held him tight to her so that he couldn't drift away. He made up thoughts of his papa drinking, his papa with women, just to spite her. He knew about women, the way they could walk along a road like to lead you, a little dog on a chain. But his mama didn't let him go, she just hummed louder, and the day wouldn't close, not until they heard footsteps and she dropped him from her lap, standing up fast as she did. It was Willet at the door with a clutch of fish, but never mind them. The boat had flipped in the Rigolets, he said. Drenched, his papa had turned blue, died before they could make it in. That was all he said, so little that it barely seemed to mean what it meant — a paper story like an obituary that only says "passed" and not how. His mama cried anyway, hugging on Willet, didn't ask for more.

Even once the rest of it came — his daddy laid out on the table he'd made — it was hard to believe it was true. Proving wasn't possible, Father Renée said in science class, only disproving, which explained why he was kneeling at the window, watching the shell road, even after his mama had sold away the trees. He believed he heard footsteps in the shells, saw the shadow of a walking man, but only believed, like he believed the man they dressed in his father's suit for the vigil couldn't have been his father — so pale he was and waxy above the scarf tied around his throat — though his mama said that was just how a body looked after the soul had passed.

He believed he saw a man approaching the house up the shell road. He believed he heard his footsteps and that they would spare him — save him from the empty house, from the trunk his mama'd packed with the clothes to take into the city, from the city house of the German, Kastenhoff, who he'd been apprenticed to, and from that man's squinting, steel-gray eyes. He believed he heard his father's feet climb the porch steps, his father opening the cabin door.

"Pop?" the man called — he believed it was his father, but he couldn't prove it. He couldn't prove anything at all.

Better Cheddar. A Coke. A sleeve of saltines. It had been over forty years, but Tess could taste them already as she idled in the Langenstein's parking lot waiting for a woman her mother's age — big gold jewelry, good facelift, starched linen blouse — to push her cart across the lane. The woman smiled and nodded, and Tess was suddenly aware of her pilly cotton tank, her makeup-free face, her hair, gray at the roots and towel-dried, but she lifted a hand off the wheel anyway and gave the woman her best Uptown smile. As she always told Cora, you've got to project what it is you'd like to feel.

She could see her mother sitting barefoot on the back porch steps in pedal pushers and a loose shirt, her blonde hair newly set, digging her cracker straight into the tub. In her other hand, she'd be holding a menthol cigarette against the neck of the Coke bottle. There would be one for Tess in the icebox, the cold lip of the glass bottle like a boy's lip. When her father was out, this was how they celebrated. Better Cheddar, bare feet. For once, no dinner at the damask-covered table. The Marleybone silver, her mother's silver, arranged like chess pieces: salad fork, fish fork, dinner fork, meat knife, fish knife, soup spoon. Even if there was just a single course, her father insisted on a fully set table, so he could turn the unused silver over, a silent protest that she did not serve a meal the way his mother's help had served a meal. So, when he was gone, her mother put on her white gloves and little hat as usual, went down to Langenstein's as usual, but only got Better Cheddar, Cokes, a box of saltines. When Tess was older, her mother would offer her the box of menthols too, and Tess would take one, practice holding it like her mother did at the very tips of her fingers, practice leaving lipstick prints on the filter in her mother's favorite shade.

They would laugh together, leaning back on their elbows on the top step; it made them so happy, to conspire.

And how did that make you feel, being left alone? Alice had asked Cora, on the other side of the door.

Beside her, the trunk of a Lexus popped open and the older lady began to transfer her groceries from her basket. Gone were the bag boys, the dime held out between gloved fingertips. Long gone, of course. Progress pushed them out of their old routines, and nowhere faster than where the routines were oldest. Whenever she went Uptown, she saw how the apocalypse would come. She heard the fish knives, salad forks, soup spoons clattering as the tide pulled them out into the Gulf, saw the net on her mother's hats hung like Spanish moss from the trees of the frayed swamp, the menthol smoke rolling off like mist on water. Since she'd married Joe, she only came Uptown to get Better Cheddar and Popeye dip or maybe a prime porterhouse for special occasions, but she still kept an eye on the butcher, the way her mother had taught her. Buddy was infamous for putting his thumb on the scale.

Do you feel like your parents abandoned you? Of course, it was what she was paying

Alice for, to ask that question. But she didn't have to like it.

The older woman slammed her trunk shut and looked at Tess as if to say: *What in God's name are you looking at?* Reasonable question. She popped down the makeup mirror and dabbed some concealer under her eyes while she waited for the parking spot to open.

As she put the car in park, she noticed a man, tall, a little salt-and-pepper, crossing Arabella towards the entrance of the store. Augie Randsell. Roused by the smell of menthol, something old in her made her thump her horn at him — *hulla-ba-loo-hooray!* — the way Madge used to do back in high school. Augie turned his head, and a thrill shot up her spine. His mouth moved to say her name. Getting out of the car, she felt faint, put her hand on the door to steady herself. An old Bonneville whisked by, fondling her skirt.

"We keep meeting like this, I'm gonna start calling you a streetwalker," Augie called, and she closed her eyes for a second, saw the headlights of his Porsche lighting up the backs of the highway signs — the nightmare of evacuation in the contraflow — as he braked into the emergency lane. She had been standing down the shoulder,

105

holding onto Vincent as he urinated into the trees. That was what had started it: Augie had left Mrs. Randsell at home, and Joe had sent Cora after her, in a boat, on the flood. *Fancy meeting you here!* his face peering over his half-rolled window, the evacuation coursing behind him.

Do you feel like your parents abandoned you?

As he turned towards her, away from the automatic doors of the grocery — opening and shutting, opening and shutting — she watched his shoes: saddle leather, polished, stiff-soled, heel-toe, heel-toe, the cuffs of his trousers breaking nicely across the waxed laces. In his front pocket, he jingled change. He had put his hand on her hand on the white tablecloth in Houston the evening after Joe had abandoned her to go look for Cora, and she had eaten the steak he'd paid for, she had let herself be consoled. It was wrong. Inappropriate. Unhealthy, like the widower she'd seen who responded to his wife's death by seeking out fetish parlors where he could be tied up like an animal, only to come into his grief two years later when nobody he didn't pay would speak to him.

It's not a question of feeling, Alice said, apropos of something spoken too softly to hear. *It's a question of fact.*

Augie was grinning so wide his lips disappeared. She had given him up thirty-eight years ago, and only once before had she felt even a twinge of regret.

It's not a question of feeling, Alice said.

But she hadn't felt this way about seeing anyone, Joe included, since she was twenty-three years old. It must be, she diagnosed herself, some sort of sublimation or displacement of grief. How else to explain it? Augie Randsell was nothing more than an aging Debutante's Delight of middling intelligence, but here she was clinging to the hood of her car.

It's not a question of feeling. It's a question of fact.

"My dear Dr. Eshleman," he said, as he always said.

"Mrs. Boisdoré to you, Mr. Randsell," she said, as she always said.

"Call me Augie," he said, laughing, and patted her on the back. "You alright?"

She shrugged and let go of the roof of her car.

"Home again, home again," she said.

"Jiggedy-jig. Glad to be out of Houston, I'll bet."

"How much?"

He blinked his pale lashes.

107

"How much will you bet?"

"It's hard to prepare, isn't it." He led her away from the car, his shoes clip-clopping as they crossed Arabella, back towards the market.

"Impossible," she said.

They went through the magic doors into the air-conditioning. The cashiers kept their heads down. The registers beeped. "It's like when Madge died —" He picked up a basket. "You understand it conceptually. In theory. You can even visualize it, think, we'll lay her out in the green silk dress, bury her in the family tomb beside the cypress tree. But then you have to live with it." He cleared his throat. "You have to live with it."

She was following after him like a small child, her hand somehow in his hand, until he dropped it. He picked up a bottle of wine from the wire rack next to the crackers.

Tess looked at her feet, at the inches of spotted linoleum between them. After Madge's funeral, Augie had drifted away from them. Had not called. Had not even sent the proper *Thank you for your thoughts,* not even a printed card. And that New Year's they had left a message on his machine, inviting him to the usual dinner, but they never heard back. Joe had taken it as

108

an affront, but it wasn't that, was it.

Augie was holding the golden bottle of chardonnay up into the fluorescent light, and it cast watery shadows over the toes of his shoes.

"I keep thinking still, you know, about your mother," Tess said. There had been no green silk dress for Mrs. Randsell — she was cremated in Houston in the T.J. Maxx pajamas she'd been wearing when she died — and as yet there'd been no burial under the cypress that shaded the family tomb. Augie had not set a date for the memorial, and she doubted that he ever would. It would have distressed Mrs. Randsell greatly, Tess was sure — she of the ten-year mourning, who wanted to talk about nothing but Eleusinian mystery cults the whole long drive out of New Orleans. Mrs. Randsell was sure Tess would be interested — *You read Jung, don't you dear?* — and so she'd gone on and on about "Golden Leaves," initiations, pennyroyal. *You have to really watch what you drink down there,* she'd said, of Hades. *Don't drink from Lethe, whatever you do!* she said, reaching from the front seat to grab Cora by the arm. *And if anyone tries to stop you drinking from the pool of Mnemosyne, you just tell them you have a right to it, because you are — wait —* She'd picked her book up from the footwell and read, with mock seriousness, *"The child of earth and starry heaven." You'll need your memory if you're ever going to get back out to the land of the living.*

If it had been up to Tess, she would have buried Augie's mother with coins on her eyes. At least burned that book with her. But it had not been up to Tess.

"It was only going to get harder for her." Augie's sigh smelled of gin.

Tess nodded and took a step closer, then a step back again, putting a hand on the edge of a shelf half-stocked with crackers. He plucked another bottle of chardonnay off the rack and, holding it in both hands, read the label.

"I do hope Adelaide is feeling better," Augie said.

"Cora, you mean."

He looked up at her, blinked, and there were broken capillaries on his nose, and it was almost as though she'd been under a spell. Time spun forward. The gilding flaked from his face.

"Del's fine," Tess said. "She's home, did I mention? Cora on the other hand —"

Do you feel like your parents abandoned you?

110

"Oh, Jesus, Tess, I'm sorry," Augie laughed and put the bottle back on the shelf. "My mouth, lately, it's been getting ahead of my brain. Too much living alone. So this daughter of yours, who saved my mother's life — the little that was left of it — whom you and I drove out of New Orleans, whom I've known since she was knee high to an ant, her name is Cora?"

"You got it, Mr. Randsell. Right on the nose."

Augie touched his index finger to the tip of her nose, and for one flashing moment, she was a girl again, perfumed and powdered, in a new gown at Proteus the night Madge was queen. Augie had her in his arms, and when he pulled her close, she imagined he might kiss her, that she was his girl, not Madge who stood on the dais in her heavy dress, that she was Augie's girl and not Joe's, who even then was waiting at the valet stand in his father's car for her to emerge from the rustling lights so that he could drive her home before the storm broke — a winter storm that was already shaking the auditorium with its thunder, though the rain had not yet begun to fall.

"Is Cora alright?" Augie said, serious again suddenly, his liquid eyes on her face.

Do you feel like your parents abandoned you?

Tess shut her eyes. He put his hand on her shoulder, a warm hand at the verge of her blouse, on her skin. She let her head fall against his collarbone and took a deep breath of his old-fashioned aftershave, his smell of soap and sweat, and he held her tight.

Del watched Cora hesitate at the edge of Alice's front porch, her head tilted back, her eyes closed against the breeze that fell through the remaining branches of a damaged oak. Dressed all in white, she looked almost mummified, her cheeks sunken, her ribs visible where they met her sternum over the stretched-out neck of her sweatshirt.

Tess had told Del to wait outside, in case Alice needed more time for the session, and so they'd set up camp in the Jeep, all the windows open. Kea sat on the rear bumper in the shade of the open hatch, while Anthony played tag with Neesa, chasing after her while she ran giggling back and forth across the quiet street.

Cora put her hands into her hair, looking from the child to the Jeep and back again, but before Del could go to her sister to explain, she was already coming down.

112

Kea pushed herself up and went towards Cora with a big grin on her face, her hand extended. "It's so good to meet you! Troy, you know, told us what you did for those kids —"

Cora, aloof as a goddess, walked right through her. She was watching Anthony and the child, but not as if she saw them, her eyes blank disks of blue.

Anthony ambled towards them, his arms out wide for a hug, but Cora ignored him and climbed into the passenger seat. Anthony's hands dropped to his sides. When he looked at Del, she saw that old familiar expression of pity on his lips. He nodded at her, to say he understood, like everyone always had. *Hey, Del, how's your family holding up?* When Cora went missing from college, when they had to send her to DePaul, her classmates, her teachers, her friends all always only squinched their eyebrows, bit their lips. *So, is Cora going to be okay?*

Del made herself get back in the car, fighting the old impulse to pretend not to know her sister. It was always Cora's show, always had been. Everything was always on her terms. In the passenger seat, her sister had her head down between her knees, and Del put the key in the ignition. She tried to call up the memories she relied upon when she needed to be kind: Cora holding Del's head in her lap when Del had fallen from the pecan tree and broken her leg, Cora stroking her hair as their mother maneuvered the car through the pines, Cora making up a story about fairies while pain glared like the sunlight that shone in a halo around her sister's head.

"So where we headed, folks?" Del asked as Kea buckled Neesa into the middle seat and Anthony shut the door.

"You know the train tracks out by Elysian Fields? Behind in there," Kea said.

Cora groaned into her hands, and Del worked her thumb into the muscle along her sister's spine. Del knew how hard it was for her to see hard things — images lodged in her, and she had trouble getting them out again. One glimpse of a TV show with an abused child or a hurt animal could send her to her room weeping. Truly, Del didn't know how she'd survived it: three weeks in the flood.

"I won't make you look," Del whispered.

Even before they'd reached the old abandoned market in St. Roch, the rest of the car had gone quiet. The little girl looked widemouthed out of the windows at the boarded-up houses as they passed, the messages in spray paint on plywood: *I am here.*

Destroy this memory. Baghdad. I have a gun.
Kea leaned against her daughter and stroked
her hair, humming.

There was nobody out on the street,
nobody sitting on their porches. Electrical
poles tilted over the sidewalks, trailing their
wires like trees brought down by vines, and
everywhere a broken gray crust of dirt
covered the concrete, the grass, the trashcans and bicycles, sofas and potted plants
strewn on front lawns. On every block,
disabled cars had been stranded along the
curb, a thick swamp of mud on their upholstery, so that when the occasional undamaged sedan appeared in a driveway beside a
flung-open house, it gleamed so brightly you
saw stars.

Del could count on one hand the number
of times she'd been out this way — the
eighth and ninth wards being off her mother's maps of safe, read "white," places to go.
She and her mother had sped down the
length of St. Claude once on the way to
some nursery in St. Bernard, her mother's
knuckles pale around the wheel, and Del
had gone to Vaughan's for music some in
college, been down to Holy Cross twice as a
teenager with her grandfather to see a
hundred-year-old ébéniste about veneers.
So it was odd how devastated she felt look-

115

ing out at the neighborhood. It wasn't hers, and yet maybe it should have been. She shook her head. It didn't matter if had it been hers. What mattered was that it was gone.

As they descended farther below sea level, the line the flood had drawn traced steadily up the sides of the houses. They passed a single person — a middle-aged woman in a stretched-out cotton shift, carrying a dresser drawer — and then it was back to nothing.

Del curled a hank of Cora's smooth hair around her hand, and Cora nodded, pulling the coil of hair tight before Del let it go.

"It must have been rough, what you went through," Kea said softly as Del turned the Jeep down towards the Industrial Canal. "Me, I can barely handle a thunderstorm, isn't that right?"

"She screams like a little child," Anthony said.

Neesa started to giggle. "She's silly. I'm not scared. I wasn't even scared in the hurricane, and you couldn't see your hand in front your face."

"Good for you," Del said to her. "You must be very brave."

In the rearview, she watched the little girl nod.

"Turn —" Anthony coughed a little on

the word, his face turned to the window. "Take your next right."

A stop sign stood off-kilter at the intersection, and though there was no one for miles, Del stopped. On the next corner, a camelback painted blue with orange shutters had buckled, its roof stove in by a telephone pole.

"I can't hardly believe it," Kea said. On her lap, Neesa's face had turned to stone. "I can't hardly believe it. The house I grew up in, the house I was raised in."

"Not this one?" Del let the car coast until she was parallel with the camelback, then tapped the brake, her hands at ten and two on the wheel.

Kea didn't answer, her face locked in an expression of refusal.

"Yeah, this one," Anthony said as he opened his door and got out into the mud-coffined grass.

Anthony climbed up onto the front porch and rattled the gate locked over the door. On the siding, the rescue patrols had marked a different sort of X, this one inscribed in a square.

"I can't hardly believe it," Kea said again as Anthony hopped off the side of the porch and climbed over the chain-link fence into the yard.

"I know how you feel," Del said as she rubbed her hand over her sister's back, but she wasn't totally sure that that was true.

When Anthony appeared again from around the back of the house, he was shaking his head. He stood for a moment looking at the telephone pole that had crashed into the house, at the floorboards snapped in half and hanging over the trash-strewn mud, then he put his hands in his pockets and got back into the car.

For a while, they continued out and down, stopping at a sister's house, an uncle's, and a cousin's — all flooded so bad the furniture lay overturned in heaps on the floor, every wall stippled with black mold. They stopped in front of a friend's house with no roof, looked for an address that no longer had a house to its name — only concrete steps with the numbers 1341 set into them in blue porcelain tile. They idled in front of it, watching fire ants build their mound beside a shipwrecked chest freezer. Anthony rolled down his window and pounded his hand twice against the door.

Kea sighed. "You want to go by Troy's?"

"I don't have the address," Anthony said.

"She does." Kea pointed her chin at Cora.

Her face still in her lap, Cora whispered, "No."

Del drew her brows together.

"Sure you do," Kea said. "Y'all been fucking for how long? Besides, that's where they found them — Reyna and Tyrone and Willy — you know."

"The child, Kea," Anthony said.

"When they got stuck in the water?" Neesa said.

Cora was humming to herself, her hands pressed over her ears, and Neesa scooted forward on her mother's knees to look at her. "She rowed in the boat?"

"It's just life, Anthony," Kea said.

"I want to rode in a boat," Neesa said.

"Troy lived right down the block from you, Cora, didn't he?" Del said.

"Row a boat," Kea repeated. "Ride in a boat."

"No," Cora was saying. "No."

"I know a song," Neesa said, and began to sing it: *Row, row, row your boat, gently down the stream. Merrily, merrily, merrily, merrily —*

"Do y'all know the house from the outside?" Del asked, turning up Claiborne, back towards Esplanade. "I can get us close at least."

When Joe pulled back the shower curtain, his father was standing inside the white

119

steam. He was clutching at the towel hanging on the door, and he lifted it off its hook,
held it out like Joe's mother used to do
before he was old enough to bathe himself.
Joe took it, dried his hair. Air was blowing
from the vent over the door, cold in the
water-beaded fur on his chest.

"You need me to get out, so you can use
the toilet?" Joe asked.

His father shook his head, his face needy
but impassive like a child's.

Joe wrapped the towel around himself,
patted at his privates through the terry. "It's
not a problem, Pop. I'm done in here."

He reached around his father's back,
struggled to get a grip on the glass knob,
turned it. Dry air flushed the room. The
smell of sawdust was still in his nose, and
he turned around to grab a Q-tip. His father
was leaning over the sink, trying to see his
face through the mirror's scrim of steam.

"You got an in-grown whisker again?" he
asked Vincent.

Joe took a Q-tip from the jar, cleared a
hole in the condensate with the flat of his
hand. His father's eyes met his in the reflection, blinked, as the fog began to creep back
across the mirror.

"Man, I look like a drowned rat," Joe said,
ruffling up the short hair matted to his scalp.

Side by side they looked like before and after versions of the same man: The receding hairline receded. The freckles become liver spots, laugh lines become trenches. The careworn hollowness of his cheeks under their three-day stubble turned into his father's permanent hangdog mouth. They were both too skinny, Joe thought. He'd have to feed them more.

His father kept looking into the mirror even as the steam whited them out. He touched his reflection, touched Joe's arm.

"They told me you drowned," his father said.

Just the aphasia, Joe told himself. "Right. I look like a drowned rat," he repeated. "So, bathroom's all yours. I might lie down for a minute."

Joe stepped out into the hall, closing the door behind him. His whole body ached, and his forearms looked like he'd gotten in a fight with a pissed-off cat. He lay himself out on the mattress, his forehead on the backs of his hands. A disk of yellow light sliced in through the windows like a hazard sign. *A baby can drown in as little as one inch of water.* He shifted, pressed his arm across his eyes, kept himself from going back to the bathroom. His father wasn't a baby.

He fell asleep, woke. According to the

clock, three minutes had passed. His father was watching him again from the door, and again — he had to shake it — he thought of a child. Cora, waking from a nightmare, waiting for them to notice her as she stood silently in the dark beside their bed. He could almost smell her, feel the heat of her little body as she climbed in between him and Tess, whispering, *There was a three-headed wolf and he chased me down a pond and I kept on going down and down and down and down until the stairs stopped working* — Abruptly, he inhaled. His father still stood watching at the door.

"Pop, what's up?" He pushed himself onto his elbows. "I was gonna take a nap, unless you need me."

His father shook his head. Joe made himself see the old man — blue polyester pants belted high on his waist, the tremor in his hands. *A feeling of usefulness can be incredibly therapeutic,* he remembered reading on one of those web forums. *If you forget who your LO is, it makes it that much harder for them to remember themselves.* He pushed himself backwards, put his feet on the floor. Everything made of wood in the cabin they'd already oiled, polished, or waxed, but neither of them had touched the hope chest, though it stood in the middle of the living

122

room floor. Joe had been waiting for his father to pick up the tools again, finish the "alterations" he'd started in Houston. But his father seemed to shy away from the chest, as if it was the chest that had hurt him. Occasionally, he would look from the chest to his inner arm in confusion, the marks Tess's fingernails had left there. He seemed malleable today though. Interested.

"You feel well enough to do some work today?"

His father nodded.

"There's Mama's hope chest, remember, needs your attention."

"You want me to polish it for you?"

Joe shrugged. "Or finish the work you started at Vin's, I was thinking. Tess's not around to stop you, right?" His father's hand moved steadily towards his pocket, trembled as he slotted his thumb in. "If you're up to it, of course."

"Anything you say," his father said.

"Good, good."

Joe put the clothes he'd worn to the store that morning back on. Change jingled in his pocket as he followed his father down the hall. At the edge of the great room, they stopped.

"That's your mama's chest?" Vincent pointed.

123

From a distance, the chest looked like an animal had been at it — a wolf maybe, sharpening his claws. In various places across the intricate interwoven carvings of wisteria and magnolia branches and roses, his father had knocked Vin's oyster knife into the wood, breaking off a petal here, cutting in a thorn there, thinning a stem. He'd heard it from the basement guest room through his sleep, a sound like gunshots. He'd rushed up the stairs, half-dressed, and when he'd flipped on the lights in the den, Tess was standing over his father, his arm in her hand. The oyster knife clattered to the floor. *No, you're the one. You're the one we should have left,* she was saying. There was blood under her nails.

"If you don't feel up to carving, you could always just patch it, right? I've got wood putty, and there's cypress scraps in the workshed and Elmer's."

"You want me to do this?" his father said, his lower lip out and trembling.

Joe took his father's right hand in his own, and turned his arm over, looked at the four crescent moon scars Tess's fingernails had made on the inside of his wrist.

"Not if you don't want to do it."

"It's your mama's chest. What if I foul it up?"

"You are the greatest living cabinetmaker in the South." He nodded. "You can make a few minor repairs to an old chest. Mama would want you to, wouldn't she?"

"She wants me to?"

Joe nodded. "I think she does."

He led his father across the room and sat him down in the rocking chair beside the chest. Vincent's hands stayed in his lap for a moment, and then they reached out, hesitantly, coming down onto the lid, where the veneer was still smooth and unbroken as the day he had left it on Sylvia's front porch sixty some-odd years ago, with a note inside asking her to marry him, should he return from the war. His white brows knit, his eyes closed behind the wide lenses of his glasses, he was running his hands over the braided stems of the flowers, the thin magnolia branches. He followed the carving over the side and across the wood he'd damaged, and then up again, and his thumbnail fit into the groove of the closed, velveteen petals, and he smiled but did not open his eyes.

Neesa was still singing when they turned up Bayou Road. *Merrily, merrily, merrily, merrily, life is but a dream.* She kept singing as Del crossed Broad and turned up Cora's street, kept singing as they slowed to a crawl past

125

Cora's house, kept singing as Anthony sat up straight and pointed at the green house across the way as Cora kept shaking her head in her hands, saying *no.*

Row, row, row your boat —

Del pulled the Jeep into Troy's driveway, just two strips of broken cement laid over the buried grass. The flood had come up about four feet here, drawing a thick line on the siding just above the house's raised floor. The window beside them was open, and on the sill, there was the corrugated mark of a duck boot's sole.

— gently down the stream.

"Doesn't look so bad." Kea looked at Anthony, jiggled the child on her knee.

He nodded as he got out of the car, leaving the door open, chiming, and walked around to the front of the house.

Merrily, merrily, merrily, merrily —

Cora pressed her hands against her ears and began to sing in round, her voice a drone. *Merrily, merrily, merrily, merrily.*

— life is but a dream.

The day was softening as it edged towards evening, and the warm air coming into the car would almost have been pleasant if it weren't for the smell. The whole city smelled acrid, with its rotten freezers, mildewing furniture, but it was stronger here — the smell of a rat in your wall. They sat breathing it as Anthony opened the front door, and the screen slammed shut.

Cora moaned and crossed her arms over her head. Del saw Anthony's shadow pass by the window, before he opened the shutters on the other side, letting in the light. He looked around, quickly, then hurried out of the room.

Del got out of the car and tilted her face up, breathing the heat, like an embodiment of the terrible, yellow stench, and shut the door Anthony had left open, closing Kea and Neesa and Cora safely in. Then she walked down the driveway towards the front of the house.

On the lawn, a Big Wheel lay on its back like a stranded turtle, coated in the ubiquitous mud, and Del followed Anthony's boot tracks up the steps. The flood had come in over the front porch, but the mud had been trampled between the steps and the door. Del went past the patrol's mark:

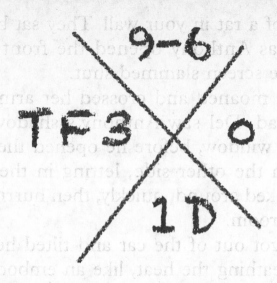

She pulled open the screen door. The stench was stronger inside — hotter, almost viscous — and Anthony was standing in front of Troy's framed Congo Square posters, breathing into the arm he held across his mouth.

"What is it?" Del said, but she understood the moment she'd spoken the words.

In the kitchen behind him, caught in a window of yellow light, was a woman's body without a face. Her jeans were crusted up to her thighs with dried mud, her feet bare. Around her demolished head, the blood had seeped into the floorboards, turning them black.

"It's Reyna," Anthony said.

"Who?"

"Troy's sister. Tyrone and Willy's mother."

"How can you tell?"

"I can tell." Anthony opened his eyes. "Just go. Please. Keep them out of here."

Del ran from the house and did not stop until she was in the middle of the street, where she emptied her lungs of the burning air.

A Mardi Gras Indian's suit was nailed to the front of the house across — the long blue and orange plumes trailing down from the finely worked crown of feathers, a sort of war yell in the middle of all this silence and mud. It was as if a great bird had been picked up by the wind and held there against the house until it died. Del stared at it as she took a few deep breaths and then went back to the Jeep and tapped on Kea's window, motioning for her to come out.

The back door opened just enough to let Kea's legs through, and she turned her head back over her shoulder and said to Neesa, "Sweetie, you sit tight. I gotta go see about something."

Neesa nodded. In the passenger seat, Cora was invisible.

Kea stepped out of the car and shut the door, and Del led her out of earshot of the car. Neesa was peering out of the window of the Jeep, her forehead bright against the tinted glass.

"What is it?" Kea asked.

"Troy's sister."

"Reyna?" Kea's head whipped towards the front steps of the darkened house.

"She's dead," Del said.

"Jesus." Kea exhaled. "Jesus. So that's where she is."

"Somebody shot her."

"She shot her," Kea said firmly. "She's been trying to for years."

"Who?"

"Reyna." Her hands slapped her thighs. "From the first time I met that woman I could have told you she was going to kill herself. She was out of her ever-loving mind."

"She was shot in the face."

"Thank God they got those boys out." Kea shook her head. "I doubt your sister even knows what she did."

"But she and Troy rescued all three of them, you said. Why is Reyna still here?"

"I don't know, honey," Kea sighed. "She wasn't acting right apparently, and they had to bring her to the police. Troy just said they lost hold of her after that. Couldn't find her anywhere."

Anthony was coming out of the house. He closed the door firmly, his eyes to the ground, and shuffled down the steps, holding his hands away from his body.

"We're not going to tell Cora," Del said. "She doesn't need to know about this."

Kea nodded, and Anthony jutted his chin out at them, his tongue curling around his upper lip. He moved around the side of the neighboring house and bent over by the hose spigot, turned the knob with both hands. The pipe convulsed against the underside of the house, but nothing came out, and he shook his head and came towards them.

"No goddamned water." He looked at them. "Somebody's been inside there since. I can't find the gun she used. I don't know if it was the patrols took it or what — motherfuckers left flowers. Didn't take care of her, but left flowers? There's tracks all up and down in the dirt."

"Kea thinks she shot herself," Del said to him.

He looked at her like she was stupid. "She's tried it before. This isn't a murder mystery."

Del ducked her head and backed up a step. "We've got to go to the police."

Anthony nodded, but Kea raised her eyebrows. "Not if there's no gun there, I'm not going to the police."

131

"We can't leave her there, Kea," Anthony said.

"They did —" Kea threw her hand at the marking beside the door, her voice going loud. "1-D. That means one dead. They came and saw her and left her be."

"We're not them," Anthony said. "She's family. I can't do that."

"Then you dig a goddamn hole. I'm not going to the police, saying there's a dead woman in a house don't belong to me, and clearly she killed herself but no there's not any note. *No, officer, I didn't see a gun, officer. How could I have taken a gun I didn't see?*" She stuck out her wrists at them. "That would be one way to get a roof over our heads, sure."

Anthony stuck out his tongue and licked his upper lip. Del turned back to the car. The little girl was still watching, the sides of her hands and her chin now pressed against the window.

"Y'all should come home with us," Del said. "Or at least send Neesa home with me while y'all do whatever you need to do."

Kea made a clucking sound in the back of her throat. "That's kind of you, but you've done enough. We've got some people out in Hammond. If you've got a telephone that works at your house, we'll have them come

132

pick us up."

Anthony had stuffed his hands in his pockets, and he looked up over the roofs of the houses. A pair of pigeons wheeled in the pale sky, settled on Troy's gutter, then lifted up again. "Moving on," he said, though his eyes had fallen to the feathered suit pinioned against the house across the street. "Alright then, I guess we're moving on."

"But what are we going to do about her?" Del asked.

Anthony shrugged. "I'll call Troy. It's his house."

"I can call in a tip, anonymously, if you want," Del said.

"Alright," Kea said.

The back door of the Jeep popped open, and Neesa's feet came sliding out onto the driveway. Anthony and Kea both ran at her, their arms out, ready to hold her back. Neesa put up her hands and stuck out her lip, surrendering the way robbers do on TV.

"She keeps saying 'No,' the lady," Neesa whined. "But I'm not doing anything. 'No,' " she repeated in a low, froggy voice. " 'No no no no no,' but I'm not doing nothing but looking."

Vincent held his bowl in one hand, held his spoon. Mr. Kastenhoff still stood at the silver stove in his baggy drawers. Vincent wanted to ask where his mother was and when she would come home, but he didn't want to sass. Instead, he sipped at the pot-likker pooled in the bottom of the bowl. It was sure his mother's string beans, tasting like smoke and pig and onion sweat and salt, and on his tongue the little beans that had slipped from the pods disintegrated like the Eucharist. He was sleepy, and deep down, in the pit of his warm, full belly, he knew that it would be all right.

It was some kind of a test, the chest he hadn't dared touch. But that was all right. Mr. Kastenhoff had forgotten about it. It wasn't like the day in the shed with the veneers, when the old man hadn't fed him until he'd gotten it right. Or the chairs, when he'd wrenched Vincent's arm for finishing the carving — finished it well, but Kastenhoff wouldn't admit that, since he hadn't trained up yet. He looked at the little marks on the inside of his wrist. He felt the bruise still. It was a test, but he'd passed. He'd barely touched the chest, and he wouldn't, unless they made him.

He knew that soon his mother would return through the heavy door and pull off her gloves and tell him about her day. She'd been into town, which was a long way, even on the new paved roads. She would tell him how the bus had smelled to high heaven, full of all the people who didn't know how to wash their selves, and how she'd had to fight through the thick crowds on Canal Street with the umbrella she carried for the purpose. She'd tell him about the doctor's office and the jingle-bell streetcar that ambled down the avenue, about the market with its mountains of yams, its flats of crabs with their wiggling claws. She'd tell him about the ladies in the street with baskets on top of their heads, hollering *Strawberries!* and then she'd take a fried pie out of one of her bags and pull off its crinkling paper wrapper, hand it to him. He would bite into the crispy sugar crust, down into the lemon cream, and all would be right-side up again, everything just fine.

But the man in the kitchen turned off the tap, touched his heart, flipped off the electric light, told him good night, and she did not come. He sat in the dark and waited. The moon rose, but she did not come. He fell asleep with the bowl in his hands and woke with the bowl on the floor. She did not come, she did not come, and still she did not come.

It was not until just before dawn, when the windows were brightening to gray, that he heard something on the path, in the shells. It was not a woman's feet, not a person's, but a creature's — the soft padding of paws up the steps and onto the porch. Then he saw Sheba come through the door. It was strange, that a dog could come through a door that was not open, but not all that strange. Sheba. His good dog Sheba came across the room, her head down, her honey ears up like she was listening. She lay down beside him, resting her head on his knee, and it was lighter than air and warm as breath. She told him everything was all right, in the way dogs have of telling you things, and he knew what she meant, and he lay his hand on her silk-smooth head and patted her, until she decided she'd had her fill and went on off again.

SATURDAY
OCTOBER 22

Tess heard the door click open at the bottom of the stairs. Which daughter was it? And was she coming in or going out? She turned her cheek onto the cold patch of drool on the Dobies' soft mattress, pushed herself up onto her elbows. Downstairs, the floorboards groaned, and the door closed again. Coming in. Across the hall, the springs of the sofa bed squeaked.

"Cora?" Del's voice struggled out of the padded dark.

Tess got out of bed, tied her robe around her, and pushed her head through the door of the girls' cluttered room. In the lamplight, Del wiped the back of her hand across her eyes.

"I've got her, sweetheart," she said, though her heart was pounding. "You go back to sleep."

Tess waited in the shadows at the top of the stairs. Below, Cora was shuffling across

137

the entrance hall in her duck boots, her nightshirt glowing in the darkness. Tess could almost hear the slow waves of her sleep lapping at the steps. Waking sleepwalkers could leave them in a state of "sleep inertia;" the better course was to lead them gently back to bed.

Tess edged out of the shadow and put her weight on the top step. The staircase moaned. Cora whipped her head to the side, her hair falling across her eyes. A mistake.

Tess pulled herself back onto the landing, waited, holding her breath, as she had done over the side of the girls' cribs on countless nights in their babyhood, her hands, her forearms slipping inch by inch from under their sleeping bodies. Cora looked up at Tess, then down at her own body. Her eyes seemed unfocused, and there was something off about her movements. *Mania,* she heard Alice whispering. *Thorazine.* It was neither of those things, but there was something seriously wrong nonetheless. Cora crouched on the rug, the nightshirt pooling out over her feet, and shook out her arms as if she was checking the fit of the sleeves. She held her hands out, examined them.

Tess ran down the remaining steps and bent over beside her daughter. A rope of hair was plastered against Cora's cheek, the end of it in her mouth, and Tess reached out to brush it back behind her ear, wishing that Cora's light body would collapse against her, hoping that she would be strong enough to scoop her up in her arms and make it up the stairs. Tess's fingers grazed her daughter's cheek, and the touch made Cora jump. Her dilated pupils were sinkholes, edged in only the thinnest margin of blue.

"You're sleepwalking, darling. I'm sorry." Her voice was so loud in the dark. "I'm sorry."

Cora kept looking at her hands, and so Tess took them in her own. She turned them palms down, palms up. The heels were skinned, as if she'd taken a tumble running down the sidewalk, and they were filthy, black dirt with the mildewed smell of the flood smeared across her palms, ground in under her fingernails.

"Are you awake, my love?"

"I'm not asleep."

"What happened to your hands?"

She shook her head.

"It's okay." She tried to pull her daughter into her but Cora resisted. "It's okay, sweetheart. It's okay. Sleepwalking is normal. Doesn't mean anything."

Cora snatched her hands back, stood up.

"I'm not. I wasn't."

"Then what were you up to, out there at night?"

Cora stood still as a statue, a terra-cotta figure out of Egypt, perhaps, like the weeping Isis they'd seen at the Louvre — her cheekbones rising as if to meet her low brows, her wide ripe lips in an eternal pout, her hair a river in flood.

"There's mud on your boots," Tess said.

Cora looked down. Del had sworn up and down that she and those people had told Cora nothing about the dead woman in Troy Holyfield's house, but Tess could sense a change. At dinner, with little Neesa running around, Cora had been so withdrawn as to be almost absent — she'd kept her eyes hooded at the table, even with those obnoxious people behaving as if she, Tess, were responsible for the fact that they would have to leave the city that night, when what she'd done was offer them a meal while they waited for their friend to drive in from Hammond to pick them up. The woman was affronted when she'd asked her to take off the child's shoes, and the man had stuck his hand out at her, *Stop!,* when she'd offered to call the medical examiner about the corpse. Suspicious, angry. They'd all had mud splashed up their calves, just like Cora

140

did now.

"Do you remember where you went?"

Instead of answering, Cora turned from her and walked towards the kitchen. Her fingernails played the balusters. Tess checked the lock on the front door, then followed. She flipped on the light. Cora was sitting on the floor. A craquelure of veins showed through her tan, translucent skin.

Tess got down a mug, filled it with milk, popped it in the microwave. It orbited in the bright yellow light, showing its smiley-face front, its frowny-face back. Cora traced her thigh with her index finger. The micro-wave beeped, and Tess stirred in a spoonful of sugar, a drop of vanilla.

"Why bother?" Cora said.

"Why do I bother?" Tess crouched down and offered the mug. Cora's hands closed around it so weakly that when Tess let go, she had to grab to keep it from falling. "Because I love you? I care about you?"

"It's pointless." Cora drank, though, holding the mug in two hands like a child.

"The point is, you need nourishment."

Nodding, Cora put the cup down, picked it up, put it down again, as if she was unsure of the solidity of the floor. "I'm sorry, but it just goes right through me."

Cora laughed, and for a millisecond, Tess

thought that she must be hallucinating: Cora looking up into her face, her blue eyes reflecting the ceiling light, laughing.

"Right through!" Her hands splashed out at her belly.

Tess grabbed her wrists. Cora fought, twisting her hands so that Tess felt her skin pulling sideways across her bones, and then she stopped fighting, and the laughter dropped off of her face. Tess felt as though her organs were being pulled through her mouth.

"You see? You can see it now, can't you?"

"What?" Tess shook her head. "Are you on something, Cora?"

"What?"

"Drugs. Are you on drugs?"

"What?" She said it the same way she had before, flatly, as if she truly didn't understand the meaning of the words.

"You heard me. Are you on something? Anything." She couldn't say out loud that she almost wanted that to be the case. "Did Alice prescribe something for you?"

"She said it wouldn't do me any good."

"Alice didn't say that."

Cora shook her head. "It would just go straight through."

"What do you mean by that, 'go straight through'?"

"It would go straight through."

"Where were you tonight, Cora?"

"Nowhere." She smiled, shaking her head. "Everywhere."

"Is it the same old — do you feel a pressure to walk, wander?"

Cora shook her head, looked down.

"Do you go walking every night?"

She bent over her knees and pushed the mug away, then stayed like that, with her hands out and her cheek against the floor.

"I see her."

"You see her? Who?"

"No one."

"Oh, Cora." Tess lay a hand on her back. "Do you see her now?"

"No," Cora said, her mouth pressed open, like a fish's.

"Where was she, this —" You did not say hallucination, did not say vision. "— this person that you saw?"

"In the lake. In the water."

"You went to the lake? You walked all that way?"

Under her palm, Cora's back rose and fell with her breathing, and Tess reached up with her other hand for the phone she'd left on the counter — 5:10 a.m.

"I'm calling Alice, honey," she said. She punched in the numbers, but the phone

143

hammered out the call-failed tone. "Did you discuss this with Alice?"

Cora's eyes were closed, her mouth stayed shut.

"I think we need to get you medicine, my love," she said, stroking her daughter's back over and over and over. "We'll get you help. We'll make it all right." She dialed her service, but still the line was down.

Joe wasn't sure what he'd expected. That Del would come bounding towards him, arms outstretched? That she'd jump into his arms and bury her head in his chest? All he knew was that he hadn't expected this glossy person to emerge from Cora's car — patent leather boots up to her knees, mirrored glasses — then stand there surveying the ruined woods like some sort of insurance adjustor. The neutral smile on her face didn't change as he came down the porch steps. She didn't move. She was apparently unmoved.

"The lovely Adelaide!" He held her tight, his arms around her hard deltoids, bony scapulae.

"Hey, Daddy."

She sounded like herself, but when he pushed her back to arm's length, there was that hard creature again. In the silver surfaces of her Ray-Bans, all he saw was a convex version of himself — this fading, disheveled thing.

"I'm sorry I forgot to come get you the other day."

"It's okay." The smile was a pose. She never let anyone comfort her, never let them apologize. Instead, she'd say, *It's okay, Daddy,* her voice cheerful like a little bird's.

"Del, Del, Del." He patted her, two hands on two arms. "I'm glad you're here."

She laughed. "I'm just glad to be out of that fucking city."

"Well, it took you long enough."

She pulled away and turned towards the house steps. "Two days. Just two days. You could have just as easily come to the south shore." Their feet were loud in the shells.

"Got a lot to do out here, you know," he said.

A-void-ing, Tess would sing-song. He lifted his chin. The last time he'd been to the Dobies' he and Tess had fought so long and so hard that Cora had begun to sob. *How can you trust me?* Tess had laughed. *The question is, Joe, how can you trust yourself?*

"How's Cora?" he asked.

Del shook her head. "Mom says she's been wandering, you know, like she used to. Out there —" She cast her hand around the

145

property as if she could see the drowned houses, the mud-cased streets beyond the trees. "She comes home all filthy with flood mud. She really freaked Mom out this morning, I think."

"Jesus." Joe put his hands up to his brow, worked his fingers across his scalp. "But we trust your mother, right? She knows what to do?"

"Obviously," Del said, sarcastic, but he knew she believed it. "God, the poor trees."

He nodded. "And don't forget your poor father who's been chopping up those poor trees."

That morning, he'd moved most of the timber to the road so that she could drive up to the house. He watched her look at what was left — the splintered stumps spread among the needles, the tidy piles of logs. Those trees were her and Cora's childhood. They had named them: The God Tree. The Little Girls' Tree. The Big Girls' Tree. The Wish Tree. The Ghost Tree. Cora had imagined subterranean pools that the pines dipped their roots in, and creatures, good and bad, that lived in the branches. She had drawn a double cosmology on newsprint — the Light Forest and under it the Dark Wood in shadowy reflection. Between them was the surface of a pool, sometimes a blue crayon river, that you could pass through only once, unless you knew the secret code. He could still see the two girls lying on their stomachs on the porch, Del's feet kicking happily as Cora wound wild, ranging stories of the magical creatures who had lived on their land, precursors of the cormorants and coyotes, bears and fawns — the wars they'd fought, the adventures they'd had. The stories were strange, rambling, and dark, and the drawings were beautiful. Cora had stopped drawing in her teens, though, stopped telling stories, and now the drawings were probably disintegrating in one of those wet boxes they hadn't dealt with yet, and he'd taken a chainsaw to the forests.

The cabin door opened, and his father came out, his face pillow creased. "Afternoon!"

Del stepped away from him, but then, remembering herself, stepped forward again and forced herself to kiss him on the cheek. "Hey, Papie."

He was holding the door open, his arm out to usher her in. "My," he said. "Aren't you a beautiful young thing."

She turned sideways to pass him, her bag dangling from her arm. "It's Adelaide, Papie," she said. "Your granddaughter."

The nastiness in her voice shocked him. Del and his father had been so close once upon a time. Even as a little girl, she loved to watch her Papie drive a chisel down the leg of a chair or pin glued pieces of veneer together in a vise, and Vincent, for his part, was gentler with her than he'd ever been with Joe or his brother, Vin. Maybe because she was a girl, he didn't expect her to automatically know how to hold a plane or what an ogee was. He was almost patient. For a time, it had looked like he might actually teach her, that the tradition would continue on. With Del's business sense, they might even open the shop in the Vieux Carré they liked to fantasize about, not far from where François Boisdoré had run his operation until he died in the late nineteenth century, one of the wealthiest Creoles of color in all of New Orleans. They had seen it so clearly, he and Del and Vincent; they'd had dinners where all they talked about were Royal Street rents and windows full of fine furniture, while Sylvia served rabbit fricassee from the big iron pot. Vincent had liked to tease Del that if she followed François's example too closely, she'd end up selling coffins for some Haitian, and Del would counter that at least they'd be beautiful coffins, and he'd be a rich and handsome Haitian.

But the summer Del came home from college everything ended. Though none of them knew it, the dementia had set in, and Vincent had forgotten he'd promised to let Del apprentice with him for the summer. He'd slammed the door of the workshop in her face. Del had been so angry — not sad or disappointed. Furious. Refused to visit, refused to talk to Papie, even on the phone. Later, when Vincent was diagnosed, her anger rounded off to a sort of embarrassed disgust, but that was no better. She didn't deal well with weakness, his Del. It was the same thing with Cora — Del couldn't tolerate her sister's sensitivity, her flights of fancy, not now that they were supposed to be all grown up. She wanted to shove reality down Cora's throat, and, like her mother, she thought Papie should just be discarded now that he was sick and old. Weakness was not something the Eshleman women really knew how to forgive.

Del was scowling now as she stomped with her bag up the stairs to the room she'd shared with her sister since they'd put the addition on, and he followed her, ready with his talking-to, but she had scuttled up the stairs too quickly, slammed herself in the bathroom, and he hesitated halfway up,

149

stretching his calves on the riser.

Above the handrail, his mother had hung the second-string family photos in a long diagonal line. He was face to face now with one, time-stamped 1998, of the girls sitting side by side on top of a ladder somewhere on Basin Street, Mardi Gras Day. Del was dressed as Monica Lewinsky, but Cora, twenty-two then, was still wearing fairy princess wings. He looked into her little square face, trying to remember that what was happening to her now was nothing that they hadn't always known would happen when she was eventually confronted with the world. Cora had never been strong, had never been able to shrug things off, had never been able to pretend something was tolerable when it wasn't. In every new place they stayed — in hotel rooms and friends' houses and here, upstairs, when the girls' rooms were new — he'd had to assure her that she was protected — locks, guns, alarm — that he'd always keep her safe. And he had, for a time, managed that trick of making her believe it: look at her, still in braces, sitting with a book in the crook of the magnolia tree.

Joe put both hands on the banister, breathed. He could admit that he had not been able to shelter her forever, that he never would have been able to. He could admit that the magnolia tree was inside the house now, and that these photographs were all they had left. All of the others, the boxes and boxes of Fox Foto envelopes stuffed with an almost monthly record of the girls' childhoods had been in his studio (Tess had packed her mother's silver, though, very carefully) and now they were gone. Del wanted him to drive into the city, lend them a hand. But was he wrong to want to hold on to the safety he had left? Was he wrong not to want to pluck the ruined prints out of the tree and admire the way the rain had washed away the pigments and pulled up the metals and buckled the paper? There were certain lost pictures he wanted to remember as they had been. Like the one of Andy Roche, who had passed away just six weeks before Joe's mother had: Andy was laughing so hard he had to hold onto Tess's shoulder for support. There was the series from their twenty-fifth wedding anniversary, when they'd reconvened the bridal party at Dooky Chase — it was the last time they'd all been together, Madge hanging onto Tess's right arm and Andy somewhere to his left, and Vin had brought him a fake moustache, and Tess had worn a toilet paper veil which she had fluffed mock-vainly all night. There were pictures of Tess's sweet mother smiling at him as he took her picture, and the video that Cora had done as a school project, in which his own mother had explained how to make her duck gumbo, starting with how you pluck the bird. There was the shot in which Del looked skeptically up at Minnie Mouse, too old for Disney World even at five, and the one that showed Cora sitting among boxes on the floor of her new house in Gentilly grinning like a child, and a square fading portrait of Tess in her lace graduation gown with a big white bow in her bronze-flecked hair. If he couldn't point out to his grandchildren — *Look, see how your mother scowled at me?* or *Here's the beach where we went on vacation.* — he wanted at least to remember those things true. *God, my friend Andy could laugh. Wasn't that just a perfect day.*

At the top of the stairs, the bathroom door opened, and Del came out onto the landing, toweling her face dry. When she dropped her hands, his eyes stayed with the cloth, expecting her face to be printed there perhaps, perhaps not wanting to look. She'd been crying, and he went to her, taking the stairs two at a time.

Del stood in the bright rectangle of the open door, and as Joe made his way up, he burned the image into his memory: the red-ness of his daughter's eyes, the embarrassed, expectant frown on her lips, the spots of wet on her shirt. There was a scab on her knee where she must have cut herself on pavement, and her hands went out, waiting to embrace him, still her daddy's little girl.

"Yesterday we went too far," Alice was say-ing on the phone. "I understand you're coming from a place of pure maternal concern, but I shouldn't have allowed a preliminary meeting. It was damaging, and now you're trying to come back into our space."

Tess smiled at the mud-encrusted sham-bles of her office, the sodden couch, the box of tissues crushed under a swollen copy of the DSM. Voici: "the hermetic, unchanging therapeutic environment." How long were they going to keep pretending such a thing could exist, or even that it should?

"I'm not asking you to break privilege, Al-ice. I'm just saying —" Her voice was pinched from breathing the mildewed air, and she coughed, then inhaled hard, feeling the tiny burrs of mold pricking at her lungs. "I want you to reevaluate whether you should prescribe something."

"Are you at your house?"

"The office. The Dobies' landline quit, but this one still works, God knows why."

Alice sighed. "It was you yourself who said that you didn't think medication was the right thing for Cora."

Holding the heavy receiver between her shoulder and ear, Tess wrenched open the window behind her desk and coughed again.

"That's not what I said. I said cognitive-behavioral had been working for us."

"*It's not bipolar:* I'm just repeating your words."

"This morning was something I hadn't seen before. Wandering, yes. Delusions, no. She thought she was out there in the flood, Alice. And now it turns out a woman she rescued has turned up dead? If she saw that — If she thinks —"

"*Lalalalala!*" Alice sang. "I can't hear you!"

"Christ, Alice!"

There was silence on the other end of the line, and Tess tried to imagine Alice, chastened, sitting in the chair on the far side of her desk. Tess was her superior, goddamn it. But Tess's desk chair was growing blue-green mold and the top of her desk was warped. Her file cabinets were overturned, her patients' files strewn across the floor, the ink running off of their names.

"You put her under my care," Alice said,

in a richly enunciated voice of authority. "If you want me to see her, I will be available tomorrow morning, unless you believe this is an emergency? In which case I can re-arrange my schedule and see her today."

Tess shook her head. "The episode's over. She's asleep again." She picked up one of the pictures of the girls from her bookcase. The color had washed out of it, leaving only coppery outlines of the two of them wearing Christmas dresses on her mother's silk sofa. She turned it over, pried out the velvet back, and peeled the photo up off the glass. If they could all have just stayed there, in the wash of those lights, their bellies full of filet and bordelaise and chocolate mousse. "She was walking all night. She goes walking every night, I think. Out in the flood zone."

"Well, then, tomorrow at nine?"

She rolled the photo up in her hand. She coughed again. "Alright."

"You should get some fresh air," Alice said. "It's not healthy, breathing that shit."

"I won't be long."

Tess replaced the receiver in its cradle, leaned her head through the window into the breeze. Goose bumps went up on the back of her neck as she imagined Cora tracing the paths she'd taken in that pirogue during the flood, repeating the trauma. She was sure that's what this was: compulsive reenactment. Most places, the lights were still out, and who knew where she was going, into the houses where people — like Reyna — were still turning up dead. She remembered the time Del and Cora had found that injured raccoon on the batture and brought it back to her mother's house in a cardboard box. It had bitten Del, and they'd had to send it off for a brain biopsy, to be sure it wasn't rabid. When Tess — fool that she was — told them what had happened, Cora had cried for weeks. Tess looked out onto the wasted boulevard. Wind was barreling down Canal instead of traffic, racing across the facades of the deserted houses. She had her own prescription pad, of course, in the top, locked drawer of her desk.

Pulling the hank of keys out of her pocket, she stepped over the file cabinets and slotted the little silver key into the lock of her desk drawer. It wouldn't turn. She worked the key out, slipped it in, wiggled it. Crouching down, she tried again. She pounded against the key. Her hand slipped. A splinter broke off the desk and stabbed her.

"Fuck!" she screamed into the uninhabited air.

Mold was filling her lungs, and she held her breath as she yanked the key so hard the head of it bent back. Lightheaded, she kicked the desk with the heel of her boot, and as it groaned to the floor, the window fell closed with a guillotine swish. Tess sank down onto one of her fireproof file cabinets and pulled the blade of wood out of her wrist. Slowly, the rain began, drops falling against the cracked window, darkening the stucco columns, joining to form rivers that ran down the glass. She used to love the rain.

"If something's broken, what's your first step?"

His grandbaby, Adelaide, looked up from spading putty willy-nilly into the new cuts in the hope chest on the living room floor. Looked up, blinked, like she'd forgotten he was there.

"You take it apart," he said, answering the question for her.

She had that set to her mouth she always took when, long time ago now, he'd tried to teach her something. Mulish, just like her father. Never believed anybody could know better than their own mighty self.

"You've got to study it."

She nodded, but just stuck that putty knife

157

back in the tub, and, a little more careful this time, filled in a gap in the old cypress. He never could talk to them in terms they understood, women, always cooing to one another about how they felt this way and believed that. Him, he never could think except in terms of the physical. Didn't matter if it was divorce or destruction, failure or death, you could dismantle it like a slow clock and lay the parts out on butcher paper, examine them all for the little spot of rust or the chipped tooth on the bevel.

The thing with clocks, though, is you had to be very careful to label each and every small part, and lay a clean drop cloth down under you, in case you dropped something. He'd had a clock come in once, a German clock that sang a song and had a shepherdess that went around and a little sheep after her. He'd marked the dials, taken it apart, laid everything on the paper, cleaned it, and left it with the heater on to dry. But the next day, when he put it back together, it didn't work. He took it apart again, put it back together, and on and on all day until Sylvia called him to supper and he was beside himself with frustration. It wasn't until he woke up at two in the morning with the ghost of this hard little thing between his index and thumb — a spring he'd missed

— that he went down to the shop and, all the lights ablaze, crawled around on the floor until he found it rolled up against the foot of his workbench, smaller than a grain of rice. After he'd put it right, the clock set to ticking — the even beating of the pendulum and the little shepherdess going round and round.

"You've got to spend your time," he said to Adelaide, who was just troweling that putty in. "You've got to study it. Think: Where did it fail? What's not meeting plumb? How, if you were going to put it back together, would you do it different? And don't you answer without a why." He raised his voice to make her mind, but the finger he pointed wouldn't hold still. Imagine, trying to put that clock back together now — he wouldn't even be able to slot the screwdriver into the screws.

We come in and out of our competence is the truth, in reverse course as we come out and into confidence in our work. Boy now did he believe this hope chest was a work of genius when he finished it, oiled it, put inside it the letter he'd wanted Sylvia to read after he'd shipped out.

Along with this piece I hope you will accept the proposal I had hoped to make you

159

in person. But as you are away at your sister's, I leave this trunk here, hoping you will see in it the light by which I worked on it — the fullness of a man's love. As you wait for my return, I hope you might fill it with something like the same.

It was a sentimental, amateur business, "a man's love" indeed. He'd made it out of cypress — rot-resistant, watertight — though it was an ugly wood, coarsely grained. Everything on it had "meaning"; he would have painted the roses red if he'd had more time, their thorns hidden by wisteria, which hung over the pavilion where they'd first kissed. The roses, though, looked like something from on top of a cake, and on the side panels, the magnolia buds were vulgar in a way he should have noticed — probably his subconscious had been in the chisel, his mind in the hotel room on Canal Street that hot afternoon before she went down to the Pass for the summer, the blinds striping her waxed mahogany skin. The corner beams, which were executed fine, were carved to look like pine boughs: *Our love is evergreen.* And so he had taken the oyster knife to it. Awake at night in that basement room in Houston his eldest son had furnished straight from a catalog, thinking of his passing, thinking that this would be all that was left of his life's work when he was gone, as the rest of it was more than likely sitting under nine feet of water. They would put the chest in a museum, in their damned reverent condescension. *What does the wisteria mean, Vincent?* Tess would ask in front of the company, though he'd answered twenty times before. And so he'd found the oyster knife in a kitchen drawer and sharpened it on Vin's good stone.

He didn't blame Tess for stopping him. The cuts he'd made were careless, done with the wrong tools in the wrong light. His hands shook. There came a time when the work wanted to be passed to younger hands. Problem was the younger hands wouldn't take it up. Everything was supposed to be easy: instant gratification, instant soup, prefab furniture, premarital sex. Not even Joe had the patience to do things right. He'd wanted to spit when they'd dragged him to that show with those animal cabinets, the pigs and cows that opened up like steamer trunks to reveal compartments Joe had filled with all kind of little garbage. *Arks,* Joe called them. Nonsense. But worse were the drawers that stuck and drooped, the visible seams between the veneers. Some little reporter for the Living section had found her way to him and wanted to know how he felt about his son turning his "métier" to a "higher purpose," how he felt about having trained such a great artist at his knee. *No comment,* he'd said. Across the room, Joe gesticulated with a fizzy little cup, and Sylvia wouldn't let him go home. *Please, I don't wish to comment.* He'd had to beg the girl to go away.

No, he didn't blame Tess for grabbing him, though Joe did. What he blamed them both for was their hypocrisy. Incompetence was incompetence was incompetence in their book, or so they said. Meanwhile, they pretended to respect him. Pretended to defer.

"I can't remember," the girl Adelaide said. "Do I need to let this dry first and then sand it down, or can I clean it up now?"

"Patience. You have to have patience."

"So I let it dry."

He groaned, his dramatic sigh, but she didn't seem to care. She had been the promising one, the one who sat with him, until they sent her north. He had given her her own mark, hadn't he: forged it late one night, a B like his B, holding an A on its upright, and she had held it in her hands and thanked him with tears in her eyes. He'd given that to her. Not to Joe. Not to

162

Vin. He did things purposefully, though they didn't like to believe it — that was the kind of learning age wouldn't strip away.

He stood up from his chair and crouched down and took her hand, as if that was all he needed to do to make her listen.

"It's never the fault of the broken thing," he said. "It is always, every time, your fault."

She smiled at him, smug as a full-bellied gator. She scraped her knife against the side of the tub. "No, Papie. I'm pretty sure it's not."

Tess stacked the staves of wood together and wound duct tape around them, threw them in the corner, brushed the hair out of her eyes. All that for a pad of useless, ink-streaked paper, when she could have called it in. Just dialed Majoria's, if it was open again, and read off a prescription for Depakote. There had been no need to destroy her father's desk, not that there had been any need to save it. Soaked through with floodwater, it would have smelled like petroleum and mildew for the rest of time. You weren't supposed to feel tenderly for heirlooms belonging to people you didn't care for, but what she saw when she looked at the desk was her mother leading her into her father's cigar-smelling study and saying,

He would have wanted you to have it. It hadn't mattered that that was a bald-faced lie.

Tess pulled out the last of the big drawers and set it on the floor, stepped on one of the sides and pulled up, ripping the dovetails free. The desk had had dry-woods twice. Been fumigated twice. Well, it was done now. The rain past, heat was filling the room, and she turned to the window to see someone in an oversized raincoat and a grocery bag on her head coming across the lawn. She flattened herself against the wall. The footsteps rang on the porch. The vestibule door slammed.

"Someone's here!" Tess hollered.

There was no answer. She grabbed the crowbar as her mind flipped through the possibilities: not Alice, and Sheila was still in Louisville. It could be anyone, hunting for Oxycontin, Percocet, needles. The main door opened heavily on its hinges.

"There are no drugs on the premises!"

The tapping footsteps passed reception, turned down the hall. The doorknob turned. She flung an arm out and held the door shut.

"Who's there?"

"Dr. Eshleman? It's Joyce." That pathetic, perpetual tone of crisis. "Please let me in."

"Joyce." Tess let the doorknob go. "It's customary to knock."

Joyce didn't make eye contact as she came into the room. Instead, she looked up, tracing the flood line that ran a foot or so below the ceiling. She pulled off the big raincoat, a golf jacket of Rafael's. Underneath, Joyce was wearing a white dress with elaborate beading, and she had a new Gucci bag slung across her gym-toned body. Shopping again.

"I knew y'all had flooded, but I couldn't believe it until I saw it with my two eyes."

"How are you, Joyce?" Tess started gathering the patient files still strewn across the floor.

Joyce's hands twitched at her tightly bound hips. "It's all gone," she said. "The house, the boat, one of the cars, all my pictures — my wedding pictures — the televisions, all the little things I've saved my whole life. My mama's house too. Rafi, he said, 'Oh, Lakeview's gonna be fine,' but he's always saying that. 'The levees are built solid, my baby.' What the fuck does he know?"

"Language, Joyce."

"Sorry," she said, in her narcissistic, wheedling voice. "I shouldn't have barged in on you, but I tried your service. They said they didn't know how to reach you.

Then I'm trying Dr. Luce, and she says I can come to groups with her, but I don't want groups, Dr. Eshleman. I want you."

Tess nodded. She put the files back in one of the boxes she'd brought over. She bent over and grabbed more of them — Jason Katz's on top. He was dead, Jason Katz.

"I told him to get out," Joyce continued. " 'It'll be okay,' he says to me. 'We'll just spray it all down with Febreeze,' like he thinks it's a joke! I told him, 'Go, be with your buddies in Texas, I ain't coming.' "

Tess nodded.

"So I'm living in the Monteleone and trying to deal with the insurance, but we're going to run out of money before we get anything. You know they don't cover floods? What's it good for then, you don't cover floods?"

"Why don't you go to your sister's in Monroe?"

Joyce waved her hand in dismissal.

"Why not?" Tess asked, before she realized she didn't care. It was profound, the depth of her not caring.

Shaking her head, Joyce reached out to touch the wall only to yank her hand back as if she'd received an electric shock. "What am I going to do in Monroe? In that house with my mama and Henri and Jasmine and all of those kids? I'd start tearing my hair out again."

"I can prescribe you more Xanax." She motioned to the lump of wet brown paper that had been her prescription pad. "I can call it in."

Joyce shook her head. "I can't go to Monroe. I'll die."

Joyce was always saying she would die, and now it made Tess angry to hear her say it as she stood in those ridiculous shoes on the mud-caked floor.

"You won't die."

Joyce put manicured fingers to her temple. "Xanax's not going to do me a bit of good. Xanax going to build my house back? Clean my things off? Xanax going to fix it? Going to make me smile at Rafi? 'Oh, yeah, honey, it sure is funny how everything we own is covered in industrial waste.' Going to take that storm, break it up in the Gulf? 'Cause that would be one hell of a drug. I'd take that drug."

Tess looked out at the cars parked on the gleaming street — her ancient Mercedes next to Joyce's new white 4Runner and nothing else for blocks. Tess had bought that car in 1988, the same year she'd gone into private practice, when everything had seemed to be on track and accelerating towards some unseen, idyllic future. With the advent of Prozac, she had more patients than she had time for and more ways to help them, Joe had just sold out at the show in Copenhagen, the girls were happy and healthy, the USSR was faltering, and the city was riding a crest of oil that seemed like it might carry them all to prosperity. The day after the act of sale, she'd driven to this perfect, discreet building she'd bought, on her own credit, in the shiny silver car with her windows down like a teenager, blasting the Bee Gees. She'd put on old jeans and painted the walls sunny yellow in reception, private mauve in the restrooms, soothing green in the offices. She'd hired her own staff, her own colleagues. She would be able to fix people who had been unfixable, and the elation she felt had made the whole world seem better. She had thought she was in control.

"They say the trees are going to die," Joyce said. "The ones that were underwater. That the roots got choked up and they're going to suffocate."

Tess looked at her hands, their raised blue veins. "There's nothing we can do, Joyce."

"God." Joyce was pacing before the shelves of ruined books. "God, God, God, God."

Tess picked up the frame holding the

ghost image of Cora, then put it back down. "I do understand," she said. "It's a shock. We didn't think — it didn't seem real. We didn't believe this kind of thing could come to us. Tragedy. It was something that happened to other people, wasn't it."

Joyce's eyes drifted up to the flood line again. She shook her head. "You sound like Rafi."

"What?"

"That's an ignorant thing to say. 'Tragedies happen to other people?' Maybe in your world, Dr. Eshleman." She laughed, and a perfume, the smell of lilies, rustled out from her sleeve.

Tess stared at this pretty woman, leaning, in a white dress against the mud-stained walls of her devastated office. She looked like a borderline-offensive Versace ad, like disaster porn.

"But maybe the way I'm thinking is no different," Joyce continued, reconsidering. "Like: we've already got it twice in a row, Katrina, Rita, so it can't happen again? But of course there could be another one. Or who knows, an earthquake? They could drop a bomb." She nodded, turned. "I want you to — Can you come to me at the Monteleone? Any time. I'm not busy."

"How could I help you?"

"It's just that — I'm not going to die, like you always tell me. It's going to be okay."

"No," Tess said firmly, and she saw Joyce look to her, desperate as a cornered doe. "I mean, how could I possibly help you? You're right. Anything could happen at any time."

"Jesus." Joyce looked like she'd slapped her.

The rain started up again abruptly, and they both looked to the window to see a curtain of water sweeping across the street as if it were a stage.

"I can still call in the Xanax, Joyce."

"No," Joyce shook her head hard. "I already told you, I don't want any Xanax." She pulled on Rafael's raincoat, dug a plastic grocery bag out of her purse and tied it around her hair.

"I'm sorry."

"I've got to go," Joyce said, then ran, wobbling in her heels, down the office hallway.

Tess watched as she flung herself down the steps and across the front yard, hunched over her purse to protect it from the rain.

Holding the phone in one hand, Del smoothed her curls up from her forehead with the other, watching in the night window as her brow went smooth, then creased again.

"The new girl moved in today," Fran was saying. "She wants the room clear."

"Hang on a minute, Fran," Del said into the phone. Behind her, at the cabin's long hand-sawn table, Papie and her father were waiting to eat, their hands folded in their laps. "Y'all go on. I have to take this."

"Y'all," Fran said. "Three days back, and you go all Southern."

Del opened the door to the screen porch, out to the loud night sounds of tree frogs and crickets, then shut it behind her carefully, reminding herself to take a deep breath. "She wants the bureau out? The Boisdoré bureau, that my grandfather and I made. Are you fucking kidding?"

"Everything."

"What else is left?"

"Your hangers, your shoe boxes, your soap, your pictures, your hair clips, your bed. Zack."

"Zack?" She picked at the screen that separated her from the forest.

"He's been over here like six times."

Del watched through the window as her father picked up his salad fork, raised his eyes at her, pierced a piece of romaine. She thought of Zack, hangdog in the corduroy chair by the fire escape, then forced herself to think instead of the houses she'd seen yesterday, the curtains blown out of windows, the mattresses on top of cars."

"There's bedbugs in the city, Del."

Del felt her face go red as she tried not to scream. She had slammed her bedroom door in Fran's face the day the levees broke, had burned the letter Fran wrote her in the bathtub: *If you would only let me help you. It's difficult for me* — this was the funniest part — *when you shut me out.* Just days before they'd been down at the Delancey, spinning around each other on the rooftop dance floor, laughing with Annabelle and Rhea and Zack. She taught the bartender to make Sazeracs, and they raised a toast to the hurricane they'd thought had passed. She had loved Fran, loved New York; they'd made her feel free and powerful and young, but now all she could think was — *A decade of friendship, and I pretty much can't stand you anymore.*

She turned her back to the window and stepped out of its light, took the cigarette she'd been saving out of her bra, twisted it — Marlboro stamped in little gold letters all around the cork-print paper. Funny how much effort goes to fancy a thing made to be burned.

"I don't have fucking bedbugs."

"Please let's not start again."

Del laughed. "Oh, I'm not *starting* a fucking thing," she said and hung up the phone before Fran could think of an answer.

Behind her, Papie and her father would be fidgeting with their napkins, watching her as she dropped the phone to her side, as she pressed her forehead into the screen, but she still stood on the porch for a moment longer, looking out into the darkness. If she could just rewind the tape, she thought, start again. If she could leave this body, like a cicada molts its nymph skin. If she could become a nymph again and burrow down under the pine needles into the forest floor. If she could be reborn every seven years, her sister next to her. If they could come running out of the forest, two children with baskets full of blackberries, wearing their old twig crowns. She would do it all differently. Not leave. Never leave.

In the orange light of the dining room, her father was bringing plates of the shrimp creole she'd made to the table, set for three. She turned around into the light, opened the door, before she had time to cry.

"Mmm." Her grandfather smiled up at her as he swallowed. "Tastes just like Tess's."

"It does," her father said.

Del sidled around the table into her usual spot, spread her napkin in her lap. He was allowed to miss his wife, she reminded herself. They should all admit what they missed.

"The way Sylvia made it was different — darker roux," Papie said.

"And more bay leaf," her father said, "and less spicy. Don't get me wrong, I like it hot," he corrected, picking up the bottle of Crystal and sprinkling it over his plate. "I'm not saying that. It's just — my mama's was a little more country, Tess's is a little more city. A little moderner."

"There's basil in here?" Papie said, picking now.

"More modern." Del speared a shrimp, stared into her plate.

Papie was humming as he cut his shrimp with his trembling hands, his mouth wet at the corners, and she tried to remember how she'd revered him once, how she had pleaded with him to teach her while he went on about how woodworking would ruin her pretty little hands. She had loved watching him, the way he'd stand back and stare at a piece, shaking his head, then sketch an ogee, then another with fuller curves. When they'd been making the bureau together, the bureau Fran's new roommate wanted to put out on the curb, he'd gotten frustrated with the way she was drawing the feet — not claws, she'd decided, but fetlocked, cloven hooves — and he had taken the pencil out of her hand. Watching him draw was even better than watching her father draw. You didn't expect those craggy, varnish-stained fingers to have so much grace, a Pan's foot flowing onto the paper almost as good as something tossed off by a Renaissance master.

She had wanted what he had to give her so fiercely. She'd wanted to wear it, "her heritage," strapped tight to her body like a suit of armor. She'd thought it would protect her against all the people who talked down to her — her supposed friends whose mothers wouldn't let them spend the night, the Jesuit boys who constantly asked her advice but never asked her out, the trustees and Garden District dads and PR ladies at Buckner who saw her as a perfect example of the sort of brown girl they allowed to wear their uniform kilts. She thought if they respected the work, they'd have to respect its maker, and she'd had fantasies of making something beautiful — a table or a breakfront sécrètaire — to donate to Buckner with a little brass plaque to show all those stuck-up bitches a thing or two: That "her heritage" was more valuable than theirs. That membership in her family was better than membership in some fucking Carnival krewe. That what she'd inherited was worth more than plantations and oil money. Instead, she'd made one chest and gone to college, and Papie had gotten old and senile like everyone did in the end.

A necrotic smell came off her grandfather now that was not quite masked by the aggressive scent of the Irish Spring, and she suddenly didn't want to eat. Along the back of the shrimp ran the dark vein no one in her family ever bothered to remove, shrimp shit not being shit, somehow. She worked the tip of her knife into the shrimp's belly and pushed it off the fork.

"Something wrong?" Papie gestured with his water glass. "Got a bad shrimp?"

"I should've cleaned them better, is all."

"Tastes plenty good to me," her father said.

She took a bite of rice and sauce and made herself swallow. There had been maggots in the freezer when they cleaned it out, her mother said, which meant their eggs had been waiting all along inside the vacuum-sealed filets of fish and bags of stone-ground grits for a good warm place to hatch.

"Think we can keep you around a little longer, chef?" Her father pinched her shoulder with his dirty-nailed hand. "I don't like the idea of your going back to the south shore tomorrow. Or back to New York in a month, for that matter. It's been a long time since we've had you home to take care of us."

She had been planning to tell him. Lay her hands on the table, say, *So, Dad, by the way, I quit my job,* though, really, the word was fired. But when she looked at him, she still saw the pride he'd taken in all her big plans: she was going to be the department head of American Furniture and Decorative Arts, put her daughters through Brearley, buy a brownstone on Little West 12th. He had wanted what she wanted just because she wanted it, and he wanted it still.

"This is all the vacation I get, and sick days too. You can't just leave," she said.

Except that you could. Except that she had.

"That's not what I'm saying, honey. You know that."

She nodded, but the shame — Phillip's nostrils flaring as he looked at his watch, then at her empty seat, then called her cell which she would not answer — made her almost sick. Fran sat red faced and silent in the kitchen with her hand cupped over Del's key, reading over her post on the alumni listserv: *Perfectly good room suddenly avail-*

able in E. Village walk-up. Help me pay the rent! Zack stood barefoot halfway down his building's stairs, squinting to make her out in the dark.

She stood up from the table to take her plate to the sink.

"You've got to eat." Her grandfather chewed the shrimp and its guts, the rice and whatever lived inside the rice.

"I don't have to do anything." She stopped, looking from her bowl to her father's well-stocked cabinets, to the chopping board, the dirty counter, the dishes piled in the sink.

"You're not hungry? I think it's delicious," her father said.

"She's too thin, Joe. Look at her — you can see her bones."

She hunched over the sink, afraid she was going to vomit. She saw Troy's kitchen again, Reyna's leg sticking out from beneath the plastic bags, her missing face. She spat once, pushed herself upright.

"I'm not hungry, no."

She ran water into her bowl. The thick sauce floated up in chunks, threatening to overflow.

"Can I fix you something else?" her father said. "We've got chocolate ice cream. Whipcream in a can like your mother won't let

178

me buy. Cookies? Oreos. Chessmen."

"Stop." It was too much. "Please just fucking stop."

His eyes fell to his food, and the smile went off his face, and he took a bite of dinner. Papie stood with his clean dish and walked, lamely, towards the stove. The rice and sauce poured over the lip of her bowl like vomit, and she leaned over the sink, clutching her skirt, her hair hanging.

"In my day, a girl was supposed to have meat on her bones."

"I never said you shouldn't have left." Her father pointed at her with his fork. "You've got to live your life the way you choose —"

You don't have to do anything, her brain said. *You can go to France like Louis Armstrong, like Virginie Gautreau. Never call, never come back.* Papie scraped up the last bit of rice from the pot. For some reason, all she could do was laugh.

"Right," she swallowed. "Right."

"Right! You're not obliged to us. Your only obligation, at this point, is to make your life the wonderful, joyous thing it has the potential to be."

"Oh, it's all up to me, is it?"

Papie's hand shook so violently that the spoon clanged against the side of the Dutch oven.

"It is all up to you."

"Bullshit!" She snatched the spoon from her grandfather and ladled sauce over his rice for him. "You know that's bullshit! What if I wanted to be here? What if that's what would have made me 'joyous'? But I was born a century too late and in the wrong fucking body. And this city —" She laughed. "I get them now, the people asking if we're going to rebuild. That fucking asshole on Marketplace? He's right. Why were we shocked? This had been going to happen. Been going to happen for a long time, and we pretended it wasn't, went on our merry way. It's our fault! It's our fucking fault, and now not even you can bring yourself to go into the city, not even to pick me up from the airport. Couldn't bring yourself to talk your way in even when Cora was here —"

Her father bowed his head, closed his eyes. "When an officer tells you to turn around, you turn around, Del."

"So you let her stay trapped here? You let Cora ignore a mandatory evacuation order, and then you gave up on rescuing her from that hell," she shouted, "because one cop said turn around?"

She waited for his face to change, but it didn't. Her mother was right: he was weak, and he didn't know it. She had friends, like Tina's husband, George, who had gotten back into the city on day four, no problem, and stayed just to check out their house. It was different for a black man maybe. But then maybe don't leave your white doctor wife in Houston.

"You don't know what it was like, Del," he said. "You weren't here."

"I am now. I fucking am now!" she shouted. "I quit my job, Dad. Or maybe I was fired. But I'm here now."

"Oh, Del." Her father clenched his eyes shut.

"Not on our account," Papie said. "I hope that wasn't on our account."

Del shook her head. Out of the windows, Cora's Jeep, grayed with dust, sat on the shells. "People are killing themselves, you know. Yesterday, down in the disaster, I saw a woman who'd blown her own face off. Troy's sister. You know Troy — the guy Cora rode out the storm with? Or maybe you don't. Maybe you've checked out so far you don't even care."

"Of course I care, Del!"

"You're being cruel to your father, Adelaide," Papie said, straightening himself up in his starched blue guayabera. As if he were still the patriarch. As if he were still any-thing.

"Oh, yeah —" she turned on him, the bile rising in her throat. "I'm the one who's cruel. There are bodies being left to rot in the streets, and apparently I'm the only one who's shocked by this! But maybe I've just been in New York too long, right? Maybe if I'd been here all along I'd be less upset? Maybe I just need time? How long, then, until I become a good New Orleanian again. Until the next hundred-year flood? Until the whole state of Louisiana falls into the sea? I guess I should just wait around for the ease to set in. Wait around and hope that we'll get a competent government, a functional economy. But tell me, while I'm waiting, what the fuck am I supposed to do?"

Papie was looking at his hands now, folded in front of his plate, and her father was star-ing straight at her, his eyes dead and fixed on her face.

"I can't do what I want — there's no one left to teach me. And, fine. People don't want our kind of furniture anymore, maybe, huh Papie? And I guess Dad had to live the life he chose. Had to leave you, leave this — him and Vin both — until there was no one around but strangers. And how could you teach a stranger your precious fucking skill? It was my birthright, after all."

"Adelaide —" Papie said, trying to stop her, but she wouldn't stop.

"You can't take care of everything, can't protect everything, can't save everything and everyone, not if you're looking out for yourself. How can you worry about what other people might need, and still look out —"

She stopped herself finally, but her father's eyes were already closed, his head tilted back.

"I'm sorry, Dad. I didn't mean that."

He pushed himself back from the table. She shouldn't have said it. It was unfair, uncalled for, but how else could she explain. She had made the choice to leave, and she had to stick by it. Otherwise what excuse was there for the fact that she hadn't been there when they'd needed her? When they were running she hadn't run with them; when they sat on their roofs, when they waited, she had lain in bed; when her sister poled a pirogue out to save them, she had taken the subway; when they held to, she did nothing, because she had already gone. She hadn't even held to when there was something to hold.

Joe turned on the lights in the workshed then turned them off again. The moonlight hung like a fog in the room, and he thought that might help — that he might actually see something if he had to work to see.

When the FBI agent had rapped on his hood that first morning back in New Orleans, it had taken Joe a while to figure out where he was: everything had looked unreal, the way reality can look when it shows itself unadorned.

Running his tongue across his teeth, he had blinked at the man. *Just coming to fetch my daughter.* Behind the agent's looming head, the sun seemed too high, too hot, too yellow. His truck was parked in front of the Walmart that had been dropped into the middle of the Irish Channel like a bomb, and just blocks away, the twin spans of the Mississippi River Bridge vaulted out of the city. They had been invisible the night before, the power still out.

Now, in the daylight, the city had regained its geography, but not its sense. The streets were stranged by silence, by the crowds on foot carrying their lives in coolers, their children on their backs.

184

He still hadn't understood what had happened. He hadn't understood anything, not even as he'd driven past the Convention Center, where people the news called "refugees" poured out over the sidewalk — mothers cradling tiny diapered babies, old people limp in folding chairs. He hadn't understood. He'd been in a daze, driving slowly, while they'd wandered up to the truck, knocked on his windows, a large man in an LSU T-shirt, a tiny girl in filthy flowered pants. Joe hadn't understood, not even when a woman in his rearview — a white woman — dropped to her knees in the middle of the street and pressed her head into the ground.

In his own house, the sheets had been pushed off of the beds and the tubs were all full. The one in the front, where Cora and Troy must have been bathing, was cloudy, with grit pooled near the drain. They had pulled the mahogany sideboard in front of the door to the kitchen, and he'd had to wedge himself between it and the wall and push it away with his legs to get through. He had wandered into the canopy of the tree — a few blossoms still clung to the branches, and their sticky sweet perfume mingled with the smell of damp heat and early rot — and looked up at the debris, the rain of shingles and lath, paintbrushes, a chair, a sculpture, the unfinished chalk *Cornelia, the Woodshed Dog.* Still, it had not seemed real. He'd been expecting chainsaws, emergency rooms, a tearful embrace.

Then someone pounded on the front door, and Joe felt his joints lock up. The latch broke through the door with the sickening sound of splintering wood, and then their heavy, mud-caked boots tramped across the floor — four men in something like a uniform of dark khakis and bulging flak jackets, semiautomatics in their arms and pistols taped to their legs.

"This is private property," he'd said, the last words he'd spoken as one of the naive.

Their mouthpiece, a broad man with a shaved head, had flicked at his ID badge the way you shoot a dead fly off a table. "We have been contracted by the government to enforce martial law," he said. "I would make you aware, sir, that in a state of emergency, the concept of private property does not apply."

It had clicked then, as one of the troops shouted out that he had a weapon, as the others closed ranks, that he was no longer in the world he'd thought he built. That whatever he'd built, it did not belong to him: nothing ever had. As the mouthpiece flipped Joe's license between his fingers like it was a playing card, he remembered the nightmares he'd had in college: The jack-boots. The card inscribed with the date of his death pushed across a wide desk by his high school principal. The rope a naked blonde woman had given him as a prize. He remembered the cold sweat, the plastic dorm mattress under the sheets, his heart beating. The girl he'd visited in Montreal who'd slapped him in the face as they made love, the dense hair on her legs like a man's, the smell of frying sausages. He thought of the e-mail Charlie Tolland had sent before Joe left Houston: stories of snipers posted on the roof of Poydras House, shoot-to-kill orders, of the Jefferson Parish cops bar-ricading the Mississippi River Bridge against the citizens of New Orleans who, as in the old days, were not really considered Ameri-cans, who probably never had been.

Blackwater had followed him as he walked back to the front of the house, close enough that he could feel the rifle butt to the ribs they would give him if he slowed down. They had allowed him to close the broken door and lock the vestibule gate, and then one of them had shaken a can of spray paint and drawn an X on the siding. The mark of the destroying angel. As he got into the truck and drove away, they had moved on to the Maestres' house, knocked once before they rammed a rifle through the door's glass. The troops went in, but their mouthpiece lingered on Wynne and Susan's steps, watching him. As Joe made a U-turn, the mouthpiece pointed a finger at him and shot, mouthing the sound of fire.

The pixelated darkness was beginning to resolve into cleaner shapes: the square of the window, the cold-headed hammers hanging from the wall. Joe stood between the sawhorses in the center of the room, waiting to know what to do.

Del was so angry, and he couldn't blame her. There was no other real way to be. But it had twanged something inside him. Kicked up a vibration, a hum that normally he could turn into something good, or at least pretty, as if prettiness had any worth in this world. He pulled down one of the pieces of plywood he'd used to board up the windows and tilted it against the table. *I appreciate work that has a use,* his father, pressed to comment, might say.

A whole life of uselessness, then, was his life. A life of rearranging deck chairs. Del blamed him for that, and well she might. But what could he have done? Held off the paramilitary thugs with Vin's 9mm? Nobly gone to jail? Hog-tied Cora and put her in the truck on that first day? Beyond that, did she expect him to raise the levees? Stop the storms? Did she really want the city to become again the golden capital it once was, when cotton money flowed and the docks were crowded with white-sailed ships? Or was he supposed to raise a rebellion in the river parishes and burn down The Royal O, tear down the scaffolds set up for the auction of slaves? Was that what she expected of him? He pushed the chair back under the desk and lay the panel on the floor.

Quincy at the gallery said that people were looking to buy things. *There's a hunger out there for relevant work. Things that resonate with the storm. With the city as it was, as it will be.* Things to tell them how to feel. Art that swept it all up, wrapped it up in brown paper, so that nobody would cut their hands. Art that packaged all the splinters and shards in a box with a tidy description on the top: *Ceci n'est pas une cyclone.* He could make that, if they wanted it. He had exactly $1,439.38 in his personal bank account and no desire to ask Tess for more money. *Ceci n'est pas une acte de Dieu.* He could make it. It would be crap, but he could make it and they would buy it. You couldn't even blame them. They just wanted to help. Something should result from this. Some good should come, and art was good.

When he was still a kid, he'd figured out that transforming the emotions you didn't want into art was best way to get rid of them. Even when his mother had died, that very night, as he was driving across the lake, he could see, beneath the reflections of the headlights and the moon on the water, the chalk figures dissolving in their pools. He created an entire show on that drive: chalk portraits of his mother, of Tess, of baby Cora, of his father, of François Boisdoré, of himself, and their stainless steel pendants — *Mother, Beloved, Descendant, Father, Ancestor, I.* He had needed a couple of years to make them, but before he'd even gotten to his studio, he understood the whole concept. He would place the portraits in pools of acidic water that would slowly dissolve them, the gasses bubbling up to the surface like breath, until nothing was left but flints and fossilized shells and photographs in a book.

It was his best work to date. The Guggenheim had bought the *Sylvia/Mother* diptych to put in storage, and others had gone to collectors across the country. Augie Randsell had bought the *Beloved* steel. Quincy had been supposed to sell them in pairs, but Augie had bought her the day before the show went up, barged in as the assistant was locking the gallery. Joe had let him have it, out of respect for their friendship, though Augie hadn't even had the courtesy to come to the opening the next day. The chalk portrait of Tess, then, was alone, sunk in the sculpture garden at NOMA, where at least he could visit from time to time. She had lost her eyelashes already, her fingernails, the careful carving of her hair. He hadn't seen her since the storm, but her pool would have taken on water in the flood, and if the flood was acidic, she would be vanishing even faster now, a stream of tiny bubbles pouring up out of her collapsing face.

He pulled the light's chain and illuminated the small sketches of Tess, clustered like sleeping birds on the high shelf. Heads and busts and full-length sculptures of her, nude and clothed, reclining with a book in tall clover, sitting primly, one leg crossed over the other: private studies he'd done since before their marriage, two or three a year. In the beginning, she would pose for him, but she quickly tired. *Could you not right now?* She looked at him from over the rim of her glasses, impatient. *You realize I work all day?* He clicked off the light. If she was here, he could have taken a hunk of something — chalk, marble, wood — and gone to her and done her portrait, to jump-start something. Despite her impatience, she had always been a good muse. He shook his head. Muse was the wrong word — she did not sing to him, did not whisper syrups in his ear. It had always simply been the act of seeing her, the lovely thing, or the act of re-seeing, if necessary, re-finding what was lovely, that hit that twanger inside him, made it hum. It was humming now, but beneath his feet, the board was still a nothing. Just a square of plywood from Home Depot.

No, he did understand Del. Who was he to make her feel guilty for doing exactly what he had done? He had gone north too, escaping to a place where people looked at him only half funny, only said "nigger" behind his back. He remembered thinking even the air down here, the humidity and the heat, were designed to keep him down, while in New York, the breeze had skipped so lightly across his arms he felt like he might lift right off 42nd Street, luggage and all. Of course, he had eventually come home. He had let Tess seduce him, lead him blindfolded back to New Orleans, but he was seduced by her to start with because she reminded him of his city, of the luxurious wetness of a subtropical summer, that dangerous fertility and somnolence, the smells of jasmine and oak and varnish and green peppers frying, the delicious languor of the days. She had explained to him that what he liked about the North was that it forgave his detachment, and she asked him if that was what he wanted, to be a marionette dancing in front of a painted scene. She told him that he would never be a part of New York except inasmuch as he was a member of its crowds, that as soon as he left, someone else would come to fill his place. She had been right.

Joe stared down at the sheet of cheap wood, his ears ringing. He pulled a paint can off the shelf and pried off the top, poured an unmixed slop of pigment and oil over the board and his bare feet. In the moonlight, it was impossible to see where the paint ended and his skin began, their color was so close — the color of river sand, cypress bark. The longer he stared, the less it felt as though he had feet at all.

SUNDAY
OCTOBER 23

Drifts of camphor berries clustered against the risers of the steps to the Randsell house. Tess crushed them underfoot as she climbed, releasing their medicinal scent. Through the leaded glass of Augie's front door, she could see work was already in progress on the decorative plaster where the chandelier had fallen. Scaffolding stood under an ugly hole in the ceiling, and drop cloths and ladders clustered in the hall. *Just a little water damage,* Augie had said the morning they'd found Cora. *Nothing that can't be fixed.*

She had three whole hours of freedom — Alice was keeping Cora after their session for her PTSD group — and so why not call on an old friend? They were old friends, after all. Together, they'd been through a lot. Slowly, she pulled her hands from her skirt pockets, rang the bell.

Tess held herself very straight as she

waited, feeling her face go red. Sparrows were twittering in the sweet olives, and she felt as she had that time she'd given Madge a ride here for a date, and Madge had said, *Oh, you don't need to walk me up,* but still Tess had, the crinoline of her party dress crunching against her thighs. When Beulah, the housekeeper, opened the door, she had given Tess a look: *Girl, don't be a fool.* But she was a fool. Now, Augie, pausing on the landing, leaned over the banister and waved.

"Dr. Eshleman!" he said, opening the door with three brass clicks. "What a nice surprise."

"Oh, I was just in the neighborhood." She rustled her keys in her hand. "Cora's at the doctor's for the morning, so I thought I'd drop by and see how you were holding up."

"Well, come on in!" Augie held out his hand. She took it.

Lying in the Dobies' big bed the night before — Cora's bedroom securely bolted now, from the outside — she had tried to put herself to sleep by remembering the way his starched collar had pressed against her cheek in Langenstein's. She had tried to imagine him pushing her up against the wall of Charmin. She had tried to reenact the fantasies she'd had as a seventeen-year-old — Augie unbuttoning thousands of tiny buttons on the back of her wedding dress, Augie kneeling down to pry a shoe off of her stockinged foot — but such things were not so easy as they used to be. She would get an image of his lips against her neck, her hands on his belt buckle, but then she, or, rather, the ghost of her seventeen-year-old self, would evaporate. As she stared up at the Dobies' ceiling, she had forced herself to remember Madge as she had been at the end, the petal-dry hand on Tess's wrist, those translucent eyelids shutting, so that when Tess closed her eyes again, it was Joe hovering over her and her own hand between her legs, and then it was no one at all.

"I got Tevis on the phone just a day or two after I saw all this mess," Augie was saying as he led her around the scaffolding. "And good thing too. He says he and his guys have a waiting list that's going to stretch into 2007, at least."

"That's lucky," she said.

"It's lucky Mother came here after her house flooded. Those French doors blew open in the wind," Augie dropped her hand and pointed. "If Mother hadn't taken it into her fool head to ride out the storm in Metairie, if Cora hadn't found her — thank God — if she hadn't listened to Mother and

196

brought her here, if she'd insisted on evacuating her or something, we'd be as bad off as you. Of course, if Mother had evacuated —"

Tess nodded. If only Mrs. Randsell had evacuated. If only Cora had. If they had only known Cora was safe here with the camp percolator and the generator and not lost somewhere in the storm. She could still see the empty rooms of the house on Esplanade the afternoon, a full two weeks after the storm hit, when she and Joe had returned to the city, having finally received mayoral sanction. Even before Joe had put the truck into park, she had opened the door, run across the sidewalk strewn with fallen leaves and into the portico, where she found their front door kicked in and a trail of boot tracks and a jumble of bare footprints on the mildew-clouded floors. Joe had hesitated outside the door, crumpling his keys in his hand. *What is it?* he said, some specific fear in his voice. Tess couldn't answer.

They had moved through their house — coolers in the dining room full of food now hot and crawling with maggots, bread on the table growing blue mold. The federal buffet Cora and Troy must have moved in front of the kitchen door had been pushed aside just enough that Tess could squeeze her body through, and in the kitchen was the magnolia, its thick green leaves coated in gypsum, sketched sculptures hanging in the branches among the unripe cones. A path had been kicked through the broken things on the kitchen floor, and a single bare footprint was printed in the dust, heading in. Upstairs, the ceilings were water damaged, and there was an odd constellation of holes in the plaster above the stairs. Cora's and Del's beds were unmade and all the bathtubs but one were drained, an assortment of shampoos and cleaners and antiseptics and bandage wrappers strewn across the tile. Cora's clothes were all there, but Cora was gone.

Her duck boots, though, were in the vestibule.

She can't have gone far without her boots, Joe said. And so they'd waited.

If the Red Cross had her, we'd have gotten a phone call, Joe said.

There's only one Boisdoré Construction in the whole damn country, Joe said.

If she was arrested or forcibly evacuated we would have been contacted, Joe said, and he took her hand in both of his, and they sat together on the edge of the portico watching the Humvees and the police cars pass in the street, waiting for the Jeep they knew would not come.

Tess had not been able to think. Panic will do that to you — it will strip away your ability to reason, your ability to say, *We told her to go looking for Mrs. Randsell. Maybe we should check her house on Northline. If all else fails, check Augie and Madge's house on Felicity Street.* But it didn't seem possible to leave Esplanade before night fell.

When twilight hung in the street and a squad car whooped its siren, Joe had stood, still holding her hand. *We can't stay after dark.*

They'd driven back across the lake, playing the Meters loud to drown out their thoughts and they had undressed each other on the screen porch of the cabin, listening to the frogs singing in the trees, and had sex in the rocking chair, had sex again in the bedroom just so they'd be able to sleep.

But Cora had been here the whole time — or for a while at least, Cora wouldn't say how long — making coffee with Mrs. Randsell in Augie and Madge's house, reading through August Senior's library, wearing Madge's clothes.

"Did she tell you — your mother — how long they were here together?" Tess said, clearing her throat. "When Cora joined her here? What happened? Did she say anything about that time?"

Augie shook his head gently, his lips between his teeth. "They took good care of each other, Tess. You saw them in the garden — Mother at the camp stove, wearing all her jewels. 'If they want the jewelry my husband gave me, they can have it over my dead body.' " Augie laughed somehow. "I think those two loons had a good old time."

A good old time: that was a new one. Tess wondered if Augie's talent for repression might be so great that he had forgotten how the jokes had stopped as soon as they had forced Cora and his mother into the car. If he hadn't noticed how Cora and his mother had kept their eyes focused through the rear windshield as they left the city, watching New Orleans sink below the horizon until nothing remained above the highway but the unresisting air. She wondered if Augie had forgotten how Cora had wept at the gas pumps outside of Lafayette and how he had tried to comfort her, how he'd said twice *You saved her life* as if he hadn't heard Cora replying, *But what's there left to save?* She wondered if Augie had forgotten the night they'd spent in that hot motel room in Galveston, lying awake listening to the wet sounds of tires on the highway, the sound of Louisiana draining of its people for the second time. If he hadn't heard his mother whisper, *They think they're getting somewhere, but we're all already gone.*

Perhaps he had forgotten, and perhaps that was the right thing to do. To keep on living, you avoided looking back. You forced forgetting to stop yourself from turning into salt.

But Tess had not yet developed that talent. Even when she tried to drink herself to oblivion, she still had dreams of houses torn apart like slaughtered animals. She had been so worried for so long — that Cora was locked up, that Cora had drowned, that Cora was out of it and lost in the system of buses and shelters that scattered New Orleans to the four corners of the earth, that she had trouble believing these things hadn't really happened — her body remembered them as true.

As Augie led Tess through the rooms, she looked around, trying to find traces of her daughter's presence, but nothing besides the chandelier seemed to have been touched since Madge's memorial. The same insulated silence lay over the carpets like a blanket of moss. In the living room, the abstract steel sculpture Augie had bought from Joe just after Madge's death still reclined on the console table behind the sofa, and the sofa was still covered in the same striped fabric she'd helped Madge choose when Mrs. Randsell had moved to Northline, to that "more manageable house" behind its high, locked wall.

From above the small server that held the cut-crystal carafes, Madge looked down from her portrait. It was a half-length piece, Madge's body severed at her slender linen-clad waist, her fingertips brushing the lower frame. Mrs. Arbor had made her turn sideways and peer back solemnly over her shoulder, and Madge liked to joke that the old lady had chosen the pose on purpose to give her a neckache, so that her expression would have "at least a little edge." It was not a perfect likeness — her features pinched, her eyes too wide set and dark.

Augie crossed the room and held open the swinging door. She saw his eyes go to the portrait too, and then he turned from her into the kitchen.

"You know it'll be five years in November?"

"I know."

"She would have hated this, just hated it." He slammed his hands down on the granite countertop. "I drove through where Hildy lived — you remember Hildy who worked

202

for us in the '80s, early '90s — and the little house we helped her buy off the derelict rolls and fix up? All its guts were lying rotting in the street. I don't know how to reach her, but Madge would have found a way. She would probably have driven out and scooped her up out of the Red Cross in Wichita or wherever and put her in the guest room and made her stay."

"She probably would." Tess nodded.

"She would have made them fix it. Hildy's house, everything. And if they wouldn't, she'd have had us all down there scrubbing on our hands and knees."

Tess smiled. She could better see Madge, her hair tied up in a bandana, bright pink lipstick on her narrow lips, storming city hall, brandishing a pithy sign in one hand and some ruined thing of Hildy's — a sofa cushion, a rusted cast-iron skillet — in the other.

"Me, all I can do is drink," Augie sighed, shook his head. He glanced behind him at the liquor cabinet, turned back. "You want one?"

Tess looked at the microwave clock — it was 10:15 a.m. and Cora would still be sitting in Alice's chair, silent as a locked room — but, regardless, yes, she did. "Gin and tonic?"

Augie leaned into the Sub-Zero for a lime and the tonic bottle, then turned around to her, shrugging his shoulders.

"You know, I used to be very strict about it. No drinking for medicinal purposes. It really ticked Madge off." He shook his head, laughing, and took down a cutting board and a knife. " 'I wish you'd have a drink. You're in such a foul humor.' I see her point, now. What's a couple of years shaved off at the end of things? And what else are you going to do?"

"I could write you a scrip for Xanax."

"Already have some."

"We could storm city hall."

"Ha! You think that son of a bitch Nagin's going to listen to *us*?" He tossed his head up, then went back to slicing the lime, very carefully, the fingers of his left hand bunched. "No, everybody's got to go back to where they were before, no matter how dangerous, no matter that it was a crime that their ancestors were sold a bill of goods on some malarial backwater a hundred years ago, it's their 'home,' Tess, don't you understand? They have the right to have it swept out to sea again!"

"You should run for mayor."

He shook his head, smiling. "You always wanted me to run for mayor."

"I did." She laughed, for real this time. "I remember spending our entire homecoming dance trying to convince you go into politics. Madge was so angry at me! But you reminded me of Barry Goldwater."

"Oh lord. I didn't know that was the reason! You told me once," he said, poking towards her with the paring knife, "you said, 'You've got a politician's charisma.' I was kind of offended, actually."

"I didn't mean it badly."

"Then how did you mean it?"

She shrugged and looked down at the vein of amber quartz running through the countertop. As Augie swirled the drinks in their crystal glasses, the ice cubes rang like altar bells.

"She had such good taste."

"Oh, in politicians?" Augie grinned.

"Ha-ha," she said. "No, I mean, this kitchen looks like it was put in yesterday, and she saw all that. She was a true classic, Madge. Elegance just dripped from her."

"You know, it's been so long since we renovated — two whole refrigerators ago — that I'd almost forgotten that old kitchen. Yellow cabinets, my God. And to think that was chic back then."

"Avocado," she said, before she could stop herself. She watched his hands pause, the cap half-screwed on the tonic bottle. "Weren't they green?"

"Oh, you know, you're right?" He slotted limes onto the sides of their glasses. "Avocado."

"It's just —" She laughed. "Do you know how many rolls I buttered in this kitchen with Beulah? Hiding from those third basemen Madge always insisted you provide for me?"

Augie had opened the French doors and was standing between them, waiting for her to come out onto the veranda. As she stepped into the shade of the green-and-white striped awning, one of the cold, wet glasses kissed her upper arm, and she turned into him and took it, and his thigh pressed hers through his thin khaki pants.

"Do you remember that New Year's Eve?" he said.

She froze. The broad leaves of the gingers waved against the lawn. Just before midnight, Madge and Joe and their other guests had gone down to the river to watch the fireworks, but Augie had stayed behind with her on Esplanade. Her feet hurt from being crammed into cocktail shoes, and Augie had offered to help with the dishes, but instead, they had gone out onto the gallery, the tiles slick with rain under her bare feet, and he had taken her shoulders in his hands. She had tilted her face up, and he had kissed her.

"I'm sure you realized that I was in pain," Augie said now, his hand still on the French doors. "Confused and in pain and thrashing about, trying to understand how life could go on if we lost her."

Tess nodded. The ice settled into her drink.

"You didn't know that she was sick yet, but you were kind to me. I still remember the way you took my hand, afterwards, and squeezed it. As if you understood everything."

Tess nodded again, pressing her body against the railing as she held her glass over the edge. That was how she felt now — as though he understood. They had been through it together, after all, the anxious drive into the city as Rita strengthened in the Gulf, the discovery, the relief. He had stood beside her at the garden gate, seen his mother beside Cora in the grass, his hand against her hand.

On the little iron table under the oak tree where Mrs. Randsell and Cora had been sitting that morning, a hardcover book had been abandoned in the rain. It was swollen with water, splayed sloppily open, and she felt something similar expanding, unfolding under her breastbone.

"What a pity," she said, under her breath.

"What?" Augie asked.

She listened to him stride across the veranda behind her, but did not turn to him. As he wrapped his broad hand around the edge of her waist, she held herself straight, tried not to react when he dipped his nose into her hair. She wanted to say, *Do you know how long I've wanted this?* But the answer would have put him off. Instead, she said,

"You've left your book out in the rain."

He took his hand from her waist and moved around in front of her, pushed the hair back off of her cheekbone, then kissed her there, kissed her mouth. His tongue, coated in gin, edged with coffee, fluttered against her palate. His hands moved around behind her back, worked themselves up underneath her shirt, and she couldn't stop thinking that this was how Madge had taught him to kiss, how they had learned to kiss together, here, on this veranda under this striped awning while, hovering over the green Bakelite dish, their cigarettes burned down to columns of ash, supported only by some vague, structural memory of what they once had been.

"Lord, I am not worthy to receive you," the priest said, holding the Host up over the chalice, "but only say the word and —"

"— my soul be healed," Vincent said.

"— I shall be healed," Joe said, the congregation said, Father Reynard said.

Things had changed. Even church, the one place that should have been safe. They didn't say "the Holy Ghost" anymore and they didn't speak in Latin and they hardly ever sang, these women — mostly women — standing in the pews with their heads uncovered. Sylvia would never have dared enter a church without a hat. He could remember the day when girls who had misplaced their bonnets would put handkerchiefs on their heads.

Joe was tapping his arm as if he expected him to join the communion line. Vincent hadn't taken communion since 1969, but his son was still an altar boy under that four-day beard. Vincent shook his head as Joe climbed over into the aisle and stood looking at his shoes.

1969. That was the year the priest had been replaced at St. Joseph with this cringing, skinny fellow he couldn't bring himself to confess to. Seemed like sin would scare him, like he didn't have the constitution for it. Father Keenan was his name, and he'd brought a guitarist with him from Oregon and forced them all to commit hootenanny mass, Sylvia in her hat clapping along. Whether this had been passed down and perpetrated by the Second Vatican Council or no — along with the banishment of Latin and the turning of the altar so that the geeky, string bean Father Keenan stood looking at you as he said things that were supposed to go straight to God — it took the meaning out of everything. The mass had been stripped naked, like those girls who took off everything but their tennies and ran across a football field. What beauty, what grace had been there turned out to have been nothing but trickery and veils. It was no wonder the girl Adelaide stayed home in bed.

He looked at Joe, inching forward, still bending his head in prayer. Vincent had believed once. His first communion, he'd gotten a tingle of something like faith, being one of a long line of little boys and girls lined up in their finest in front of the church. Before they walked, the deacon had given them all candles with a little paper circle around the bottom to protect their hands from the wax. He remembered thinking it wasn't funny the way the other boys, Francis Morillo, for one, made like they would light the girls' braids on fire. He remembered he'd been anxious the Eucharist would taste like meat — it was supposed to be Jesus's flesh after all. For the life of him he couldn't tell you now whether it had, the memory was so completely covered up by the gummy, plain flour taste of every other host in every other church of his life. It was possible that his memories of that day weren't even true, not the sharp drip of the hot wax, not Francis Morillo's missing side teeth — that the whole thing might be just a story his mother told for company. That happened sometimes. What you were told or told yourself could, little by little, change the very thing you'd lived, until finally there was no telling what was real and what wasn't. In the end, of course, it didn't matter; what you remembered became your world.

He was no fool, no matter what they thought. He was dying was all, just like everyone was bound to do. It just happened to be his misfortune to die in drips and drabs rather than all at once; they had called a poor executioner, his arm weak, the blade dull. So he had to watch as hotel rooms vanished into the air and office towers slumped to dust, as clients and great-aunts were erased, leaving pale smears where their faces should be. The song his mother sang as she rocked his cradle was muted in her mouth, as were the words Sylvia had said as she lay beside him in the night; all words in fact would soon be changed to moving mouths and whispers that failed to reach across a dining table that would eventually be cleared of all ordinary meals, until all that remained were abstractions, insults, radio music, and the burnt crust of marshmallow on the candied yams. Eventually, his baby children would be driven away in the backseat of that 1964 Pontiac Bonneville that had been either blue or gray. The house with the green walls he and Sylvia had raised them in would burn to a cinder, and Sylvia would walk out into the lake until the water closed over her head. Finally the bark of the trees would smooth to brown paper and the birds' voices would lose the birds, the lake and river would evaporate into the clouds, and the cars and streets would roll away over the edge of the earth until nothing was left but their roar.

Vincent bent his head and tried to pray.

Del got into the Dobies' tiny shower without

waiting for it to get hot. From the neck-high showerhead, water hammered on the bones of her chest. A bottle green fly flew in through the open window and knocked at the wet glass. All morning she'd felt like crying as she left her father's house without apologizing and drove across the lake, as she gathered Cora from Alice's, delivered her home. She felt queasy still, as if she might vomit. It wasn't just the fight she'd had with her father, who'd been trying so hard to please, standing in front of his overstuffed kitchen cabinets like the owner of a failing store; it nagged at her, leaving Reyna there in that house. She'd called DMORT again that morning, but the woman who'd answered had been so unconvincing — talking of backlogs — that she'd nearly driven by Troy's house after Alice's, before thinking better of it, since Cora was in the car. *Do you know what it would do to her,* her mother had said, *if Cora knew her friend's sister killed herself?* They should have wrapped the body in a rug and dropped her on the front steps of the nearest precinct. Or, like Kea said, just dug a goddamned hole. She wanted to force someone to do something. It was the most basic function of civilization, burying the dead, and if they couldn't get their acts together to do even that, then they weren't any better than the dogs scavenging in the streets.

She leaned against the tiles and watched white floes of lather drift towards the drain. The water had gotten warm finally, and she closed her eyes and tried to feel nothing but the shower pounding against her back, but the smell of the Mississippi floated around her in the steam, and she saw again the flood washing over the floorboards of Troy's cottage.

She turned off the taps and wrapped one of the Dobies' big blue towels around her. In their bedroom, Cora was lying exactly as Del had left her, her head propped up on pillows, her arms straight out on top of the coverlet. Holding the towel around her, Del climbed up into the narrow bed and lay down beside her sister. Cora's breathing was so quiet that if it weren't for the gentle rise and fall of the sheet over her breast, Del wouldn't have been sure she heard it at all.

"Cora? You okay?" She placed her hand over her sister's brow, but Cora's eyes stayed closed.

In the dark around the bed, their furniture huddled like ghosts. There were the armoires that had come out of Oma's house, which they had climbed into as girls, looking for Narnia between the hand-sawn boards. There was the vanity that her mother would sit at before she went out at night, dabbing the stopper of the perfume bottle on her throat. There was Cora's cheval glass, its face turned to the wall, which had reflected their teenaged bodies, silvering the blades of Cora's hipbones and the overturned bowls of Del's breasts. There was the sideboard their mother had bought at Neal's, attributed to Mallard, and the blanket chest where they'd always kept their Mardi Gras costumes — the painters' smocks and sequined tutus and old duck-feather wings. Then there were the Boisdoré pieces: the marble-topped side table, its legs an Art Nouveau riot of vegetal forms, and a third armoire, classical and austere in her great-great-grandfather's style. There were the beds that Papie had made, all three of them, for her and Cora and, before that, for their father, all gifts on their tenth birthdays. Her father's and hers leaned, dismantled, against the wall, her palm-fronded posts intermingling with his arrow-headed spears. She and Cora lay in the third bed.

She could smell, rising out of the headboard, the old woody perfume of her grandfather's workshop, the same smell that had probably lingered in the workshops of all the Boisdorés who had come before, even down to the back rooms of the shop that Theodule set up when his grandmother, Adelaide, purchased his, his uncle's, and his mother's freedom from the estate of the white widow Boisdoré. Though Del had done research into their genealogy in college, she could find no record of where the money had come from; Adelaide herself had been a slave, and her children were the result of a "liaison" with a white man named Dubuisson, who might well have paid for his children's manumission. But Del liked to imagine that Theodule's uncle François — listed on his free papers as a *bon maçon* — had been building houses all along, and that he had given Adelaide the money for his own liberty and that of his sister and his sister's child. She liked to imagine Theodule tagging along with his Uncle François as he built houses in the Quarter and the Marais, picking up a hammer first, then a chisel, and then being taught to use them by François's apprentices and slaves. By the time François owned a stretch of Esplanade between Marais and Treme and three lots at Villere and Bayou Road, Theodule had his own shop, where he later made fine coffins that his cousin, François *fils*, used to bury the best of colored Francophone society.

The Françoises, *père et fils,* and their descendants had all the money, but better than money was what François *père* had left to Theodule, and Theodule had left to Homer and Homer had left to Augustin and Augustin had left to Louis-Vincent and Louis-Vincent had left to Papie. He had taught them how to create not just beautiful objects, but their own freedom. They learned how to rescue something rough and mortal, something that, if felled, would otherwise just be left to rot, and turn it into something exquisitely beautiful, something that would last longer than the lives of many men.

Del turned away from her sister and looked at the bead of green light that ran between the Dobies' Pottery Barn curtains, suddenly and deeply afraid that out there beyond the old-glass windows was the end of all that. The way things were going, everything François and Theodule had worked for would just be allowed to decompose. The way things were going, there would never even be a funeral, much less a horse-drawn hearse, a beautiful coffin, a brass band.

As she rolled over again towards her sister's body, the bed groaned familiarly, and Del wanted to press her hands against her ears.

"I think we should go," she whispered to Cora. "I think the only thing we can do is leave."

Cora just breathed, in and out, through her high Choctaw brow.

"It doesn't have to be New York. We could go to San Francisco, Oaxaca, Tokyo. I don't care, just somewhere we can make our own lives. We'll get a little flat, and you can cook, and I can find some shop to work in, and we can start over. That way we won't have to watch everything die." She propped herself up on her elbow and brushed the hair back off of Cora's face.

"I just want to forget," Cora said without opening her eyes.

"I know, I know." Del pulled her hand through her sister's long, silky hair. "And you won't be able to if we stay here — neither of us will."

Cora turned her head from side to side on the pillow, and Del pushed herself up to sit, her back against the cold wooden head-board. "I can't go."

"You can, though." Del searched for Cora's hand under the blankets. "Let me help you."

"You don't understand," Cora whispered.

"I —" Del started. She reached over and

turned on the lamp. On the bedside table, their mother had left a small vase of roses, the red-tipped yellow ones that grew along their back fence. Del tugged one free, its thorns and little side leaves clutching at the others, and put her nose in it. "That's not fair, Cora. I'm from here too. I've loved this city and suffered by this city too. This is hard for all of us."

Cora shook her head again. "There are things I still need to do."

It was hard not to laugh. "You're very busy, clearly."

Cora's eyes opened, and their blue-haloed pupils searched Del's face. "Can you help me?"

"Of course I can. Anything."

"She's waiting for me."

"Who's waiting?"

Cora's mouth dropped open, and she looked at Del, confused for a moment. "No," she said, and she closed her eyes again. "Nobody. I'm sorry. I was confused. It's just a dream I had."

Del sighed and turned the rose between her fingers, the tiny thorns on the stem pricking her lightly. "Do you want to tell me about it?"

Cora shook her head. Her skin was draped over her face like a veil.

"You can tell me. Please tell me. I want to know."

"There's a dead woman on the kitchen floor. Because of me."

Augie still had Madge's pictures on his bedside table: Madge in a dotted sundress holding someone else's baby, Madge smiling with her green-lit eyes, Madge making a funny face in her going-away suit. Next to them was a half-full flacon of her perfume, and the smell of wilted gardenias leached into the air, so that Tess had to avoid turning to that side of the bed.

Augie stood up and began to unbutton his shirt, his fingers trembling, and Tess pushed herself up onto her elbows. He was watching his hands as he pushed each yellowed button through its hole, and when the second to last button, broken by the cleaners, snagged, he glanced at her and smiled apologetically. She had to bite her cheek to keep from crying. Intimacy was so cheap these days — all these Tulane girls with tears running down their cheeks telling her about how they'd hooked up with him and him and the other guy, so why were they still so lonely? — that it had almost ceased to exist. Even in her marriage, it had become mundane, then taken for granted, then finally lost, like a set of keys that was in your hand one minute and gone the next.

Augie's shirt fell open, and his eyes went to her again, though they looked behind her, at the drawn curtains, maybe, or maybe the bureau, maybe nothing. So far, he was less naked than he would be swimming laps in the Country Club pool, but in a bedroom with one other person, those inches of flesh, this tangle of fur, those pink, useless nipples become something private, something deliberately shared.

She shook her head. *Now, Tess,* she told herself. *Now, now, now, now.* She inclined her neck towards him, put her fingers into his chest hair. She lay her lips on his sternum. She touched the skin of his belly, his chest, his smooth, cool collarbones. She licked at the salt in the crux of his neck. He was holding his arms rigid, a little bit out from his sides, and when she looked up into his face, his mouth was open in a dumb O.

She pulled herself off of him — to ask, as it was only right to, whether this was something he actually wanted — but pulling away, she felt again that heat radiating up the back of her thighs, prickling across her abdomen. Her hands slid over his shoulders, around the sunburnt, hot back of his neck. It didn't matter if he wanted it: what was done was done. She pushed his shirt away, and it slid down over his out-flung, unmoving arms and fell to the floor with a rustle.

His hands fumbled for her elbows, and she felt his penis stiffening on the other side of her panties, and she moved her fingers up into his hair. His eyes were cottony. She kissed him on his hairline, his ear, the edge of his neck. She closed her eyes, and the sound of a car passing on the street crackled along her skin. He was touching her, and she leaned back to let him put himself inside her, and the light flashed and dimmed, flashed and dimmed — oak branches ducking in the sun — and she remembered how Augie's headlights had flashed in her rearview mirror as they descended the rural highway into El Dorado, Arkansas, leaving New Orleans as the storm approached. As far as she'd been able to see down that highway, there was nothing in front of her and nothing behind but that silver Porsche, glowing dully in her taillights and the blowback of its own high beams.

His eyes were closed, his pink body moving heavily against her. Tires whispered on asphalt, and down in the valley the lights changed in series, yellow to red to green.

Del put her nose into her plastic cup of

bourbon and inhaled hard. It was only four o'clock, but already she was two bars and four drinks in. She'd stopped seeing the faceless woman on the kitchen floor, her sister standing over her in her nightdress; she had convinced herself, with the help of the bourbon, that that couldn't possibly be what Cora meant, that it had only been the nightmare Cora said it was. But now she was hearing things — her sister's laughter, her own name. She kept looking behind her at the door, feeling someone looking at her, smelling Fran's smell of Easy Mac and cigarettes, imagining Zack's tongue in her ear. He'd kept calling her all afternoon, but she couldn't remember what she'd wanted to say to him, how to say it. His name lit up the screen now, and she pressed her finger into the red button, lifted her cup again, drank the shot down, signaled to the bartender for another.

"Del?"

She looked up. The early band was getting on stage, the sparse crowd chattering. The drummer hit the drum, and the room spun a quarter turn. The bartender poured another shot, and she slid off the stool with it and pushed past the crowd coming in through the door. Frenchmen Street was abuzz with the shrieks of the do-good tourists who wandered up and down on their day of rest in an alcoholic stupor, hunched under the weight of paid-for Mardi Gras beads. In the middle of the street a sun-burned blonde with a Hand Grenade was jumping up and down and squealing. Del stepped off the curb, and a vet in dog tags ran smack into her, the sweat on his shirt-less chest smearing across her arm.

"Motherfucker!" Del screamed as he pushed off her, kept walking. "Fuck you, motherfucker!"

In the middle of the street, the bouncing girl fell giggling against some jock's chest.

"Del!"

A hand fell on her shoulder, thumb on the back of her neck. She jumped away, turned back.

"Zack? What are you doing here?"

He was grinning a stupid, big-toothed grin, and she stepped towards him, hit at his chest with the flats of her hands.

"What in the hell are you doing here!"

His lower lip between his teeth, he walked into her beating hands, brought his arm over her shoulders, and then she was burrowing into him. A shudder of comfort suffused her body, and she was pissed at herself for feeling it, pissed at him for making her. How could she change anything if she couldn't even stop herself from doing again the things she should never have done?

"We were worried," he said. "And Fran needed your stuff out of the apartment. I volunteered to drive it down."

His face was so full of pity his eyebrows nearly touched, and he smelled of Tide and fast food, his T-shirt tight across his chest. *I volunteered.* No different, really, than the do-good tourists in the Livestrong bracelets and new Timberlands. At least he hadn't bought Mardi Gras beads. *I would feel so much better,* Fran had whined on the other side of her bedroom door, *if I could help.* She almost laughed.

"Thanks." She turned around, stepped back. "But I was going to take care of it."

"Oh, really?"

"I've got things under control."

"Well, let's lay out the facts then, baby. You bailed on your job, your lease, your friends." He was actually counting on his fingers. "You weren't picking up your phone, except to yell at Fran. You kept calling and hanging up. What were we supposed to think? I went by your house. I've been sitting on your parents' front steps all afternoon, but the house seemed abandoned. I didn't know what to do —"

She turned away from him and walked

into the crowd.

"Adelaide Hortense Boisdoré!" He grabbed her by the shoulder, and she was forced to make the face she made whenever he said her middle name.

Zack was dead serious, however. "Please, Del," he said. "Please. I've got to fly out in the morning. Please, just talk to me."

She bit her lip and turned away from him, hoping the crowd would separate them. He jogged after her, hands on her shoulders again, then off.

"Del, I'm sorry. I'm so sorry. I shouldn't have taken advantage of you like that. You came to me to talk —"

She put her hands against his cheeks, tried to shut him up.

"I don't know why you came to me, why you come to me."

"Stop," she said. "Stop. I'm the one who's sorry."

"No, Del."

"Really."

He opened his mouth to speak again, and she took his hands.

"Stop," she said, more gently now. "Just stop. Let it go."

Inside the club, the drummer beat a test riff on his drum. The shirtless vet came back through, his dog tags bounding against his pecs.

"I can't let it go," Zack said, from under his stupid lashes.

She closed her eyes and nodded. A little breeze moved through the street, moving the hair that lay against her neck. "Then come inside and dance."

Flames leapt from the grill, and the bald man whose name Vincent should have remembered stood back, holding a bottle of lighter fluid up in the air. The long day was closing down on them, and there seemed to be a firelit flicker to everything stained by the falling sun. It lit the edges of the cut grass and polished the coats of the ponies trotting in the sandy paddock. Five girls in total were taking a lesson, three mahogany ponies, one ebony, and another the dingy color of whey. A pretty brunette stood in the center of the whirling girls, yelling instructions, while Joe hung on the rail.

For some time now, since he'd been sitting here under the barn's overhang, Vincent had had the phrase "inheritors of the earth" stuck in his brain like a piece of gristle, though it hadn't been the Beatitudes today, so far as he remembered. In no sense were these little girls meek, but he supposed that was what Jesus had meant, that the Second Coming would usher in a sort of Opposite Day when high would be low, right left, up down. That was what the woman in the arena was saying, over and over. *Up, down. Up, down. Aubrey, watch those heels. Up, down.*

The girls seemed to know what they were doing, better than he would, that was for certain. The ponies lined up politely and hopped over the crossed poles like there was nothing to it, while the girls popped up to put their hands into their ponies' glossy manes.

"Up, down. Up, down. Up, down. Release a little more next time, Maggie. Up, down."

Maybe someday the low would be brought high and the high low, but not anytime soon. Around the table near the grill where they had the chips and dip and carrot sticks, the mothers and fathers had been talking about some poor child who'd had her head stove in by her horse's hoof. They didn't know how the parents could stand it. There was supposed to be a limit on how many bad things could happen at once, they said. Their own darlings needed better helmets, more supervision. He'd had to walk away. No one wanted to hear what he had to say: you protect your children too much, it only makes them less capable of handling trouble when it comes.

He watched Joe watching the woman who paced the sand in her tight pants, beating time against her thigh with a short whip, and hoped it was the girls his son had turned his attention on. Hard to deny that rear end, but this was another one from an alien planet, just like the one Joe was still married to. He knew the boy was aggrieved, but a man's place was beside his wife in bad times. It was his bound duty to forgive. He himself had forgiven Tess — she'd misunderstood was all, never had any real discernment when it came to furniture anyway — but Joe expected her to come back on her knees. That was the thing with marriage, though: sometimes you had to swallow venom for the other's sake.

Vincent just wanted them to be happy, but he couldn't get involved. Maybe it was that he had gotten too involved in the past, or tried to, or Sylvia had. They had seen this coming for miles. The boy too much in love, the girl too high above. You can't put a woman on a pedestal, especially when she thinks she belongs up there. They had gotten this idea that they were charmed, that nothing could touch them, as if their differences — white vs. colored being the least of them — could just be laughed away. It was for damn sure they'd never expected to run into real problems, and when they had finally gotten knocked off balance, well, it turned out they were so far apart, they couldn't even hold each other up.

The lesson was finished, and the girls on their ponies filed out of the arena. Joseph turned with them, walking alongside the whey horse and still talking to the girl, a little redheaded boy's body in a green shirt. Joe pointed to him, and the girl turned her pony without moving so much as a finger. *Inheritors of the earth.* The smell of horse and sweat and leather came ahead of them, and Vincent took a good deep breath of it. It was a wholesome smell, like the smell of new cut lumber.

"Pop," Joe said. "I want you to meet Maggie."

"Maggie," he said. "Princess Maggie."

The girl giggled, and her teeth were straight and perfect under her smooth upper lip. "Do you want to pet my pony? His name is Buttercup."

Vincent pried himself out of the dusty chair. "That's what I would have named him. He looks just like a Buttermilk." He patted the animal's hot, damp shoulder. "He's a good horse?"

"Yes." The girl smiled and scrubbed her fingers in his mane. "The best."

"Did you see them take that jump at the end, Pop?" Joe had on his visiting face, a mask of sunshine. "What did you call it, Maggie. A boxer?"

"An oxer."

"An oxer. The wide one." Joe looked at him, apparently serious. Blinking.

"No, I did not, I'm afraid."

"Well, it was impressive."

"Not really," said Maggie, inheritor of the earth. "I jump ones that are higher *and* wider."

"Oh, well, it looked impressive to me," Joe said and Vincent knew he missed this, the easy banter one can have with a child. He had loved his babies, Joe. "But I've never been on a horse."

"You haven't?" squealed the princess. "Why not?"

"Some of us are not as lucky as you, missy," Vincent said.

"You either?"

"No, me neither."

He'd sat a mule once, he remembered, so long ago now that he couldn't tell you anything about it except that it had felt funny to be up so high, to be able to see through the top panes of windows and into

231

the fruiting lower branches of the pecan tree.

"Do you want to ride Buttercup?"

"Oh, no, Maggie. Thank you." Joe slapped the pony's meaty neck and took a step backwards. "We're just going to have a couple hot dogs and then head home to bed."

"I'd like to try him," Vincent said.

Before Joe could stop her, Maggie flung one long, thin leg over the saddle and let herself down gracefully in the grass. She took the reins over the pony's head and looked up at Vincent, expectantly.

"Do you know how to get on?"

Joe moved between Vincent and the horse. "I don't think this is the best idea."

"Why not?" asked the inheritor of the earth.

Vincent knew why not. Joe was afraid he'd fall or hurt the horse, afraid he'd take off with it into the fields, and Joe would lose all the power over him he'd worked so hard to acquire.

"We're both too big for Buttercup, Maggie, but thank you." Joe made to take hold of Vincent's hand. "He's little-girl-sized, not old-man-sized."

"Monica rides him all the time, if he's being bad."

Joe looked over to where Monica — that pretty brunette in the tight pants — was replacing the cover on the grill, and opened his mouth, but Monica was a tall woman, and the child had defeated him.

"So, what you do —" Maggie looked authoritatively at Vincent as she pulled down the buckle of the stirrup strap, adjusting it. "— is you put your left foot in here, and then your hands on the saddle, and then you jump up and swing your other leg over his back."

Vincent nodded. He felt steady and good today — this was something he could do. He approached the pony, and though Joe followed closely, he did not interfere. The girl had lengthened the stirrup strap so that it hung halfway to the ground, and slowly, Vincent used his hands to lift his leg and slot his foot in place. He put his hands on top of the little girl's saddle and stood up on his stirrup, leaning into the animal's musty side. Under the new weight, Buttermilk stepped forward, and Vincent's right foot dangled helplessly alongside his left, and the bulging top of the saddle dug into his stomach, and he knew now that this would end in disgrace, but instead he felt Joe's broad hands underneath his right thigh, and then he was vaulted up and over and into the saddle.

He was not as tall as the mule had been, Buttermilk, and yet Vincent felt high. He was over his son's head now, and he could see the flames flickering in the barbeque pit and the last thumbnail sliver of red sun hiding behind the black trees at the bottom of the sky. Around the grill, the mothers and fathers had lifted their heads to look at him. They pointed. They raised their eyes up over their hot dog buns and stared at the old man on the little pony, and so it was absurd. Of course it was absurd, but between his legs the pony's warm sides rose and fell and his smell was good and true. Vincent took the reins from Maggie and turned the pony's head away and let him walk across the gravel driveway, out towards the long, rolling meadow. In the pasture beside them, a herd of full-grown horses, oaken, silver, and maple, saw Buttermilk at their fence and galloped up, snorting and kicking their heels. Buttermilk, inheritor of the earth, did not let this bother him. He looked at them, twitched his ears, and then walked on, taking Vincent farther from Joe, farther from the worriers and the children. He had a stream in mind, maybe, or a patch of clover, and Vincent let himself be taken there. The crickets had started singing, and the light was fading, after all.

Zack didn't know quite what to do with the funk. Four hours in, he still wobbled against the beat, his feet not quite syncopated, his hand flashing out to repeat a cymbal clash, a long high trumpet note, but Del still liked having him near her, even though she saw the other locals up front smiling at them. A large woman passed them on the way to the bar, winking, and said, "Where you from, baby? New York?" and he tried harder for a minute, bobbing his head from side to side, until Del came up behind him and showed him the way.

She took his hips in her hands, and he pressed back against her. She laughed, though it wasn't funny. She closed her eyes and put her face into his back, and she could feel his muscles tense beneath his T-shirt as he stopped dancing and stood, letting the music scatter across them. In New York, he had taken her wrists and pinned them behind her head, held them there with one hand as he kissed her neck, pushed her shirt up, pushed his other hand under her still-clasped bra, took her nipple in the rough tips of his fingers, and she had lain there quiet, her mind spinning. When he took his hand from her wrists she had kept her arms up above her head, and when he grabbed the waistband of her panties, she had lifted her hips into the air, and when he'd gone down on her, she had come in such hard, high waves that she had to fight to breathe. Now, she moved her hands under the hem of his T-shirt. Kermit blew his horn: *Do you know what it means, to miss New Orleans?*

Zack took a step away from her.

And miss her each night and day?

Del couldn't stand to look at him, that look of solicitous concern on his face again, and so she pulled him to her and kissed his slow, wet mouth.

Then, they were walking down the middle of Royal Street, distant cars whispering from the avenue.

Del was sobering up, and her ears rang — she kept her eyes on the asphalt. Zack walked along beside her, and she felt his gravity the way she imagined the sea felt the moon's. She veered towards him, away. Every so often, his hand fluttered out and brushed her elbow, and she walked him right past the Dobies' and onto Esplanade, looking up at the branches of the still-living trees.

"I loved that magnolia tree," she said.

He rubbed her back with the flat of his

hand. "I know."

They stopped in front of her house. The Ryder truck with her stuff in it — the bureau and her mattress, the wooden hangers rejected by the new girl who didn't hang up her clothes — was parked out front, but Zack was looking at the façade of her house in the darkness.

"It's still a beautiful house," he said.

She walked up the steps, and reached for the vinyl-wrapped chain. She fished in her pocket for the little lump of keys, dangled them in the streetlight. Only the big keys were there; she'd put the padlock key back in the Dobies' kitchen drawer.

"I don't have the key."

Nodding, he kissed her on her hairline with his wet whiskered mouth. "It's alright, D. Let's just go get some burgers."

"No." She jumped off the edge of the portico. "I have the key to the garden gate."

The broken bottles along the top of the fence glowed amber and green in the moonlight, and Zack looked up at them as he walked through. The lower gallery was deserted — the rockers gone — and over the toolshed, the moon had risen, a coin on the belly of the naked sky. From here, only the disk of the tree's roots and an upward slash of trunk were visible. A little burst of wind shot through the air, and she listened for its rustle in the leaves. She felt Zack's eyes on her neck. On the street, a car passed, and the shadow of the fence tilted against the house, bars of gray and yellow.

"We're going to be in the shit if a cop drives by," he said.

"This is my house. I grew up here," she said, staring into the wide black V the magnolia had cut through the siding. On either side of the gash, the windows of her father's studio banked sideways, and the walls hung slack, the house open to the sky. Del took Zack's hand and led him to a place where the tree leaned close to the ground, and then she vaulted onto its trunk.

"They don't know it's your house," he said. "Come on, it's alright. Let's go get something to eat, and then, if you're good, you can drive me to the airport at four."

Ignoring him, she began to shimmy up the trunk. He pressed his hands into the tree and followed her.

The broken staves of siding were thrust at wild angles into the gap, and the wiring had tangled in the branches. The kitchen glowed dimly with light from the street, and Del climbed over the low branches, easing across the wide crux in the trunk where as a girl she'd used to sit and read, and ducked under the canopy of broken twigs. Once she was sure the floor was steady beneath her, she let herself down. Zack came after her, his heavier movements making the tree quake. He dropped down as soon as he was over the kitchen floor, bushwhacked his way through the splintered branches and glossy leaves until he reached her. For a second he just stood there, his arms limp, his red mouth parted. Under his brows, his eyes darted towards hers and then away. Quick, like jumping into cold water, she moved towards him, put her mouth on his mouth. For a moment his lips resisted hers, his tongue heavy as clay. But then he stepped into her, warm in the hot night, his hands on her ribs, his leg up between her thighs. She heard the leaves above them stirring as the wind began to shift them on their branches, and she too began to tremble. Wrapping her arms around his neck, as if he could be more solid than a thing rooted in the earth, she pushed him down into the fallen branches. Kneeling, he ran his fingertips up the backs of her calves, her knees, her thighs, and up, until a heaviness seemed to rise through her like leaves rising to the surface of a pool.

MONDAY
OCTOBER 24

Empty room, empty house, empty street. Tess ran her tongue around the inside of her sleep-wooled teeth. Empty wineglass, empty air.

The cluttered room was jaundiced with street light, still dark, and the wing of the chair was rough against her cheek. It was unclear how long she'd been asleep there, how long since she'd come back to the Dobies' smelling of Augie Randsell and Tanqueray and showered, poured herself a glass of wine, and went into the girl's bedroom to find the beds unmade, Del and Cora gone. She had wandered a while over the padded floor looking at things — all these familiar objects defamiliarized, only themselves again now that they were out of context in this new and temporary place. Eventually, she'd sat down in the parlor armchair beside Cora's bed to wait.

Now, she pushed her hands up across her

face — her hair was dry, the wine a film in the bottom of the glass. She thought that, sometime in her sleep, she'd heard a door closing, footsteps, but the house still seemed empty, something too light about the air. It made her skin prickle.

Lacan was right: it was a thing, emptiness. She felt it driven through the center of her, as if Pan could take her to his mouth like a flute and play. Women were better adapted to it, reminded as they were of their own inner emptiness every time a man put himself inside them, and then by the babies that sometimes followed — creation ex nihilo. A consolation, that was supposed to be, until they clipped the cord. After that it was nothing but abandonment. No shoes on their feet, they left you. They grew up, they left you. Their faces painted with powders and pastes, they went out into the streets, they left you. No note, no phone call, they left you, they left you.

She pushed her hands into the chair arms, levered her heavy body upright. The yellow streetlights and the moon in Pisces fought with each other in the darkness. She had no idea what time it was, except late. The girls should be back by now — had to be. She figured they'd gone out for dinner, walked down to Port of Call for a burger like they used to do in high school. Del would have thought she was being a good sister, dragging Cora to that pirate ship of a place, the tables overhung with nets and ropes. When you got drunk down there on twenty-ounce hurricanes, you could almost feel the ocean.

Tess went out into the hall, calling for them, but no one answered. They were probably asleep in the Dobies' big bed — they would have tiptoed up the stairs, seen her in the chair, then retreated, so as not to wake her. But when she opened the door to the master bedroom, there was nothing but the tangle of sheets that she herself had left that morning. She heard her own lungs filling, emptying. Take what you need, need more.

Still, she hesitated at the head of the stairs, listening, thinking she heard talking in the kitchen, but even as she went down, clutching the banister, she knew it was just the voices of drunks passing on the sidewalk, and that the kitchen would be empty, as the sofa was, as was the courtyard. 1:38 a.m. The microwave's clock branded the air. Curfew had begun over an hour and a half ago. They would be home soon, or the police would bring them home.

Del had taken her mother's car to drive

Zack to the airport for his early flight. For a little while, they had lain in the mess of leaves on the kitchen floor, she with her head on his damp chest as he slept, listening to the slow beat of his heart inside its cage of bones. The branches swaying over them, she had traced the lines of his body, the twisted muscles of his abdomen, his hip bones, keeping her fingers just above his skin. He shuddered in his sleep as if touched, and she wondered what touch was, really, whether it began at contact or if, millimeters apart, a person could still feel another's polarity — if wanting were something transmitted physically through the air. She was trying to decide if it was possible for her body to know what she needed better than her mind when the alarm on Zack's phone went off at quarter after three, and he recoiled from her, rolling out from under her and standing up, before he remembered where he was, who she was. Then, of course, he'd apologized for the sex again. But in the very words *I'm sorry, you were drunk,* she heard accusation. Anger, even.

In the car, he wasn't talking, and so she babbled, pointing out the blocks of Esplanade François Boisdoré had owned before the city built streets on them and the derelict storefronts along N. Claiborne that had been the center of African American commerce in the city, until the city decided it needed the I-10 overpass instead. Zack watched out of the window, nodding from time to time. She kept talking, to avoid silence, to avoid hearing herself think, as she nosed the car onto the highway. She talked about the flood of 1927, when the levees at Caernarvon had been dynamited to save the city, and about the river's intention to jump into the Atchafalaya, about the trenches the oil companies had been allowed to dredge through the marsh but had not been required to fill, until she was tired of hearing herself. Just plain tired really.

"It's going to be okay, you know," he said as the city dropped away behind them.

"No." She wrapped her hands tight around the wheel. "I don't know that."

"Look, this has happened before — to other people, in other places. Worse things, actually, have happened." He paused, waiting for her to look at him, acknowledge his losses: father born in a displaced persons camp, village in Poland gone. She would not participate in that, some kind of Olympic Games of suffering. "People get back up again. They manage."

She shook her head.

"I don't get that, Del. Truly. You're not a

person who gives up! I thought you always said, you were not a people who give up. So how come you guys have gone from not giving enough of a shit to see to there being buses to evacuate people to having this hardcore existential crisis? Okay, so the city flooded. People died, and it's tragic, but now you've got to dust yourselves off, clean up, get it right this time."

Del laughed. Below them, the cemeteries spread out along their dark grids. "You don't get it. You weren't here. You're not from here."

He turned to the window, shaking his head. "You either."

"Excuse me?"

"*You* weren't here. You were in New York getting drunk and fucking everything that moved."

She looked at him, her mouth open, feeling like she'd been punched in the gut. They were passing under the overpass at Causeway, where the helicopters had dropped off people to wait days for buses, and in the air that came through the open windows, she could smell the swamp rushing towards them: the end of civilization.

"Cora was, though. Here. She was here," she said, and suddenly, as she sped away from the city along the smooth highway, she saw how much she didn't understand of what Cora had lived, why she couldn't bear to look around her. There were no night-mares anymore, she realized. None of this had been dreamed.

"I think she might have killed someone," Del said, surprised by the words coming out of her mouth.

"What? Why?"

"I don't know why. Her friend's sister was shot dead. There was something — she said something about it being because of her, about —" She felt nauseous, the reflectors on the side of the highway skipping light up over the hood of the car. "I don't think even she really knows. She's just been sleeping, sleeping and walking through the city in the middle of the night. I don't know. All I know is it's not just a garbage-removal problem, I don't care what you think. You can go back to New York and pretend life begins and ends there and forget this ever happened. But that's not possible for us."

Zack was silent. She looked over at him, at his pale face reflected dimly in the dark window, the tattered billboards ticking by behind it. The road ripped away under the tires, and, for a second, she took her hands off the wheel. The car tacked in towards the oncoming lane of traffic, the lane markers flared up in her headlights, and she wrapped her hands back around the steering wheel again, ten and two. Zack ducked his head towards her, his eyes not meeting hers, then turned back to the window. He did not look at her again, not as they went up onto the exit, not as they sped along the airport road, an airplane landing beside them. The lights were on in the departures area, people getting out of their cars in their bathrobes. Only when she'd pulled up to the curb and put the car in park did he turn towards her.

"I'm sorry," he said. "For everything. I shouldn't have come."

She kept both hands on the wheel, looked ahead of her. "Thanks for bringing my stuff."

He nodded, and she watched him in the rearview mirror as he took his satchel out of the backseat and closed the door gently, as if there were someone in the car he was trying not to wake.

"Take care of yourself."

She nodded as he turned, shutting the passenger door behind him.

Joe woke into the early morning darkness out of a dream in which he'd been buried to the neck in sand. The arm he lay on throbbed, but he couldn't bend it. He felt paralyzed, but when he ordered himself to breathe, his lungs opened up and gathered air. With relief, he raised his arms, and the bird started up again with a high frequency trill. When it paused, the night squeezed in around him, releasing him only when the bird started a new song.

When he was studying in New York, living in that swelter-box of a sixth-floor walk-up on Hudson, there was a mockingbird who made frequent stops on the water tower across the street. He would land, raise his beak, and carry on. Joe couldn't recollect the last time he'd heard one in New Orleans, though they were common. Probably he just never distinguished it from the songs of the birds it imitated: the cardinal, jay, gull, crow. Outside his window now, though, a mockingbird was singing. The double low-high, low-high followed by an obnoxious shriek, a *wow-chickie-wow-chickie,* a *SEEE-saw.* Around the calls went in rotation. Once, twice, five times. Joe got out of bed.

The canvas curtains were so soaked in light that he thought it might already be dawn, but when he pulled them aside, it was only the full moon hanging at the far edge of the pasture, right above the dead pecan where the little bird perched, like some kind of Egyptian stele to destruction.

Joe lay back down and closed his eyes but the mockingbird kept at it. He began to feel hot, desperate, the way he had that last summer in New York, when, fed up, he'd buy ice from the bodega and crawl through the window onto the roof. As he melted the cubes on the back of his neck, trying to catch a breeze, he'd watch the mockingbird come and go, watch it argue with the pair of crows that visited his water tower. The mockingbird would lift his narrow gray head and caw, his tail feathers wobbling sassily, as if he really was mocking them. *You can't come up with something better than that?* he seemed be telling them. *Untie yourself from convention, man.* The bird was a beatnik, apparently. Joe had a professor at the time who was urging the same thing, that he break away from received ideas of sculpture, and so, as he stood with the ice on his chest, he tried to interpret the mockingbird. Critical, the creature certainly was, but he was a slave to his influences too. *Whence novelty, birdie?* Joe would inquire, but the mockingbird only filled his throat and announced that there was nothing new under the sun.

Later, sometime after autumn had arrived and the crows had overtaken the water tower, he found a dead mockingbird seventy blocks uptown, on the sidewalk in front of

Café des Artistes. He was rushing to meet Tess and her mother, who was taking them to lunch to celebrate their engagement, but he lingered outside for a minute, looking. Could this be his bird? He crouched down, very nearly picked up the soft gray body. There was no blood on the feathers, no signs of violence — no indication of whether it was the crows or old age or a misguided migration attempt or what. Inside, at a table beside a mural of frolicking nymphs, Tess's mother cocked her head at him, as if he were a teenager who'd just asked an embarrassing question to which he should have known the answer. *Mockingbirds are very territorial, you know,* she said. *If they see even their own reflection in a mirror, a window, they'll fly right at it.* Goofing around, she'd pounced his forearm with her long red fingernails, and he'd laughed as Tess swatted at her, blood blooming in her cheeks.

That day Tess had worn a green dress that pulled the auburn lights out of her hair, and Manhattan had smelled of woodsmoke. After her mother left, they'd lain in Sheep Meadow for hours, his hand inching up her stockinged thigh.

Too-wee, too-wee, the mockingbird called from the top of the dead pecan. This line of thinking would not do. Down the hall, the toilet flushed. Joe sat up in bed, dropped his feet onto the floor.

He found his father in the kitchen, filling the filter of the coffee machine with grounds.

"Damn bird," Vincent said.

"I can't get to sleep either." Now that he was standing, though, his eyes were heavy, his legs like stone. "Decaf?"

His father sighed. "It's past four already. We might as well start the day."

"Got big plans?" he said, but maybe Vincent was right — it was no use trying to sleep. If he hauled the rest of the logs to the road today, maybe he could get some of his own work done. They could watch the dawn from the chairs on the screen porch, talk some. His father didn't seem to want to talk, though. He shook his head, his face stern.

Neither of them had turned on the lights, but the moon pulsed in at the window. *Doo, doo, doo,* the mockingbird sang. His father waded from the cupboard back to the dripping machine, his hands weighted with mugs.

"Pop, what say you we go night swimming?"

His father, mid-pour, looked at him. "Now how do you propose we go to the swimming hole at this hour? I'm not trudging through brambles in the dark, just because you feel like it."

Joe felt a weight sink slowly through his gut. "Not in the hole, Pop. In the pool."

"Whose pool?"

As Joe dragged himself across the kitchen, his father's eyes seemed to cloud over.

"Our pool, Pop. We dug a pool."

"You dug?" his father asked, not a question so much as a sarcastic accusation.

Joe picked up his mug and sipped at the coffee. It was scalding and weak.

"Son, I've got work to do. I don't have time for this silliness."

"Pop, do you know what year it is?"

Caw! Caw! Caw! mocked the bird from the top of the dead cypress.

"That damn bird!" His father's mug cracked down on the stone counter. "It won't let me think."

"It's 2005. We've had the pool almost twenty years now. Since the girls were little. Remember how Mom taught Del and Cora to swim?"

That was not what he was supposed to say. To avoid further agitating your Loved One, the Internet forums said, you were to supposed to lie: Let the delusion stand. Walk the LO to the swimming hole if possible. By

252

all means prevent him from seeing the pool. But Joe didn't want to lie. He wanted to drag his father into the present moment, to force him to share it with him. When was the last time they'd gone down to the swimming hole back in the pines? It probably wasn't even there anymore, but filled in, with a Payless shoe store sitting on top of it.

"I have that dining set to finish for the governor by next Thursday."

"No, you don't, Pop. You mean that four-leaf table, right? Those sixteen Chippendale side chairs and the armchairs with the pious pelicans? You finished all that in 1978, which makes twenty-seven years the governor's been having his — well, it's a woman now, so her — dinner at them."

Pee-yew, pee-yew, pee-yew.

"Stop your foolishness, boy. I don't have time for it." The last word sharp as a blade.

His father cinched up his bathrobe and took another gulp of coffee. Joe let him go on down the hall into darkness, towards his bedroom. He waited. The door did not close, and the bedsprings made no noise. Instead, a drawer slid out, a key entered a lock, a latch clicked open. The mockingbird warbled. Something clacked — Tess's father's shotgun. His father had opened the bolt.

Joe ran down the carpeted hall.

By the time he'd reached the bedroom, his father had climbed out of his window onto the porch. A cold breeze brushed the old lace curtains against Joe's bare arms as he went through.

"You seen the bastard?"

"Who? Pop —" He stepped forward, his hands out, pleading. "You want to give me the gun? I'll get him."

"The bird, you idiot."

Doo-wee, doo-wee. Pew pew pew pew.

Moonlight tracked over his father's bald, liver-spotted head.

"Go around by my windows. I'll show you — he's at the top of the dead tree," Joe said, still creeping towards his father, "but why don't you let me do it? I've always been a better shot than you. You wouldn't want to just scare the thing off."

His father flapped his hand as he clomped down the porch steps, and Joe was obliged to follow as he walked the length of the house, turned the corner.

"What dead tree?" Vincent stopped short, looking out across the property at all of the felled trees. "What is all this?"

An act of God, Joe wanted to say. *This is an act of God.* The shambles of their stand of pines stood starkly against the sky. On top of his tree, the body of the little bird trembled as he crowed.

His father hobbled a little ways into the field. He scanned the sky, the ground. He walked out farther, in a diagonal, until he was beyond the far corner of the house.

"What is all this?" he said again. "What is all this?"

"Wind damage," Joe said. "Bitch was a Cat Three."

"A cat?" His father's eyes were no longer on the trees. Around the side of the house, they could now see the big, red-bean-shaped pool. On its surface, the silver face of the moon wobbled among the leaves, and the old man crouched and lay the rifle in the rimy grass.

The mockingbird cackled, *Ah ah ah!*

It sounded just like a human laugh.

On West End, a mountain of rubble rose on the neutral ground — warped boards and bricks, TVs, toasters, baby shoes, toilets, magazines, and books — and Del idled past it, her foot off the gas. She was so tired, but she knew she wouldn't be able to sleep. She had clicked off the radio, and now the world was oddly silent. Even in the dark early morning, the city should have made some sound — a low moaning, perhaps — but there was nothing, no crickets, no frogs, no birds. She could hear the blood in her ears. The stoplights were still out at many of the intersections, and she went into them with her foot on the gas. She kept seeing a woman in wet clothes hunched over, peering through Troy's cracked-open front door, water lapping at her ankles. She was trying to imagine what could have made Cora shoot someone, someone she was supposed to have rescued — it was unfathomable, and yet, somehow, driving towards the edge of everything, it had suddenly come to her that that must have been what Cora meant. In the flood, the woman with no face pushed opened the door or came at them with a brick, a broken bottle. She threatened Troy, threatened the children, and Cora removed the safety from their grandfather's shotgun, the water tightening around them like a noose.

You weren't here. You don't know. When she got back to the Dobies', she would climb into bed and bury her face in Cora's hair and say that no, she hadn't been and she couldn't know, but she was here now and she would try to understand.

She was here now.

She looped around the park, still strung with water, then turned around the Fair-

256

grounds. At Troy's house, there was still no crime scene tape. She pulled through the intersection, looking in her rearview mirror to be sure that none of the neighbors had come back, before slowing the car down. All of the driveways were empty, as far as she could see.

She parked the Mercedes on the next block and got out, leaving the keys in the ignition, the door open, pinging. Dusty venetian blinds hung crooked in the open kitchen window, and she reached up, jumped. Her feet thumped against the siding, and she fell back into the driveway, pulled her shirt up over her nose and breathed — one, two, three. Her mouth was full of warm saliva, and she spat as she moved around to the front of the house, where everything looked exactly as it had before. In the crust of dirt over the lawn, her own footprints veered diagonally towards the sidewalk to the place where she and Kea had stood, the scales of dried mud trampled to a powder. Across the street, the Indian suit crackled in a breeze. Red and yellow feathers like flames.

She placed her feet in her own footprints as she climbed onto the porch. Around the door, the dirt had been trampled down, and she toed a flake of green paint up off of the concrete slab. She pulled her shirt up and wrapped her hand in it, tried the door handle, but it was locked. *Burned all my bridges,* her brain said, and without thinking, she stooped, picked up an empty flowerpot, and crashed it through the windowpane above the door. She looked behind her. The street was completely empty. The flowerpot rolled, rough voiced, across the wooden floor.

Glass stood in flat fangs around the frame of the window. She wiggled a few out, then reached her arm through and turned the knob. In the cool of the night, the stench hung like lake fog. The moon looked in at the windows, glancing off the edges of the framed posters on the walls, the bottle caps littered on the coffee table. As she waded in, she withdrew the matchbook from her purse, bent back the cover, ripped out a match and struck it, her thumb pressed hard against its head. Phosphorous and sulfur bit into the air. In the haze of orange light she could just make out Reyna's shape under the oily trash-bag shroud, her left foot showing, the long second toe seeming to point at her across the room. Beside her hip were the flowers Anthony had complained about, three red-tipped yellow roses in a full water glass, somehow not yet gone brittle in the heat.

She strode across the kitchen and through the next door into the bedroom, where she pulled the top sheet off of Troy's unmade bed. The match had burned down to her fingers, and she dropped it on the mattress, the flame snuffing as it fell. In the dark again, she went back into the kitchen and held her breath, bent down, and pulled the trash bags off of Reyna's body. The smell jumped up at her like an animal, and her throat clenched shut. She held her breath as she ballooned the white sheet out into the darkness, whispering the funeral psalm: *The Lord is my shepherd, I shall not want; he makes me lie down in green pastures.* As the sheet settled over the body, she lit another match. *He leads me beside still waters; he restores my soul.* Gulping in breath, she banged open the cabinets until she found Troy's lighter fluid and soaked the roll of paper towels on the counter, then threw the almost extinguished match inside the tube where it died. *Yea, though I walk through the valley of the shadow of death, I fear no evil; for thou art with me.*

Outside the open kitchen window, she heard feet approaching, crunching through the crust of mud, and she crouched down

259

beside Reyna, below the windowsill. Her pulse thudded in her neck, and the dull ache in her pelvis spread out through her thighs. She stared at the pale square of the window. The footsteps came closer, shuffled near the edge of the house. *There is a dead woman on the kitchen floor,* her sister whispered. *Because of me.* But then a dog barked somewhere, shook itself, tags jangling against a chain. She stood back up and put her head through the window. There was no one — nothing — there.

"Thou preparest a table before me in the presence of my enemies; thou anointest my head with oil, my cup overflows," she said aloud as she gathered the heap of paper — old *Times-Picayune*s and magazines, bills and letters and advertising fliers — off the wooden kitchen table and rained them over Reyna's body, and then she settled the roll of towels in the center of them. She took one last gulp of the outside air and pulled the roses — blown yellow blossoms edged in red — from the water glass and laid them over Reyna's chest. She struck one more match and lit the edge of the cardboard matchbook. The match heads flared. She crouched down and set the book inside the soaked tube of paper towels and watched as the flame grew stronger, a yellow sheet licking the roof of the cardboard. At the stove, she turned on the gas, one knob after the other, and sprinted from the house, not stopping until she'd reached her mother's car, its door still open, the alarm still chiming.

On the next block, a dog wandered out into the street and started scraping something off the asphalt with its teeth. When she'd slammed the car door, the dog lifted its head to her, its ears perked, then ran off in a slow lope down the middle of the road, slowing every so often to look over its shoulder, as if it was hoping she would follow.

Tess stepped back into the girls' room, pulled the sheets up on Cora's bed, folded them over the blanket, plumped the pillow. Cora loved a freshly made bed — little princess with the smooth black hair easing down into her feathers.

"There," Tess said aloud, but in the silence that followed that word, her tinnitus struck its bell, a sustained high A, and she dropped to her knees.

She imagined Cora in her nightdress striding barefoot across the wastes of the drained swamp while Del spun across a tile floor, her mascara smeared, men holding her up, holding her. She wished, almost, that Cora would stumble through the front door, her pupils dilated, her hands skinned and dirty, or that Del would appear, wasted, on the porch on the arm of some strange boy. Tess rocked back onto her heels. They could be together still. Down at Del's friend Tina's house or in a booth at Snake and Jake's, Cora huddled in the Christmas lights over her sleeping sister, chewing on her thumbs. They could have run away together, like they did once as children, barricaded themselves inside the playhouse at the top of the park's jungle gym. Or they could have been abducted off the street, taken away into one of the abandoned buildings to be tied up and raped and killed. They could have gone to Troy's house to dig a hole in the mud, bury that poor woman, like Del kept threatening to do. Hadn't Antigone tried to recruit her sister into burying the bad brother? Del was just like that — idealistic to the point of irrationality. She wouldn't understand what she was doing when she pulled her sister down.

Tess grabbed the Dobies' phone from the bedside table and hit redial — one ring, then Joe's voice mail. She called Del. It rang, and then her voice sang, clear and competent on the line: *You've reached Ade-*

laide Boisdoré. I'm unable to take your call right now, but please — Tess hung up, tried Cora's number. *Hi, this is Cora. Thanks for calling. Leave me a message and I'll get back to you as soon as I can.* She hung up, re-dialed Del. *You've reached Adelaide Boisdoré* — She hit END.

"Goddamn it! Answer your goddamned fucking phone!" she screamed, and the darkness soaked up her voice like a sponge. Her chest vibrated. She pushed herself upright, flashes of Augie's $800 sheets, his mouth on her rib cage. This was enough of this. The white pages were in the kitchen. She should be sensible, call Del's friends. Tina was Christina Barth, her husband was George Powell. So, Christina Barth Powell. She staggered to her feet, barked her shin on the flared back of a chair fitted upside down over a tea table. She'd call Tina first, and then Alice, to find out what Cora knew, whether Del had told Cora about the body in Troy's house. Then she would go there, except that she didn't know his last name — Troy from the restaurant, whom she'd met in Cora's kitchen once when he was helping serve grillades at that Christmas party Cora had thrown on a whim. Tess would drive around the neighborhood, calling out the window. She would need her medical license to get past the police, because of the curfew. She should take Dan Dobie's gun.

Halfway down the stairs she stopped. She heard, she thought, the rustle of keys. Footsteps. Something occluded the street-light, and then, on the front porch, through the small window in the door, she saw her — a dark head in the darkness. The lock clicked.

Del waited, her hand on the door, the smell of smoke in her clothes.

"Where in God's name have you been?"

"Sorry," Del said, sarcastically, but she was trembling.

"Where is she?"

"Who?"

Tess was already in the foyer somehow, her hand on the door, then she was out on the porch. The streetlight buzzed yellow, and she looked beyond the hedge — cars parked on the asphalt, the distant whoop of a squad car.

"Cora?" Del asked.

Tess was down in the front yard, pushing the gate open.

"Cora?" Del said again. "She's not here?" And even through that ever-present veneer of cool, Tess could hear her daughter's panic.

"She's been sleepwalking, or —" Tess said. "I don't know. I don't know."

"Oh, Jesus." Del had followed after her into the street. "Oh, Jesus Christ."

Tess stood for a moment on the sidewalk, looking one way and then the other. How far could a girl go in six hours on foot, in a city covered in toxic mud, strewn with jagged debris? She could be anywhere. Nowhere. She could have fallen through the center of the earth. Beside her, Del was taking hard, deep breaths as if she'd just swum the length of an Olympic-sized pool. Tess stepped away from her into the middle of the street, her hands opening and closing in the empty air. At the corner of Kerlerec and Pauger, the light flickered and went out, and then the brownout cascaded down the street like a wave, the houses going black one by one until the whole neighborhood was submerged in the liquid light of dawn.

■ ■ ■ ■

PART TWO:
INTO THE
TREMBLING AIR

■ ■ ■ ■

One Day Before Landfall
AUGUST 28

For most of her life, when Cora thought of floods, she thought of Old Man River, that wrinkled white guy dressed in shredded blue-gray linen out at Jean Lafitte. His name was Mississippi, from the Ojibwe word for Great River, and he would explain to the gathered children how he heaped up soil along his banks as he writhed his way to the sea, building the Delta — the very land they stood on. When there was enough dirt, some Frenchmen planted a flag, laid a grid of streets, built homes. But Mississippi liked to wash that land he'd made, and so they built levees to contain him. Here, the actor would moan and shake his tattered linens: it really made him mad to be hemmed in! He was *old*, remember, and his joints were stiff, and though they smoothed his bed with their slow-moving dredges, he didn't like working so hard; he preferred to roll down a nice gentle slope to the sea. He told the children how he thought sometimes about jumping his banks and destroying the cities of the people who imprisoned him, about trying out the Atchafalaya Basin for a change. At any time, he warned the children, he could tunnel through the foundations of their levees, make a crack wide enough to run through. And once he'd escaped, they could send their hounds, their helicopters, but they'd never get him back, no matter what they tried to do.

When she thought of floods, Cora liked to remind herself that they had been warned, to tell herself that disaster anticipated was disaster forestalled. The government made the rounds, after all. Crunching along the shell road, officials wearing hard hats and orange jackets came to inspect the levees, driving trucks marked ARMY CORPS OF ENGINEERS. They traveled the length of the river as it moved through the parish, circled the seawalls that protected the island city from the lake — called Pontchartrain — where resurrected pelicans gathered, grunting and squeaking over their nesting grounds. Cora loved the lake. There were egrets and whistling ducks there, thick oily clots of cormorants and flocks of swallow-tailed kites, snake birds curled in oaks, and sapsuckers too, drumming in the trees as if they had some news to share. The lake was so wide that from the center of it — mile twelve of the longest overwater bridge in the world — the horizon would vanish, as though the painted veil of the far shore had been raised just an inch, leaving a strip of empty air like a rent in the fabric of time.

Today the water shone with heat, but Cora walked under the trees, where the shadow of the leaves and the breeze off the lake made the morning almost cool, the earth damp under her bare feet. She liked to go off the grid on Sundays when she didn't have to work brunch — turn off her phone, turn off the radio, take a walk somewhere alone. After a hard week in the kitchen, she sometimes played a game with herself where she tried to spend the entire day without hearing or saying a single word. So far today she was winning. She hadn't seen a soul. On the way up the land side of the lake levee she had filled her pockets with clover, and she meant to sit on a rock at the shore and make a necklace out of them, the way she and Del used to do when they were little girls.

As soon as she came out from the copse of trees, though, the levee patrol caught sight of her. A cruiser moving slowly along Lakeshore Drive threw on its flashers, and before Cora could put her hands over her ears she heard them say: *Lakeshore Drive is currently closed to the public. A mandatory evacuation order for Orleans Parish is in effect. Vacate immediately.*

The flood was coming, then, after all.

Cora drove to her parents' house, under the slowing interstate and past gas stations where long lines of cars strung from the pumps. Going, going, everyone ready to be gone — in the low pressure, she felt light, as if she might float up into the quickening air, as if she'd turned into one of those cormorants at the lakeshore. Fly, if you can fly. But fleeing wasn't cool. *No true New Orleanian* — Her grandfather would curl his lip: something cowardly about it, something disloyal. Abandonment's just not a thing you do.

In the house on Esplanade, the clocks were ticking, and from the kitchen came familiar voices, television voices.

"Mom?" Cora stepped over the threshold. "Pop?"

She dropped her keys on the mail table where they settled slowly, jingling. The AC compressors clicked on, and the chilled air carried the smells of pecans and bacon. Breakfast had been eaten; in the kitchen, three placemats were on the table, two crumpled dish towels, two plates smeared with yellow egg. The reporters' voices scattered from the television.

—the highest temperature ever recorded in the Gulf and the lowest pressure since the National Weather Service began keeping records in —

Last time a storm had brushed near them, years ago, she and Del had gone to the river and leaned from the crest of the levee into the wind, so solid with speed that it stopped them from falling, though they had been trying to fall.

To repeat, for anyone just tuning in: a mandatory evacuation order is in effect for the river parishes.

The great red arrow of the storm curved towards its own beginning like one of those snakes that means eternity, but the woman reporter was smiling. They liked scaring you, reporters. That was what they lived off — catastrophic weather events, terror attacks, murder-suicides, soldiers killed by roadside bombs. Two days ago, when the storm was already brewing, the woman had been at Eleusis in her helmet of silvering hair — Table sixty-two: dressing on the side, medium filet hold the béarnaise — and all night long she'd laughed, her on-screen guffaw so loud they could hear it in the kitchen.

Now, if you do choose to stay, please be prepared. Fill your bathtubs, make sure you have batteries for flashlights, non-perishable food items, first aid kits, duct tape, an axe. I know many of you don't need a reminder, but if the water starts to rise — and if we get the kind of storm surge the models are predicting, it may well rise that high — an axe may be your only way out.

Cora twanged the TV off. Her heart was beating too fast. She closed her eyes, tried to take the three deep breaths Dr. Nemetz prescribed, but the reporter was waiting behind her eyelids, axe raised over her head. She picked up her parents' plates and brought them to the sink. On one of the burners, her mother's pecan coffee cake sat cooling, and there were two eggs and three slices of cooked bacon lying on a greasy paper bag. They had expected her. They had not meant to go without her, but they had. They'd fled headlong.

She called out again, but there was no answer. There was an axe in the toolshed, though.

She took a handful of cake to the back door, opened it, left it open. If they had gone without her, so be it. It had been a thrill once, being alone. Her parents would go out, perfumed and buttoned, and once she'd locked the door behind them, she was free. Alone, she could walk naked through the rooms of the house, lounge in bed, sit on the front steps for as long as she wanted, watching the wind move the leaves of the trees. Now, behind the high branches of the magnolia, the sky was rushing past as though the earth had sped on its axis, but that was all right: the house would hold her. She teased apart the swirling crumb of her mother's cake. She breathed in the damp green air.

Cora finished the cake before fighting with the shed door — reluctant old thing, she had to lift it up on its hinges, wrench it back. The smells of gasoline and rust mingled with the taste of pecan. She pulled the light chain. Over the workbench the axe hung on nails, its sharp edge painted red like it had ambitions.

The back door of the house slammed as she came out, axe in her hand.

"Goddamn it, Cora." Her father stopped at the edge of the veranda. "Thank God! Where have you been? We've been calling you since six o'clock yesterday. We were about to send a search party!"

Workmanlike in his belted jeans and tucked-in shirt as always, he looked her over, and, as always, she felt judged: braless in an old tank top that bared her long bird's neck. She shifted the axe, one hand at its throat, one at its waist.

"Well?" her father said.

"You weren't here."

"We went to pick up supplies. Why do we pay for your cellphone if you never turn it on?" He waited.

"It's Sunday," she said.

"Fuck, Cora." He rolled his eyes. "We've got a hell of a lot to do before we can get out of here, and I've got to go get your grandfather too, before the nuns run off with him to Mississippi. Are you packed?"

She shook her head. Of course she wasn't packed. They weren't going anywhere. They had never gone. She waited for him to tell her that nothing was wrong, that the storm wasn't coming. That they would go close the shutters, set out the candles, the playing cards, make a pitcher of sangria and listen to the rain. When the eye passed them — if it passed — they would go out for a walk and look at the stars.

"This is unacceptable, Cora. It's going to take us hours to get out as it is." His hands fidgeted. Only once before — when she walked in the front door after leaving that bullshit college in a hurry — had she seen him scared. "And what's that — an axe?"

"Yes."

The axe was heavy, even for two hands. She hefted it, like she was practicing hacking a hole in the roof, except that there was nothing above her but the sky.

"You don't intend to stay?" he mocked her.

She was not sure "intend" was the word. She had always stayed.

She lay on her back on her bedroom rug, her mouth open to catch the rain. With her eyes closed, she could see it better: The huge dark mass of water revolving slowly in the sky. The roof — rafters and all — lifted off the house and set down like a jaunty hat on top of a large tree. Old Man River rising from his bed and striding across the city, trident in one hand, Bengay in the other. Her father was outside, hammering plywood over the big kitchen windows. She spread her arms out wide on the carpet, palms up, and waited.

At least her mother had stopped trying to get into her room. The thumb latch Cora had finally been allowed to install when she was sixteen had jumped every time Tess put her shoulder against the door, while she'd gone on and on in her loud shrink's voice about necessary truths, defined the word "mandatory," listed wind speeds, all the while carefully avoiding the words she thought Cora was too feeble to hear: *overtop, surge, drown.* Meanwhile, Cora lay on the rug repeating them to herself like Dr. Nemetz had taught her to. You were supposed to say a word until it lost its meaning, replay a nightmare — a rape, a burial-alive, whatever — until the images started to look funny to you, like some kind of demented joke.

When her father had come back from picking up Papie, Cora had listened through the floor while her mother shouted at him about sedatives. It amused her — her mother's conviction that nobody give Papie anything, when she used to come into Cora's private home, open her private medicine cabinet, put the unopened plastic jars on her kitchen counter like accusations. Now it was all: *Did you allow them to give him something? A single Valium could set him back years, Joe. Years.* But when it was about *her* mind, *her* reality, that fucking orange prescription bottle had clacked against the linoleum: *I don't know why you refuse to help yourself, Cora.* She had often imagined her mother would lock her up if she could, keep her in an upholstered cage, stuffed on roast chickens and cream cakes.

"Cora?" her father was calling from downstairs. She held still. "Cora!"

She listened to the risers groan as he climbed slowly up the stairs. She closed her eyes, breathed through her nose. As the storm approached, it would be rising like a coil of proofed dough.

Her father knocked on the door. "You packed?"

She rolled her head against the carpet. She would not be strong-armed. She tried Dr. Nemetz's other method: she pictured the storm breaking apart like foam on milk, a cormorant asleep on a calm lake, her mother laughing out of the window of the truck as they sped home.

"You know that your great-aunt was swept away during Camille," her father said through the door.

She saw Pauline of the oval picture frame wiping her hands on the front of her apron as she walked to her front door, under the entrance hall's low ceilings, beside the long, mirrored wall. Pauline peered through the peephole, shot back the bolts, and when the water rushed in like a crowd of hungry guests, she fell back onto the floor, her hand up in a wave.

"Go away," Cora said.

"We didn't have the tools that we do now," her father continued. "Back then, we had to wait for them to call a storm in from Havana. We couldn't see it on the radar. Aunt Pauline didn't leave because she didn't have the chance to leave." The doorknob turned, the door caught against the lock. "Honey, would you please let me in."

Cora knew the story: How Mamie had kissed her St. Christopher medal as Joe backed out into the street to go find Pauline. How the trees in Mississippi had been pressed down in flat spirals as if by the wind of a landing helicopter. Her father always digressed at this point in the story to sing a paean to croakers — how, before Camille, Pauline would dust them in cornmeal and fry them up crisp, bones and all — but then he'd go on again. How he had driven around Mississippi for hours unable to get his bearings. How, when he had found Pauline's house at last, there was nothing left but the concrete steps and a single overturned dining chair. How he had walked along the swaybacked fence until he found all they'd ever find: Pauline's favorite church hat — aqua, with a spotted veil — plastered against the chain-link. How he had picked it up, brushed off the sand.

"Go away," Cora said softly. She closed

her eyes and imagined him going. Putting up his hand, waving good-bye. Positive visualization, this was called. This hurricane would veer off at the last second to become sideways rain across the darkened beaches of Mexico. Her parents would go, but she would be locked down safe here. Key, latch, and bolt. She did not hear footsteps though, and so she repeated herself, raising her voice on each iteration. "Go away! Go away! Go away! Go away! Go away!"

When she finally stopped shouting, he was gone.

She got up and went into the upper hall. Above the stairs, light came through the stained glass tinged blue and orange, making the air into water. Tomorrow, the wind would only be strong enough to blow the dead leaves from the oaks and some of this heat off the streets, and she would go walking through the shade down to the restaurant, where she'd have Bobby make her a plantation punch, and Troy would come in from prepping in the kitchen and nestle a little too close to her on the next barstool, and they would laugh at the foolishness of all these cowards who'd spent hours in traffic escaping nothing. She would lean her elbows on the bar, and Troy would rub her shoulders while Bobby refilled her glass.

■ ■ ■ ■

Her mother stood at the head of the dining room table, cradling an armload of felt-bagged julep cups. At her feet, the hope chest was filled with silver — Ziploc bags rolled around the fish forks, salad forks, oyster forks they never used.

"Well, well," her mother said. "Look who's risen from the dead."

Papie slumped in a wingchair shoved up against the wall under a portrait of one of the pasty Marleybone ancestors, looked at her blankly. In the kitchen, the TV was rambling: *Fifty dollars down will get you a bedroom set living room set today!*

Her mother crouched and began nestling the julep cups inside the chest. "Your grandfather and I were just discussing the possibility that there might be looting."

Cora doubted it. She looked at Papie, his mouth open like a sheepshead's.

"This evacuation, regardless of whether the storm turns —" Outside, a pot rang against the concrete steps like a gong. "This evacuation is going to be its own disaster. An empty city is not a safe place."

Cora rolled her eyes. An empty city sounded pretty great to her. It was something she'd always longed to see. Since childhood, she'd liked imagining herself as one of Bienville's crew, stepping out of a rocking pirogue onto the shores of Bayou St. John. When the duke and the Indian guide turn away, she parts the curtain of willow leaves and crouches down in the sand, waiting to unbutton her heavy coat and high boots until the crew have shouldered the dugouts and walked off in the direction of the unnavigable river. Once they are gone, unburdened of her heavy European clothes, she builds a house of palmetto fronds and cypress, learns Choctaw and Chitimacha, raises a litter of orphaned raccoons.

"Goddamn it!" her mother whispered as she stomped past Cora into the hall and out the French doors. In his armchair, Papie was listing sideways, as if the house had already started to drift.

"You lived through Betsy," Cora said to him. "Do you remember it? What it was like?"

"Betsy." He nodded his head heavily. "Betsy Frazer. Nice bosom."

"No, Papie. Betsy the hurricane."

"Hurricane? An act of God you call it."

The French doors slammed behind her, and her father, bringing the heat with him, stalked into the dining room.

"Your mother tells me you still refuse to come," he said. "This is fucking impossible, Cora."

She just stared at him.

"Why do you have to make everything a struggle?" He actually wanted an answer to that, his hands on his hips. "Why are you acting like this?" he shouted.

"Joe," her mother said.

"We don't fucking have time for this," he spat at her, taking Cora's wrist in his hand.

Her mother shouted, speed-walking behind them as he hauled Cora up the stairs and down the long hall, out onto the upstairs gallery where the sun sprang off the tin and past the old servants' quarters. Unclipping his keys from his belt loop, he unlocked his studio and opened the door.

It had been so long since she'd been invited up there, she'd forgotten what it looked like. The walls were pasted with sketches of wiry trees and angry imaginary women furnished with her mother's mouth or nose, while the tables and chairs overflowed with half-finished things — an armless nude, a dog with pinned-back ears and log legs. Her mother had stopped in the doorway as if there was a force field there, but her father suddenly didn't seem to care if she saw these things that had been off-limits, *not for public consumption,* her whole entire life. He yanked on her wrist, pulled her through.

"Dad?" He was fumbling with the steel door that led to the attic, and she didn't like any of this. Didn't like that he wasn't saying anything. Didn't like being here. She didn't like that he seemed to want to bring her to the windowless attic, where she wouldn't be able to keep her eye on the weather. The very thought made the skin prickle on her spine.

"Joe!" her mother shouted from outside, but he had the attic door open. He was going through. He was crouching in front of the gun safe in the dark. "I don't like this, Joe!"

"Come in here, Cora."

She shook her head, aware she probably looked to him like a three-year-old child.

"Come. In. Here."

She came.

"If you want to be foolish, you will at least learn how to protect yourself."

"Scaring her is not going to work, Joe!" From the gallery, her mother was shouting. "We don't have time for games. Already, the traffic —"

"Forty-five. Twenty-five. Twenty-three,"

he said. "Cora!"

She looked at his hand, clawed around the knob of the combination lock.

"Repeat it."

"Forty-five. Twenty-five. Twenty-three."

"Forty-five right, twenty-five left, twenty-three right." He spun the dial, and then there was her mother's father's old duck gun.

Above the too-still branches of the oaks, the sky was turning green like a frying oyster, and the truck was gone. Her parents were gone. Papie was gone. Everyone was gone or going, the city's noise fading as fewer cars sped to the bottlenecks, as the hammering stopped, the shops shut, as those who stayed took a last look at the sky before battening down to drink and wait. Everybody was so sure it would come, but storms didn't like to be caught in the trawl nets of probability the forecasters threw. It was their nature, Cora thought, to flout our science, to laugh at our attempts at order. Still, she had to go home and clear out her fridge and pack her most valuable things to bring them to the big house, where there were more places to hide.

She rolled down the windows of the Jeep to let the wind run its fingers through her hair. The shadows of the oaks caressed her car. She breezed through the lights at the empty intersections and under the interstate that was holding all the cars, the frightened people, the panting dogs, the birds in cages, the overnight bags, the family photos, wedding silver, flat-screen TVs, and frozen redfish up to the heavens like an offering. The air shimmered with burning fuel.

On her block, Mr. Franklin's broken-down Buick was the only car left, and nobody was out on their porches. The only soul in sight, a man walking towards the corner, turned around as she stepped out of the Jeep.

"Cora! Yo!" It was Troy from the restaurant. He jogged towards her, wearing his guest face. "Damn, I'm glad to see you, baby."

"What's up?" she asked.

His hand swirled in the air, conjuring her porch ceiling, the green sky, the smudge of dark cloud out beyond the I-10. "I came looking for you. You leaving?"

She made a face.

"No? They're saying *mandatory* on the news now. You didn't hear Nagin?"

"I'm'na start listening to him now?" She laughed. "Nah, I'm going to go stay by my parents'. Better pantry. You're not going?"

"I've been trying to find a way —" His eyes darted to her face, then up again at the sky. "My aunt and Anthony and them lit out this morning, and I can't find out anything about buses."

"What about your sister?" She cast about in the air for her name, saw only the tall woman sitting cross-legged in the middle of Troy's floor, flipping through magazines in her hospital scrubs. "The nurse?"

"Reyna?" Troy looked at her like she'd lost it, she had no idea why.

"She left?"

He shrugged. "She doesn't have a car."

"Still, though. She's got little kids, right?"

"They're at summer camp." He looked at the toes of his shoes for a second, tapped one against the cement. "Shit, Cora —"

"I heard the Superdome's taking people," she said quickly, then tried to turn it into a joke, "— if you're scared."

He kept staring at his shoes. "I tried that once before. That's not any kind of place."

When she looked at him, she saw roofs caving in under the weight of water. She didn't like seeing him scared — the man had a face like a mountainside. When Chef was bitching like they'd all be murdered if they didn't get out of the weeds and fast, she used Troy as cover, but now his eyes were jumping from her face to the Jeep and back again, and she was scared of an avalanche. She started shaking her head. She really didn't want him to ask. Since she and Nemetz had decided sex was too much for her — three years of abstinence and counting — she'd had a hard time being alone with him, with those broad hands that were so good at touching, with that back that mantled over her like a protective shell.

"Want to come in where it's air-conditioned?" She motioned to her house. "I was just going to grab a few things."

She unlocked the door. The couch creaked as he took his usual place on it. Normally when he waited for his lift to work, she babbled, he laughed, he joked, she hit him, playful as you can only be with people you used to fuck, but now it seemed like neither of them could think of anything to say. The TV popped on, popped off. Cora folded dresses, skirts, her best tops into the hampers, hangers and all.

"You don't think you can stay in your house?" she called out to him.

She could hear him shaking his head. Off the bookshelf, she pulled the journal she'd kept the year she'd tried to live away at college, opened it, began to read a page — *who want to touch you with their hot hands, all the rinsed pasta and plastic dressings, all the drones in professor suits —*

"You aren't staying in yours," he was saying, "and I don't care if there's caviar and foie in your mama's pantry, that's not why."

— a play they put on to try to convince you what's "real" is real.

"You know how deep it got down here in Betsy? This place used to be a swamp, baby. Should've stayed a swamp."

"But this ain't Betsy, baby," she said, putting the journal back on the shelf. "We're not gonna flood. It'll turn and we'll just get blown a little." She picked up the hamper. "They always turn."

Troy came into the doorway, and as he put his arms out for the hamper, she saw his face — his brow weighing on his eyes, his mouth dragged down by invisible sinkers.

"You don't know the first thing about it." He thrust out his chin. "How old are you?"

"Twenty-eight."

"I was seven years old in '65, and I remember paddling out of there like yesterday. You don't want to take your chances with a storm like this."

She took a deep breath and tried to calculate his age. Forty-two years old. She'd met his grown-up daughter and his forty-year-old sister who queened around like Phylicia Rashad in shiny satins, but it had never occurred to her to think of him that way, to think of his experience. She trotted behind him while he hauled her things to the car and told herself again how, tomorrow after the storm had changed course, they'd go to the restaurant for a drink. Bobby would laugh while the ice crashed up and down in his Boston shaker, while Troy hunched in the shadowed corner, holding her father's axe.

"So you're the kind of person lives in this kind of house," Troy said as he stepped into the heavy cool of her parents' front hall. "I had a dream once I lived in one of those mansions in the Garden District. There were dogs in every room, big dogs I had to bribe with Snickers bars every time I wanted to pass."

"This isn't the Garden District," she said.

"No shit," he grunted. "Nah, the rich people around here're even longer dead."

She wished she hadn't invited him. All she'd wanted was to be alone. Now, Troy was looking at the house the way she'd seen him watch a seagull once when they were smoking outside the kitchen, all mouth-open, uneducated awe. She wanted to elbow him, tell him you were supposed to pretend you saw glorious shit every day, but the way his eyes followed the crown molding as it looped across the ceiling in sweeps of cypress made her see it new. At every joint, the plasterer had made mud into a silk ribbon, crinkling and neatly bowed, all of it lifelike but pale as the faded sculpture of the Greeks.

She was up on her toes trying to shoot the bolts on the front doors. "Hey!" she said. He turned towards her, slow as molasses. "Help me with this."

He dropped his bag and laid a hand on her waist to move her aside, and she stepped away from it, but not before she'd felt a blush bloom across her skin. She and Dr. Nemetz had figured out that it was too hard for her, in a sexual relationship, to know where she stopped and the other person began, but that didn't stop her wanting; instead, desire appeared out of nowhere, apparently at random.

She breathed Troy in as he reached up to wiggle the bolt into its notch. She liked his smell, like cloves in rendered fat, and it calmed her a little bit. Out of the corners of his eyes he looked at her, then brought his arm down and wrapped it around her shoulder. Whenever he hugged her — sneaking up behind her in the walk-in or drunk at Pal's after a shift — she felt overtaken, and usually she fluttered away like a spooked pigeon. Now, though, she thought it might be nice to have him take over.

She leaned into his chest, let her legs go slack. "I'm glad you came to find me."

His body straightened and relaxed. He danced her two steps backwards into the house, and when he let her go, he picked up his bag and followed her up the stairs.

"How'd your daddy afford a place like this?"

She felt her mother behind her, hands on hips — *A lady never talks about money* — and it was like she was in one of those stiff dresses Tess insisted be buttoned up to the neck.

"It's her money," she said. "Her daddy was in oil and gas."

"My oh my."

"Well, son of a bitch drank most of it, and we lost half the rest in the crash," Cora tugged at the neck of her T-shirt. "Besides, this place was a real shithole when we moved in. Had been a boarding house. There were holes in the roof, rusty old bathtubs. It was built way back when we were still France — or Spain maybe, I don't know — by a free man of color. He built the next door house too, but it was torn down."

Troy's fingers traced the upright grooves and viney swirls carved into the newel post. "Your granddaddy makes furniture too, right?"

"Used to."

She ducked into her mother's bathroom to fill the tub with emergency water, and when she came out again, Troy was leering at her room as if he saw her teenage self in there, unbuttoning her monogrammed school blouse, unzipping her plaid skirt.

"That's my room," she said.

He turned around to her with a big grin and made like to throw his bag backwards onto her bed. She crossed her arms over her chest and made a harrumphing noise, but he could never really be shut down. He still waited on her front steps to be invited in after their shift, still put his hands on her when he found her at the drinks station. Two months ago, at Bobby's party, he'd started unzipping his fly in the hall, and she'd had to elbow him in the ribs.

"This isn't a quid pro quo me giving you shelter," she said. "You can stay for free."

His face cracked open, then shut tight again. His phone was buzzing in his back pocket, and his hand moved, reluctantly, to pick it up.

"Reyna," he said into the phone. "It's about to be too late to change your mind."

Cora was close enough to him that she could hear most of his sister's answer: something about meaning what she said, something about Troy finding an evacuation car.

"Nah, I found a friend, I'm over by her place," he said, his face closed up, holding something back.

You nasty man. Reyna's voice came loud through the phone as she laughed the funny hooting laugh Cora remembered from the last time they'd met, when she had given Cora and Troy a ride home from a deb party they'd catered. Cora liked her — she seemed to live her life at full throttle, singing loud along with the radio as she punched the old Thunderbird through yellow lights, her hair an unmoving helmet in the wind.

"You should get out of here, Reyna, you really should," Troy said, in a stern, condescending voice like the one Cora's parents reserved for her. "This is not going to be pretty."

Through the phone came the word *Charity* then *children in this city* then *You think I don't know from ugly?*

"No, no, Rey, that's not what I'm saying."

Then don't say it, she responded, and then said something else, something muffled, that Cora didn't pick up.

Troy's face changed — melted, as if it had suddenly lost all muscle tone. "That's not Willy, is it, Reyna?"

Cora couldn't hear her respond.

" 'That's not Willy?' I asked you. I thought they were at camp, Reyna! You told me they were at camp!"

"The little boys?" Cora whispered.

Listen, we're fine here, Troy, stop worrying, Reyna said, her voice raised high, then dropped low as she talked about locks, about water.

"I'm coming to get y'all," Troy said. "Just hang tight. I'll be there in fifteen."

There's no place to go, Troy, Reyna shouted. *You know damn well there is not a single place —*

Troy snapped the phone shut like a clam in his palm, and in the quiet, beyond the boarded windows, they could hear the wind beginning to kick up, leaves and loose boards rattling.

"She's got her kids with her?" Cora asked. "We can go get them — we've got plenty room."

Troy turned away from her towards the

disapproving portrait of Imogene Marleybone.

"You don't want her here," Troy said.

"Why not?" She looked down at Del's bedside table, cleared of all the hair ties, pencils, art books Del used to keep there. Del would be plugged into the TV in New York, fretting about her, she was sure, the same way Troy was fretting about his sister. "I had a good time talking with her when she picked us up from that cater gig Carnival time. She seemed cool."

"Seemed," Troy said.

Cora clicked on the lamp, but the bulb had burned out. She clicked it off. Reyna had been on her way home from a ball, wearing this long gold dress and black eyeliner that made her look like an Egyptian goddess, and Cora had looked at her own face in the rearview mirror, thought how much they resembled each other. Hoped that she'd look that good in ten years.

"What happened to her car?" Cora asked.

"That was the river pilot's car." He clucked his tongue, looking into the distance like he was remembering something. "Back when she was with the river pilot." He lifted his bag up onto Del's bed. "She's in Calliope, Reyna. They'll be fine."

"Calliope? I thought she was a nurse."

Troy shrugged. "You said the storm would turn."

LANDFALL
AUGUST 29

Cora lay across Troy's body on the kitchen floor, trying to rename the storm's sounds. It was a freight train lumbering. An old man's moans. The big bad wolf's huff and puff, his howl.

She was sticky, her mouth and her thighs. Naked and drunk, like Troy snoring under her, his head on a chair cushion. When the rain started, he'd been dancing in front of the stove, licking béchamel off a wooden spoon, until she took the spoon away. She was feeling every raindrop fall like it was falling on her head, like the bullets that rained from the sky on New Year's Eve, so she put the milky spoon down on the counter, wrapped her hands around Troy's wrists and worked them up under her shirt, staring into his pecan eyes as she did.

He shook, Troy. Every time she put her mouth on him — on the padded bones of his pelvis, on his rib cage, on his cock — he flinched, shuddered. Soon, she was able to stop thinking, and she let the little sparks he lit on her neck, her inner thighs, spread until she was on fire. She pretended that this fire was what was making all the noise. But her body had eventually grown cold, and now she could hear the rain again.

You scared? he'd asked her, but scared wasn't it. Scared you ran, you hid, but she was still there. They say a deer on a night road will stand transfixed by headlights, that he'll just let the car come. Now that the storm was here, working over them like a huge engine, she understood the deer's wisdom. The world would do what it would do to you; what you did didn't change a thing.

Something hit the house with a twang — metal, bending as it hit, then another something driven against the driveway side. She stood up, and the house began to sway on its foundation, or maybe she was swaying. She reached for the counter. It was like being chained in the hold of a ship that someone else was sailing, some homicidal asshole of a captain.

She looked down at Troy. His eyes were open.

"I'm going out," she said.

"Don't tempt, girl."

Like being chained in the dark all the way across the Atlantic, everything black, especially the new world you're headed to.

"No, I've got to," she said. "Got to see it. See about it."

Troy put hands to the ground and pushed himself up. "Not by yourself, you're not."

The roar of the wind seemed to diminish when she opened the door onto the screen porch. Now that she could see the sideways rain, the magnolia tree bending like a penitent, sound and reality matched. If she could be inside it, blowing with it, she thought, maybe the wind would go quiet — if she didn't resist, if she let the wind flatten her, if they all stopped trying to hold themselves up straight, if they became the storm. She put her hands flat on the screen. The rain stuck her like hypodermics.

Troy had stopped inside the door. He was zipping up his pants.

The wind howled down, driving leaves and branches and plastic bags like hell-bent ghosts. She pressed into the screen, straining it, and the cold needles pierced her, and the wind pushed the wire mesh into her breasts and her thighs. Under the arches of her bare feet, the porch floor shifted as Troy came up behind her. Dry hands closed around her upper arms.

301

"Got the idea, baby? We got to go in."

She forced her fingers into the screen's tiny holes.

"Cora, come on."

His hands came up under her arms and pulled her back as if he thought he could separate her from the storm. His body was tight against her back — the warm dry skin of his chest, his hard pelvis, his cock, the cables of his legs. She strained forward, and when the middle bar of the screen snapped, she fell sideways, the wind holding her almost upright, almost airborne. She landed palms down in the grass, and Troy, holding her hair in his fist, fell next to her. The wind was throwing things at them — branches and shingles that flapped and veered, bottles that skittered along the ground — as Cora pushed up on her stinging hands and tried to stand. Maybe the wind would throw her too, she thought, but Troy had ahold of her hair, and his other hand grabbed her shoulder and pulled her down under the porch.

Behind the old brick piers, the world seemed to snap shut. The sound of the storm seemed to be hers, now, something her body made. The sound of blood rushing through her veins. The roar of her nerves firing. Troy hung over her. Rainwater rolled over his brow. She reached up to touch his cheek. Fingertips on water on skin. His hand flashed up, grabbed her, and the world opened, the storm rushed in.

"What the fuck is wrong with you, girl?" His hand held her wrist. "Jesus. We should've got you out of here. I should've known."

But here they were, weren't they. Crouched in the dirt. Below sea level. Underground. At the edge of the chain wall, rain drove in, and she wanted to be out there in it again. She struggled against his hand on her wrist.

"Stop it!" he yelled, his hand tight as a vise.

Above them, the house swayed, creaking, and again she thought of a ship, thousands of bodies crushed together in a lightless hold for the six weeks it took to cross the sea. She stopped struggling and pulled Troy into her. She would at least have the pleasure of his body against hers if that was what they were in for. The moisture between his skin and hers had warmed, and she felt cold, suddenly, as if all the blood had left her.

Troy looked to where rain crashed over the chain wall in waves. "I didn't know you were so drunk, Cora. I should've locked you in."

She tasted vomit at the back of her throat, swallowed. "I'm cold," she said.

He let her go, his fingers moving to the buttons of his shirt, but Cora didn't want the clammy fabric against her, she wanted his body. She pushed her head into him, tried to wrap her arms around him again, but he only hovered over her in the dark. One hand on the ground to steady herself, she put a hand on his neck where she could feel his blood pulsing. A thin slick of water moved across the backs of her thighs. She worked her hand down Troy's body, tracing the riverine muscle that wrapped around his side and rushed down under the waistband of his jeans. Her head tilted up, she licked at the water running down his chest, until he lowered himself onto her carefully. Just heavy enough to hold her down.

"You are out of your fucking mind," he said, and his lips were so close to hers, but then a loud pop like the crack of a whip ripped through the howling of the wind, and his hands lifted up off her, and she pushed back away from him along the ground as the house quaked, thundering with the impact of something huge and hard.

The house above them crackled and groaned as if it might founder. Troy was out in the rain already, calling for her, but she had crawled away behind one of the piers, and she did not answer, and when the house keeled again and thundered, amplifying the voice of the storm, Troy's eyes flashed white, and he ran away through the rain.

She woke in water. A cool brown lake that stretched around her as far as she could see, beyond the house's piers and the porch steps and out over the side yard, where it lapped against the bricks edging the rose bed and glowed with a woozy sunlight that had something wrong with it, that was coming down more strongly than it should. Somewhere beyond, dogs howled in chorus, and the sound made the water riffle and the hot air shudder between the surface of the flood and the subflooring above her. Footsteps passed over her, and a shudder ran down her spine: someone walking over her grave. She sat up straight, water sucking at her skin.

The water was only about four inches deep, but there shouldn't have been standing water at all. It never flooded here, not if the pumps were working. Esplanade was a ridge, the portage Bienville's Indian guide had led him down, showing him the best way to bring small craft from the gulf into the river. It had always been high ground.

She pitched forward onto her hands and knees and crawled out, floor joists scraping her back. Out in the open, she stood, surveyed. The water seemed to go on and on.

There was something very wrong with the light. The water, placid, rippled against the trunks of the crepe myrtles along the side-walk, against the piers, a sheet of water printed with the brilliant sky that reached beyond the fence posts, across the streets, as if she'd awakened on a new world cloaked in glass. On Esplanade, a car tore past, and the wave it made climbed over the tops of her feet, then continued along the backyard, under the house, rode over the wobbling reflections of the parlor windows, and then was gulped up into the bright sun of the side yard. That was what was wrong. All the shade was gone. The wind had picked the magnolia up and thrown it down, bashed its green head through her parents' roof. That explained the deafening crack, the dream she'd had of the earth breaking open, of fall-ing down through rushing water, falling and falling without end.

"We've been trying, honey. All day — your phone, the house phone, Troy's phone. I even called next door, to see if the Maestres were in, but nothing. Nothing, nothing, nothing until now."

She looked up the stairs at the shuttered windows, the blue light now coming through the slats. It was seven o'clock, maybe eight. It would be dark soon.

"But the magnolia —" she said. "I'm sorry. I'm so sorry. The doors are closed now, but I don't know what else to do."

"Sweetheart, sweetheart, it's alright," her father said again. On his end of the line she heard a truck go by, the sound of suburban crickets. "It's no big deal — we've got insurance. Wind damage. They're crying about wind damage on the TV, like that's the worst that could happen. Who cares about the goddamned windows at the Hyatt? Anyway, we'll be home tomorrow. All that's important is that you're okay. You feel safe now? You've found the flashlights?"

"Yes," she said, except that Troy was still collecting — stalking around, opening all the drawers and armoires. The dining room table was a thicket of lanterns, matchbooks, candlesticks. She'd been watching him pace all day — trying Reyna's phone, his aunts', his cousins', while he moved back and forth between the broken kitchen and the safe part of the house, dragging coolers full of food and hampers of plates and Mardi Gras cups. Except when he'd needed her help moving a buffet to barricade the kitchen door, she'd just sat on the steps and watched him, the towel around her shoulders he had put there that morning. So worried about his sister and her kids. As if he hadn't abandoned her under the house at the height of the storm.

"Sweetheart, listen, we'll be back as early as we can get there tomorrow. Maybe noon, one o'clock if I can get your mother in the car early and we get lucky with the traffic. But meanwhile, why not see if Troy will let you put him up an extra night, just so you'll feel safe. You can put out all the candles, pretend like it's the 1800s, have a good old time."

"Okay."

He seemed like he didn't want to hang up. They were out to dinner with Aunt Zizi and Uncle Vin and her cousin Kevin. Her mother had apparently drunk too much gin and puked on the side of the road.

"We ran into Uncle Augie on the way up," he said. "Shared notes. His mother's an old mule just like you — wouldn't evacuate — and so now she's all alone at her house in Metairie without power, which is no good when you're an old person. Your mother and I were thinking maybe you could go check up on her?"

Troy had come into the dining room again and stood there, punching something into his cellphone. Without the sound of his feet, the house was quiet as a closed mouth — no refrigerator hum, light-buzz, air-duct rumble.

"Look, I know she's a nasty old witch — the last time I saw her she waved an empty water pitcher at me like I was the help — but can you just check on her? You've been to that house with your mother. Maybe bring some water with you, food, whatnot. You gassed up the Jeep?"

Her father just kept talking. She could see him, turning to the window of the restaurant, holding his finger up to ask her mother to wait just one more minute. He was still in the former world, air-conditioned, clean.

"Honey, I remember Betsy — water came through the seams in the doors. But after it was over we stood up, dried ourselves off —"

Carefully, quietly, she put the phone back in its cradle, while he went on talking.

"What happened?" Troy said. "Line cut out?"

Yes, she thought. The lines cut, the bridges blown, the boats burned, the ladder pulled up between this world and the world of the living.

"I can't get anything to go through. Not even texts. Nothing. Not even to you, apparently." He came towards her, into the stair hall, and she moved up, a couple steps farther away from him. "I told you I was sorry. I'm sorry I left you there. But you weren't listening to sense, and I got afraid the house was going to come down on top of us both."

She remembered falling through the rain, and with her eyes closed, fingertips against her eyelids, she felt like she was still falling. She opened her eyes and watched Troy's biceps twitch as he took a box of matches in his hand, slid out the little paper drawer, selected a match, struck it. His neck was something made of meat. She shook her head to set it straight. No, she would visualize that the storm was over, the house intact, her parents on their way home.

"Look, Cora," Troy was saying as he put the lit candle on the newel post. "I think I better — I got to go see about Reyna. She's not — I don't trust her to keep it together in a situation like this. And I got to see about my house too. I don't want to leave you, but you understand. I need to go see if the roof's off or something, see about my nephews. You'll be alright," Troy said. "You've got plenty food. You've got water. The power'll be back on soon, and we'll all go back to normal."

She almost laughed. As if normal was a place on a map — a place you could go back to. No, as soon as you left, the rope was cut, the boats burned, and time rushed in like a river in flood. Home was a place beyond the rain and the long night. There was no way back. Not unless you were willing to swim, and from what she'd heard, the current was strong, the waves high and crested with fire, salty as tears.

Sometime after dark, the front door rattled, then knocked against the jamb. In the bathtub, sunk to her neck in tepid water, Cora stayed still. If she could just be totally quiet, the man outside would give up and go away. All she had to do was pretend she didn't exist — or that the world didn't. She had already taken the batteries out of the radio, and the phone had ceased to ring. Her parents would be back tomorrow, and the man outside would leave if she just held her breath. With each knock, the water shuddered. What if he was the government — mandatory meant mandatory — and would break the doors down and drag her, naked, out of the city? What if he never went away?

As slowly as she could, she peeled herself from the water. There was no change in the knocking. She placed her feet in the bath mat's soundless pile. She wrapped herself in a towel, picked up the emergency lantern, turned it off.

She had learned the sight lines of the house when she was thirteen, the first time her parents left her home alone. The closed shutters made it easier — the leaded window in the front door was the only unblinkered one in the house, and from it, you could see no higher than the landing of the front stairs. To see who was at the door, she could creep halfway down the back stairs and, from the twelfth step, bend over and look down the hall to the front door.

Out in the city, alarms were going off, sirens sounding above the growl of generators. She shimmied along the hall from the bathroom towards her bedroom. Downstairs, the man was kicking the door. The wood fibers cracked. She thought about the duck gun in the attic. *Open the breech, load the magazine, close the breech.* At the stairhead, the prisms on the chandelier touched one another, tinkling. *Cradle the gun, lock into your shoulder, remove the safety.* She lifted her foot over her bedroom's threshold and landed lightly on the rug. *Ready.* No clean clothes — the armoire door would creak. *Aim.* But if she shot someone, she would never stop seeing him, lying bloodied in the vestibule. *Fire.*

As she pulled the damp shirt over her head, the man began to yell a word that sounded like her name.

She remembered herself. She was a capable, twenty-eight-year-old woman in good health standing on the second floor of a locked house just hours after a hurricane. Her neighbors' roofs had caved in, she imagined, their windows had blown out. Some of them had been caught in the storm and hurt, and here she was hiding like a coward, doing nothing to help. The man was yelling, though. He seemed angry. Walking heavily down the front stairs, she showed herself.

Between the leaded glass and the screen of the vestibule doors, Troy was pacing like an animal in a cage. Cora hesitated a minute longer before opening the door.

"Goddamn it, Cora —" The outer air rushed towards her, hot as breath.

"I'm sorry." Her body still barred the entrance. "I was scared. I didn't know it was you."

"It's flooded," he said, spreading his hands away from his pants that were wet up to the middle of his thighs. "My house, your house, the whole neighborhood — I didn't even get to Reyna's. And it keeps getting higher, like it's still coming in somewhere — not just rain, it can't be. The levee's breached. I hear them saying it's in the Ninth too, and Lakeview, and St. Bernard. Ten feet deep some places, some places more. It's coming up through the manhole covers. I need your Jeep, Cora. As soon as it's light out. We need to go find them —"

She backed away from him, from the city, from the heat. The flood had come. She could still bar the doors, give Troy the keys, and wait here, high up on this ridge until the city had drained and it was safe to venture out again. But if she stayed inside, the flood would find her. She could feel it rising, snaking its way through the sewers. She could feel it bubbling up in her throat.

One Day After Landfall
AUGUST 30

On Martin Luther King, they stopped the Jeep and got out into the early morning damp. Up ahead, in front of Calliope, a tree had fallen, a tangle of power lines and rough-barked limbs frozen at tortured angles. Two men in wifebeaters stood on the corner, leaning against the chain-link, and Cora glanced back at the Jeep and the pirogue they'd stolen from the Maestres' garage strapped to the top of it. They would have to walk from here.

Last night, Cora had kept dreaming the same dream. She was floating in the middle of a river as wide as an ocean, watching the muddy banks. A wind stirred, and dead oak leaves eddied towards the water in a tumbling gust that changed into a murmuration of clamoring birds. She woke, fell back asleep, and the beach was there again, but this time the birds had transformed into a horde of people rushing towards the waves.

Men and women, little boys and girls in Carnival clothes and masks reached out their hands to her, but she stood paralyzed in the prow of her rudderless boat, and every tear that fell from her face made the flood rise higher.

She didn't need Dr. Nemetz to explain that one.

After the last dream, she'd rolled over on the mattress and taken Troy's phone from his nightstand, found Reyna's number in his recents, pressed send an uncountable number of times, listening to the alarm sound of the failed phone line as she drifted off again. Half-asleep, she felt a hot pressure in her lungs as if she were diving under water, her webbed feet pushing her towards the muddy riverbed, her feathers pressed to her sides. She needed to find something before she could rise again, surface with it held in her beak. A faceless woman and her children climbed out of the water through the hole they'd chopped in their roof with an enormous axe, but then they fell, floating limply towards the riverbed, facedown.

When she finally elbowed Troy to wake him, he just rolled over, growling. She'd come close to hyperventilating, waiting for the dawn. *Breathe through your nose, deep down. Think about the task in pieces: what's your first step?*

So far, they hadn't seen the water. All through the Quarter and down Tchoupitoulas, Annunciation, Melpomene, she'd had to maneuver the Jeep around branches and torn wires that basked like snakes on the asphalt, but the streets had been dry. Even here in Central City there was no water, but the men at the chain-link still looked at the pirogue, the Jeep, with desire. Troy nodded at the men. One nodded back. The other, a bandana tied tightly around his head, just threaded his fingers through the links of the fence and kept looking.

Between the brick buildings, the grass was spongy with rain. The paths that led up to the doorways had been broken up in places by weeds, and devil vine reached up towards the railings on the porches. Two women sat on a stoop, fanning themselves with magazines. It seemed no one was talking, no radios playing here on the other side of the rain.

Someone had broken the lock on the door to Reyna's entryway. It hung open, letting a strip of daylight into the otherwise dark hall. They climbed the stairs, listening, but they were alone. Troy knocked on Reyna's door.

"Reyna! It's Troy, come to pick you up!"

From the way his voice sounded, bouncing off of the stairway's hard surfaces, Cora knew already that there was no one inside. As soon as he rammed his shoulder into the door, the door yawned open. Troy called out again, but the apartment was obviously empty. The six locks on the back of the door — a chain, three dead bolts, a slide bolt and the knob's lock — were all undone.

"Reyna?" Troy called a last time. No answer.

In the kitchen, sandwich makings were spread out on the counter — peanut butter, a slimy cold-cut box, mustard and mayo jars, the wrappers from a package of Velveeta squares. The refrigerator door hung open, and its dank interior was littered with half-full juice boxes and cartons of milk, a tub of cream cheese, a bunch of limp celery.

"They left," Cora said. "I guess they found a ride or something?"

Troy didn't respond. He walked towards the bedrooms, one done up in yellow on yellow flowers, the other in blue stripes on blue. Clothes — T-shirts and winter coats, socks, a single child's sneaker, a package of Underoos — were laid out neatly on the floor of the blue room. Cora bent over and picked up the package of underwear, little boys' Superman briefs, size three.

"They're so little —" She looked up, but

Troy had left the room.

In the bathroom, Troy had opened the medicine cabinet and was throwing its contents into the sink. He didn't speak until he found what he was looking for, an amber prescription bottle, which he opened, then shut, before ripping the whole cabinet from the wall. It crashed into the bathtub, the mirrored door cracking from top to bottom.

"Stupid bitch!" he yelled, and the building's silence swallowed it up. "Stubborn, goddamn, stupid, fucking bitch!"

Cora backed into the hall. He shook the golden bottle in his blanched fingers.

"You think it's a good thing she left?"

Cora looked away from him — at the construction paper drawings of superheroes taped to the doors, at the bamboo mats laid over the linoleum floors. He was close enough to her that she could feel his breath.

"Off her meds and wandering around a flooded city with two tiny boys? You think it's a good thing?"

"But she can't be just wandering around —" She moved away from him, half-sure, suddenly, that the children and Reyna must be hiding somewhere, that they couldn't be out there in that. "She has to have gone somewhere safe. To the Superdome, you think?"

She stepped into the blue bedroom again, casting her eyes around for a child hiding under the covers, behind a standing lamp, in the overflowing basket of clothes. A pair of action figures stood in battle on the dresser, a dinosaur puzzle waited, half-done, on one of the beds.

"If she left," she said, "if she took them with her, she has to have gone somewhere safe."

"No way she went to the Superdome." Troy shot up his chin. "She hates places like that. Hates crowds. Hates the police. And she doesn't have a car, doesn't have anybody's going to take her in. Those boys were supposed to be away, goddamn it. She tells me they got a scholarship to summer camp in Mississippi, and I believe her like a fool, until the storm is on us, until it's too late — Willy giggling in the background. She told him to hush! She told him to hide from me!"

He shook the bottle and she heard the tense little rattle of the pills as they hit the top and fell back down — nearly full. He laughed.

"You think she got herself in good hands, Cora? Last time she went off her meds, Tyrone had to call me from the closet she had him locked into 'cause she was afraid the police were going to come and take him.

Thank God he'd stolen her phone. I filled this prescription for her three weeks ago, and she gives me a look like butter wouldn't melt. You think she got those kids to someplace safe, Cora, do you?"

"What about her boyfriend? She could have gone to her boyfriend's, couldn't she?"

"Who, the river pilot? Darryl? Darryl doesn't give a shit about her," Troy said, walking back through the piles of clothes, through the living room where the windows were X'ed over with duct tape, and out of the open door. Cora ripped a picture from the refrigerator — Reyna as she remembered her from the day they'd spent at Troy's apartment five years or so ago, when Reyna had come in her nursing scrubs to help them paint the ceiling. She'd brought beer and her eyes had sparkled when she laughed, and none of them had done much painting. In the picture, she was laughing like that, holding two round-headed little boys in her glowing arms, and Cora folded it into her pocket as she went after Troy down the stairs.

"Besides, Darryl's in the East," Troy was saying to himself, "so unless you want they drowned in my man Darryl's attic —"

Out in the daylight again, Troy strode across the grass to where the women still sat on their stoop, still fanning their glossy magazines.

"Excuse me," Cora asked them, "is there any chance you've seen Reyna? Reyna Holyfield?"

The women were shaking their heads.

"Or the little boys?" Cora held up the picture. "Two little boys."

"Tyrone and Willy," Troy said.

The younger of the women, wearing a purple sundress, her hair scorched, tilted her head to look at the photograph. "Oh, you mean Queen Madam." She twirled her finger beside her head. "I saw her leaving here with the little princes and a Hefty bag of their shit yesterday, seemed like the storm was just about getting ready to blow."

"You know where she was headed?" Troy asked.

The young woman just shook her head, her lips disappearing between her teeth.

"Maybe to go find you," the older woman said, looking from him to Cora, "she knows where you can be found —"

"Thank you," Cora said, but Troy had already begun to walk away, leading her out to the sidewalk over the wet grass and onto Martin Luther King. This was the way Reyna had gone. Cora could see her walking out into the storm — a fine, tall woman striding into the street, clutching her belongings to her chest, pushing against the wind under the flailing power lines, the boys following, fighting their way towards something better than the apartment behind them gone dark as night, soon to be filled with thunder and rain.

Beside the Jeep, the two men who they'd seen coming in were sitting on the curb. The one in the bandana turned his head and watched them.

"Give us a lift?" the other one said when they'd gotten close enough. He didn't raise his head from the street, only jiggled his foot in its sneaker.

"Where?" Troy asked, lifting his hand and flinging it out across the city. "You know the levee's breached. It's flooded bad."

"Can you take us to the Convention Center?" the man said. "They're going to have buses leaving."

"Get in," Troy said.

Cora got up behind the wheel and watched the rearview as the men climbed into the backseat, then put the Jeep in gear and turned it around. The men sat silently, watching the city pass. She drove slowly, pulling up onto the neutral ground in places to avoid telephone poles, trashcans, pieces of torn roof, until she saw it there in front of her for the first time, the real flood, the lake itself spreading out over the streets and under the highway, an infernal body of water from which the scalped Superdome rose like a volcanic island. She stopped the car, got out into the street and watched the brown lake come towards them.

With each stroke of the oars, the clay surface of the flood cracked, and dark mud spun up from beneath the pirogue. Flotsam littered the water — milk jugs and chair seats, rubber dolls, plastic bags, books, and ice chests. Troy pulled them forward past the waists of telephone poles and the trembling whiskers of car antennas, past house after drowned house.

Reyna and her children were not at Troy's house. Not at his aunt's or cousins'. It was impossible to look for her at Darryl's, in the East, and so now they had launched the boat near the cemeteries and were heading for Mrs. Randsell's. After that, they would begin in earnest.

It was already two o'clock — a stinking mist rose off the flood into the sun. All day long, dogs had been crying out in their broken dog-tongues when they heard the boat come near. Everywhere, animals were trapped behind walls and spiked fences.

Now, when the oars splashed down, there was a crash, a whimper. A Labrador and two little puppies pressed their faces against an X-taped window. And then all at once there was shouting. A gun fired, and Troy dropped the oars in their locks and brought his hands up to the back of his head. Cora squinted into the sun glaring off the shingles, but she couldn't see a soul.

The shouting resolved to words. "I said: State your business."

At the corner, a big white man stood on his roof, pistol flashing at his hip. A little girl and a woman with sweat-pasted brown hair huddled in the shade of a flowered bedsheet behind him.

"We're out saving people," Cora said.

"You ought to speak up, girl!" The man's voice was shaky, like he was drunk, his face red and tight. "You're gonna want me to hear you, I think. So I don't decide to go ahead and waste another bullet."

"I guess you don't want to be saved?" Cora's voice sounded so foreign to her — calm and haughty — she wasn't entirely sure she was the one who'd spoken.

The man's finger left the trigger. "You preaching to me, young woman?"

Cora closed her eyes, channeling Tess in a fresh green suit, standing in front of the disciplinary committee at school. "Far be it from me."

The drunk man laughed, and his wife lifted her leg and toed him in the ass.

"You tell him, honey," she said to Cora.

"Who you out saving?" the man asked, but now in that teasing voice older men liked to use on her when she was dressed nice. "Beggars can't be choosers, you know."

Cora didn't answer, and Troy kept staring straight ahead as a helicopter swooped over them, low enough to riffle the water. A man was leaning out of the open door, shooting pictures.

"Are you the looters?" the little girl asked, peeking out now from behind her father's leg.

The woman shushed her, and Troy, for the first time, looked up at them.

Cora squinted at the water line riding the house's eaves. "There's been looting?"

"Y'all haven't been listening —" The man waved his gun at their radio. "We're just sitting here waiting on the war."

Troy began to nod as he put his hands on the oars. "We've still got some of our own folks to see to, but we'll come back. Y'all are doing fine —"

"You'll come back?" The woman's voice went high, an odd sort of jubilant whine.

"We'll come back," Cora said.

The woman clapped a hand over her chest as the oars rose, dripping thick flood.

Troy kept his eyes on the rooflines, but they didn't see anyone else. A boat motor started in the distance. Troy worked the oars. Finally, the way widened out, as if they'd left the cypress passages for a backwater lake, and they floated onto a body of water that stretched out between an avenue of treetops. Behind them, beside the flooded canal, the dry asphalt of Palmetto rose over Airline Drive. Northline ran beneath them, and as they turned up it, the world seemed almost right, as if the trees and low houses lined the banks of a natural river. Cora squinted through the high branches of the oaks at the silent, sealed upper stories of the houses.

"You ever been out fishing?" Troy asked.

Cora nodded. Years ago, they'd gone out in the Rigolets in the Maestres' motorboat. The sky was a saturated blue, and there had been blood on the deck as the men slit open the red sequined bellies of the fish.

"Chef took me out when he moved me up from dishwashing," Troy said. "Said that was how I'd learn to respect the product, understanding where it comes from. But all it made me want to do was fish. Quiet and peace, quiet and peace. Saw a lot of pelicans too. Pterodactyl-looking things."

In front of them, the sign for Stella Street poked above the water, and Troy nodded towards it and pulled them closer. As they neared the curb, the boat snagged on something, and Troy swung an oar underneath the hull. The sound of a plastic trashcan hitting pavement bounced through the water as the pirogue wandered into the canopy of an oak. Suddenly, the light went dim, the day calm and almost cool. The shadows of the leaves rained down. Troy made to move them out again, but Cora reached up for the branch that hung overhead. The tree creaked as she put her weight on it, releasing its earthen perfume. Resurrection fern was greening along the lower limbs, and the upper branches lifted up over the fence of Mrs. Randsell's house, leafing out above its low-pitched roof.

"Wait for me," she said.

Before Troy could answer, she had climbed into the tree.

The wide branch ramped up gently, and Cora shimmied along it on her hands and knees like she'd used to do as a kid, up and over the fence and the swamped garden. Even looking down at Troy, who was tying up to the tree's trunk, she wasn't dizzy, wasn't scared. She dismounted onto a narrow windowsill and, holding onto the gutter, looked around.

She had only been to Mrs. Randsell's house once, when she and her mother had gone to bring her a housewarming gift one of those days Cora was suspended from school. She remembered entering through the gate in the high fortress-like fence. The fence top was jagged with broken glass, and the gate had spears for finials. Mrs. Randsell was safe here, Cora remembered thinking, so much safer than she herself was at home on Esplanade, where the old windows rumbled at all hours with the chaos-bringing voices of the drunks. As she watched her mother chatter away about how to care for the narcissus she'd brought, Cora had thought she'd like a wall like that, with a gate to which only she had the key.

Cora knocked — "Mardi Gras Mambo," something cheerful — on the shutter slats.

"Mrs. Randsell, can you hear me? It's Tess Eshleman's daughter? I'm here to fetch you."

Through the shutters, Cora could see the bolt that held them closed, but the window was open behind them. Holding the gutter tight, she raised her foot and kicked, and the slats broke with a damp crunch.

Even on the second floor, up above the flood, the house felt like it was drowning. It kept its mouth shut like a girl playing dead at the bottom of a pool. The closed shutters muffled the outside world; the barking dogs and helicopters sounded far away. Through the floor, she heard the water slapping the walls. There was a glassy clinking as if toasts were being raised, something hollow that filled and emptied, something like a clock ticking.

In the filtered light, the sitting room looked like it belonged to the Titanic. A yellow armchair, an empty ashtray, a lacquered screen drifted in the crepuscular currents that pulled on the chair's skirt, the chain of a Chinese lamp, the telephone's cord. The chair cushion was still indented from Mrs. Randsell's weight, the ashtray full of butts that would slowly lose the smell of smoke. The sour smell of the flood was seeping in. Cora found it hard to move. Twice she opened her mouth, twice said nothing. Then, somewhere among these upper rooms, a clock struck one.

"Mrs. Randsell?"

She would not think of the old woman floating facedown by the kitchen door or trapped against the bathroom ceiling. Instead, she would imagine Mrs. Randsell crouching in a corner, frightened at last.

Cora opened the door to a small, orderly closet. The clock's chime wound itself.

"Mrs. Randsell, it's Cora Boisdoré. My mom, Tess Eshleman, sent me to find you."

All the doors were open wide. She circled them: A guest room with two twin beds made up in blue. A marble bath with frosted stars around the mirror that reflected her shadow. A master bedroom with a tall half tester piled with pillows — Cora ran her fingers down its posts. The spore-pocked fern fronds might have been her grandfather's work.

At the top of the steps a door with a dead bolt and a security chain was wide open. The track of a stair lift ran down the wall and into brown water. The chair was submerged.

Leaning out over the brass banister, Cora moved down to the level of the flood. A palm in a plastic pot rocked in the clutches of the curtains. A china rabbit floated, ears up, beside a jug of bleach. The gray sludge that covered the water outside had not entered the house, and Cora could see clear to the bottom, where foam matting lifted the edges of the rugs. Above her, the floor creaked, and she turned around to see the old woman standing at the head of the stairs, holding a silver letter opener like a dagger.

"Mrs. Randsell?"

"What are you doing in my house?"

"It's Cora. Cora Boisdoré." She put her hands up. "I'm here to help you. Your son, Augie, my parents' friend? He asked me to help you. Can I help you?"

"Boisdoré?" The old woman nodded her head, the letter opener falling to her side. "Oh, that's right. You're Tess's daughter." She sighed. "This is bad, isn't it?"

"We have a boat tied up outside," Cora said. "We'll bring it in."

From the Jeep, they watched the two teenagers they'd rescued climb up and over the fence of what they claimed was their aunt's house in the Riverbend. Not that it mattered whose house it was, so long as it was dry. When one of the boys came out of the front door to wave good-bye, Mrs. Randsell rolled down her window.

"You all be careful," she yelled at them, then rolled the window up. "Our corporal act of mercy for the day."

Mrs. Randsell's linen slacks were still wet from when she'd tripped on the stairs getting into the pirogue, and her arthritic hands seemed to hurt her, but she had commanded that they fill the Jeep with people before they left the flood.

"Now, you'll bring me home," the old woman said. It was not a question.

Her hand on the gear shift, Cora looked at her, but Mrs. Randsell didn't seem confused.

"But your house is flooded, Mrs. Randsell," Cora said carefully.

"Oh, I don't mean back to Metairie." Mrs. Randsell's hand flapped. "I mean *home* home. *My* house. I suppose your being Tess's daughter, *you* think it never belonged to anyone but Madge."

"Don't you think you're better off coming back with us?" Troy said from the backseat. "We're planning on leaving, soon as we find my sister and her little boys. You come on with us — we'll get you to your son."

"You'll do no such thing." Mrs. Randsell just stared through the windshield as Cora began to drive them downriver. "You don't think I sat alone in that flooded house through the storm and two days of heat just to go to Houston now? I'm no fool — when they say a storm is coming I believe them — but there comes a time when a person is too old to leave her home."

"You heard the radio," Troy continued.

"They're serious about getting us all out of here."

"And they'll come get me once they're finished with that out there." She flung a jeweled hand behind her. Before they'd left her house, she had emptied her jewelry box onto her person. "No. You can take me out in my coffin."

"That's the thing, ma'am. We don't plan on taking you out in your coffin."

"Don't talk back to me, Mr. Holyfield," Mrs. Randsell said.

The car fell silent.

So far, uptown, the streets were dry. The storm seemed only to have brushed across the neighborhoods, tossing branches into yards, littering the streets with shingles.

"I was born in that house, you know. 'Madge's house,' 'Augie's house' — it was my grandfather's house. My father put the addition on, where the kitchen is, and he left it to me and August Senior when he died. My mother died in the bed I was birthed in. My husband courted me there. I'll tell you — that was the hardest thing about giving it to Augie. After Madge went around 'renovating,' I couldn't hear his voice anymore." She sighed. "Every time I stood on the landing where we'd used to have our tête-à-têtes on my mother's little settee, I could hear him talking — even before he died. Of course, I suppose that was why I moved in the first place. I got to where I couldn't stand to listen anymore."

"I'll take you home," Cora said.

"Thank you, dear." Mrs. Randsell's hand covered Cora's, and her touch, despite all of the diamonds, was as light as air.

The sun had started to set, and its light slanted across the city. When they entered the Garden District, the day seemed to shake loose from the tight fetters of the heat, and the silence lifted. Through the closed windows, Cora heard a chattering as if someone were throwing a party on a nearby lawn.

"Invasive," Mrs. Randsell said as a cloud of green parrots lifted from the top of a palm tree. "Drive out all the songbirds."

In the rearview, Cora watched Troy watching the birds.

"Three generations in that house and now —" Mrs. Randsell made a popping noise. "I should have had more children is what I should have done, but we can't always control those things. I know Augie couldn't either, I'm not saying that. Madge wanted them, just couldn't have them, and he was so in love with Madge. Still is." She sighed. "A mother can't say, 'Marry again, boy!

Hurry up and make me some grandchildren before I'm dead.' He's still handsome, though, don't you think? Even if he is getting old. He could still find a young enough woman, but he won't. It's just that I always thought — old-fashioned of me, but I saw the house passing down into the future, to my grandchildren and their children's grandchildren."

Mrs. Randsell allowed herself one sigh before going quiet. Cora counted — Augie's children her age, their children having children in 2030, those children's grandchildren taking possession of the house in 2090, when, according to the most recent climate models, the sea level would have risen three feet. Cora was crying when they finally pulled up in front of the house she'd gone to so often in party dresses, holding boxes of almond petits fours in her lap. Mrs. Randsell's hand patted her rhythmically on the arm.

"It's been a rough day, dear. All that you went through to come find me, out on that terrible water. Why don't you all come in, and we'll see what my son has for us to eat."

Inside the wrought-iron gate, a bough of the holly tree had fallen, scattering golden berries, and Cora picked it up and carried it with her, laying it down again beside the steps. Bees were murmuring in the azalea bushes, and Mrs. Randsell unlocked the door onto the house, which exhaled its pent-up cool. For a few hours, she could stay here, let Mrs. Randsell feed them, pretend that she was one of those phantom grandchildren, that she, Cora, was meant to inherit this house and pass it on through inexhaustible generations. For a few hours, she would try to believe that the world was only what she saw through the Randsells' kitchen windows — a bench under an oak tree, a clear swimming pool, a swath of grass. She would forget about the people on their roofs grateful for the coming night, forget about the crowded beaches in her dream. The Jeep waited in the street, the pirogue on the roof still dripping.

Two Days After Landfall
AUGUST 31

They had been down this street already — there was the mannequin in the hot-green fishnets again, floating like one of the drowned. All morning, every time they turned a corner, there would be an SOS spray-painted on the side of a house or telegraphed by a white T-shirt hanging from a closed window, and the people they rescued had gotten worse by the hour, more tired, more upset, as the helicopters buzzed across the rooftops like carrion flies. The rooftops were empty now — they had done that much — but Troy kept calling, making up little heatstroke songs.

> We've got your ride right here,
> His name is Paul Revere,
> and he's ready to take you away from here.
>
> We got water here for the water-weary!
> Water for the water-borne.

Anybody there to hear me?
Call out if you're home alone!

The sound of the oars took up where he left off, and Cora turned them off their well-traveled street, down into the deeper water.

There was no one on the rooftops here either. She turned right, and cars rose up out of the flood like stepping-stones. There had to be people somewhere nearby. She kept expecting to turn a corner and find the remnant of New Orleans clustered on the roof of a school like it was a cruise-ship dock, Reyna and the boys waiting front and center with their luggage.

When she turned to the left again, Troy suddenly stopped singing, and his hands moved out as if he wanted to take away the oars. A shadow moved across the pirogue and suddenly, she knew where they were. She looked up as the façade of their neighborhood church rose up serenely from the water, intact even to the stained glass.

Cora began rowing backwards towards their houses, and Troy started shaking his head.

"They're not there," Troy said. "And I've already seen my house. I don't need to see it again."

"But I haven't seen mine, Troy," she said.

"We were in such a hurry yesterday, we didn't look."

He reached out for the oars again. "You don't need to see that, baby. You know what it's going to be."

"Don't patronize me," she said as she swept the boat around the corner, across Troy's lawn, looking towards her little house across the street, flooded to the middle of its windows. "I know what I need."

"I don't think you do."

He grabbed hold of the oars, but she snatched them away. As he stood up, the boat rocked and water sloshed over her legs. His hands reached out to push them backwards and away from his front porch — he was being idiotic, he was too worn down — but when the pirogue butted up against the house, they heard the sound of splashing, of feet running inside.

"Reyna!" Troy hollered. He leapt from the boat onto the porch, his feet splashing. "Reyna? Is that you?"

His hand spun on the locked doorknob, and then he began pounding on the door with the flat of his hand.

"You leave us be!" a woman yelled. "You will not take us! You cannot make us go!"

"Tyrone! Willy!" Troy shouted. "It's your Uncle Troy. You come on out now."

On the side of the house a shutter flapped open and banged against the weatherboard, and the yelling started up again, accompanied now by the sound of furniture being dragged across a floor through shallow water. From the window, a hand extended, a little arm waving something orange.

Troy bent close to the door now, talking, his hands flat, and Cora pulled the boat backwards and up along the side of the house. In the window, a boy, no more than four, stood naked except for a pair of water wings, his brown legs covered in weeping red pustules. Behind him, Troy's kitchen was lit with dozens of candles that sent a perfumed stink out over the smell of the floodwater. The little boy blinked his sticky eyelashes and held out his arms, but before she could reach him, he leapt out at her in a flurry of plastic and skin. The pirogue keeled one way and then the other, but she caught him, an arm between his damp legs, a hand clapped to his back, as floodwater sloshed across them. She could feel where the water had touched her, as if she'd been burned. The little boy must have waded through it for some time — the gasoline and industrial waste and sewage — and he must have trailed his hands in the water, because they too were covered in sores. In the house, running feet splashed and a calmer voice interrupted Reyna, who was still yelling at them to go away. Quickly, Cora settled the boy in the bow and picked up the oars.

"Stop! Stop!" Reyna yelled, thrusting her head from the window, just as Cora made it to the edge of the house. "Stop! That is my child! You can't take my child!"

Troy looked at Cora from the porch. "Do you see Tyrone?"

Cora shook her head. Inside, the running feet changed direction, and then the door opened against the security chain. Reyna tried a softer tone. "You tell that woman to give me back my boy. He's not going back to that hellhole of yours. That's no kind of place for children. Full of rapists, killers, and all you do is stand around and say the buses are coming, the buses are coming, the buses are coming, the buses are coming —"

"Reyna, Reyna, it's me. It's Troy, Reyna, we aren't going anywhere like that. We're going to get you out of here."

"Mom, that's Troy, it's Uncle Troy," the other boy was saying, somewhere behind her in the house. He sounded oddly — frighteningly — calm.

"What do you know?" she'd begun to shout again. "How do you know who he is? You know how they are, people claim to want to help? They'll kill you as soon as look at you."

"Don't you listen to her, son. Come on to me, baby. Come on."

Cora bent towards the little boy and put her hands over his ears. It seemed true that Reyna was ill, but who was to say, given the state of things, what was insanity and what wasn't, when the sea walked on land and mechanical buzzards swarmed over houses capsized like ships. She looked into the boy's frantic yellow eyes as they searched her face. She struggled to keep her expression blank, free of the horror she felt as she listened to Reyna yell, though she knew that if she'd been in Reyna's position, forced to walk for miles across a flooded city in search of safety for her children, she would be yelling just the same.

Troy had finally gotten the door open, and Reyna waded out onto the porch, followed by a gangly older boy, maybe ten. Reyna was wearing Troy's kitchen jacket and nothing else, and her legs — and the older boy's too — were ulcerated like the baby's. She leaned against the porch rail and stared at Cora, her eyes almost completely red, and Willy hid his face in Cora's lap.

"We're just here to get you home, Reyna," Troy said. "That's all we're trying to do."

"Who's this bitch, then? That's what she's trying? She's got my child in her boat."

"She's a friend of mine from the restaurant," Troy said. "You come on in the boat too, and we'll get you out of the water, get you cleaned up, get you some food."

"They just want to help us," said the older boy, who held a backpack across his chest.

Reyna looked at Cora with such intensity, Cora could feel it on her skin. "You know what help gets you?" she asked, as if it were a real question. "Fucked."

Eventually, they had to lie to get Reyna in the boat. They told her Calliope had not flooded as it had done in the last several hours, that her neighbors were already home. They told her that what she'd heard were just malicious rumors, that the city was returning to normal and she would be safe at home with her children. They'd told her they would take her home.

After they'd made it to shore and Reyna, Tyrone, and Willy were safely inside the Jeep, Troy had taken Cora by the shoulder and whispered that they had to get Reyna to a hospital, that he had seen her this bad only once before. After her first child was born, she'd called from the hospital screaming that the nurses had taken the baby away.

It turned out that the little girl had died in the night, and in the next few days, Reyna had tried four times to take her own life. Cora had not been able to ask when or how before Troy opened the car door and pushed Cora in.

Now, Reyna talked nonstop as Troy drove them away from the margins of the flood, her exhaustion-sharpened face turned out the window, her arms and legs wrapped around the boys who squirmed like puppies in her embrace.

"Don't look, boys, don't look. There's nothing but filth out there, like I always told you. It comes up from underneath. And once you see it, you'll never stop. You'll never get your eyes clean."

Cora watched the boys in the rearview mirror. Tyrone was staring out of his window, watching the filth roll by, but Willy had his head cradled against his mother's breast, his hands over his ears. He was humming.

"No-city no-place nothing nothing nothing."

"It's going to be alright, boys," Cora said.

"Don't you talk to my children, bitch. Don't you start lying to them again. They know it's not true. They know not to listen. They know what you —"

"You'll see," Cora continued. "We're going to get out of here just as soon as we can. And the first thing we do when we get out of the city is we're going to go to a Burger King, and we're going to get hamburgers, milkshakes, whatever you want —"

"You're not taking us anywhere!" Reyna yelled, hitting the back of Cora's seat so hard that she jolted forward. "Not anywhere! We're dead already. Dead before we died."

"Hey!" Troy yelled. "That's enough."

In the rearview, the boys huddled against each other, Tyrone looping his arms over his brother's shoulders. Cora stopped. They would be at the checkpoint soon enough, and Reyna would be gone, and Cora would be able to reassure them.

"— trying to tell me what I'm going to do with my own children. What I'm going to do, how I'm going to be, when they're the ones, with their yellow rooms, their overflowing toilets, their pills in little cups —"

Reyna kept talking, but she had turned her face to the window again, and Tyrone began stroking Willy's back. His hand ran up and down, quieting his little brother, and Cora tried to visualize Del sitting in her lap, running her fingers through her hair the way she did when Cora couldn't handle things.

346

Finally, they reached the checkpoint, and Troy stopped the Jeep. "Reyna," he said. "Can you give me a hand with something? I want to get some flats of water."

For some reason, she didn't argue with him. She just got out and followed him across the streetcar tracks, towards the tents and military Humvees. As soon as Cora thought she was out of Reyna's line of sight, she unbuckled her seatbelt and bent into the backseat, reaching under the driver's seat for a jar of peanuts.

"It's going to be okay." She opened the jar slowly, desperate for Tyrone's eyes to stay on her hands. "It's going to be okay. I promise. We're going to go back to my house, and take a bath, and bandage you up, and get fresh clothes."

She tapped peanuts into Tyrone's hand, risking a glance up to the encampment where Troy was speaking to the guardsmen.

"We've got lots of good things to cook for dinner," she said, while Tyrone pushed the peanuts into his brother's mouth as though he were feeding a puppy. "Baked beans and some steaks in the freezer should be thawed out now, and canned peaches. You like peaches?" she tried, but just then Reyna started screaming.

Tyrone looked up. She couldn't stop him.

He watched the guardsmen put his mother in handcuffs, watched his uncle walk away with his hands in his pockets as though he had nothing to do with it.

"Row, row, row your boat," Cora started to sing, desperate to drown out Reyna's screams, desperate to keep Willy from looking through the window. "Gently down the stream. Merrily, merrily, merrily, merrily. Life is but a dream. Row, row, row your boat —"

Even as she sang, she felt the impact. She'd been falling ever since the rain had started, but now she felt herself land, hard. She watched Troy hitch his jeans up and wait for a Humvee to pass before crossing the street. His face was blank — shell-shocked but resolute. The air was suddenly as clear as still water, and she could hear Willy chewing his peanuts. He smiled up at her as his hand reached into the glass jar for more. Tyrone was still looking through the window, and she scrambled into the backseat and threw an arm across his eyes. His mother was trying to jerk her manacled hands away from the two guardsmen who held her, her head lowered, showing the spirals of her braids.

"It's just for now," she heard herself saying as Troy opened the door. "Those men are going to help her, so that she can come back home healthy and look after you right." She didn't even know if she was lying, like the bitch Reyna said she was. Regardless, Tyrone nodded and put another peanut in his mouth.

Troy was at her father's grill cooking the steaks from the thawing deepfreeze, and smoke twisted across the firelit yard, tangling with the moss hanging in the trees. Cora sat on the lower gallery with Willy in her lap, bandaging his legs. The smell of soap was strong on his fuzzy head. She'd washed him three times with dish detergent then orange oil then shea butter shampoo, and she breathed him in, talking about clean streets, freshly made beds, red leaves on a bright blue day. Her hands worked rhythmically as she laid on the fabric tape and ripped it with her teeth.

"There you go."

He played with the buttons on her blouse. "Where?"

There was no point answering that. Tomorrow they would be somewhere else; she and Troy had agreed. They would take her car and drive north. Thinking about the malls they'd stop at to buy new clothes, the bleach smell of fast-food restrooms, the thin motel towels made her sick, but it had to be done. The boys needed to be gone. Tyrone leaned against her leg, pressing his thumbnail into the decking. He had let her bathe him, but he wouldn't look at her now. He didn't trust her, and she didn't blame him. In his position, she wouldn't trust a goddamn thing.

She scooted Willy off her lap and held her arms out to Tyrone. "Let me do you now, honey."

The boy shot his legs out, but he kept looking at the floor. On the wood, he had carved a row of angles, like roofs without houses. She squeezed Neosporin onto his sores and gently rubbed it in.

Sitting on the magnolia's fallen trunk, Troy poured a can into a pot on the grill, and the liquid hissed and sputtered. Neither boy had asked about their mother. Presumably, they'd seen it all before. Presumably, they understood, though Cora could not really say that she did. She did and she did not. While the little boys were in their bath, Troy had pulled her into the hall, apologizing. After the death of Reyna's daughter — SIDS, the coroner said — she'd taken pills, and when that didn't work, she tried a razor, then a knife. He couldn't manage her if she got like that again, he said. Not and take

350

care of the boys. He didn't say: not and take care of Cora too. It had already been hard enough — getting her to get help, getting her to take her medicine — but she had eventually gotten well enough to go to school, get her nursing degree, take a job at Charity. Still, when Tyrone was born, he had called family services. They'd told him there wasn't much they could do beyond sending a social worker out once to check up, and so he'd tried to let it go. He'd tried to be a good uncle to them.

Cora started another roll of gauze, holding the end gently against Tyrone's shin, while her other hand circled. *Help gets you fucked.* It was true, Cora thought. Everything Reyna had said was true. When you were at the bottom of your hole, they came and took away what agency you had left. They called you weak. They dragged you from your house. They inserted tubes and instruments into your body. They gave you pills that took away your reality and replaced it with their own. Yes, help was a disrespect. Help was a fucking, and this time she had been complicit. More than that, she had been glad to see Reyna grow smaller as they drove away. She would have been glad to see Reyna completely disappear.

When they had gotten back to Esplanade,

there was the graffiti X on the siding, the door kicked in, boot tracks on the floor. If they hadn't been out, the patrols would have dragged them out, pushed them out at gunpoint. Maybe locked them up, especially if Reyna had still been with them, acting like that. They were lucky — they could leave tomorrow on their own accord. The rescuers would carry on without her, and that was probably for the best. Earlier that afternoon, she'd pried an old man's fingers off the arms of his rocking chair, and when a woman had begged her to turn the pirogue around so that she could go back for her wedding album, Cora had kept rowing. She had been high on helping them. Each person she found felt like a missing piece of herself, but now she understood that they each belonged only to themselves.

She should look out for herself now as everyone was always begging her to do. She should pack her things, get on the road, have a Frosty and some onion rings, stand naked in front of an air conditioner. She imagined a hotel shower, the water stripping the dirt from her skin. Her body wanted those things — rest, pleasure. She and her body were one. *Accept that the world is telling you the truth,* Dr. Nemetz would say. The truth was that the city was flooded.

The truth was that the government would rescue the people who were still out there. The truth was Troy and these boys needed her help, and she needed to accept that and go.

In the yard, Willy was running naked around the stalks of the tiki torches. Troy looked up at the tree, at the knotted moss and the ropes of smoke that dangled into the sky like the promise of escape. Cora rubbed Neosporin on Tyrone's other leg as Tyrone watched his brother run.

THREE DAYS
AFTER LANDFALL
SEPTEMBER 1

Tyrone was sitting up in bed, his wet eyes shining in the near-dawn darkness, when she heard it: a rustle of leaves, a scrabbling like the sound of an animal's claws on slippery ground. She reached for Troy, but he was no longer in the big bed, where they'd all fallen asleep together in a hot pile. Willy still lay curled beside her, thumb in his sleeping mouth.

"Where's your uncle?" Cora asked Tyrone, but he didn't speak, didn't move.

Twigs were breaking inside the house. Something was in the magnolia — an animal, a burglar. Tyrone's eyes were fixed on the door of the bedroom, which was open onto the pitch-black hall. Wind rushed in, a smell of ozone. For a second, the scrabbling died, and they heard only the clattering of the leaves.

"It's nothing." She patted Tyrone's arm as she got out of bed. "Wind just blew the door open."

The air licked her skin with its rough tongue, and Cora waited with her hand on the edge of the door. Somewhere in the house there were footsteps.

"Troy?" she called out.

The footsteps stopped, but Troy didn't answer. She wanted to retreat to the bedroom to wait with the children — if it was a looter, they would be safe hiding under the bed in the dark. They would simply let the person take what he wanted and go away. But the person was not opening drawers, not picking up any of the heavy, valuable things scattered around the house. He was walking slowly, trying to get his bearings. Cora went into the hall, closing the door behind her.

The footsteps were coming across the lower floor — barefoot and light. She wanted to call out again, but her mouth wouldn't open. Instead she flew to the back of the house, threw open the door to the gallery, and then she was in the open air, under a heavy blanket of stars, her feet tearing off the tin floor as she ran. Down in the garden, Troy was going into the shed, where the axes were. There was no time to yell down.

In her father's studio, magnolia branches

thrust up through the broken floorboards and against the toppled sculptures. She shimmied around the walls and ran into the attic. Her heart was beating against her neck. For a second, she closed her eyes, her hands on the warm metal door. *Forty-five right, twenty-five left, twenty-three right.* She felt around for the bullets in the bottom of the safe. *Open the breech, load the magazine, close the breech.* She checked the safety and, clutching the duck gun by the barrel, went back down and through the studio and along the gallery under the stars.

Inside the house, there was screaming — a cacophony of shouts and high-pitched yells that would not resolve into words. At the head of the stairs, Cora stopped. The door to her bedroom was open now, and Troy was blockading it with his body as he struggled against someone whose face Cora could not see, someone who was trying to get into the bedroom, where Tyrone lay on the white sheets, oddly still. Outlined in the moonlit window above him, Willy stood and wailed.

Her father's voice was in her ears: *Cradle the shotgun, lock it into your shoulder, remove the safety.*

The axe blade gleamed at Troy's thigh.

This was a nightmare then. How else

could everything she'd feared be coming true. The smaller figure, whose bald head shone featureless in the dark, was grappling with Troy, who had stopped fighting back, who only stood with his arms and legs pinned into the doorway as if he were a wall. He seemed to think he could protect the little boys from the terror that was coming at them, but there was no safety here: only screaming, only sobbing, someone yelling *no,* someone with a curdled voice yelling *Let me in.* Safety was impossible here, on this side of the rain.

Remove the safety.

"Mama! Mama!" Willy was screaming, silhouetted against the moon, but his mother was gone, and the axe was in the hand of the other person now, who struggled and kicked, trying to push past Troy. Troy didn't move.

Remove the safety.

"Stop!" Cora yelled, but they could not hear her through their own shouting.

Remove the safety.

"Stop!"

Nothing changed.

There was only one way out. *Open the breech.* To leave this place, this hell on the far side of the rain, you had to break through the sky.

She pointed the gun at the ceiling, pulled the trigger.

In the light of the blast, Cora saw Reyna's face turn to her as the axe fell from her hand. All the voices stopped, and beyond the explosion's echo, all she heard was plaster falling around them like hail. Troy groaned and grabbed his arm, and Reyna collapsed to her knees, then slumped forward, her newly shaved head cradled in her hands.

"Mama!" Willy yelled, and Tyrone flipped on the lantern beside the bed. Troy slammed the door to their room, shutting the boys in, before he dove upon his sister, picked her up by the armpits and threw her against the wall. Her head hit the top stair before she began to tumble, heavily, from one step to the next.

Troy staggered backwards against the door, his face blank with shock. He clapped a hand over his forearm, where he was bleeding from a constellation of tiny wounds.

"Oh God." He staggered towards the stairs where Reyna sat slumped, her head bent on her chest, her eyes closed, her lashes heavy against her cheeks. She looked like she was sleeping. But you could not sleep in a nightmare.

"Oh God, what have we done?"

Tyrone pushed the door open a crack, the hinges creaking, and Cora realized that she was still holding the gun, her finger still on the trigger. She crouched and laid it on the floor as Tyrone left the bedroom and moved past her. At the head of the stairs he stopped and stood, looking down through the banister rails at his mother. Reyna's mouth hung open as if she were sleeping. But you could not sleep in a nightmare, because where would you go in your dreams?

"She was just trying to come to get us," Tyrone said. "She was just trying to be with us. She was just coming to be with us, Uncle Troy."

Willy had come out into the hall now, holding the lantern up to illuminate his full moon face, and Cora went to him, gathered him into her arms.

"You're so scared of her," Tyrone said, his face pressed into the balusters. "Why do you have to be so scared?"

Cora carried Willy to the stairs. As they descended, Troy came to the banister, put his bloodied hands on Tyrone's shoulders. Blood ran in long rivulets from the wounds on his arm, fell with a soft *tap tap* on the floor. Cora could hear them all breathing: Troy's heavy exhalations and Tyrone's quick, panicked pants. Willy sobbed quietly against her shoulder as she tried to take deep breaths. But only once they had come beside Reyna and sat beside her on the stair, only after Willy had reached out and pressed his small hand against his mother's smooth brow, could Cora hear Reyna's lungs filling, emptying — a crackling breath like the sound of the wind.

"Mama?" Willy said, running his thumb up the ridges beneath her razor-scraped scalp where her skull had once been delicate and unformed.

"She's alright," Cora said, "She's just sleeping."

But you could not sleep inside a nightmare; you'd only go deeper down.

A sliver of the moon nested in the rooftops of the Quarter, and Cora pointed it out to Tyrone, who still had not closed his eyes. They had been sitting in the portico for hours it seemed like, waiting for Troy to come back. Long enough now that their fear had evaporated in the night air. Willy slept draped around her neck, and Cora's breathing now matched the little boy's, her heartbeat slowed from its frenzy. Every so often, Tyrone's long lashes would droop over his cheeks and his body would relax against her, but he always woke with a start the second he began to drift away. Now his eyes followed her finger to find the moon.

"To wane," Cora said. "That's the word for the way the moon gets smaller."

Tyrone nodded and coughed roughly, rubbing his long throat.

"Tomorrow, it'll be gone I think." Tomorrow, as they drove north, the earth would float right in front of the sun, and the moon would be invisible against the vault of the sky. "They used to believe the moon caused madness, you know."

Tyrone dropped his eyes from her finger, craned his close-cropped head to look again down the empty street for the Jeep.

"But it doesn't —" She stroked Willy's narrow back. "The moon's got nothing to do with it. Just the tides. It pulls up on the ocean. 'Madness,' even — that's a stupid word. What your mama has is just a disease, something wrong with her head. Something broken we can fix. That we're figuring out how to fix."

Tyrone's dark eyes blinked in the lantern light.

"Even the scary things she does, that's not her doing them," Cora continued. "That's the broken part. The malfunction."

Tyrone set his jaw, and as the sinews in

his cheeks tensed, she saw what he would look like in a few years, as he became a teenager, a young man. He would need someone to help him learn softness. Teach him to believe in the lies you had to believe if you wanted to live.

"You were so scared of her," he said. "So scared."

"You don't have to worry." She adjusted Willy on her shoulder and reached over to touch Tyrone's shoulder, but he pulled away. "You're safe now. Your Uncle Troy and I are going to take you and Willy away from here, and when your mama is well again, she'll join us."

"Not you."

She tried to remember what had happened — the screaming in the dark, the grappling, his mother's hand on the axe. She had been right to stop it, hadn't she? But a boy's mother is his mother is his mother is his mother.

"Okay."

"Not you."

"If that's what you want."

The boy nodded, a sharp jerk of his chin, and his shoulders relaxed as they had when he'd watched Troy carrying Reyna's unconscious body out to the Jeep, her eyes closed as if she were asleep. Tyrone had worked himself out of Cora's arms by the time Troy reached the bottom of the stairs. He leaned over the banister and Troy looked up at him, hitching his sister's body higher in his arms. *I'm going to get her in the right hands this time, buddy. You just wait for me, you hear.*

After the door was closed and locked behind him, Cora had packed the bags, filled them with everything that mattered — some clothes, her diaries, a toothbrush. The boy was probably right, though; she had no business going with them. Out there in the daylight, her wrongness would show.

Tyrone stood up and walked down to the sidewalk. Between the trunks of the oaks, a set of headlights strobed. *Help gets you fucked,* Reyna said, speaking truth. Troy parked the Jeep in front of the house.

"She's gonna be all right," Troy said as he came across the sidewalk, the engine still running, the duck gun under his arm. "Got her to the medics, and in the morning they're going to bring her to the hospital in Lake Charles, make sure she gets all the right kind of care. I gave them her history. Names of the doctors and all that."

Cora avoided his face. Weighted with the sleeping child, she stood up and descended the steps. She freed a hand to open the back door of the Jeep and laid Willy down on the seat, kissing him lightly on his sweaty forehead. Troy went into the house and came out again carrying the bags, but Tyrone was waiting, hanging from the column at the corner of the portico, holding his backpack across his chest. Troy opened the hatch, and Cora grabbed her bag from him.

"I can't go with you," she said.

Troy tensed. "What the hell are you talking about?"

"I'm not coming," she said loudly, then lowered her voice. "You've got to try to understand. Their mother —"

He looked to Tyrone then back at her, shaking his head. "This is not about her."

"It is, though, Troy. It is all about her. All about them."

"What kind of man do you think I am, going to take your car and leave you here by yourself? You are out of your damn mind."

She was not out of her mind, however. This was not what madness felt like — her heart beating steadily, solidly, inside her chest, the moon tethered in the sky. She would stay and he would go, and everyone would be fine. He and the little boys belonged on the highway, and Tyrone was right, she did not belong with them.

"I won't come, I'm sorry."

Troy buried his nose in her hair. "Please, baby. Let me look out for you." And as his lips moved against her scalp, she wanted to let him.

"No," she said. "I've got to look out for myself."

He walked past her into the vestibule and came out again with the gun, put it into her hands. "You keep this with you then."

She tried to give the gun back, but he wouldn't take it. "If something goes wrong, if there's an emergency, I'll go to Mrs. Randsell at Augie's house. Madge's old car is still there. We'll be alright."

"If there's an emergency." He shook his head. "Like this isn't an emergency already."

"I'll go if I need help. If I get scared. I promise," she said as she turned away from him.

"I guess you're a grown woman," Troy said. "I guess I can't stop you."

Tyrone plodded down off the portico and, without looking at her, settled into the front seat of the car.

She watched her Jeep until the galleries of Royal Street had swallowed it, kept watching as the leaves went still on the trees and the mark of the tires evaporated from the street, and then she stood up and went back inside the house.

Cora shut the door behind her and climbed the stairs. On each step, little drops of blood glistened. She set her bag down and pulled a T-shirt out of it, wiping as she climbed. At the top of the stairs, on the ceiling between her room and her parents', birdshot had pocked the plaster, and a small puddle of blood was soaking into the rug. She lay her T-shirt down over it. The white cloth gathered red. From the back of the house she heard ticking, like the sound of a dog's feet on wood.

The gun still in her hand, she went down the stairs again. A pale wash of dawn spread across the hall from the cracked-open kitchen door where the buffet had been pushed aside, and she heard the sound of claws again — just the magnolia, she reminded herself, just twigs tapping against the house. Nevertheless, her heart was pounding, her head reeling as she went to the open door.

A dog, its ears pressed back against its skull, snarled at her from the magnolia's branches. She jumped back — just one of her father's unfinished sculptures, fallen from his studio, the dog's head and raised hackles carved carefully, his lower half ordinary, bark-clad wood. Around it were the downy cones of the magnolia tree, not yet bleeding their bright-red seeds. But the tree's broken branches shook in the light, casting strange shadows, and she saw Troy holding Reyna's limp body in his arms, her mud-blackened feet dangling lifelessly at his hip.

As he carried her out of the house and across the sidewalk, his feet silent in the mud, Reyna lifted her face to Cora, lifted her heavy lashes. Beneath them were blood-ied sockets, her eyes plucked out by birds.

■ ■ ■ ■

PART THREE:
THE CITY OF DIS

■ ■ ■ ■

FIFTY-SIX DAYS
AFTER LANDFALL
OCTOBER 24

DAWN

Fire had consumed the center of the house. The window Cora had used to climb through on her nightly visitations, the kitchen, and the roof above were nothing now but a black stain that seeped across the siding like blood on cotton. Inside, the ashes smoldered.

When Cora had rounded the corner and seen the house in flames, it had seemed right. Necessary. She had been glad to watch it burn, and as she watched, as the firemen came with water, her mind repeated Ezekiel: *I brought forth a fire from the midst of you; it has devoured you, and I have turned you to ashes on the earth.* She remembered the flash at the muzzle, Reyna's shorn head in her hands. She remembered Reyna singing loud in her lamé dress, punching the river pilot's car through the intersections. She remembered the photograph of Reyna

371

she'd taken from the apartment at Calliope
— a woman obsidian with summer, encir-
cling her babies in her arms. She remembered the first time she'd come here, seen
her lying on the floor — Reyna's face so
wrecked that it could have been anyone's
face, could have been Cora's own — and
beside her the gun missing from Esplanade,
and in her head she heard a flapping, like a
page being flipped: Her long lashes on slack
cheeks. Her eyes plucked out by birds. She
began to cough, and as she bent down over
her legs, she saw that her hands were glowing in the moonlight. Living. Clean.

She staggered into the street now and
turned towards the old portage, let the new
roses she'd brought for Reyna fall from her
hand. Her throat burned. On the corner
ahead, a cypress, its trunk entwined with a
chain-link fence, trailed its shrouds over a
pool of rain. She crouched beside it, her
nightdress hanging over her feet. She
plunged her arms into the puddle and
cupped the water to drink, but it was so
black with mud that her hands disappeared,
and she pulled them out of the pool, afraid.

She passed through the neighborhood and
along the walls of the cemetery until she
had reached the open gate. As far back as
she could see, the little marble houses stood

side by side, rain-washed to a high white that glowed against the mud. The black doors of the tombs were locked tight and safe, and there were no windows in them that could be broken, and their roofs were made of stone. She walked until the granite wall ended at a little copse of oaks, shaking clean air from their leaves. Cora pressed herself between the mausoleums and under the heavy branches of the old trees. Before her, a field stretched down to Bayou St. John, and she walked through the broken chain-link gate and across the road, and crept down through the dead grass to the water.

The black neck of a cormorant cut across the trembling pink surface of the bayou. Near the far bank, two men were fishing from a canoe. She fell on her knees by the chilly water, splashed her hands down. The bird dove. The men turned towards her into the light of the rising sun, which blanked their faces, their features misty as wraiths'.

One of them whistled. "Hey, lookie here."

"What you doing out here before dawn, child?"

She splashed the water up over her face, over her arms. She was so thirsty. She lifted a mouthful, cupped in her hands.

"Hey hey! Don't drink that, girl, you crazy?"

The men had begun to row towards her, and the water ran through her fingers. Their boat cut a fast wake in the bayou's surface.

"You must not be from here. This water's nasty. It ain't to drink."

"Not unless you're some kind of raccoon or something —" The men chuckled.

Her hands sank into the water. Out beyond them, the cormorant resurfaced, dove again.

"I am the child of earth and starry heaven," she said, strange words faintly remembered, and yet the men, just feet from her now, pushed their oars forward. The boat halted in the water.

"What?"

"I am the child of earth and starry heaven."

They pushed the bayou towards her, moved away.

She brought the water up to her mouth and drank, and it tasted cold and clear. Once upon a time, this bayou had drained the city's swamps into the lake, and the Choctaws, the Bogue Chittos, the Biloxis, having traversed the lake from the gulf, had rowed the length of it in their birch bark canoes to make portage into the river. She remembered this as clearly as if she had done it herself: the pole in her blistered hands bending as she pushed against the muddy bottom of the channel, the water coursing across her feet as the pirogue knocked against the banks. She had reached for a willow branch, and it brushed her head with its long leaves as she swung up out of the water and hauled the boat ashore. She bent down. She dipped her hands into the water again, drank again. She remembered a drift of leaves rolling across an island that changed to a flock of gulls, a flock of gulls that changed to a horde of people waving dirty cotton flags. She had gathered them up into her skirt, she had rowed them out across the lake and left them on its farther shore.

MONDAY

OCTOBER 24

Tess sat in the portico in her bathrobe, watching the shadows move across Esplanade. She had gotten as far as to open the door to the house, but the air that poured out with its dank smell of mildew and dying vegetation made her afraid of what might be waiting for her inside. Yesterday afternoon — Augie's hands on her, that mist of gin and distraction — seemed like ages ago, though it had been less than twelve hours since she'd come back to the Dobies' house to find her girls missing from their beds. Cora could not have gone too far from home in twelve hours, not in the state she was in.

Not that this place was "home" any longer. She ran her hand across the tiles, still as smooth and vibrant as the day she and Joe had set them there, drinking beers and listening to the radio, while Cora played below them on the sidewalk. The thousands of tiny blue and green tesserae spelling out a Minoan sea, its waves and jumping dolphins, would soon pass into other hands, but they had always been meant to outlast her, outlast the house's four walls, outlast perhaps even the city — Joe studying the pictures of Lycian mosaics after a sun-struck trip to Turkey, Cora only a twisting in Tess's gut she mistook for bad kebab. *We were so happy,* she had said to him when they'd last sat there, waiting for Cora to come home with the Maestres' motorboat trailered behind her Jeep, when she hadn't come home. *Were?* he'd asked. But even the question had been a lie. Because of course Joe knew that it was over, just as they knew, as the sun went down on the drained city, that Cora was not coming back — mold on the bread, the kitchen door shoved open against the sideboard, the drawers overturned — and that they would have to leave without her again, and that nothing would ever be the same.

Tess stood up and went into the house. She paused to lock the vestibule doors then picked up a lantern and snapped it on, illuminating the blooms of yellow and pink mold on the garlanded ceiling. As she skirted the dangling chandelier, the swollen floorboards moaned beneath her feet. Something somewhere rustled. The hair went up on the back of her neck.

"Cora?" Her voice bounced against the high ceiling of the hall.

The rustling stopped with a thud, followed by a strange, hoarse cry. Somewhere, the hinges of a door were whining.

"Cora!"

Tess got no answer. She ran to the kitchen door and unbolted the padlock. In the gash of warming sky, the tree hung its melancholy head. The leaves had been disturbed again — a space had been cleared, big enough for a body, and a sticky smell, like sex and sleep, drifted in the air — but the countertops were clear, the cabinets closed. She took a deep breath, and then she heard it again, the rustle, accompanied by a sound like someone fighting for breath.

She ran up the front stairs, her heart hammering so hard that she had to wait on the landing for a second while the blood returned to her brain. The rustling was louder here, but the rasping sound had stopped. The latch on Cora's door had not caught, and the breeze that slipped through the hall made the door move gently on its hinges. She pushed it open.

The bird came at her in a green flurry, the dark ripping open as lime wings tore through it. A feather touched her cheek, and she heard herself scream, and the bird shrieked back in a voice she recognized as one from the multitude of Quaker parrots that lived in the palm tree. She dropped her hands, and the bird landed in the middle of the floor then hopped onto a pile of boxes at the end of the hall. It lifted its Day-Glo wings, squawked.

From the doorway, she threw the lantern light around the room. It was empty of any evidence her child had ever lived there. No clothes, no dolls, none of the sentimental treasures she kept arrayed on her mantel-piece, no ribbons or books or trinket boxes. No furniture, even, for Cora to hide behind. She opened the door to her own room, to the closet, to the bathroom where the tub sat empty, to Del's room. The hole in the roof had gotten bigger; now she could see the sky. She returned to the hallway, where the palm-sized stain on the carpet had faded to a dull brown, and the parrot flew to the banister. She opened the door that led outside onto the upper gallery. From the downed magnolia, out of the broken staves of wood and loose shingles, midges were rising into the fog of early sun, and she re-alized that this all was only the beginning. Soon, flowering vines would push their claws into the chimneys' mortar, and roaches would crawl up out of the drains. Mice would chew through the cabinets, and the cats who brawled on the back fence at night would stalk them through the limbs of the fallen tree. As the swamp advanced, nutria would amble out of the reeds, and cypress trees would bow their heads and pull up their knees beside the big Rococo bookcase. Eventually, the lake, then the river, then the Gulf would wash across Joe's mosaic of the sea, and the mangroves would wind their snaking roots through the floors. Eventually, the lichen-covered walls would tremble as the muskrats moved inside them, and the termites would accomplish their slow work of ruin.

That would take years, though. It was important to focus on the now. *Now, now, now.*

She crept along the hallway past the bird who was still perched, skinny, on the banister, its head cocked, considering an escape through the oculus. She spread her arms and ran at it.

"Out!" she yelled, and the bird took off, darting towards the open door and the sky.

Downstairs, she heard rubber soles shuffling across the front porch, keys rustling. She wanted to believe it was Cora, but they were a man's steps. She picked up a broom and held it across her chest. The padlock clicked, and the chain knocked against the frame of the screen doors. She came halfway down the stairs.

"Tess —"

Joe was standing at the edge of the Minoan sea, the sun rising behind him. Just Joe, once again alone. Once again without their missing daughter, just like that night in Houston when they had looked up from their dinner, laughing and naive, at the sound of his truck in the driveway. Vincent had been going on about how porky Zizi's green beans were, *so porky,* when Joe came up the front steps, once again alone. He hadn't called them from the road back from New Orleans to warn her — to say, *I couldn't get in,* so that she wouldn't have kept up hope — and so Tess had run out into the street and away from him, her breasts in their lacy bra banging against her rib cage, sure that when he did open his mouth, he would tell her Cora was dead. She was sure that the looters had come and tied Cora to a kitchen chair. Sure that that was what he was going to say.

She had stopped under a streetlamp, looked up — the lantern painted green to make it look like oxidized copper — and it was as though something had just imploded, like the grain elevator across the river in '78 when they'd sat up in bed, thinking the Russians had finally dropped the bomb. As the after-sound of the boom rang in their ears, a silence descended in which you could've heard the chaff floating down to earth if you'd known that there was chaff. *I couldn't get in,* Joe said finally. And she'd known then that he was a coward. She could see him standing at the entrance to the bridge, requesting passage in his polite, ingratiating way, being denied. She saw him step back into his truck, put a finger to his hat brim, thank them. *How could I have trusted you with this?* she'd screamed, and the only answer he had for her was her own name.

"Oh, Tess," he said once again, standing alone now at the edge of the sea.

Joe had had the key in his hand since they left Esplanade, but as he lowered himself into the street, he put it back in his pocket. The front door to Cora's house yawned inwards, and the screen door gawped, propped open with a cinder block.

At the curb, beside Cora's refrigerator and the sofa and mattress he and Tess had hauled out those first days back in the city, stood the rest of Cora's things: her melamine kitchen table and four mud-painted shaker chairs, boxes of dirty china and CDs, books, pots, and pans. There were six giant garbage bags that must have contained everything else: her mildewed clothes, her floor cushions, dried beans, dish towels, rugs. At the Dobies' too, Cora had packed a bag — snuck in while Tess and Del were out in the Marigny hunting for her, must have been. She had taken her toothbrush, her folded clothes. But Tess wouldn't believe that that meant anything. She'd had a patient some years back, Jason Katz, who had packed a suitcase in preparation for hanging himself. Running shoes, Dopp kit, jeans, two clean shirts, four pairs of boxers and four pairs of socks neatly folded into a carry-on he'd set near his front door. Tess had spent months obsessing over whether it was a just-in-case hospital bag or some sort of Egyptian provision for the land of the dead.

Now, Tess pressed the car door open with her fingers and slid her thighs across the seat.

He stepped into the street and looked down it. "The Jeep isn't here either," he said.

Smoke threaded the air — a house fire smoldering down the block — and the neighborhood was beginning to wake. Lights went on in upstairs bedrooms and trucks rattled in with their tool chests and sheets of drywall.

"The Jeep isn't here," he said again. "She's gone somewhere then. Thank God. Thank God."

"Doesn't mean a goddamned thing," Tess said.

Clutching the handhold, Tess lowered her slippered feet onto the curb. She looked up at the open door of Cora's house, coughed.

He could feel the smoke in his throat too. "Well, shall we go in?"

Off in the distance, a table saw screamed on, ground to a stop. His feet cracked through the crust of lake mud into the sticky, wet earth underneath. He half expected the mud to creep up his legs, his belly, his back and neck until it had encased even his head, and he knew that if it did, he would wait patiently for it to petrify him, as if he were waiting for a cast to set. The table saw spun, ripped, spun down. He dislodged his feet from the mud, crossed to Tess, held out his hand. But Tess stepped over the pile of Cora's things without taking it, her robe parting over the blue skin of her thighs. She walked out over the lawn, her head down.

Her hands opened and closed, opened and

closed as they did when she fretted, though fretting was not the word. He took her arm, opened her fist, threaded his fingers between hers. Cora had left every door in the cottage open. The floors had been swept clean, but the gray marks of the flood still lodged deep in the wood. An electrical cord dangled from the air conditioner in the window. A poster for the Rebirth Brass Band curled up from the back of the closet door.

Tess's hand tensed for a moment, went limp. "The bathroom," she said. A green feather clung to her robe. "Why is that door closed?"

Joe squeezed her hand, let go. He took the four necessary steps, turned the knob. From the ceiling hung the Moravian star light. Dead termites clustered in its lowest point.

Tess's hands, balled into fists, were pulling her towards the ground. He went behind her, closed his arms around her, held her up.

"You didn't want to find her. You didn't try."

Joe shook his head. "I did. I do."

"What happened to us?" she said. "Where have we gone?"

"Nowhere." He pressed his nose into her hair and breathed its smell of dust and dampness and the summer ghost of her lemongrass shampoo. He wanted nothing but to wrap himself around her, press up against her back, his knees into the crux of her knees, and bury his nose into her neck until there was no space left between them, until she could hear his thoughts. *We are nowhere. We haven't gone.*

Papie kept craning his neck over the wing of the Dobies' big armchair and squinting at their front door, as if he were waiting for a train. They might as well have been strangers on a subway platform, Del thought, though they weren't waiting for anything close to the same thing.

"What's taking so long?" Papie glanced at her, then looked back at the door.

She shrugged. The kettle she'd put on when her father had dropped Papie off hadn't even boiled. She looked at the clock — still only ten — but that meant she'd been awake for over a day.

"What in God's name can be taking so long?" Papie said again.

Del shrugged. "Track fire."

He cocked his head. His flannel shirt was misbuttoned, and mismatched socks peeked out from under the high cuffs of his pants. "What?"

The kettle finally began to whistle, and

Del got up. "Excuse me."

He pushed himself to his feet to watch her leave the room.

In the kitchen, she turned the burner off under the kettle and brought it to the tile counter where she had sliced the lemon and laid out the mugs, tea bags, honey. The courtyard was still in shadow, and in the window over the sink her face was reflected as clearly as in a mirror. She reached behind her head and undid the knot of her scarf while the tea steeped, let her hair spring free. Her mother had sent her to check on Cora's house after they'd searched the Marigny, and now they'd gone back again. Del was glad. She hadn't looked properly, distracted by the flames whipping the dim sky, the neighbors clustered around. It looked like a decent fire she'd set, but she hadn't gone close enough to see if it had accomplished its purpose — she didn't like being there, at the scene of the crime. She was afraid someone would put it all together, the smell, the burning, Cora and Troy. But she really looked nothing like her sister: her face was round where Cora's was angled, her skin darker but more freckled, her lips riper, roughed up now from kissing.

"They all want to do it fast these days,"

Papie said when she came back into the room.

"Do what?"

She held out his mug, and he took it in two hands. Her whole life, his nails had been ragged and jammed with sawdust, his fingerprints highlighted with stain. Now, they were pink-padded, raw pecan-brown, like babies' hands. It had been years since they'd taken him away from his workshop, but she'd never seen before that his hands had changed.

"Fast. Instant gratification. Like a bouillon cube. Don't want to take the time to learn."

She sat down on the Dobies' too-soft leather sofa and closed her eyes. Her head hurt, and her eyes watered, the smell of smoke stuck in her nose. She should turn off some lights, but she didn't feel like standing up again.

"If you do find someone good, then they want to learn everything you know as quick as they can and then run away before you've got your use of them, make their own profits. They don't care for the hard work, the real work. *Shit work,* I heard one of them call it, the job I paid him to do. Want to hire their own men to do it for 'em, and I'm not going to be a party to that. No, ma'am."

Del nodded. Furniture, he meant. Actually, she had always enjoyed doing the little things Papie had tasked her with: rubbing wax into the surface of crosscut mahogany, blowing sawdust out of precisely drilled holes, gluing together long strips of ebony and oak. That wouldn't have lost its meaning, she didn't think. Not even the little things. Not even now.

"It's not to my taste to train my own competition."

"Your tea okay, Papie?"

"No, ma'am." He examined his cup. "Too hot. Don't want it to burn me."

"Mm." She took a sip of her own and smacked her lips. "Mine's cooled off pretty good."

"My mouth is burned." He looked up at her. "My mouth is burned!"

"No, Papie, no — you're okay."

He was looking around, suddenly startled, at the Dobies' oak bookcases, at the paint-dulled medallion around the Noguchi lantern, at her bare feet, at his clean hands on the chair arms, at the steam lingering over the lip of his mug.

"It's burning me." He dropped the mug, tea flooding out over the rug.

She stood up, as if she could push him back to wherever he'd been just seconds ago

— his workshop? 1989? She held his shoulders, steadied him, and he dropped his eyes to the brown mark the tea had made on the rug.

"It's a mess," he said, shaking his head. "It's all in a mess."

Through the long front windows of the house, Del saw that her parents had returned from double-checking Cora's house. Her mother walked delicately, weaving and watching the sidewalk because of her bare feet, and her father had his arm around her shoulders. He looked at the air in front of him, speaking, filling his cheeks with air between each set of words.

"It's going to be all right," Del told Papie, taking his hand in hers. "We'll fix it."

"You?" His eyes traveled around on her face, searching for something.

"Adelaide," she said.

Her father followed her mother up the steps, leaning towards her terry cloth back, yearning towards her.

"I had a girl apprentice once went by that name. Made a pretty little chest, some marquetry on the drawers I showed her how to do."

Del nodded and smiled at him as her mother unlocked the front door. There was a bitter, smoke-laced edge to the air — the smell of autumn.

"She wasn't there, like you said," her father said as he came into the house. "But she had been there — all her furniture was out on the street. Was it like that when you went?"

Del shook her head. "No."

"Are you sure?" Her father was wide-eyed with worry and exhaustion.

"If her furniture was outside? Yes, I'm sure." So, Cora had seen the fire. So, she knew.

Her mother settled into the hall chair as Del picked up the photo of her sister her father had brought from across the lake, a photo from last Christmas, when it had snowed. Snowflakes clung to Cora's lashes, to the tips of the old fur pulled tight around her neck. She was looking up, trying to catch snowflakes on her tongue. She'd been getting so much better.

"If you know where she is," her father said, "you've got to tell us."

"Oh, Jesus, Dad. Obviously."

Del walked clear across the room, looked through the far window. A woman and her Irish setter walked past the wrought-iron fence that surrounded the Dobies' garden, the dog's coat flickering between the black bars. "I told you about Troy's sister —"

Her father sighed heavily. "I know, baby." He strode across the room and hugged her tightly. "I know. I'm scared of that too."

She tried to look him in the face and say it, but he kept ahold of her. She dug her chin into his shoulder, stared at the sickly azaleas. If Cora had seen the fire before disappearing, then that was confirmation: Reyna was the dead woman from her dream. Her dream was not a dream. And if the fire was what had released her — allowed her to leave — then they had to let her stay gone.

Del decided that once the police got there she would steer the conversation towards suicide: tell them how sick Cora was, list the names of her doctors. That way nobody would put a trace on Cora's phone, no APB's would go out with her picture and license plate. Even if they did end up connecting the Jeep to Troy's house, the bone fragments in the ashes would confirm their suspicions. There were too many other bodies, too much else going on.

"Suicide is not what I'm scared of," she said to her father.

He shook his head. "We can certainly pray."

"I did something." She looked at the rug. "No one had come to get Troy's sister, and —"

Her mother looked up from her hands. "You didn't tell Cora about her, did you?"

"No."

"Are you sure?"

"Jesus!" She stomped her foot, and the teaspoons rattled on the glass coffee table. "Of course I'm fucking sure! I'm not the one with dementia. She knew already. She already knew."

Her father picked up the tea tin and stared at it.

"She didn't kill herself," Del repeated.

Her mother swallowed, her unwashed hair flat against her scalp. "What did she tell you?"

"Cora said she had dreamed of a dead woman on the kitchen floor. She said that it was her fault."

Tess stood up from the chair so fast its back hit the wall behind. "I can't believe you! She tells you this and you keep it to yourself?"

"She told me yesterday. You weren't here, remember? I tried your cell. I had no idea where you were."

"And so you left her here alone?"

"Tess —" Her father tried to corral her, but Tess was pacing in a fury, walking straight past his outspread arms. "Calm down, honey."

"Don't fucking tell me to calm down! You left her here alone, Adelaide. You left her here!"

"I did. Right. I'm the one who left her."

Her father backed against the sofa with his hands out, signaling *stop.*

"Please, Tess," her father said. "Del, please."

She listened to her blood course through her ears. "I don't know why I even bother. We should all just fucking take the Fifth."

There were, however, some things that could not go unsaid. Some things that, kept bottled up, would poison you from the inside. It was necessary to say it. Necessary like vomit.

"I think Cora knew about Reyna," she said. "I think she's the dead woman in her dream. I think it isn't a dream. I think Cora's been to Troy's house since the storm. I think that's where she's been going at night. I think that's where she went."

"God — Jesus — that's where she's been going," her mother said. "She told me, she tried to tell me that that's where she goes when she leaves the house at night. Mother of God."

"Well, let's go there then," her father said.

Del shook her head, and her mother

stared at her, her lips locked between her teeth.

"What the hell do you mean?" her mother said.

Del looked outside again. A squad car had turned the corner and was rolling slowly towards them, the driver looking out of the window at the house numbers.

"She won't be there anymore."

"How could you possibly know that?" her father asked.

"Because the house isn't there anymore."

"What?"

"It burned down last night."

"Oh, God."

"The fire trucks were there when I went to see if Cora was at her place this morning."

"That burned house across the street?" her father said.

"I didn't want to tell you."

"Why in God's name not?" her mother shouted.

"I didn't want to scare you."

Her mother laughed once, a gutteral *ha*.

"Did she set it?" her father asked. "Do you think Cora set the fire?"

"I don't know," Del said, and it sounded like the truth as it left her mouth.

She didn't know anything, she realized.

All she knew was that there were roses there and roses here, Reyna burned and Cora gone, the Jeep missing and the bed cold. She didn't know when Cora had gone to Troy's last night, if she had. She didn't know if Cora had seen Del set the fire, or if she'd come only after, or when she had gone or where or how far. She was relying on words that had floated up out of someone else's nightmare. There had been no gun there, and she had only seen Reyna's body briefly, in the dark. Anyway, she didn't know how a shotgun to the face looked any different than a pistol, a grenade: there'd been no traces of the shot, only a face that was no longer a face, but more like an enormous wound. All she had were Anthony's words, *Shot herself full of buckshot,* and her father's weeks ago, *Well, the shotgun we thought was stolen has magically reappeared.* But she didn't have any more reason to disbelieve than to believe.

"You gave Cora the shotgun," she said to her father.

"What?"

"Troy's sister was killed with a shotgun."

It was as if she'd stuck a pin into a balloon.

"You think your sister killed the woman." Her mother said this flatly, the way Del

396

imagined she repeated things back to her patients, so that they would hear how crazy their thoughts sounded.

"I don't know what to think. You said the shotgun was missing when you came back to the city. And then you found it in Cora's laundry basket."

Her father wrapped his fingers around her wrist. "My poor baby."

She pulled her hand away. "Cora's strong. That's what you don't get. You think she's suicidal. You think she's gone." She threw her chin at the street, where the cops were slamming their doors, getting out onto the sidewalk. "And you better the hell tell them that. But just know that you're wrong. She was down here by herself, saving people in the heat. Burying dogs. Bringing people water. She's not going to give up now."

"That's not how trauma works," her mother said.

"I don't care how it works! I don't think we understand at all what she went through or what she's going through now. I don't think we have the first fucking idea."

"Language, Del." Her mother sank down into the little side chair by the door, and Del wanted to grab her. Wanted to wrap her hands around her mother's bony chest and shake.

"It's not like something's not been going to happen," her father said. "We've been waiting for something to happen. It just finally has."

"Listen —" Del said. "I'm just trying to help! I'm telling you it's possible Cora might just have left. She might have had a perfectly rational reason to go."

"Murder?" her mother laughed. "Arson?"

Her father sighed. "You're some hard on your sister, Adelaide."

"It's you who's hard on her. You defeat her! You already called the morgues."

"We can't turn our faces away from reality, Del," her mother said.

Del laughed.

The police were shuffling up the porch steps from their car, the creases of their pants shining greasily in the sun. The woman officer turned a knob on the radio clipped to her belt, and static pushed through the windows. Del went to open the door.

Tess had been so grateful for Joe's presence as they'd discussed suicide with the police, discussed the river, the lake, the bayou — all the places you could drown — that she'd invited him to stay the night. As he put his hands on her back, helped her up from a chair, she almost physically felt a weight lift off her. It was like the old days when, on the parade route or at the zoo, he would grab Cora, riding piggyback, and lift her up — little legs kicking — and settle the giggling girl on his own shoulders. Just the fact of his broad back in the worn-in undershirt, his hands opening a Barq's or scrubbing the stupid tile counter, had been a relief, and she'd felt herself go limp. Grief was infinite, though, wasn't it — something like love that, divided, did not diminish. And now, in the Dobies' bedroom, as he teetered on one leg pulling off his shoe, he seemed so burdened that she worried he might collapse.

She watched him in the mirror. She was brushing her teeth, the lines permanent now around her eyes, and she considered making a pact with God: to repent, to forgive, to ask forgiveness. If it would bring Cora back, she would fall on her knees in front of him, reciting the Act of Contrition. *Deus meus, ex toto corde paenitet me omnium meorum peccatorum.* She spat the toothpaste, rinsed. To bring her daughter back, she would put their home back together, regardless of what he had done, what she had done. She would move to the Northshore. She would make breakfast. She would keep her mouth shut. If it would bring Cora back, she would walk across the bedroom carpet, put a hand under his arm. If she did that, she knew Joe would straighten up and hold tight to her, and half of her wanted that badly. She was tired of hurting him, tired of the way his hand trembled on the back of his shoe. She would do penance. Did it matter that it wasn't really for their sake that she would do it? Did it matter that, in her heart, she knew that she would commit all her sins again?

Yes, her heart said. Yes, it mattered.

She dried her face, turned to him.

Joe, barefoot, straightened up and went to close the bedroom door.

She moved her lips, trying out the words: *I have sinned against you, whom I should love above all things.* Should love. Father Patin would tell her that sin drove one out of the embrace of God's love, and that was why she couldn't feel it, because she had not yet asked for forgiveness. Human love was only borrowed from the love that God had for us, he would say, but she still loved her children, didn't she?

When she looked at Joe, she felt only pity.

He looked at her from across the Dobies' bedroom, not taking his shirt off, not unbuckling his belt, like a houseguest. He knew he needed her permission to undress, to get into Laura and Dan's bed beside her, to regain his place. He was right, and then again, the fact that he was right made the wrongness of it all manifest. The fact that he would even ask, waiting there across the room, meant that this could not be fixed. He would always cede control. She would always take it.

She looked at him, not in the eyes, but at the fuzzy hair growing out of his scalp.

"I can't." She shook her head. She hedged. "Not tonight. Not yet. I'm sorry."

All he did was nod, and then he picked up his shoes and wandered into the hall, closing the door softly behind him.

FIFTY-SIX DAYS
AFTER LANDFALL
OCTOBER 24

SUNSET

Cora drove east out of the city, along Lake Borgne. During the storm, the Gulf had surged into the lake, and the lake had broken, foaming, over its banks as the wind drove it headlong across the marshes. The water had thrown its creatures up on land, and the deflated carcasses of snakes, nutria, muskrats, and alligators now lay among the shivered planks and bricks that had once been the stilted houses of fisherman.

As she passed through Bayou Sauvage, a sounder of wild boars wading in the water among the trees lifted their heads to watch the Jeep. Beyond the low, weed-eaten walls that bordered the bayou, the hulls of ships came into view — a whole flotilla beached like the navy of a vanquished nation. Wide-bottomed trawlers lay on their sides against the salt-dead shoulder, and the rusting riggings of shrimpers flew against the sky. One steel-hulled ship had been thrown high into the roadside cypresses, breaking through their heavy branches, until it had settled down onto the trees' trunks as if they were pedestals. Here, huge rags of saltwater prairie — four-foot deep, block-wide sections of marsh grass that the surge had torn out of the swamp — lay across the road. By now, they had been crushed and rutted down to the asphalt, but she still had to slow to cross the deep mud, watching the green marsh float by over the dry land while the blushing, still water of Lake St. Catherine glistened in the distance.

Finally, up ahead, the trusses of the bridge that would lead her over the Rigolets and out of New Orleans rose above the wreckage of the highway. Her hands began to shake. She pulled off along the rutted path that ran between the bridge's pilings and the red brick walls of the ruined fort. She got out of the Jeep and walked down the bank, past a storm-stripped tree and towards the water, until she was standing on a thick mat of driftwood, littered here and there with red milk crates and plastic buckets.

The surge had risen yards above her head, depositing sand and broken branches on top of the fort, crashing down on the ramparts, splitting them. White streaks of salt like dried tears striped the brick, and black stains poured from the cannon emplacements and into the water. She looked across the pass, low now, a narrow channel of calm water separating here from away. Out in the water, a cormorant stood on the post of an ancient pier, drying its wings.

Sheltered against the landside of the ruined fort, a dogwood shrub had survived the storm, flexible enough to bend down before the water and rise again when it had passed. Though everything around it was dead and fall was coming, she thought she saw glimmers of green on its red branches, and she picked her way to it over the flayed logs. At the end of each twig, new leaves were budding, and some had already unfurled. She reached out her hand for a shoot to keep as a charm. When she broke it, white sap oozed out, and she heard a cry.

Staggering back, Cora tripped, falling down on her knees in the drift of dead wood. A dog — brown chested with black fur matted to its back and jowls — was limping towards her from out of a cannon emplacement in the wall of the fort. She started to rise and run back towards the Jeep, but the dog was whimpering. It flinched every time it put its right leg down.

Just a yard or so away from her, it stopped, holding its leg up in the air, a thin line of red blood trailing down its foreleg from a ripped dewclaw.

"Come," she called to it, whistled. "Come here, buddy. Lemme see."

The dog came, but when she reached out to touch it, it shied away again, pressing its body against the ramparts. Cora went back to the Jeep. In the glove compartment, Troy's cousins had left beef jerky, Cheetos, a bottle of hot spring water, and she took them, opened up the dried meat, and called to the dog again.

"Look —" She held her hand out to it. "Come see what I got for you! I know you're hurt. I won't hurt you again."

The dog came. It wolfed the jerky, butted its heavy head against her leg, its hurt paw lifted. Opening the bottle of warm water, she crouched down and lifted the dog's paw onto her knee. When she poured the water over it, the dog flinched back but waited, and Cora poured the whole bottle out over the wound, rinsing the blood off into the sand. From her hair, she untied her bandana and wrapped it around its leg for a bandage.

"You want to come with me?"

The dog tilted its head, listening.

"I'm going away now. You wanna come?"

She opened the back hatch of the Jeep, threw her bag, full of all of the clean clothes she'd taken from the Dobies' and the money — the nearly ten grand she'd pulled from its hiding place in the ceiling of her closet — into the backseat, and patted the floor of the car, inviting the dog to jump.

"Come on now. There's nothing left for us here. We can be something else now."

The dog, though, backed away from her, then turned, trotted several steps towards its cave in the wall of the fort, and paused, lifting its injured paw and looking over its shoulder at her.

I am already dead, she thought she heard it thinking. *Dead before I died.*

But she was not. From the surface of the water, the bloody wash of dawn had lifted, and the cormorant beat at the air, taking flight across the pass. The dog loped off, hiding itself in the ruins. There was no hope of helping it, and so she gave up, got in the Jeep and crossed the bridge towards higher ground.

TUESDAY

OCTOBER 25

In Tess's dream, Cora stood on one of the turnarounds near the middle of the Causeway. The smoke hung thick around them as fog often did on fall mornings, obscuring the wavy dark line that would otherwise have been all that was visible of the distant shore. Tess was driving out to rescue her, wheels thumping rhythmic as a heartbeat over the breaks between the floating sections of the bridge. She kept passing mile marker eleven over and over again, and eventually, it occurred to her that she had gotten off the bridge itself and onto the disused cloverleaf that had served as a turnaround before the second span of the bridge was built — a closed loop just feet above the lake, which spread out under the overhang of smoke like molten pewter. She began to look for exits, but every ramp was flooded with a glassy film of water. She meant to plow through, but she could not gather the nerve, and so Cora waited. Up ahead, on that far turnaround, she stood, still as a statue, until she could wait no longer, and Tess had to watch as her daughter stepped over the concrete barrier and into the lake.

Tess had had patients who had experienced such things: a wave of cold passing through the skin on a hot July day, or a sudden bout of disorientation, an abrupt falling feeling that they recognized as announcements of loss, they said, even before the police came to the door. Early in her career she had believed them. Those stories had seemed to confirm something important, something that she increasingly strained to believe — that the world was of a piece, that an organizing principle greater than plain physics held sway over our lives. It was what had drawn her to Jung in college, his belief that future wars could enter dreams as yellow floods spreading across Europe and that golden scarabs could fly out of patients' heads to tap against the windows of his examining room.

At some point she had shed it all, though, or so she thought. She'd grown up, stopped going to church, stopped having patience for the mystical. Synchronicity became coincidence and confirmation bias. If a patient came to her with a story of "confirmed" premonition, she would explain that we project meaning backwards onto things that would have passed unremarked were they not followed by landmark events. She had settled into a more mature understanding of our minds — that our memories were constantly revised to reflect our present understanding, that any experience of order or wholeness was a construct created by our consciousness for its own comfort. The world did not signify, it was only given significance.

Still, she was having trouble seeing this morning, as if she had smoke in her eyes.

The day was beautiful, one of those bright blue, crisp autumn days that did their best to make up for the humid summer just passed. Del sat down on the sawn edge of the Dobies' porch and tried to let the sun wake her up. She had been half-asleep on the leather sofa, trying to recover a dream — a hot orange square surrounded in black metal — when Mrs. Fuller from around the block had knocked on the door with Cora's phone in her hand. The old Nokia looked like it had been backed over, and Del tried to imagine Cora letting it fall from her fingers onto the street. She would have had to put the key in the ignition and hold it in place while the engine turned over, then shift into drive. She would have heard the plastic cracking under her tires. At the end of the block, she would have had to decide whether to turn right or left, and somehow she couldn't see Cora doing all of this and then jumping off of the Mississippi River Bridge, as her mother had started saying she must have done. She rubbed her finger over the phone's cracked screen. She had to admit that it was reasonable for her parents to be afraid — that the fire might not have come as a relief, but only a release from her final obligation — but Del couldn't believe it. As Cora would have said, she couldn't feel it to be true.

She turned the phone over and stared at the street, quiet now — the clubs all closed, everybody off attending to their business. The musicians would be sleeping off their hangovers, and people all across the city would be sorting out the salvageable from the ruined. In New York, it was ten o'clock already. Magda would be slipping off her shoes under her desk while Phillip stalked through the showroom. Zack had told her he was preparing for a trial this week, so she imagined him hunched over files or leaning forward towards a conference table, his tortoiseshell glasses on. She liked it when he wore his glasses.

She took her own phone out of her pocket. Zack answered on the fourth ring. "Adelaide Hortense Boisdoré. Well my, my."

Hearing his voice, she felt his tongue move against her upper lip. She put her hand to her mouth, took it away.

"Hey, Zack." She wasn't sure what she'd meant to say. Really, she'd just wanted to remind herself that he still existed. "How are you?"

"How are *you*?" he said.

"I'm really sorry."

He cleared his throat, and she could hear him nodding, feel his hand at the back of her neck. "We should probably dispense with the apologies and just stop doing that."

"I guess so," she said, and her voice broke on the word.

"Mmm-hmmm."

She waited, listening for something on the other end of the line that she could read for his expression, his posture, whether he would have stepped into her then, negating everything, and let her feel the heat of his body against his skin. But all she heard was an insulated door closing.

"I want not to lose you more than I want to fuck you, you know."

411

"I know," she said. She would not cry.

"I want it to be okay for you, when NOLA is spick-and-span again, to come back. I just want everything to go back to being the same."

On his end of the line, an arriving elevator chimed its electronic bell.

"Listen, Zack —"

"Do you think spick-and-span is some kind of racial slur against Latino domestics?"

The elevator disgorged a hubbub of voices.

"This was a stupid time to call." She swallowed. Her face was getting hot. "You're at work. I'll let you get back."

"If you hang up now, I'm never speaking to you again," he said, so matter-of-fact she believed him.

"Okay."

The lobby doors opened, and more people passed him, talking. *Rubenstein,* a woman said. "Dailey." She could see his half-ironic, half-respectful nod. "So, look. I do think I owe you an apology for the car. I wasn't listening. I was railroading you. And what you said about Cora —"

"She's missing," she said.

"Fuck."

"Just thirty-six hours or so, but that doesn't mean anything."

"I know you're worried."

"I am."

She listened to him breathing, the patient slowness of his lungs filling, emptying. On Royal, a car passed, throwing up dust.

"Zack, I think she left because of that woman, because of Reyna. I did something —"

"Do you need me to go to my office?"

She nodded and stared down the empty street.

"That's a yes?"

"Yes."

She listened to him walking down the hallway, his feet on that diamond-patterned carpet. She'd used to love meeting him for lunch at his office. They would sit on the floor behind his desk, basking in the sun that came straight in through the big windows, and look out over the Hudson at the breadth of New Jersey, dotted with cities, smokestacks, bridges like snagged threads, scuffed patches of swamp and parkland. Her own office had been a windowless cube, no escaping from it, except through the art. There, if she needed to get away, she had to slip down to storage, into the cold, humidity-controlled air. On her last day, she had run there, her hands shaking, feeling like she was escaping to a bomb shelter

413

where the headlines, the phones, the designers bitching about install dates, couldn't get to her. *I think you'd better take a break,* Phillip had clucked. Downstairs, the only sound was of the freight elevator going up, its chain uncoiling from the ground.

She had kicked off her shoes and walked up and down the aisles of archival boxes. She'd just needed to look at something beautiful, to breathe, to be nowhere. When she found lot 503, she climbed up on the lower shelf and clawed down the box. Hokusai's *Thirty-Six Views of Mount Fuji,* a rare, complete, and undamaged set. *Ukiyo-e* prints, Magda had told her, had fallen out of favor for a while, and people had used them for packing material, like old newspapers, their headlines now meaningless: *Nagin: Entire City Will Soon Be Underwater. New Orleans Shelters to be Evacuated. Katrina Destroys Entire Towns.* This lot was in perfect condition, though, and as she lifted the top from the box, she saw the bright, barely faded colors through the scrim of acid-free tissue. *Under the Wave off Kanagawa* was the first image of the series. Fran had had a poster of it in her dorm room at school, and Del had spent many hours, stoned, staring at it. Fuji, someone had told her, was the Japanese symbol of

414

immortality or the fountain of youth, something like that, and she'd liked to gesticulate with the joint while she interpreted the image, claiming that the wave, towering up like a mountain to crash down on the fishermen in their boat, represented mortality, but that Mount Fuji — small, distant, but at the compositional center — was a reminder of a solid and permanent world beyond. Under the scrim of paper, though, she could hardly distinguish the fishing boat from the wave itself, and Fuji was lost in the distance.

She wasn't wearing gloves — she hadn't even washed her hands after lunch — but still she plucked at the corner of the tissue with her fingernails and pulled it off. The real woodblock was so much better than the reproduction: the blues were strong, and up close she could see the slight stippled variations in color that showed how the block had been re-inked and reapplied. She had never noticed before how the streaked snow on Fuji's peak reiterated the ripples of the water below the boat or how the death's-head faces of the fishermen recapitulated the foam breaking in gouts off the head of the wave and the snow falling in the distance on the mountain.

She saw, then, that the mountain was not

a counterpoint to the wave but a reflection of it, and that its distance, its smallness, the way the wave wrapped around it made it a weaker reflection — it was part of the mortal world. Nothing was exempt, after all. She'd picked up the print and laid it on its face in the top of the box, then pulled the next sheet of tissue off the *Red Fuji*, whose lower slopes were flooded by a blue forest. In the next print, Fuji was threatened by clouds while bright red lava fractured its shoulders. She turned through them all — Fuji hidden under a bridge, Fuji disappearing into the snow, Fuji reflected in a lake, drowning in a river. Magda had told her that *ukiyo-e* meant pictures of the floating world, and she finally understood what that meant: that even a mountain was ephemeral, something that existed as we perceived it and so disappeared when we turned away. More than that, though, the mountain — everything, even love, even home — was mortal. Snow would eventually wear Fuji away, its eruptions would break it apart. Eventually even the stones would turn to dust. Nothing could go back to being the same, but she couldn't say that to Zack. He wouldn't want to hear it.

She got up off the porch and went back inside. On his end of the line, a door shut

416

with a click. Zack cleared his throat.

"Is this a landline?"

"Yeah," she said.

"I gotta say, I was happier when I thought you were calling me for me."

"I was." If she had been there in his office, she would have put her hand on the back of his neck, she would have laid her head on his shoulder. She took a deep breath. "I was, Zack."

"But you have a legal question."

She let the breath out. "The body, it was in her friend's house. So I burned it down."

"Wow?" She heard the creak of his desk chair as he fell into it.

"Yeah. After I dropped you off."

"Did you use an accelerant?"

She almost laughed. "That's your question?"

He paused. His mouth would be twisted inside his neat beard. "You asked my advice."

"Lighter fluid." She walked to the end of the Dobies' hall, walked back again.

"Did you spread it around? Toss it on the couch, the walls, et cetera?"

"I dumped it on a roll of paper towels and lit a matchbook and opened the gas and left."

"Good," he said.

Now she laughed.

"Yes, that's good. This all went down in the kitchen?"

"Yes," she said.

"And this is where the body was."

The smell of the house was still in the back of her throat, and Del pressed her arm across her face, closed her eyes.

"Yes." She ran herself a glass of water. "Reyna. Her name was Reyna. She was on the floor of the kitchen."

"How was she killed?"

"Shotgun." She said, through a mouthful of water. "My dad gave Cora a shotgun to protect herself with, before they left her."

He sighed through his nose. "Why are you so sure Cora did this? Aren't there hundreds of shotguns in New Orleans? I mean, it's the South, right?"

"Cora told me she was responsible. Now she's missing."

"She told you what, exactly?" Zack expelled a heavy breath. "Look, even if you burned the house down, they'll find the shot. And the remains will be identifiable."

"I know, but I couldn't just leave her there. She was a woman. She had children. And Cora had been going to visit her at night, walking across the city alone." Del stared through the window at the Dobies' dying garden. "I don't know if Cora really killed her or if she just thinks she's responsible for it. I don't know what actually happened, but I called the police, I talked to the DMORT, and Reyna was just being left there. It was wrong. It was so fucking wrong, Zack."

"So you committed a felony," he said. "You burned down somebody's house. You could have set fire to the whole neighborhood."

"There was no one else around. The neighborhood is flooded out."

"So you committed a felony," he said again.

"Yeah."

"Did you give the DMORT people your name?"

"No."

"Okay, and did anyone see you there?"

"I don't think so."

"But now Cora's gone."

"Yeah."

"And the cops are looking for her."

Del closed her eyes again. "If I only knew where she was. If I could just reach her, tell her to stay away. Nobody will come looking. They think she's jumped off a bridge or something." She pulled Cora's phone out of her pocket, pulled out the SIM card, and put it down the garbage disposal. On the other end of the line, Zack was quiet.

"Are you okay, Del?"

Nobody had asked her that, she realized, since she'd arrived. She had to think about her answer as you might take an inventory of your pain after an accident, to see if any bones were broken.

"I don't know."

"I'm sorry to scare you, but you need to know that if they do decide to bring it, shit may go down."

She nodded.

"You might be okay. From the news, it doesn't sound like they're too concerned right now about tracking down individual bad actors. Are you sure the house went up?"

"Bad actors," she repeated.

"Did you see the house actually catch on fire, Del?"

"Yeah. I went back afterwards to look for Cora. The fire trucks were there."

"Fuck, Del. You went back?"

The tears jumped into her eyes, and she had to swallow to keep him from hearing her cry.

"I'm sorry," he said, talking in his lawyer voice again. "Del, I'm sorry, truly. Like I said, it may not come to anything. The

420

police have their plates full and the insurance adjustors sure as hell do. You just sit tight. Keep your head down. I'll try to get there as soon as I can."

"That's okay, Zack. Really. Stay where you are."

"I don't think it's really your prerogative to tell me what to do."

He laughed once, bitterly, and she listened for a while to the noises the house made, the ticking of its clocks, the creaking of its boards. Zack's chair squeaked lightly as he swiveled.

"I've got a trial going on right now, but when it's over, I'm coming back down."

She stayed quiet. She could almost smell him, his sharp blue smell of deodorant and Tide.

"And meanwhile answer your fucking phone."

"Yes, sir."

"Alright then?"

She nodded. "Alright."

The line went dead, but she listened for a little while longer, as if, with the phone against her ear, she might be there with him on top of Manhattan, watching the sun slant across the river, and they could see ahead of them for miles and miles.

Vincent had been watching the cars pass from the portico, where he was sitting in an uncommonly comfortable rocking chair. Esplanade Avenue, think of that. Drinking a glass of good ice tea on Esplanade Avenue. Inside, they were talking, Sylvia yammering away, he imagined, but he was content to rock and wait.

Cars passed, Sunday driving, their tires peeling — *woosh, woosh* — off the pavement. He listened for the sound of distant hooves and hoped the vegetable man would pass, the horse cart with its music of iron and leather, the voice calling *Sooweet potatoes. CoLARDS. CreOLE tamatas.* He had a wild hankering for a sweet potato pie. Not Sylvia's, though hers were good, creamy, just enough of that spice. He wanted a pocket pie from Moe's. He could taste it — a crackle of icing sugar, the crust crumbling into the thick filling. He got out of his chair — damn knees acting up — and went down the steps. No need to tell the ladies good-bye; he'd be back before they finished chatting, and with a nice surprise.

He passed under the oak trees, jingling the change in his pocket. He had plenty money, if a pie was still a nickel. Could maybe even stick around 'til Sheep's opened and get him a stuffed crab. He couldn't remember the last time he'd had one of those pies. He knew they'd gone for one not long after Joe was born. He'd smeared a little of the russet cream across the baby's lips before Sylvia could swat away his hand.

He couldn't recall, but it seemed to have been a while since Joe had been so little. Even the trees had gotten older. They seemed sickly, their leaves turning brown. Just across Rampart, they stretched up their arms like mourners over an empty lot, but when they'd torn that building down he couldn't say. Up ahead was the gray rise of the damned interstate highway they'd built over top of Claiborne Avenue. Already, the houses closer to it were in a bad way, alligator vine pulling them plank from plank. He wasn't going anywhere near that highway, though he realized that was exactly what he'd been planning to do: thinking to walk down Claiborne, catch the streetcar, when anybody knew the tracks had been pulled out of the ground in 1953. Shaking his head, he turned up a side street where the trees were replaced by telephone poles — a line of them like Greek crosses. He worried where to put his feet.

Once he was deep into the neighborhood, the day went quiet, almost too quiet, like something had sucked the sound out of the air. There were no Sunday drivers, and the parked cars were scarce and sad looking, dirt on their windows. It was a fine day, but all the porch swings and rockers he saw were empty, and as he put one foot in front of the other, he realized that one thing contributing to the quiet was the softness of his own footfalls. A crust of earth maybe an inch thick covered the sidewalk and spread into the grass of people's front lawns. He shook his head to loosen his cogs. He looked up at the sky — bright blue.

Moe's was on Claiborne, a corner shop with little bells that bashed against the glass door, and when the pies were coming out hot, there'd be a line it seemed like had the whole neighborhood waiting in it. Outside on the neutral ground under the oaks, there'd be men in suits bringing their pink tongues up to catch a flake of sugar from their moustaches, a lady in a church hat dabbing a handkerchief at her painted lips, beribboned children running around hollering and their minders watching out the bottoms of their eyes like let them play because sure there would be time enough for solemnity.

Yes, it did feel like he was carrying a whole barrow full of rocks around in his stomach, and he couldn't be sure of why. He wasn't wearing a hat, and sweat worked in itching rivulets through the little hair he had left. Maybe he was dreaming. Only in dreams and graveyards were things so quiet. Marching on he saw somebody had painted crosses on the houses. One house, painted pink, even had written on it what passed for an epitaph: *Dead dog under porch.* He could smell the death too, but he couldn't hear his feet touching down on pavement. He must be dreaming, he reckoned, except he didn't feel like he was dreaming.

Here came St. Bernard, and he turned, watching his feet for something to go strange, but the shadow just lengthened, his laces flopped against the sides of his shoes. All was as it should be until he looked up: a highway roaring above where Claiborne should be. He wasn't sure if he'd be able to eat. Had they? They had. They had built it here, despite who all had gone down to city hall and pleaded with the women there who just shook their heads. He himself had had his hat in his hands, but it had been like talking into the wind — you could just about see your words whipping away. Boh Brothers had come with their wrecking machines, and the oak trees' roots had clawed the air. He kept walking. That day he'd been to Moe's in that great crowd, hadn't the dark-skinned shopgirl cried, while outside the wrecking machines lifted pieces of steel into the sky?

Here he was come to the edge of the freeway. Here was the gray roadway running above and a blue sign, marking the surface road — N. Claiborne. N for Not. Not Claiborne. Claiborne dug up. The neutral ground turned to cement. The oak trees bulldozed. To his right — he could barely bring himself — Moe's stood shuttered. Plywood boards on the windows, on the door, where the spray-paint cross said *9/12, RATS, 2 DB, D-MOR* meaning something but not signifying, and as he stood looking up at the cars running over the interstate over the concrete over the killed grass and the gone trees, he realized that he was a long way from home.

They sat on the lower gallery of their house together, looking at the fallen magnolia, because that's what Tess wanted. He had promised himself that he would stop bending to her, but he'd still let the branch spring back up against the kitchen ceiling when she asked him to, laid down his saw at her say-so. She thought Cora was going to just wander back into the yard, maybe scratch at the door to be let in. But *Let's just sit for a minute,* she said, and so he sat. The leaves shuddered as a breeze moved through.

"Tell me," he said.

She shook her bent head — a knob of bone above the boatneck collar, two impastos of white running almost to her shoulders. "I called again just before I left. Her phone's going straight to voice mail, and the cops have nothing on her license plate. They think we should print posters, hang them on all the telephone posts in Christendom."

"Like a lost dog," he said.

She looked up, as if she could still see the magnolia where it used to stand, the cones studded with ruby seeds like a twelfth-century mace, but there was only sky there, crisscrossed with distant power lines.

"They're going to call with even the tiniest hint of anything, but I wouldn't hold my breath." She slapped her thighs and went back to looking at the empty piece of sky.

"Her car," he said. "It's technically registered to you. If we called it theft, would that —"

"No. Are you kidding?" She licked her

lips. The light glinted off her varnished skin. "We're going to keep mum to the police about a fire she most certainly set, but you want to have her — if they can find her — arrested for auto theft? You must be out of your fucking mind."

"I shouldn't have assumed, last night —"

"You didn't assume. I invited you."

He tried laying his hand on her thigh, but her quads tightened. She was hard, as if she were encased in a smooth shell, like a pecan. He wanted to squeeze her in his fist against a stone until she cracked. Instead, he took his hand back into his own lap.

The yard was desolate. Oak leaves were strewn across it, and the grass had died in the places where water stood, but the roses were blooming. Hard little blossoms had opened among what leaves remained on the canes, as if the bushes were determined to bear one last crop of fruit before dying. It had been nearly two months now since they'd left, and he suddenly remembered the herbs that he had pushed under the porch where they'd be safe. He got up, bent down, and pulled loose the section of lattice. Powdery gray sticks and limp leaves flopped over the terra-cotta.

He clutched the porch and laid his head on the backs of his hands, his stomach tightening like a fist. She didn't ask him what was wrong. He stood up and walked halfway across the grass. She just stared at the place where the tree was not, and he wanted to bear down on her, the stone biting into the meat of his hand.

"Tess, you need to talk to me. If we're going to get through this, if we have any hope —"

She grimaced so he knew he had done it — and if you didn't peel it properly, the pecan, blades of bitter pith would slice between your teeth.

"If you want to talk to me, that is," he tried, backing off, but it was too late. "If that's what you need."

"I slept with Augie Randsell," she said.

He walked away from her, but before he'd even reached the fence, the words caught up with him. He crouched, as if to inspect the grass, and tried to smile. Jamming his knees into his belly to smooth out the sudden pain in his gut, he slotted a piece of split-end grass between his fingers and looked at the brown and sandy grains of the soil. It had to be an ulcer, something. It wasn't like a person could actually feel his heart break.

"I'm sorry, Joe. I am," she said. "I didn't mean to hurt you, but I can't seem to avoid

429

it. And I don't think I'm going to be able to avoid it going forward, even if I do everything right from here on out."

He had expected this all along, he supposed. From the very first moment, when he'd noticed her sitting on the edge of the bathtub in Marty Hopkins's living room in SoHo: a displaced Uptown girl unclasping her gold bracelet and hiding it in her pocket. He had never had a secure grip on her, whoever she was. She had only ever given him coats to hold, furs and skins. Sheep's clothing.

"I never could. Unless I tried, tried, tried. And I've got to say, I'm exhausted from it. The whole weight of everything has always been on me, and —"

He looked up from the grass to see her hand, scissored at the base of her throat. He was a harness, she was saying, a millstone. She had always been the provider, according to her; even when he'd had successes, it was her "connections" (she'd never dare say race) and her money — her daddy's money — they lived off. He should have rejected it out of hand, that day she'd put the bank book in front of him — a quarter of a million dollars, just lying there, not worked for, not even by Millard, but harvested from other people's sweat and dying, while Millard sat at the top of the Plaza Tower in the air-conditioning. It was obscene, and he had felt dirty, looking up from the number scribbled in the vinyl book at her, standing across the kitchen table, her robe gapping. *Gold digger,* he called himself, but that was a word for women. *You can do your work,* she'd said, and he'd listened to her, *Yes, ma'am*'ed her like a fucking houseboy. He told himself the money had nothing to do with anything. Told himself he'd married her because she smelled like jasmine. Told himself he loved her because she was the kind of person — she'd been the kind of person then — who leaned over, her robe wide and breasts hanging like ripe figs in the lacy neck of her slip, and said he could quit his mind-numbing job. He'd believed it, even: believed love was her sun-buttered body on the floor of his hot attic room, her finger tracing the lines of his sculptures, her face in the auditorium when he graduated art school and no one in his family had come. He'd believed the money was their money, the house their house, had greeted his father at the front door with a Baccarat tumbler in his hand. *Set yourself up right, boy,* his father had said, and he'd believed that too, despite the snarl in his father's voice. He'd believed it though he himself had brushed the passbook from the table and bent Tess over it and pushed her robe up and screwed her like he had something to prove.

She was still talking, and he wondered if she would get around to asking for forgiveness. Whether she'd blame it on her stress, whether she would say it was some sort of accident, as if, had the fence rail collapsed at Sol's party on Sunday, he might have wound up with his dick inside Monica Selvaggio. Tess was too smart to claim this was some new thing, that it meant nothing. He'd seen them through the window of that McDonald's on the evacuation route, she and Augie sitting at an orange table in the overwhelming lights. When she'd begun to choke on a piece of crouton, he hadn't been able to reach her, so quick was Augie's attentive leap, and when Augie brought her water with his alcoholic tremor, her hand had covered his on the paper cup. They had looked into each other's eyes as if they'd forgotten Joe was out there, guarding his sleeping father in the dark parking lot. You could be sure that they hadn't seen him watching through the window, blinded as they were by their own reflections in the glass.

Joe put his head between his knees, into

the dirt-salt stink of his blue jeans — it had to be some sort of stress-related ulcer. Maybe they'd been fucking since Madge died, and Augie had been snubbing them this whole time in order to avoid having to face him in public. Maybe it had been going on for years, and they'd only been waiting to tell him until there wasn't anything left to lose. But did it really matter when they'd started fucking? She had always blushed at the sight of Augie, a middle-aged woman in a middle-aged haircut blushing when a middle-aged man laid a hand on her crêpey arm. If she was walking towards the door, still in her apron fifteen minutes after the party started, and if it was Augie and Madge, Augie double fisting bottles of "claret" from his "cellar," Madge in one of her sweaters, Tess's face would light up like Rudolph's red fucking nose.

He vaguely heard the words his wife was saying: "— capable of surprising myself. I don't have to be president of the damned universe. I know you think I do, but I don't. It's not interesting. It's not pleasurable. And I think I deserve some pleasure in my life. Even now. Even still. We don't have all that much time left, Joe."

Joe knew he had been settled for — she didn't need to say it. *Dr. Eshleman,* Augie would greet her. *Mrs. Boisdoré to you, Mr. Randsell.* It made him livid. She thought Augie was her better — certainly his better, because of the money, the name, the skin (though she'd never dare say it), the god-damned tacky way he flew his Rex flag out of season — but Augie was not even her equal. Still, Tess had only left her clan for Joe's because Augie had chosen Madge instead of her. She had wanted Augie from the first, and Joe knew it. He'd seen it the first time he'd seen them together, known it maybe even before then, since that night he'd picked her up from the Proteus ball, just before the rain. As he'd stood beside the door to the Municipal Auditorium, holding the umbrella like some chauffeur ready to escort her safely into his father's car, he'd seen her come tripping from the far end of the long, plain, lamplit corridor, looking back again and again as she clutched her half-fallen mink against her shoulder. She had never stopped looking back.

Del quit picking at the grout between the tiles on the Dobies' kitchen counter and finally put her hands on the keyboard. *Cora, I hope* — she typed, deleted, typed again, and waited for the words to come. She had been staring at the cursor for so long that her heart had synchronized with it. She deleted her sister's name, retyped it.

She reached into her pocket and fingered the sharp edge of Cora's phone, then clicked back to her inbox: a flyer from Bloomingdale's, an invitation to a loft party in Williamsburg, a note from Zack, saying his trial would probably last another week or two, but that she should call him anytime. She searched for the last e-mail Cora had sent her when they were all still in Houston, but she only got as far as *My Adela* before she had to go get herself a beer. She could hear her sister's voice as clearly as if she was in the room.

On 10/10/05 Cora Boisdoré, <thegoldenwood@hotmail.com> wrote:

My Adela,
So Mrs. Randsell's dead. Mom comes out to the pool where they've put me with a bucket of rum and sits down on the lounge chair, says, Honey, she didn't make it, I'm sorry. Puts her hand on my head at least before she started bitching about sunscreen. I knew it was going to happen. I knew it. Even before the stroke, Mrs. Randsell said — when we were still on Felicity Street — that it

would happen. Said she'd never see the city again. I won't either, of course. None of us will. Even when we were sitting out on Uncle Augie's lawn, drinking coffee every day before I went out into the flood, I wasn't there anymore. None of us were. We had already stopped existing.

I'm trying to forget it all, like she said. If I could, I'd like to replace everything I saw — everything I did — with something else: histories, the world before we ruined it. To see, instead of Vin's suburb, a copse of sweet gums at the end of a row of cotton, strung with spiked fruit. To see, instead of cotton, the swamp that was drained to plant it — bald cypresses bending their knees above the water, tossing their wispy heads. I don't really get anywhere, though. A blink of a better world, then nothing. Just blank. Just fine. "Fine, fine, I'm fine," I say until I almost start to think it's true. That's the way Mom and Dad are, constantly. As if they're oblivious to the fact that for weeks their lives have been draining into the Gulf with the floodwater. They don't understand that this is the way ghosts live, among the memories of the things they've lost, haunting houses and neighborhoods that are no longer theirs, maybe no longer there at all. A haunting of brass bands and churches, a haunting of buttermilk drops and purple plastic pearls strung from telephone lines. Soon, though, they'll see. They'll understand the quick shock of ruin.

Dead already, she said. Dead before we died. We thought she was fucking nuts, sent her away, but it's true: you only have to look in the mirror to know it, look around at these exiles who keep coming by with jambalaya and tissues, dressed up in lipstick and sunhats to look like the living.

It turns out sacrifice doesn't get you shit, you know. Whatever you do — it doesn't matter. Even with your heart raised up in the priest's hands, the crops fail. And it continues to beat, they continue to serve you chicken, expect your "participation," expect you to shower and dry with the towels they wash and fold. Mom takes me to buy shoes appropriate for a funeral, and I nod my head. I am trying to tolerate, you see. Since you asked me how I was.

C.

Del pushed the stool back and ran up the

stairs two at a time. In Dan's gym, she turned on the light and looked around. Her own wide-eyed face stared out of the foggy mirror of the disassembled vanity. Her suitcase yawned open, and her shoes were kicked off between the door and the bed. There was Cora's empty rose vase, Cora's mug of cold tea, Cora's laptop in plain view on a side table jammed into the corner, just sitting there next to a couple of books, an untouched newspaper, a jar of pens. She fought her way through the furniture and popped the computer open. The screen was clouded with mildew, but it turned on with a hum. She wiped it down with her shirt, opened Cora's Outlook. A long list of boldfaced e-mails appeared on the screen.

She wanted to shake the computer in her parents' whining faces. *I don't know what else you want us to do, sweetheart. We're just going to have to prepare ourselves.* She picked her way back across the room and closed the door, sat down on the floor with the computer. She opened Cora's sent mail folder and watched the messages load — just a dozen or so, dated between September nineteenth and the twenty-ninth. She hit the reload button once, then again, but nothing new appeared on the screen. She clicked on Cora's final reply to Troy, on the twenty-ninth — just one sentence, *I told you I can't* — and as she scrolled down, trying to see what Cora couldn't do, Mrs. Randsell's name leapt out at her, then Reyna's. She took a deep breath, closed her eyes, and pressed the down arrow. She would start at the beginning.

On 9/6/05 Troy Holyfield, <troyward7@yahoo.com> wrote:

Cora, we are safe in Rome by my auntie. Please reach us as soon as you can at (319)709-6984 to tell us that you are okay. Don't try my mobile because they are not working. I am feeling a lot of guilt for allowing myself to take your Jeep.

On 9/8/05 Troy Holyfield, <troyward7@yahoo.com> wrote:

We have not heard from you and there is no answer on your house phone and this makes me worry that something happened. I ran into this friend of mine Russell who just got out and he says the police are going house to house forcing people out and they're arresting some, I guess for ignoring the evacuate order. I hope this is not the case with you and that you just went by Mrs. Randsell, like

439

you said you would do in case of an emergency. Call me if you can. My mobile is not working, so use the house (319)709-6984

On 9/10/05 Troy Holyfield, <troyward7@yahoo.com> wrote:
Please call if you can. (319)709-6984

On 9/14/05 Troy Holyfield, <troyward7@yahoo.com> wrote:
Listen, Cora, maybe you are not getting these messages, or you don't want to get them, which I understand as what we went through together was like being in war where they say you either become brothers or you never want to see them again, but I need your help. I called the place on the card the medics gave me to check in on my sister they don't have record of her. No way of saying where she has gone to. I call the police, I call Charity. The line's disconnected. I put her name on one of those boards they have on the internet for people who are missing, put her name with the Red Cross but nothing's turned up. Call me, please. I am at (319)709-6984, and I also got a new mobile (319)867-3852.

On 9/14/05 Troy Holyfield,
<troyward7@yahoo.com> wrote:
I know you feel guilt, Cora, but there is no need. You should see how good the boys are. It's all over their face. All I need you to send is one word that you are all right and I will stop trying to reach you.

On 9/17/05 Troy Holyfield,
<troyward7@yahoo.com> wrote:
They say they are letting people back in to check on their houses, and I wish for you that this is what has happened, that your folks went in and found you and now are in your dads car on the road going out of town, at least you have dry feet and clean clothes and water. For me I wish that you were here with us. The boys are starting school again and I am looking for some work. I wish peace for us all and health and safety and air-conditioning and a plate of Wallace's fried oysters aioli. I don't know if what I wish is possible or ever will be but I wish it anyway.

On 9/22/05 Troy Holyfield,
<troyward7@yahoo.com> wrote:
Please contact me to let me know you

are safe and that you have gotten out before this next hurricane touches down.

On 9/24/05 Cora Boisdoré <thegoldenwood@hotmail.com> wrote: Troy, please do not worry, I am safe in Houston with my family.

On 9/24/05 Troy Holyfield <troyward7@yahoo.com> wrote: Thank the lord girl. The boys want to hear your voice. They have been asking if you call, and I tell them, like I tell them about their mama, that you call after they're in bed and are going to come up to see them soon. I haven't told them I don't know how to find her. I don't know really what to say. So I say you and their mama both call and ask after them and you want to know how they behave in school and that you are going to bring Tyrone his blanket he left at your house when you come visit, which might be some time since I told them the airport is down and you have to see about your own folks. Willy came home yesterday with a picture he drew of you and his mama, both of you with wings on like angels and he said it was so you could fly here to see us. If you could call after they're in bed I would appreciate.

House: (319)709-6984
Cell: (319)867-3852

On 9/24/05 Cora Boisdoré <thegoldenwood@hotmail.com> wrote:
Troy, you should prepare them not to see me or Reyna again.

Del exhaled hard. She had been holding her breath, she realized, barely reading, just scanning for that name. She backed up, reread Troy's e-mail, realizing she'd barely understood half of what he'd written. *Like I tell them about their mama. Both of you with wings.*

In the eye of a storm, there was silence. Unlike other so-called silences, with their ticking clocks, bird noise, distant engine rumble, this silence was true and total. The cloud walls rose up to meet a perfect patch of sky, and you could hear your blood rushing in your ears. Joe had heard stories of people who'd lashed themselves to trees after their houses went under, who lifted their heads when the winds died to find their families gone and the branches filled instead with animals: alligator and squirrel,

443

bobcat and goat, moccasin curled up beside muskrat like the lion and the lamb. This was no eye, but still all he heard was a constant ringing in his ears.

Tess's mouth was moving. Her hands gripped the back of the empty rocking chair they'd stationed in the portico, where his father had been sitting when they'd last seen him. She pointed at his shirt pocket. Her shoulders rose and heavily fell. Joe looked at her fangs, the fur on her bony arms. He backed away, down the stairs, across the lawn. He started the truck. She was moving towards him, slowly. Stalking him.

On the forums, they said that wandering could be occasioned by a hallucination or by a need. Hunger, thirst, lust, habit. The belief that the LO was expected at work, the suspicion that home was not really home. You, the CG, were supposed to label the doors of the house — BATHROOM, KITCHEN, BEDROOM. A stop sign might discourage outdoor journeys. You were supposed to purchase a packet from a company called Home Safe, with iron-on labels for the LO's clothes.

Joe idled the truck down Esplanade, looking down the side streets. When they had walked around the corner to Esplanade from the Dobies', his father had seemed to

know where he was. *It's a fine house, Joseph.*
He had squeezed the slice of lemon into the
go-cup of ice tea they'd picked up from Port
of Call. *You got anything sweet?* Maybe it
was the caffeine that had done it. You were
supposed to keep the LO hydrated and fed.
He'd had a boiled egg for breakfast but it
was past lunchtime now. In the distance, a
church bell tolled one, two. His father
always liked to talk about how they would
go down Claiborne after church when he
was little, back before the city destroyed it.
Get a stuffed crab at Sheep's, maybe a
pocket pie. *You got anything sweet?* Joe put
his foot on the gas, ran the blinking yellows
all the way down to the I-10. Sheep's had
been to the right. He turned.

Under the interstate, the corpses of
flooded-out cars sat in long lines of eternal
bumper-to-bumper traffic. Their windows
and paint jobs were all clouded with a thin
coat of mud, and doors and trunks had been
left open — an exodus caught in the mud
while the parted sea towered trembling
beside them, the Israelites running, the red
water crashing down on the heels of the last
child pulled up the bank. Waking in the hot
cab of the truck that morning he'd come
searching for Cora had felt a little like waking in the Sinai — families burdened with

445

trash bags and coolers picked their way across a desert of mud crisscrossed with torn power lines. But there was no Moses here leading these people out of bondage, no milk and honey on the other side. Those were all just fables — lies to get you through.

He'd told Tess they'd turned him back at the bridge because he knew she wouldn't believe the truth, but even that she hadn't believed. A woman of the water, Tess would never know deserts. She thought he should have tried harder, thought he'd backed down. *Why didn't you tell them about Cora?* she wanted to know, as if Blackwater would have sent out a search party. She wanted to make everything about responsibility. About trust. She believed that what separated them was thin and moveable — Du Bois's gossamer veil — but it was more like a barrier of bulletproof glass. The truth was, she had her world, he had his, and their words came to each other muffled and distorted by what stood between. That was why he'd lied to her: there was no way he could ever make her understand. He honestly hoped she never would. That she would never have to watch him be pushed, handcuffed, into one of their prison vans.

You didn't want to find her. Tess kept saying. *You didn't want to find her.* Implying: *You don't want to find her now.* But he did. His foot was off the gas, his eyes were wide open. He wanted to find his people, hold them close, never let them go again. Could she say the same?

As he approached St. Louis No. 1, he spotted a gray-and-brown figure moving out among the disabled cars, and he pulled the truck up onto the sidewalk, rolled down the window and squinted through the shade. The old man had his back to him, and he was moving away through the cars, trying one door handle after the other, peering through the windows. Joe got out of the truck, stood a minute while his eyes adjusted to the shadow. Blue shirt, serge pants. It was his father, alright. Thirty yards or so away, Vincent was reaching in through the broken window of an old Lincoln, fumbling for the handle.

"Pop?"

He withdrew his hand, looked at Joe, reached in again through broken glass.

"Mr. Boisdoré?" Joe shouted. "Vincent Boisdoré?"

His father looked towards him, then turned away.

The fenders pulled at Joe's pants legs as he wove between cars. His father was still popping handles, looking at his right arm from time to time, occasionally fondling the antennas of the cars as if he were wading through cattails on a riverbank. Joe quickened his pace. His jacket pocket caught on a mirror, ripped. He got stuck between an SUV and delivery van, had to back out, go around, and by the time he'd found a clear channel, his father was almost a block away.

"Sir!" He jumped up onto the hood of a Miata and yelled it.

"Just trying to find my car." His father spoke loudly, in that voice Joe remembered from childhood — the traffic cop leaning in through the window, the lawyer in the seersucker suit waiting for the two of them to get out of their seats on the streetcar so that he could sit down. No matter his anger, Vincent always, eventually, complied.

"This is an impound lot, sir. None of these cars is going anyplace."

"I didn't park illegal." That voice again, the edge of defiance. He hadn't stopped walking. "It was Boh Brothers, moved the street."

"That's right, sir." Joe walked across the hardtop, and off the back of the trunk. "But the fact remains these cars are in the possession of the city."

But his father had stopped listening. He'd

gone back to trying the doors. Joe could see it all play forward: If one of them opened, he would sit down in the driver's seat and lock the car from the inside. Joe would have to kick the passenger window in. His father would be frightened, maybe hurt. Joe might have to call 911.

"I got a call, for a taxi pickup," Joe tried. "A Mr. Vincent Boisdoré?"

His father just shook his head, rubbed his right arm, moved away.

"Your wife's looking for you. Wants you to come on home."

"You know my wife?" He turned towards Joe, and Joe pushed his way towards him.

"Sure do. Sylvia," he said. "Great soul."

"You're going to give me a ride home?"

On one of the forums, a CG, someone's daughter, had written that for the LO home might not be a physical place, the way we usually thought of it. That it might instead signify the world where they had felt like themselves, and therefore might not be something anyone could provide. Still, Joe nodded as he sidled between the last cars that separated them. The backseat of the Trans Am beside him was full to the roof with ruined suitcases and cardboard boxes, its drivers'-side window smashed. His father stepped towards him.

449

"You know the way?" Vincent asked. A long cut ran across his forearm. Blood was congealing in the tiny springs of his hair.

Joe nodded. "I can get you home."

So far Del had gathered this: That if anyone had killed Reyna, it had not been Troy. That he had left New Orleans with her children after some sort of incident that involved bringing her to the medics. That some emergency had happened to make Cora leave Esplanade for the Randsell house. That, meanwhile, Reyna had gone missing, and though Cora knew, or thought she knew, where she had gone, she wouldn't say.

Cora was writing other e-mails around this time — to Del, to her therapist, to her chef and her landlord and her small handful of girlfriends — but to Troy she would say very little, though Troy was the only one begging her to speak.

On 9/30/05 Troy Holyfield <troyward7@yahoo.com> wrote:
Cora, I tried your uncle's house in Houston he says you cannot come to the phone. Please let me know how I can reach you.

On 10/03/05 Troy Holyfield
<troyward7@yahoo.com> wrote:

Cora, I have a favor I don't know who else to ask. Will you call please.

On 10/06/05 Troy Holyfield
<troyward7@yahoo.com> wrote:

I thought I was doing right getting her help. I mean, she got WELL for a while, Cora. Had a job at Ochsner, was working on getting her medical assistant certificate. But in that situation, I don't know. I don't know if there was any right thing we could have done. Maybe she shook herself loose. Maybe bringing her to the authorities for a second time that night was not the right thing to do, but I had to think about the boys and would they have been safe with her? Could we keep her safe from herself if we tried? I was trying to do right by them, and I guess I did wrong by her. Maybe I should have made you drive the boys out of town, stayed there with her myself, nursed her back. Maybe if I'd brought her meds out of Calliope, shoved some down her throat while she was knocked out on the stairs, we could have all left in the morning together, easy as pie. Lord knows there's been enough pain in her life, in all our lives. Enough babies stolen away from enough mothers. Enough of this badness. I'm worried about the likeliest scenario to have happened, and like you said I'm trying to prepare Tyrone and Willy, except I don't know if they have any more room in their heads for badness.

You don't call and that's all right. But I'm getting nowhere with looking for her, and I am beginning to be afraid that you are right. I don't know why, but I get this sense. Did you go by my house again before you left? If not, could you go again when you're back and check to see if she there and also go by her place in Calliope?

Del felt Troy's fear building in her, the bottom falling out of your faith in the solidity of things, in their ability to hold you up. If there had been anything to learn from the last few months, it was this — that you could rely on nothing, that no one would protect you. You couldn't necessarily even rely on yourself.

On 10/14/05 Cora Boisdoré <thegoldenwood@hotmail.com> wrote: "Help gets you fucked" she said to me. I pretended like I didn't understand, but I think I always have. You don't say that sort of thing to yourself if you can help it, not

452

and try and live in the world but help does fuck you over. Sometimes what and who and how you are and what you've done and what you're going to do can't be changed, not by anybody, even with the best intentions. They think they've helped me by bringing me out to Houston. We thought we were helping the little boys. We thought we were helping Reyna by putting her in hands we thought were good, but what good did it do. Mrs. Randsell is dead, Reyna gone. The storms just keep coming. One day the seas will come to walk on land, I don't care how far you go. Run, little chicken, run, run, but the sky's still gonna fall. And it'll fall regardless of if you're in the flood or in a new built house with the air-condition running, because what does being in the air-condition change except how quickly you remember reality when you wake up in the morning. It's still going to fall, and so you're just putting it off, and all putting it off does is make it worse when it does happen.

I could live here, presumably. My auntie circles want-ads in the paper for line-chefs. I could buy a little house, live a fake little life on the dry land. Some days I try to pretend none of it happened. Try to forget.

Blot it out, like Mrs. Randsell tried to tell me to do. Blot it out blot it out blot it out she said when she took me in, took me into her arms the night I went to her. And so I tried: You and me, we drove away from New Orleans that night, before the storm came, right? We saw nothing, did nothing but drive. Nothing but fuck, right? In that little Motel 6 by the side of the highway. Nothing but pig out on Arby's and Dairy Queen and fuck and watch Pay-Per-View. Nothing else. Nothing else happened.

Some days that feels better to me — sometimes it's all I can take — but some days, I'd rather have the flood. At least in the flood things are coherent. So, yeah, help is a fucking. Your sister was smart. It's better to stay stuck in the shit if the shit is what you're destined for.

We're going back to New Orleans, whatever that means, tomorrow. I'll look for her, but I don't think she's anywhere, Troy. I'll let you know.

On 10/14/05 Cora Boisdoré <thegoldenwood@hotmail.com> wrote:
You asked me how I know what I know. How I know that she is gone. It's because while I was still at home I couldn't sleep

454

because I kept thinking I heard her coming in through the magnolia, looking for the boys. I had dreams where I saw her come prowling through the house, disguised as a dog sometimes, sometimes as herself. Sometimes, there was only the feeling that she had been there, laid like a veil over something else — a fawn torn apart, its throat ripped open, or a tent filled with those boys' screams. I was scared so bad I was sleeping with the duck gun, though what a gun could do against a nightmare, I don't know. But it wasn't just dreams, was it? Not that there's really much difference between nightmares and what we're living anymore.

This was the last e-mail in Cora's sent folder, and Del turned her face away from the screen. She felt cold, as though freezing water were pouring down her back. She reread the last e-mail. She had seen footsteps printed in the dust at their parents' house, the little feet with the long second toe — the footsteps of a real living person. Their house creaked loudly when you walked through it; if Cora had awakened at the sound of Reyna's footsteps, would she have picked up the gun she slept with and gotten out of bed?

Cora had gone back to Troy's house like she told him she would, and she'd returned every night until Del burned it down.

Del shut off the computer now, pressing down on the power button so hard that her thumb went pink, then shoved it under the mattress of Cora's bed, ripped back the curtains and cranked up the blinds. Dust swarmed in the spears of sun thrown between the shutter slats. It hung like gauze over the mirrors. She wrapped her hand around Cora's bedpost and tried to concentrate on Papie's carving. Solid things, real things. Ivy, jasmine, devil vine.

Tess sat over her drink, warm Knob Creek with a dash of Peychaud's in a plastic cup that left no mark on the copper bar. The dining room in front was full, as were the tables behind her. For the last hour, she'd watched people walk by on Dumaine, stop, put their cupped hands to the glass.

The noise in the room was strange — a bustle of voices without any background clatter of wineglasses and knives on plates, since the water pressure was too low to wash real china and silverware. Tess kept looking behind her to be sure the restaurant was still there, that the people she heard talking were not actually an audience murmuring amongst themselves while they watched her sitting in front of the mural behind the bar — swans on a lake and the colonnade of the Peristyle — like an actress in a one-act play. *The Lady Escapes* she'd title it.

Because she had escaped, hadn't she. She could admit that she had long had fantasies of being free of them all, and now she had in fact stepped out of the house she and Joe had built, leaving her husband to deal with his missing father all by himself. She would solve only her own problems now. She'd gone for a drink.

Ideally, she would have walked across the Quarter to Galatoire's, where there would have been chipped ice in a real glass, a Pernod wash, a twist of lemon. Ideally, it would have been Friday lunch, and the tablecloth would have been strewn with the crumbs of one of those hot, crackling loaves they served only at dinner. Ideally, she would have had béarnaise with her soufflé potatoes and fried eggplant with powdered sugar and silence, while in front of her the mad society put on their tableau in the seersucker suits and bright silk skirts of summer. Ideally, Nelson would have bowed, a starched napkin draped over one arm, and said something mildly wicked while he placed the drink in front of her. Ideally, there

457

would have been frost on the glass and the air would have smelled like garlic and the ceiling fans' brass blades would have spun over the mirrored room. Nelson was dead, though, the chipped ice gone, Galatoire's closed, for now at least, and so this would have to do.

She picked up her cup, shook the last drop of bourbon onto her tongue, and lifted it into the bartender's line of sight. He had been keeping his distance, not giving her a menu or chatting her up, seeing something in her face, maybe, that said it would be too much effort and ill spent at that.

"I'd love another if you could."

He nodded. "I hope you haven't been stood up."

She laughed and took her purse from the empty stool beside her, settled it in her lap. "Nope. I am all alone."

"I'm sorry." He reached under the bar to grab a menu. "As you'll see, we're not totally up to speed. The kitchen's about half-staffed and no oysters."

"No?" She gazed down at the offerings, handwritten on a sheet of blue Xerox paper — four appetizers, four entrees, two desserts. She was not hungry, though she knew that she should eat.

He shook his head. "Storm surge got into

the beds."

"I heard P&J's going to be getting in sacks from Nova Scotia." Clucking his tongue, a bald man in a bow tie came to take the empty stool. "Sure you don't need this?"

She relinquished it with a wave of her hand.

"Read in Tom Fitzmorris they had forty thousand pounds of oysters go bad," the bald man said. "Can you imagine?"

She shook her head and gathered her new drink, put her nose in it. "I don't want to."

"Me neither." He brushed the thought out of the air. "Shouldn't have brought it up. It's best to get back to the business of enjoying ourselves as quickly as we can."

Tess nodded at him, smiled, though she could feel her eyes going dull. "Made out all right?"

He laughed, making his martini slosh from his cup. "I've got flood insurance if that's what you mean. No? But what you gonna do."

She considered the damp bar. Crumpling the paper napkin in her hand, she blotted up the vodka he'd spilled. Shadows of the drops remained on the copper.

"I don't know about you, but I'm not the type gets worked up about things I can't do anything about. The minute I saw the pictures, and I'm right off the 17th Street Canal, mind you, I said to myself, *Verg, you take this in stride now.* Nothing you can do about it, so — equanimity. Always wanted to move to the Quarter. Look at it that way." He stuck out his hand. "Vergil Ferguson."

"Tess Eshleman," she said. "Good to meet you."

"Not Dr. Eshleman?"

She would have stepped into the mural then if she could, walked right up to the man in the boater standing on the edge of the lagoon and let him row her out among the swans.

She nodded.

"I know a patient of yours. Shouldn't divulge the name, though, should I? Ruin our tête-à-tête with doctor-patient confidentiality."

"Maybe that would be best." She looked down at the menu, rubbing her right shoulder with her left hand so that he would see her wedding band, that lying little ring of gold.

"I'll bet your services are much in demand, these days. Even I could maybe use them." He laughed a hiccupping sort of laugh. "You probably think I'm so deep in denial I may never claw my way out."

"No." She shook her head. His eyes, a

460

damp, well-lit blue, were set inside merrily wrinkled lids. We put too much emphasis on sanity, she thought. On reality. You could not change reality, but you could change your perception of it. Make accommodations. "You seem to be doing just fine. Anyway, I'm not practicing at the moment."

He nodded. "Doctor, heal thyself?"

The bartender rubbed the places in front of them with a rag and set out two placemats, two napkins, two forks, two knives, and she started to push herself away from the bar.

"Something like that."

It was hard enough just to be here without being expected to help someone else manage it. They said, in New York, that the towers had made them kinder to one another, but here, they had already been kind. When you turned up the volume on that kindness, it blared. She pulled her purse into her lap. She should go, anyway, help Joe find Vincent, deal with telling Del about the divorce, get in bed before she gave herself a headache. She reached inside her purse for her wallet — she had the right small bills to pay for her drinks and make a quick exit — but as she was pulling out the money, there was a thump against the plate glass, and the bar went quiet under a fusillade of curses.

"Don't you try and run again, mother-fucker!"

A green windbreaker was shoved against the window, pulled back up, slammed back again. The man's brown skull knocked against the glass.

"You think I don't know what you been up to? You fight me, we will taze you, you hear? Don't you make me taze you."

The policemen had their nightsticks out, and as they leaned in to turn the man over, Tess saw their faces, one white and one black, fat as hogs, lit up by the dining room's chandelier. The alleged criminal's cheek was smeared against the glass, his eye swollen shut, and his shoulders jerked while the white cop yanked one wrist and then the other into the handcuffs.

"Should have kept running," the bartender said.

Tess nodded. They all should have. They should have taken the opportunity the storm provided, each started over again, each put their FEMA money down on their own little house on their own little hill. Bought a cow, a bag of flour, a box of salt. Gone down to the village church and confessed their sins to a strange priest and started fresh as newly baptized children. He could have gotten free, this man in the green

462

windbreaker. They all could have gotten free. They could have vanished into the chaos, into the records lost into the water, into the refrigerated tractor-trailers full of unidentified bodies. The storm had been like Bourbon Street on Mardi Gras Day — if you lost your grip on whoever was following you, if your hand slipped out of your husband's hand, if you lost sight of your daughter's hat, the crowd could come between you and sweep you both on, in different directions, away from each other, then farther away.

The cops had pulled the man onto his feet and were hauling him to their squad car, and the hubbub of disembodied voices rose again in the tiled room. A server came out of the back with two plates, and the smell of beef — *Grilled Tenderloin, Cauliflower Gratin* — intermingled with the smell of the bleach they must have used to mop the back bar when they'd returned after all those weeks of heat. Vergil was talking again, and she put her wallet back in her purse and turned to him, smiled.

"You know what Tom said — I used to come here a lot when he and Anne were still running the place. He was really broken up about going, but Anne was so sick —"

"A brain tumor, right?"

He nodded, his eyes on the painted lagoon, on the arched bridge that spanned its two yellow banks. "It really puts it into perspective, and, when you get right down to it, it sums up how I feel about it too. He looked at me and said, quoting Lafcadio Hearn I think it was, 'I'd rather be here, Verg. I'd rather be here in sackcloth and ashes than own the whole state of Ohio.' "

Tess closed her eyes. *Here.* And where else, really. Even if she went away to her imaginary hill, to a cabin on the salt flats of Brittany, they would come after her. One morning, she would open the door and find them all standing there in a dense little knot — Joe, Vincent, Del, Cora, her mother, Joyce Perret, Jason Katz — all of them shivering in the cold, all of them needing her. She looked down at her hands wrapped around the copper rail at the end of the bar. They were smooth in the dim light, young looking. Then the cops turned on their blues.

"That's where they went, isn't it?" she asked. "Ohio. Where Anne's from."

The bartender laid down their bread basket. "Maybe I should go ask her for a job."

"Ain't no ersters in Ohio," Vergil said.

She looked down at the menu and noticed

that Anne's squab dish — the crisp-skinned bird over that bed of woodsy, rich dirty rice — was still there. She did have to eat.

"I'll have the squab then," she told the bartender.

"Atta girl," Vergil said. "That's the way to do it. And one for me."

Del had dialed Troy's number four times from the Dobies' kitchen phone but pressed send only once — and then she'd hung up on the first ring. Cora's words had been stuck in her head for so long that they were beginning to make sense. *Help is a fucking Help is a fucking Help is a fucking.* Like the tiny FEMA checks that didn't do much except keep people from coming home. Like the volunteers rebuilding houses that would just flood all over again. She imagined Cora in her nightgown, wandering down the aisles of a fluorescent-lit pharmacy, a little plastic cup brimming with pills in her hand. Del had been running away from everything that was fucked up and damaged for so long — this place, her sister — she had never looked at it honestly, never realized that, sometimes, brokenness was the only way to be. She opened Cora's computer and did a search and deleted anything that included an occurrence of the words *Reyna* or *sister*

465

or *gun,* and then she shut it down again.

Just then she heard a key in the front door and froze. The hard soles of her mother's flats clunked against the floor.

"Adelaide?"

Del picked the computer up off the bed and tucked it under the mattress again. Her mother was calling her name, a little hitch in her voice as if she was crying or drunk.

When she opened the bedroom door, her mother was holding onto the banister, climbing the stairs. She was, in fact, wasted.

"Where the fuck have you been, Mom?"

This made her mother stop, two feet on one riser. "Peristyle."

Even from here Del could smell the bourbon on her breath.

"You've eaten?"

"I did. Squab." She straightened herself, ready to put on that attitude she took every time she was in the wrong — an armor of arrogance she must have learned from her racist drunk of a father.

"Well, I was waiting for you, but I guess I'll eat now."

Her mother let her blow past her, and Del could practically hear the slow wheels of her brain turning as she shuffled around to follow. Del went through to the kitchen, opened the refrigerator to pull out the tub of congealed red beans. Her mother stared in at her from the dark hall.

"I've left your father, Del."

"I am aware."

"For good. It's for good. I — I'm seeing Augie. Your father and I are getting a divorce."

"A divorce. Good."

"I'm sorry, Del."

Del shrugged. "Yeah, well —" She dumped out the rice into a bowl, scooped out some beans, ran a little water over.

"You haven't heard from your sister?"

She threw the plate in the microwave. "Of course I haven't fucking heard from my sister."

"Oh, Adelaide," her mother sighed. "Do you have to be cruel to me about it?"

"I'm the cruel one?"

Opening and closing her mouth like a goldfish, her mother came into the room. "I'm sorry."

"You said that already."

"Do you think I'm not torn up about this?"

"Honestly, you look like you've got some pretty good painkillers on board."

"Oh, goddamn you, Del. I'm a grown woman. I can have a drink."

"Sure, sure." The microwave whirred,

467

spinning her dinner around.

Cruelty — Del supposed it balanced out, her withholding versus her mother's withdrawal. When there was no right thing to do, you could only choose between different varieties of wrong. She'd said everything already, after all, and they hadn't believed her. The only piece of useful, nonincriminating information she was keeping secret was Troy's phone number, and there was no reason to think he had any idea where to find Cora, or, more importantly, that Cora would be better off if she was found.

The microwave beeped, and Del sat down with her plate at the counter. Her mother was skulking along the cabinets. She took down a rocks glass then stood staring at the freezer. Del wasn't going to give her permission. As she said, she was a grown woman, she could have a drink if she damn well wanted one.

"So, this thing with Uncle Augie," she said between bites. "It's been going on for a while?"

Her mother opened the freezer, dug her glass into the ice bucket. "We were already separated, Del."

"You were on a break!" Del heard herself turning into some sort of idiot teenager. Her mother opened the liquor cabinet. "Seriously, though. If this is the new state of things — oh, Dad found Papie, by the way, in case you care — we might as well bring it out into the open. You and Uncle Augie went down to New Orleans and found Cora together, his mother died and you comforted him — it's understandable. Really."

"That's not how it happened, Del."

"Oh, no? Then tell me, how did it happen?"

"I ran into him at Langenstein's the other day. It's been over with your father since Houston. Since he gave up on getting your sister out of the city. I sincerely wish that weren't true, but it is."

Del laughed. "So you grabbed a prime porterhouse and a bottle of wine and fell into bed —"

"No, not exactly."

"— picked right up where you left off."

"Excuse me?" The bottle of rye stalled at half tilt over her glass, and now she poured, one finger, then two. "What in God's name are you talking about?"

"Oh, we knew." Del speared a piece of andouille, put it in her mouth. "We saw you. What year was that? The year Madge was diagnosed? We were little enough still that you probably thought we wouldn't understand. We were hiding behind the curtains, waiting for the fireworks, and suddenly —" She spread her hands for effect. "— all was made clear. Why Dad hates Augie, why you always worked yourself up into a tizzy when they were coming over, why —"

"That's right, Del, just get it all out."

"Oh, it's not like I've been holding some grudge. Like I'm all damaged. My idyll of monogamy shattered! Everyone deserves a fling or two. It's just that your generation with your antique morals had to wait 'til after you were married. It's more complicated that way, you know, but so be it." She took another bite. "I'd say your best friend's husband wasn't the best choice though, especially when your best friend had cancer, but it's cool."

"That's not what happened, Del, but think what you like. I can see I can't fall any farther in your estimation than I already have."

Del nodded, digging into her red beans. "Maybe you're right."

Her mother put her drink down on the counter, and Del reached out and took it, raised it in a toast.

"Chin chin," she said and took a nice big gulp of burn.

FIFTY-SEVEN DAYS
AFTER LANDFALL
OCTOBER 25

Cora held the button down and looked out over the motel parking lot as the ice thumped into the plastic bucket. The night was wide and unprotected. She put a hand against her bare neck. Beyond the last ranks of cars, the asphalt tumbled down towards deep ditches, and she felt eyes on her, a creature clutching the edges of the grassy banks, watching her as she stood under the yellow light. She backed up out of the glare, kept her finger on the button. The parked cars crackled in their loneliness.

She'd been doing so well. Had eaten a roast beef and three things of onion rings, downed her Dr Pepper, but now she had a flash of that last night on Esplanade: The hammock rocking her awake. The light in the house. Running until her lungs burned. Her heart sped up. She could pass through to the motel's courtyard, out of sight, and come around the far stairwell and press herself to the unlit railing of the balcony, run into her room and lock the doors, but the windows would still be made of glass. All it took was a brick, a fist, a length of cord.

The ice machine ground out another handful of cubes, and she released the button, took a deep breath. *Tu m'en veux?* her brain said. Nobody wanted anything of her here; that was why she'd come. Still, she moved to the edge of the walkway, out of the light. The two older women in the room beside hers were still up. She'd noticed them coming in — Tulane T-shirt, box of chicken. The curly-haired one sat against the headboard of her bed, doing something on a calculator. The other lay on her stomach in a long flowered nightdress, eating a biscuit like an apple while she read. As Cora passed, she looked up from her book and through the window. Cora ducked her head, fumbling for the key card in the waist of her pajamas.

The one in the nightdress swung the door open, and Cora jumped away. "You the Jeep with the Louisiana plates? We keep seeing you on the road!"

The key had fallen to the concrete floor, and Cora bent to pick it up, tried to catch her breath, act normal.

"What?" she asked, straightening back up.

"New Orleans —" The woman pointed with her biscuit. "I can hear it in your voice. Us too!"

"No." Cora slid the card into the slot, out, in again, but the lock would not catch.

"Come on —" The woman was whining like a little kid. "Come on in and have a drink! I'm sure you need the company as much as we do."

"I'm sorry." Cora shook her head as the door finally opened. "I'm from North Dakota."

She slipped inside, locked the three locks, placed the ice bucket on the table, drew the blinds, then opened her side of the communicating door.

"North Dakota —" one of them was complaining.

"Far way to drive."

"Bullshit. She's Seventh Ward as the day is long." A toilet flushed behind the wall. "I kind of want to go knock on her door. That's some hard-core denial, North Dakota."

Cora put down the ice bucket, closed the communicating door. She remembered reading somewhere about a native woman who had been rescued from a tiny island a very long time ago, after eighteen years of living alone. When the Spaniards found her, she was clothed in a gown made of cormorant feathers stitched together with the sinew of whales. Seven weeks after the ship brought her back to California — seven weeks in which the woman danced and ate among the colonists, while the missionaries searched in vain for someone who could speak her language — she died of dysentery. A priest of the mission buried her, baptizing her corpse with a name he chose himself, in a language she had never learned.

Cora climbed into bed, turned out the light. The woman in the nightdress was right. Hard-core denial was what she was aiming for. A new land, a new life. It was as she had been counseled, Mrs. Randsell at the door pulling off her housecoat, wrapping it around Cora while she stood there shivering on the porch. *Hush now, baby. Hush. You can't have. You can't have done a thing like that.* Her weak hands patting at Cora's scapulae. *Just forget it. Blot it out.*

But when she fell asleep, she dreamed of nothing but the little boys: Tyrone and Willy sitting among the colored papers and paints on a table in her old art classroom. Tyrone and Willy plucking flowers from a box of Jujubes. Tyrone and Willy standing on the edge of a planet consumed by the roots of huge oaks. *Mais si le mouton mange la fleur, c'est pour lui comme si, brusquement, toutes les étoiles s'éteignaient,* Willy said, though he didn't speak French. He and his brother were wearing cardboard Burger King crowns. They giggled as they pelted her with flowers which filled her mouth like sticky candy, until her head exploded with a hollow bang.

Cora sat up and waited for a minute in the cold air, listening to the sounds of the itinerant world: a woman's heels on concrete, the reverberation of a steel door's slam. The words translated in her head, *But if the sheep eats the flower, it is as if, suddenly, all of the stars were snuffed.* The little prince wept. Though usually he lived very happily on his private asteroid, he felt lonely here, in the desert of the earth. *I will make a muzzle for that sheep,* the jet pilot promised. *I will make armor for your flower.* Cora wrapped her arms around herself, but the motel air encased her like a block of ice. She thought of her mother, of nestling into her chest. She thought of her father's smell of wood and aftershave. She thought of her sister laying her soft body beside hers in the narrow bed. She thought of Troy, of the boys, of the dog who had come to her out of the ruins and let her cradle its paw in her hands.

She got up and went to the bathroom, steadied herself on the vanity. In the mirror, her hair hung down lank around her tear-stained face. It bothered her that, when the woman had spoken to her, she hadn't acknowledged her home. It wasn't like her, as her mother would have said. Mrs. Randsell was right, you could try to destroy your memories, but she had been wrong to think it helped. You were built from the bricks of your past; if even a few of them crumbled, you risked collapse.

She had to look, then. She gritted her teeth, and Tyrone sat up in the big bed, listening to the creaking darkness. *Dead already. Dead before we died.* Reyna's words coagulated in the air, and Cora pulled the trigger. Troy carried her body down the stairs, stood there on the dawn-lit sidewalk with her grandfather's gun. *She just fell out.* She had believed him. *She'll be good as new soon, you hear.* But he had lied. She had seen it: The exploded face. The pool of black blood that whirled, driving through the floor like a drill. *You just sit tight with Miss Cora,* Troy had said to the little boys. *Everything'll be right-side up again in the morning.* But it hadn't righted itself, had it — the way a reflection, reflected again, retains the water's wobble, the mirror's warp. Reyna visited her dreams, her eyes plucked out by birds.

That final night, she'd gone to sleep in her hammock on the upper gallery, the house unbearable now with heat. Startled awake, she opened her eyes to raindrops spinning down from the sky. When the wailing did not return, she nestled back down into her net, her body wrapped around the shotgun. The wails she thought she'd heard could have been anything — a gate opening, a dog's whine, her own voice in her sleep. Still, Cora clutched the gun in her arms as she rolled to look over the gallery rail. Below, a shadow staggered back and forth across the garden, as if blind. Cora leaned farther and the hammock spun and she fell, the gun fell, banging, on the gallery's tin floor. *Boys!* Reyna cried as Cora made for the fire ladder, the rain coming down harder now, the tin loosening under her feet. In her mouth was the taste of rust. Cora vaulted over the railing in her thin nightdress, began to climb down. She could no longer see the woman in the garden, and the wailing had stopped. As she struggled to keep her grip on the wet rungs of the ladder, her vision flashed: white column, gray house, a bar of light moving beyond the shutter slats. A face pressed against the inside of the window glass, its eyes plucked out by birds.

Dead already, Reyna said. *Dead before we died.*

Cora let go of the ladder and ran.

Barefoot, in only her T-shirt and underpants, Cora ran through the Quarter. Through the high-rises and the parking lots and under the freeway she ran, and she did not stop until she found herself on the front porch of Uncle Augie's house, ringing the bell. Mrs. Randsell wrapped her in her housecoat. *Hush now, baby. Hush. You can't have. You can't have done such a thing.* The dying smell of Mrs. Randsell's petal-soft arms. *Just forget it all, my darling. There's no use dwelling on a thing like that. It's like thinking about the expansion of the universe, like thinking about the sun burning out. Blot it out,* she said. *Blot it out.*

She had entered in the middle of a blink. Vincent's eyesight was going, of course, but he'd swear she was gone one minute, there the next. He squeezed his hot eyes shut and looked again.

From where he sat in his recliner, Vincent could see Sylvia lying in the middle of the bed, curled up in her housedress, pretending to sleep. *What did I do this time, my love?* She liked to pretend to be sleeping when she was angry, leave the vacuum in the middle of the floor, the stew bubbling, go hide out in the bedroom until he apologized. He must have really done it this time — her face closed up tight like an oyster.

He turned his hands over — that right arm swollen tight as a tick, the left, holding the TV remote, a mess of wrinkles and spots. He flipped off the TV, its jabber and brightly painted rooms.

"I apologize," he tried. "I can't say I know

479

for what, but I apologize."

"Not to worry, Pop. We all have our days."

Vincent looked down at the floor so fast he wrenched his neck. He hadn't known Joe was there — butting in — sitting on the floor in the middle of a pile of women's clothes, his nose all red.

He looked back at the bed, at the bedspread — the one with the design of castles made of little knots — swirling under the weight of his wife's curled body. If he managed to rouse her, if he found the right words, she would push herself up ever so slowly, open her eyes with a smile like the world was dawning fresh, and on her cheek would be imprinted a mirror castle, pale pits on her dusky skin.

"Pop," Joe sighed, wiping a hand under his nose. "I'm the one owes you an apology. I let you down the other day. Next time, you tell me when you get a hankering for a pocket pie, and we'll go down to Barker's Corner and get a Hubig's, alright. Chocolate, lemon, cherry."

"What has got into you, boy?" Vincent said. The mirror over the bureau reflected an old man's face twisted in confusion. "Get on out of here with that mess."

Quieter, the boy said, "Okay, Pop," swallowed. He had a stack of receipts he'd pulled out of the pockets of the clothes on the floor. He picked them up, struggled to stand.

Vincent watched the boy leave, desultory, the mess of clothes still on the ground, and when he looked back to the bed, his wife was gone. He pushed forward in his recliner, and it levered him upright. He followed the hallway. Joe was sitting on the living room sofa now, counting his receipts out on top of Sylvia's hope chest. He'd been getting closer on the carving. Closer to getting it right.

"Where did she go?"

Joe shook his head. "That's what I'm trying to figure out."

She was not in her chair by the fireplace, not in the kitchen. He went to the front windows and saw her, far out in the windless moonscape of crashed pines, lying on a bed adrift in the early morning fog. He could almost see her face — soft and ripe with sleep, her skin downy with fine hairs — and he wanted to wrap his mouth around her, like she was a peach. He went for the door, tried to open it, found it locked.

Behind him, the boy stood up, the receipts crinkling in his fist. "Where you going, Pop?"

"Out," he said.

"Alright, let me come with you."

But he didn't want the boy to come with him. It was a private moment he was looking for, out there — he wanted to run his fingertips over the castle imprinted on his wife's cheek, wanted her to hook her fingers over the waist of his pants. He fought with the door handle, rummaged in his pocket for keys. He had nothing — a short pencil, a rubber band, a bit of lint. They were trying to keep him prisoner. Through the window of the door he could see her sleeping in her white bed in the white fog, like a fairy tale maiden in a dream. The boy came up behind him, put a hand on his arm, which filled suddenly with a sharp, searing pain.

"Let me loose!" he yelled.

The boy backed away, holding up his hands. One of them held a key. He watched the key enter the lock with a near sensual pleasure, watched the door open, went out of it and down the steps so fast he nearly tripped. He heard his own hard breathing.

"Pop, you okay?"

His vision was watery, like he was walking inside a cloud. She was still asleep on the white bed, waiting for him to cross the fallen trees.

"I'm coming," he said. Suddenly, he realized he didn't know her name. "I'm coming —"

"Pop, you talking to me?"

"The girl," he said, as if the boy couldn't see. But now, he looked back to where she had been, where he thought she had been, and he couldn't find her for all the ruined forest. He pushed on, his feet crashing down through the branches of the pines, their scent spiking the air.

"The girl?" Joe was following him, his head whipping around as he stared through the wreckage of the forest, looked back at the house. "What girl? Cora? Do you see her? Is she here?"

"Cora?" He blinked. He was trying to remember where the bed had been. Trying to call back the image of a woman waking in a square of sun, the sensation of her hands fumbling at his belt, but he couldn't find her on the forest floor. He wanted to call for her, but he didn't remember her name.

"Cora! Do you see her?"

"No!" he yelled, walking faster, trying to escape. "That's not it! That's not her name!"

The more the man talked, the less he could remember. Now he couldn't recall her face. He touched her wrist. No, her neck. He lay his palm against her neck as you would against the brow of a feverish child. He opened his mouth to say her name — the curtains were puffed with sunlight like breeze. Her name clotted on his tongue. He had to shout it out to her if he wanted her to lift her arm from her face, brush back her dense hair.

The broken forest unrolled towards the road, and for a second, he saw the bed covered in shadow, a lighter gray on the black asphalt, her dark form sinking into the mattress. He rushed forward, twigs popping underfoot. The broken trunk of a pine tree snagged his pants leg, ripped it. The light was fading. Soon it would be night, and he would have to let her sleep.

"Cornelia Sylvia Boisdoré," Joe said.

"Sylvia," Vincent replied. His heart began to slow, but there was a taste of copper in his mouth. His lungs were burning, his legs shook. He closed his eyes — his wife raised her face from the coverlet. Her hair hung over her cheek like a shadow in the darkening room.

"Cornelia Sylvia Boisdoré. Remember, Pop, we named her after mom."

"Sylvia!" he shouted into the dark room. She lifted her head and brushed her hair back from her face, a featureless face, shining and pitted like the moon.

■ ■ ■ ■

Awash in the flickering light of the Dobies' big television, Del slept curled up into a corner of the sofa, her arms hugging her knees. The coffee table was littered with balled chocolate wrappers, a dirty fork sat beside a dirty bowl. It was nine thirty already, and Tess had intended to wake her, but autumn had happened overnight, and Del looked cold. From the arm of the sofa, Tess grabbed the plaid throw and laid it down over her daughter's bare legs. Gently, gently. Even so, Del shifted and mumbled in her sleep like a child, smelled like a child — the heat in her hair and milk chocolate on her breath. When she slept, her face had always locked itself into an expression of sternness which Tess read as self-protective, but now, even after a night of sleep, her eyebrows were knit, her wet lips half-open, as if she was trying to work something through.

Tess dropped onto her knees on the carpet and bowed her head. Poor thing, she didn't deserve this. Del had always done everything they'd asked, done everything right, gotten into the right school, taken the right job. None of them deserved this, but Tess should

485

have tried harder. Should have remembered what was so hard to remember: that once you had children, your life was no longer yours.

She put her hand over her daughter's hard ankle bone, and Del, startled, turned her head sharply into the pillow. Tess dropped back onto her heels. The cold television light trickled across her daughter's face, and Tess took the remote and pinged it dark. She gathered the foil pebbles from the chocolates, poured them into the bowl. The phone rang. She ran to pick it up, pressed the on button, went into the kitchen, set the bowl down on the countertop with a click.

"Hello?" the woman repeated, her voice older, Southern and raspy.

"Hello," Tess said.

"Who is this?"

"I'm sorry?" Tess said. "You called here."

"No, I have three calls from this number yesterday afternoon. Three hang ups."

Tess sighed and looked at the microwave clock — 9:32. "I'm sorry, I don't know what you mean, and I'm rushing out the door. I'm afraid I have to —"

"First you tell me who you are," the woman said.

Del turned over on the sofa, and Tess opened the back door and stepped out onto the bricks. "This is Mrs. Boisdoré," she said. "And if you could identify yourself?"

"Cora Boisdoré?"

"No."

Muffled now — a hand over the receiver — the woman called, "Troy! It's that girl Cora."

"No, I said," Tess repeated. "Cora is my daughter."

There was a papery flutter as the telephone changed hands. Troy spoke: "Cora, is that you?"

"No." Her voice was breaking. She struggled to pull it into line. "This is Tess, her mother."

"Oh. I see."

She remembered this voice — the fear and sadness in it when he'd called Vin's house in Houston, asking if Cora was alright, if they would please give her the phone. Tess walked into the garden, into the midst of the scorched plants.

"Is she all right?" Troy asked.

"I don't know. She's missing. That woman —"

"My aunt."

"Your aunt called me," Tess said. "She said you'd gotten calls from this number?"

"I apologize. She's worried it was my sister Reyna."

487

"Oh. No. You weren't told?" Tess took a deep breath. At least this was something for which she'd been trained. "I'm so sorry. Your sister passed away. Your cousins were supposed to call —"

"No, no, they did." Troy sighed. "Kind of y'all to give Anthony and them dinner. I thank you. It's just, my auntie —" He sighed again. "They had a run-in, her and Reyna, when Reyna was living with her. Reason why my aunt moved up north. And now that we've heard there was a fire at the house, my aunt's on edge. Seems like she can't rest easy with Tyrone and Willy here until she's got positive ID on the remains."

"I see," Tess said. *The remains.* An elegant word that had lost its elegance. Something brutal about the plural. *What remains.* "I'm truly sorry."

"Thank you," Troy said. "But Cora, though — did you say she's missing?"

Tess shook her head. She would have to ask the police about the fire, though Del had been adamant that they not mention it when they first came. It didn't matter: she needed to know everything, even if they would know then what she knew. She wasn't quite sure what that was, anyway: her mind fuzzy like her unbrushed teeth. They used dental records to identify burned corpses, didn't they? She thought of Cora's perfect, chloride-shored incisors.

"There was nothing on your machine?" she asked, grabbing hold of the dried bouquet of a hydrangea. Could Cora have come here, just to use the phone, and then left again?

"What, you think it was Cora who called us?" Troy said. "She left out of there today?"

"Yesterday. Or no, the night before that."

"Then how is she calling me from your phone?"

"I don't know, Troy. It wasn't me."

Tess brought the papery blossom to her face and breathed in its smell of dust and dew.

"You don't seem surprised," Tess said, "that she's gone."

"No." A door clicked shut. "I guess it's like for me she's been missing a good while."

"I'm concerned —" She drew in a deep breath. "— that what happened to your sister —"

"Cora didn't have anything to do with that."

Tess felt the world dilate, the blue sky yawning over the courtyard fence. *You gave Cora the shotgun,* Del had said with wild conviction. *Troy's sister was killed with a shotgun.*

"What?" she said.

"Cora kept saying to me — back when she was still e-mailing — that she didn't believe Reyna was still alive. And then she turned up dead. But Cora didn't have a thing to do with it. She couldn't have, I know."

"Why? Why would she have had anything to do with it?"

"Look, there was a tussle." Troy cleared his throat. "She came back to y'all's house, Reyna did, looking for her boys. But that was my fault. My actions. My decisions. I chose to bring my sister to the authorities instead of taking care of her myself. I chose to take those children away with me, and I would have done it if Cora'd been fighting me tooth and nail. Reyna sure as hell was."

"I thought —" Tess said, fighting for sense. "I thought your cousins said you'd saved her, that you and Cora had saved her and the children."

"I thought we had too." Troy sighed heavily. "Or that we'd at least done the best we could. But we didn't, we didn't help her. We couldn't help her. I don't know if anybody could."

"She was ill — suicidal — your cousins said?"

"She'd gotten treatment," he said. "After

what happened in the house that night, I brought her out to where they had medics set up. Tried to get her back to a doctor. But there was nothing there for anybody. A tent full of screaming kids. A bunch of men with guns."

"Oh, no," Tess said. "Oh, no. I'm so sorry."

"I left her there anyway. I left her there, unconscious, and I took her boys."

Tess settled back against the patio table, looked at her feet, blue veined and bunioned from her pregnancies. Persecution complexes did not mix well with real persecution. How many times had she arrived at Charity minutes before they'd shackled one of her patients to a bed? How many times had she seen a commitment backfire therapeutically, though, practically, there was no other option?

"I'm so sorry, Troy." She had failed him. Her profession had failed him. The government had failed him. Civilization itself had failed him. "I am truly very sorry."

There was nothing on his end of the line but his slow breathing. How little comfort there was in the world. How meager our ability to care for one another. She thought of Cora, sitting on the kitchen floor, refusing even sweetened milk. *It just goes through,* she'd said. *It goes straight through.*

"Are you sure she knew?" Tess asked. "Are you sure Cora knew your sister had passed away?"

"She said — after we left she said she kept hearing Reyna coming in y'all's house. Said she kept dreaming about her, like she was a ghost. And, me, I couldn't find her. Not in anybody's records. Not in the Red Cross's. Not in the prison system. Nothing. I got scared. I sent her —" he said. "When y'all went back to New Orleans finally, I sent Cora to my house to check and see if she was there."

Tess closed her eyes. She saw Cora's skinned palms, the mud on her boots. She'd been alright in Houston. They never should have brought her home.

"She had nothing to do with it," Troy was saying. "It was my decision to get those children from her. My own."

"Troy —"

"There was nothing else to do. There was nothing else I could have done. It was the boys I had to look to."

Tess nodded at the shadowed bushes along the fence. "Oh, Troy I'm so sorry. I don't know what to say. I don't know what's happened." Something viscous, toxic was rising in her throat. "What's happening?" A bubble of drown. "I don't know what to do.

492

All I know —" She coughed. "All I know is I'm afraid."

There was a silence on Troy's end of the line, and Tess pressed her fingers into her eyes.

"She had her troubles, Cora," Troy said. "You could lose her so easily. You'd think you knew where she was, what she was thinking, but you'd be wrong. I didn't want to say so, but when you said she was missing — my sister being how she was, that's where my mind goes to. Dark places. Like, if things get bad, you don't know how the badness can find a way to stop."

"Yes," Tess said.

"And you can't do a thing about it, it's like dropping sandbags in a river."

"Yes."

"I should have never left her. I don't know what happened down there, after I left with those kids. She was pushing her keys in my hand, telling me I had to go. I should never have left her."

"She wasn't your responsibility."

"She was all of ours."

"Yes. We are all each other's." Tess tilted her head up to the pale sky where the dim moon still hung beside the fronds of the dying palm. "I suppose that's right."

"But you couldn't stop her," Troy said.

"She was going to do what she was going to do."

"A force of nature."

"Yes."

"She was a force of nature," Tess said, realizing that they had been talking about her daughter in the past tense. Above her, clouds were scudding past towards the gulf, and she sat down on the mat of palms and tilted her head up to the sky.

The attending — a petite woman in a taut white coat — turned over the laminated card Tess had made, looked down the list of forbidden medications, and then handed it back to Joe, without saying a word. According to Tess, Joe should be hovering at her shoulder, asking questions about every medication ordered, every monitor, every note she was making in her chart, but he couldn't bring himself to get out of the chair. His father lay in the bed, his red eyes closed, mucus dripping from his nose. Joe took a tissue from the box on the laminate table and dabbed at his father's face: no reflexive response. The monitor said 104.3, and Joe didn't need to listen to what the attending was telling him — infections, MRSA, the high risk of sepsis among the elderly — to know that it was bad.

His father had wept in the car, after Joe told him that Sylvia was dead. He'd had to say it, to make him stop fighting for the road, stop staggering over the broken pines. He'd sobbed, wiping the tears from his face with that red, infected arm. Joe tried to snap him out of it, tried to talk about other things as they sped down the highway towards the emergency room, but his father would not hear him. Joe supposed there came a time when the dead had more gravity than the living, when they became so many that the balance tipped on its fulcrum and you fell towards them, down.

The nurses bustled around his father while the monitors beeped — a tall young black man and a round-assed white woman, someone's mother. You could not deny that caretaking was needed; you yourself would want it in your turn. But sometimes it looked like waste, didn't it: a void that pulls you in. Already his father rarely remembered him, and half the time, when he did remember, he seemed not to care — only spat at him to get out of the room. Joe wondered where the memory went sometimes, the mule his father remembered so vividly Sunday gone by Monday morning. Of course, he knew — proteins choked the neurons, plaques broke the synapses — but he preferred to think of a hard rain, the mule plodding out of a dense forest and into a field the second before the storm clouds broke, a curtain of water sweeping across the stage. Regardless, Joe knew that in the end he would have nothing to show for all his trouble, nothing other than his own satisfaction, if you could call it that, and his pain.

"You had him in assisted living, you said?" the doctor was asking. "Where was this?"

"In Gretna. But it's been shut down since the storm."

"I'd be happy to call Belle Maison for you, with a referral," she said.

His ulcer made a fist. "I'm not going to put him back in one of those places."

"This is a really nice one of those places, though." The doctor looked at him from between her penciled eyelids, serenely wheedling.

It was hard for him not to yell. "No, I said. No thank you."

"So, after he wandered off —" She blinked. "— he cut himself on a car window? This was in New Orleans proper?"

Joe reached out to take his father's hot hand. "I had to go into the city to be with my wife."

"Alright. I'm going to go look into what

we're dealing with," she said. "That's a nasty kind of dirt now, down there."

Joe nodded. A nasty kind of dirt, as if the dirt of the "Pleistocene uplands" was somehow clean. It was true that the flood, full of farm runoff, that high nitrate sludge, had raised creosote, lead, arsenic from the soil into plumes of petroleum and benzene, but that was what the world was made of now, wasn't it? That was what we had made of the world.

"I hate to say it," the doctor said, "but once we get you all set up and ready to go home, I'd try to keep him over here as much as you can. He's in a delicate condition. Even just the mold alone —"

Joe tuned her out. He would have liked to hop her in his truck, pretty doctor in the plum lipstick, and take her through the flood. On your left, my house, Doctor. On your right, my wife. You'll notice, perhaps, the space beside my younger daughter where my eldest daughter should be. But she is out walking through the desert, Doctor, as am I. As you watch our tires spin on the cracked surface of the earth, I recommend you pull your pretty cotton blouse across your face to protect you from the dust. Terrible, isn't it? It makes us all choke. But there is no time for concerns like those in the desert. See Cora adjust her sunglasses over her eyes as she rolls down her windows to bathe in the hot air? See my father pulling himself over the broken trees with his trembling hands, now that the mule has vanished into the rain? We don't have time for the future, Doctor. We hardly have time for the past. The only thing to do in the desert is keep walking. Otherwise you will die of thirst before you make it to higher ground.

Her mother was sitting on the courtyard steps in her bathrobe though it was already eleven. She held a cigarette pinched between her thumb and forefinger like a joint, and her hand was shaking.

"Mom?" Del said.

Tess nodded but did not turn, exhaling a thin stream of smoke that floated up over her head. The pack lay open on the brick, only the one cigarette missing from the honeycomb, and Del picked it up, pulled off the cellophane, crumpled it.

"Smoking?"

Tess shrugged. She sat slumped on the step like the St. Peter's *Pietà,* her knees rounded up under the terry cloth like mountains, the Dobies' portable phone resting in the basket of her lap. She hadn't showered yet that morning it didn't look like, hadn't even run a comb through her hair.

Tess took a drag from the cigarette, let out the smoke. "We got a call here from Troy." She glanced up at Del. "He had some missed calls from this number."

Without makeup, her face was puffy and white, as if someone had tried to erase it, and Del felt a sudden pity. Her mother lifted her trembling cigarette and inhaled again, peering at Del like an expectant dog. She had never been a natural mother, her mother, always straining to provide more than she had to give. Del had known that at least since she was six, when Oma had hired an ironing lady who would crouch down and crush her and Cora against the ample bosom of her uniform saying *Hello, my babies. Oh, my good babies.* Del had known even then that her mother would never have that in her, that open generosity of love — she was too afraid of what her children would take from her, of what they had already taken.

"Yeah, I called him, Mom," Del said.

"Oh." Her mother watched the smoke tumble from her mouth, shook her head. "Of course. Okay."

"I'm sorry. I should have told you I found

his number."

Tess nodded. "Well. It doesn't matter. He hasn't heard from her. He doesn't know anything. The police —" She fondled the phone in her lap. "They're coming over soon. They said they have new developments, but not to get our hopes up."

"New developments?" Del slotted her thumb into the gap in the cigarettes. The smoke burned her esophagus. "They didn't give you an idea what those were?"

"They said not to get our hopes up." Her mother shook her head. "He said she knew — Troy said Cora knew Reyna was dead, just like you told me. Said she thought it was her fault, because they took Reyna's children. He told me too —" She swallowed. "He said there have been investigators at the fire. That they're working towards identifying 'the remains,' he called them. I've already accepted it." Her ash was growing long. "She's gone."

Del nodded. She pulled out a cigarette, looked at it.

"Don't, Adelaide —" Her mother reached out for the pack, looking beside her as she stubbed her own out in the potted holly bush. "I don't know why I bought them."

"I've got to go," Del said. She looked at her bare feet, the cut-off cuffs of her sweatpants. She should tell her mother she'd set the fire, hand over Cora's computer, comfort her somehow, if only for the minutes they had before they learned something new. But she couldn't speak to the police again. Couldn't ask her mother to lie for her. "I'm going to see Tina. I haven't met the baby yet."

"Stay with me, Del, please. Just until the police are gone. I know what they're going to say. I've already accepted it."

"She's — I'm overdue to visit. You tell me what they tell you." She leapt up the steps, went in through the banging screen and upstairs, thumbing her sweatpants off as she entered the bedroom.

The computer was still tucked under the mattress. She grabbed her jeans, took out her big purse. Downstairs, the screen door creaked open again, banged shut.

"Del! Please. They might have questions. Just call Tina, tell her you'll be a little late."

She pulled her jeans on and tugged an old Buckner sweatshirt over her head, thrust her toes into her Chuck Taylors.

"Del!" She was at the bottom of the stairs, the banister creaking under her hand.

The doorbell rang. The computer just barely fit in her bag. Downstairs, her mother was opening the door. Del went out onto the landing. The policewoman, Costa, looked up at her from the doorway, smiling and squinting her eyes.

"Hey, Adelaide," the woman said. "You on your way out?"

Her mother was out on the front porch. Del pressed her purse against her chest.

"I'm sorry," she said, "I'm late for something. Have you found her?"

"Not yet, but we'd love it if you could stay and talk. You never know what you know."

"I'm sorry, I'm late."

Del went down the stairs and breezed past them, her head down. She felt her mother's eyes on her, smelled her mother's perfumed body balled up inside the robe. The police stood like ramrods in their pressed blues. She went out the door, down the street. At the end of the block, she looked over her shoulder. Her mother looked after her as the cops stalked into the house.

She pulled the sweatshirt's hood up over her head and put in her earbuds, though she didn't turn her music on. *Keep your head down, girl,* she told herself, *and keep walking.* In the ratty old jeans, walking on the heels of her shoes, she passed, unnoticed, across Rampart. For once in her life, she was glad of the invisibility granted her by her skin. As the traffic slowed for the intersections, not actually stopping at the flashing red light, no one looked up at her. A woman in a Mercedes stared at the road, tapping her teeth. A man in a pickup truck tossed his Popeye's box near the overflowing trashcan on the corner. The traffic broke, and she crossed into the shadow of the raised highway.

Above her, the traffic on the highway thundered. The computer was getting heavy. She thought for a moment that the best thing would be to walk out among the abandoned cars, find an open trunk and throw the computer into it. The police had ways to undelete things, recover hard drives; hell, even Fran knew how. But what if there was something in those old e-mails that she'd missed. What if Cora wrote to Troy, or Alice Luce, anyone, to say where she was? She pulled the sweatshirt strings tight to make the hood pucker around her face, then clasped the computer to her chest again and stepped off of the curb. A Suburban was speeding through the intersection. She sprinted. The horn blared, and wind whipped her heels.

She started to run, flopping in her half-on shoes until she'd turned into the Seventh Ward. Her phone started to ring, and she stopped, bent over to catch her breath. She was afraid even to reach into the bag to silence it, and so it kept ringing as the person, transferred to voice mail, hung up and tried again. On Esplanade, cars whispered past. She was safe here, camouflaged as a rabbit in brambles. The streets were still empty. In front of most of the houses, the lawns of dried mud remained untrampled — no one had even come back to look. At the corner of Onzaga, she stopped and readjusted the computer, then turned toward the track.

She could already see up the block to Troy's house, which was still standing, ringed in yellow tape. The terra-cotta ridgeline of the roof arrowed towards her. She kept to the far side of the street as the front door emerged from shadow, then the house's flank. Burn marks spread like smudged ink across the siding. The fire had eaten a hole out of the center of the house big enough to drive a truck through. She backed up, looking around her for fire trucks, cop cars, anything. Far down Paul Morphy, a couple of women were getting into their SUV. Del sat down on the stoop of Cora's neighbor's house, pulled out her phone, nonchalant, like she was waiting for someone. Three missed calls from her mother. Two voice mails: *The Jeep was picked up by a red light camera in Arkansas. But that could mean any number of things. That she's driving around. Or someone just found the car with the keys in the ignition in Gentilly and* — The machine cut her off, and the next one began: *It doesn't mean anything. And they won't say anything about the fire. About the remains. I don't know the address, Del, I don't even know how to ask. Please call* — Del deleted the message and pocketed the phone.

The women down the block had driven off now, and she stood up, crossed the street to the burned house, went under the cordon. Between the jagged teeth of the broken siding, she saw that the floor had caved in, but the cabinets still hung from the wall, their singed faces shining dully in the sun. Below them, the refrigerator, vomiting a mountain of bottles and jars, lay on top of a pile of shivered floorboards. Her phone rang again, stopped. In the center of the house, a piece of black plastic shuddered, but she could see no white sheet, no fragment of body or bone.

"It's just not possible right now, Tess."

Alice held the door almost closed behind her, standing in her kitten heels on her front porch. An acrid, buttery smell was leaking

505

out of the house.

"Gerry burned the popcorn?" Tess said, then cleared her throat. She would not cry anymore. She would be done with the crying.

The corners of Alice's mouth went up. "Sweetheart, what I should have said is: I think she's probably all right. If you want to wait, I can see you after groups. I know you're having a rough time, but I've got a whole room full of people in there." She waved a hand at the house behind her.

Tess nodded.

"Their time is ticking," Alice said, with a sympathetic smile.

"No one will speak to me, Alice. Joe hangs up the phone. Del's run off to hide with her fucking high school friends. This sister of Troy's, that house was burned down the same night Cora goes missing. They've found remains. I'm praying they're the sister, but no one will tell me anything. No one will say anything to me at all."

Alice shook her head. "It's like living inside a police procedural around here right now."

"I just need to work through some of this, say it out loud. I keep thinking about Jung's scarab. Thinking this has to mean something: The fire and the flood. A corpse gone the same night a living girl — my girl — goes missing. But it's not acausal, is it —" She was going to cry, she caught her breath, squeezed her eyes shut. "It's all real, Alice."

Alice's hand left the doorknob and came to Tess's shoulder. "I would have you in there with everybody, but Joyce Perret is with us. I don't think that would be good for either of you."

Tess nodded again. "No."

"Listen, do this for me. Go to the park. Go look at the ducks. Count your blessings. I mean it: Number one, Cora is probably okay. Number two, you've got money to live. Number three —"

"You don't think Cora could have burned down a house, do you? Del thinks she killed the woman — but that can't be. That can't be true."

"Del thinks." Alice rolled her eyes, blowing air out from between her lips. "Honestly, no. I can't talk about that with you though, Tess. You need to talk about your fears with someone else. This —" She waved her hand back and forth between the two of them. "— has got to stop. We had — have — a professional relationship. And I just, sweetheart, I think you are a good doctor and a good mother, but I can't be all this for you.

Boyd is back, you know. Or Bruce Siger-son?"

"I'm not looking for therapy, Alice."

"Okay. We all should be getting help, though." Alice nodded, blinking her eyes heavily. "Regardless, you've got to stop this prying. It won't get you anywhere. I'm a locked safe." She made as though to zip her lips and throw away the key. "Okay? No chance. I have to get back inside, but I will offer one more thing, which is that you've experienced a major rupture, and like any fission, it's going to produce a huge amount of energy. Spend that energy wisely. Not in sleuthing or regret. 'Why' is pointless. The question is: what now? I know you like a good fixer-upper — that's your life now, okay?" She leaned over, took Tess's face in her hands and kissed her on the top of the head.

"Thanks for that."

"You owe me forty bucks, but I'll take it in martini form when you're feeling better."

"Alright, Alice."

Alice started to open the door, but then stopped. "Tess, in my opinion there is no possible circumstance in which Cora could have done any violence to anyone but herself," she said.

"Thank you."

Alice nodded and closed the door.

If any energy had been produced, as Alice said, from her fission with everything important in her life, Tess felt it leaking from her now, catastrophically. She could pinpoint the fault now, the moment that had occasioned this meltdown. It wasn't Cora's disappearance or her sleeping with Augie, it wasn't Joe's failing to rescue Cora from New Orleans or her being rough with Vincent, it wasn't their allowing Cora to stay when they evacuated, or even the storm itself. It had not been the moment of Cora's conception on the floor of Joe's studio, or the day she'd married Joe, or the day they'd met. No, it had been the afternoon in 1965 when she'd gone to watch baseball with Madge, the two of them in their pedal pushers, cracking gum. They'd both just had crushes on Augie Randsell at that point, and when he came up to the plate, twirling the bat around, she'd been too shy to cheer, but Madge stood up. Madge yelled, *Augie! Augie! Augie! Oi, oi, oi!* the color mounting in her cheeks, and Augie hit a home run off the first pitch. As he came around third base for home, he threw his hat to Madge, and she caught it, *clap,* in two hands, and that had been the moment that began the chain reaction that led her here. Tess had had to go far away from them to make a life for herself that was so different it couldn't be compared to theirs. Had to go to New York. Had to marry an artist, and a Creole one to boot. Had to take a job. *Dr. Eshleman.* Move downtown. *Mrs. Boisdoré to you, Mr. Randsell.* She wouldn't necessarily have even married him, but the fact that she had never even had the chance had ruined everything.

Stretched as far as she could see down the street were houses she could have lived in with other men, other children. With an ordinary man, the kind her father would have chosen, there would not have been mosaics laid on her porch nor stained glass made for her birthday. There would not have been dozens of images of her worked out of wood and marble and clay. There would not have been obscure jazz records booming through the house at ten in the morning, or sex on the roof when the children were in school; an ordinary man would have gone out of the door at nine and returned at six, kissed her dryly on the mouth as he loosened his tie. But they would have had children together, her and this ordinary man. Towheaded, unremarkable children, whom she could pat on their uniformed bottoms as they went off for school, without worrying about what insults they might have to endure, what misinformed generalizations. She would not have had to push them so hard — Del could have rested on her laurels, and Cora — as fragile as she was — Cora might have turned out differently if her world had always been completely safe, completely stress-free. Actually, with a different father, Cora would have been completely different. A different girl with a different name.

From around the corner, a little boy came squeaking on his tricycle, all alone, and Tess stepped down from the porch and went down onto the lawn. She watched the little boy wobble past, then watched his father, a portly redheaded man in a golf shirt and Dockers, shuffle out from behind a big hydrangea and follow after him. Blue flowers on the hydrangea, which meant the soil was acidic. Basic soil made pink. The father wiped sweat from his brow with the back of his forearm, nodded at her. Tess nodded back, smiled, then crossed the sidewalk and got into her car. She rolled down her windows, rummaged in her purse for her cellphone, and dialed Augie's number. He answered on the first ring.

His father was behind the privacy curtain, mumbling in his sleep. Joe sat in the vinyl recliner and watched Vanna turn the letters over on the muted TV. The whole hospital wing was quiet, as if sound had been bleached out of the world. She turned over three B's, three T's, one S, one Y — a gap-toothed "Before & After" phrase that refused to mean anything, even after the contestant had mouthed the words. He didn't get it until Vanna turned over the last white square: BEAUTY AND THE BEAST OF BURDEN.

Visiting hours were over, but, like a good boy, he'd made them let him stay. Even from across the lake he could feel Tess's scrutiny. She had called him to give him the Cora update — Tess scrambling for a reason to hold on to her suicide theory, even as Cora's Jeep was speeding on traffic cameras — but, despite her despair, she'd still gotten on her high horse about his father's treatment plan. No matter the situation, no matter her own state of mind, Tess always knew best. She had rattled off facts — *If your father goes septic, there's a forty percent chance that he will pass within the year* — and big doctor words — *immunosuppression, reinfection* — to establish her authority. Her opinion was the only one that ever counted, but he thought he might be finished counting it.

The Wheel of Fortune went around and bankrupted all three contestants in a row. *You can put me out on the street.* He was humming. To shut himself up, he pulled out his phone. Del or his brother Vin: those were his only options now. *Put me out.* In the past, he could have called Tess, Andy, his mother. *Put me out.* But you couldn't make a cellphone call in a hospital anyway. *Put me out of misery.* He stood up and went out of the room, down the hallway, down the stairs, through emergency, out the doors.

He walked across the ambulance lane and into the slanting red of the sun. An empty breeze was blowing, the kind that said they might drop a few more degrees in the coming days, and it pulled a fine spray of water from the fountain that played in the middle of the lawn. Joe tried to enjoy the sensation, but to do that, he'd have to feel it first. Instead, the longer he stood there, the emptier his mind became, as if the breeze were stripping thoughts from it like dead leaves from a branch. He looked at the pines standing guard over the sky. He stepped into their needles, smelled nothing.

Across the street, an old roadhouse hunkered against the ditch. It was the kind of place he and Vin would go to when they were kids, sneaking out in their mother's

Buick, drinking a couple of beers at the high bar until some redneck got it into his head to quarrel with their presence there among the nice country girls in their bell-bottomed riding pants. He thought of Monica Selvaggio the other day at Sol's farm, bending across the folding table for the hot dog buns. You could roll a marble across that thing, and if she wasn't married, maybe she would have let him. He was hardly married anymore. He could go into that roadhouse no problem now, pitch a hip against the bar, grab a longneck by its throat. He could corral some pretty young thing and get her talking: tell her about his dad, tell her about Cora, spin out a story about how she'd left all this behind — the mud and the mold and the coming water — how she was on the road now, her head out of the window of the speeding car, hair whipping around her face, the radio turned up loud. Maybe the girl would have pity on him, maybe take him out to her truck the way they did now, or so he'd been told, no wooing, no waiting. He tried to remember how that felt, a girl's body against yours, all sinew and lubricated joints, but he found his mind stopping short at her hand on his zipper, her lips on his cheek. He found a hard refusal in his heart, a fist clenched in his chest.

Above the rise of the I-12 a band of cloud was moving in, tossing the spindly branches of the pines. The breeze snapped with ozone and resin, but he put his hands in his pockets and trotted down the hospital's long lawn, towards home.

Del had taken herself to a party. Tina's high school boyfriend, Little Joe Alpharetta, was moving to Dallas the next day, and his boxes were all stacked up along the walls, his entire liquor cabinet — everything from rye to crème de banane — lined up on the counter. A "house-cooling," everybody was calling it, but the living room was packed so tightly that Del was sweating through her clothes.

She had done three circuits of the room, through the kitchen and out to the keg and back, without managing to attach herself to any of her old high school friends, and so she was back to Tina and George and George's old crew. Rob Walker was talking about MRGO, and she rolled her eyes at Tina — all dolled up in a skintight dress despite the nursing bra — as she turned sideways to slip between her and the big brown couch. As she straddled its arm, Rob put a sweaty hand on her shoulder. She couldn't figure out how to make him let go.

"— not to mention the cypress forests it killed, which is only a fraction of the swamp that's dying every day," Rob said. "A football field's worth. Every. Single. Day."

Del gulped at her beer. "Can we talk about something else?"

"I'm sorry, Del, if I'm traumatizing you, but it's just the truth. What with saltwater intrusion and the increase in storm activity we're expecting with the warming oceans —"

"Come on, man, let it go," George said.

Tina smiled at him. She had lipstick on her teeth. "Yeah, Rob, Del only just got here. Can you give her some time to get drunk before you purposely make her cry?"

Del would allow him to do no such thing, but as he kept talking, she felt the anger welling up in her chest again, and she reached up and pulled Rob's hand off her. She scooted backwards a little and looked out across the party, which seemed to be approaching its zenith. The house was so full that the boxes were no longer visible, and people trying to move through the crowd had to raise their drinks up above their heads as they squeezed between knots of conversation. She spotted Isabelle Franks and Megan Rosier hunched together in the kitchen, and Howie Richard was sitting alone halfway up the steps to the camelback, balancing a paper plate of Doritos on his knees.

"Well, sure it's criminal," Tina was saying, "but who's going to sue who? The Corps is the government. Can the government even sue itself?"

"You're missing the point," Rob said, and, almost without meaning to, Del stood up again, downed the last warm slug of beer, and pushed herself into a clogged channel that wound behind the backs of some Buckner husbands into the kitchen.

She paused a moment in front of the food, which the party guests had littered with balled-up cocktail napkins and foam-streaked Solo cups. Isabelle stared at her for a good three seconds, blinking her big brown eyes that had become even more cowlike since they'd graduated.

"Del Boisdoré?"

"Hey," Megan said, the sparkling fringe on her top trembling. "You're in town?"

Popping a handful of Zapp's in her mouth, Del shrugged. "Kinda."

Isabelle was still looking her up and down. Del jutted out her hip in her distressed jeans and forced a smile.

"Tina said you quit your job in New York?" Megan said, raising her penciled eyebrows.

"They wouldn't give me leave to come home."

Isabelle's mouth bunched up in one corner as she unconsciously smoothed the pleats on her Lily Pulitzer housewife dress, its pastel seashells like something one of her two kids might have drawn. "Good for you."

Megan raised her plastic cup of wine.

"I could never live in New York," Isabelle said.

"Yeah, you'd go broke," Megan said, pinching at the fabric of Isabelle's sleeve.

Isabelle blinked rapidly. "It just wouldn't suit me. It's too fast-paced. I'm not one of those mothers who's going to let a nanny raise her child."

Del smiled, nodded. "It's not really —" She looked down at the white bottom of her cup.

"Oh, look." Isabelle pointed at the door, an old Trinity friend of theirs coming in. "McGrath!"

"I heard Julie's still in Macon," Megan said, nodding.

"McGrath!" Isabelle yelled in her rough old catcher's voice.

Megan had pivoted around to the bar and

was pouring Pimm's straight into her cup.

"I'm going to go refill my beer," Del said.

"McGrath!" Isabelle barked. "Mic Grath!"

The blood beating in her neck, Del pushed her way out of the kitchen and through the dark laundry room. On top of the dryer, a Buckner girl from the year above was perched, her eyes closed. A tear had rolled down each of her cheeks, leaving trails that glistened in the light off the kitchen.

Out in the yard, a satellite party was taking place within a nimbus cast by the lights strung up in the holly tree. Hearing the screen door bang shut, Little Joe looked up from the tap and nodded.

Del tripped down the steps and stood beside Courtney Bain, her cup out. "You seen Tina?"

"No." Courtney shook her head. "Have you seen Lauren?"

"No," Del said. "How'd y'all make out?"

"We're alive, I guess. By the grace of God."

Little Joe took Del's cup from her and tilted it into the dying stream of Bud Light, then reached over and pumped the keg. Courtney wandered over to the tree and sat down, and a pair of guys in scrubs got in line behind Del and peeled new cups off the stack.

She tilted her face up and let her eyes adjust to the thinner light. The night was moonless, but the stars bored bright holes through the ebony of the sky. A rapping came from the house, and she looked up to see Tina standing in the window of the kitchen, knocking her fat diamond ring against the glass. Tina motioned at her, but just then, Del's phone buzzed in her back pocket — Zack's name on the bright white screen. She held the phone up to Tina, then walked out beyond the pool of light, pressed the green button, and brought the phone up to her face.

"Zack," she said.

"Hey."

She gulped a sip of beer. "Hey."

"They convicted my guy today."

She sat down on the steps up to the laundry shed and put her feet on the rim of a pot containing an aloe plant whose spikes had gone limp, sick from too much water.

"I'm sorry," she said.

"I'm not," Zack said, like a shrug. "Stupid motherfucker. Thinks because he has a trust fund, he can get away with literal murder."

"There's a lot of that. Well, not literally," Del said, just to respond, and the line seemed to go dead for a minute. Away from the hubbub of the party, she could hear the tree frogs chirping on the batture. A ship blew its horn, and she closed her eyes and breathed in the smell of the ligustrums.

"So, how are you doing, sweetheart? I didn't really understand your 'coded' e-mail. You guys found your sister? And the other thing, something about Troy's house?"

"Yeah, I think it's going to be okay. Cora's driving too fast through Arkansas, and the house was really burned to a crisp when I went to look. But it's over. It's gonna be okay."

" 'It's over?' So, you're a stupid mother-fucker too."

"What?" The aloe pot rocked under her feet.

" 'It's over,' like you don't even remember what you said to me in the car — or maybe you didn't mean it? 'It's not over, it'll never be over. It's not just a garbage-removal problem.' You were right, of course you were right. They're building your levees back to pre-Katrina strength? Well, that's great. And they got all the water out, so you're all good now, you're going to stay. It's all hunky-dory, huh? You're like — it's like you've never seen a movie. The bad guy's got the cop tied to the radiator, and he thinks he's safe, so he confesses everything, starts mak-ing a cup of coffee, and that's when they get him. Because he is a stupid mother-fucker."

"I'm not stupid, Zack."

"Then stop doing stupid shit, sweetheart."

"Okay, first thing is stop calling me sweet-heart," she said.

"And the second thing?"

"What the fuck is wrong with you?"

She felt the party turn to stare, but when she looked back towards the lit circle around the keg, Courtney Bain was talking to Lauren Farrow as she redid her ponytail, her Solo cup held between her teeth, and one of the football types was doing a keg stand. Tina was the only one looking in her direction; holding the screen door open, she squinted through the darkness, her head tilted to the side. Del held the phone up again, and Tina finally turned away.

"I don't want to be your lawyer, Del," Zack said.

"I don't need a lawyer! I never asked you to be my lawyer!" Across the yard, the screen door clapped shut. "I asked you to be my friend!"

"I don't want to be your friend."

Del rocked herself once, twice. She bent her toes around the rim of the terra-cotta pot, leaned forward, her elbows digging into her thighs.

"Okay," she said, unable to keep the hitch out of her voice.

The screen door swung open again, and Little Joe came dancing out, waving a piece of paper towel in his hand, trying to get people to second-line.

"You know what I want to be, Del."

She reached her arm out and pried a piece of the flaking paint up off of the bleached siding of the shed and looked at it, a thick but flexible thing, like a snake's scale.

"I'm not coming back though, Zack," she said. She looked across the yard to where Tina's husband George was ripping paper towels off of the roll and handing them to Courtney and Lauren. Tina was holding the screen door open, and it seemed like the whole party was pouring through it. Someone had turned up the stereo on "Hey Pocky A-Way" and opened all the back windows.

"You say that," Zack said, "but this is all going to end at some point. You're going to find Cora, and soon the rest of things will go back to normal."

"That's not what it's about. Or it's not just that," she said. "I can't leave, Zack. I've already lost too much. Maybe half of it? Twenty-seven thousand acres of cypress forest? A football field a day? My sister's gone and my grandfather's halfway out of his mind and my parents are done and the house I grew up in — they're going to gut it, fix it up, sell it — and I have literally two friends here, but I'm not going to lose the rest of it, okay? I can't."

"Then I'll come there," he said.

She laughed at the absurdity of that statement. "No, you can't, dummy. You're from there as much as I'm from here. 'New York is the ancestral homeland of the Jewish diaspora,' you said, like six weeks ago."

"I can come there."

"Don't be ridiculous. I'm going to be all right."

"Del, I —" He sighed. "Del."

In the silence, she stood up and went halfway back across the lawn. From the screened doors and windows of the house, the Meters were shouting *Hey pocky way, hey pocky way,* over and over to end the song, and she watched the jumping napkins die in the hands of the dancers as the track cut out and was replaced by the sound of Louis Armstrong's plaintive horn playing the first notes of "St. James Infirmary." At the front of the parade, George took a stutter step, then raised his hand again with the napkin in it and started to lead the second line again in a slow march around the holly tree and out of the haze of light.

"It's not about you," Zack said. "It's not just about you."

George was dancing towards her, and as he approached, he reached out his napkin at her, then held the dancing in place as he tore it in half and handed one part to her.

"I'm at a party, Zack, can we talk about this later?"

"I'm done talking," he said, and suddenly she knew that he would come. They would find each other some night soon on the damp bricks of the Dobies' courtyard, and he would flick his cigarette into the monkey grass and say again the things that he kept saying, and this time she would say them back. She imagined them sitting on the front porch of a house they'd fix up in Bayou St. John as their teenaged children came back home from the parades, tired and satisfied, carrying glittered coconuts in their arms, their necks bowed under the weight of thousands of strands of plastic pearls.

Little Joe and Vita Barron were singing, *Let her go, let her go, God bless her; Wherever she may be; She can look this wide world over; But she'll never find a sweet man like me,* and the girl who had been crying in the laundry room held out her hand to Del, and she stepped in along the side of the line.

"Dance with me, then," she said to Zack, and she raised up her phone in the hand she held her napkin in and started to sing along with all of them, though she didn't entirely remember either the music or the words.

FIFTY-EIGHT DAYS
AFTER LANDFALL
OCTOBER 26

Cora found Tyrone on the swings in the schoolyard, a black Saints beanie pulled low on his head. He held the chains twisted so that his feet dangled high off the ground. Behind him, other children in hats and puffy jackets were playing tag, screaming wildly, their snow boots pounding the painted asphalt. The pair of girls next to him swung high enough to make the chains buckle in the air. Every so often, Tyrone released a link so that he bumped down half a turn, and then he wound himself back up again.

He hadn't seen her yet. She stood under a leafless tree on the other side of the street, waiting to know what words she needed. She checked the plastic watch she'd bought — fifteen minutes had already passed. She crossed the street. Tyrone didn't look up, but the girls looked at each other and shrieked, their dresses flying as they flung themselves into the air and across the playground. Cora looped her fingers into the fence.

"Tyrone?"

He looked up, his brow bunched under his hat's gold fleur-de-lis, and let go of the chains. His spinning sped up as they untwisted and then slowed again as the swing began a counterturn. She expected him to run away from her, but he didn't run.

"Tyrone. I came to say I'm sorry."

His hands caught the chains and held them separate for a moment, his back to her.

"I know it isn't enough," she said. "I know it doesn't matter what I meant to do, but all I wanted was to protect you. All I wanted in the world was to protect you, but still everything that shouldn't have happened has happened, and I am sorry. I am sorry about your mother and sorry for what you lived through, and I'm sorry you lost your home."

He began to wind the chain back up again, crossing hand over hand. Each time he turned to face her he closed his eyes.

"And that's all," she said. Her heart was beating hard and fast. "I'm going now, unless you have something you need to say to me."

She swallowed a mouthful of acid spit, listening to the swing's hinges creak as he adjusted himself in the seat, and then she pushed off the fence and began to turn away.

"Don't." He took his hands off the chains, spun down three revolutions, stopped himself.

"I'm here."

He held still, his head bent. "She used to get us Milky Way bars from the K&B sometimes, when she was feeling good. She called us little prince, little prince."

"Because you are. You are. You are a prince."

Tyrone let himself drop a turn and looked up. "We got a dog once. He was big, colored like tinfoil, with no ears. We dressed him up in her clothes before she came home one day, and she didn't even get mad. She laughed. But we had to let him loose. He bit Willy. Just a little bit. So we took him down to the big park, and we let him go loose, but I saw him again once hanging around the trashcans. But he didn't know who I was. He growled at me. Forgot to take his medicine, Mama said. I knew it. Seemed like he didn't like the taste, even wrapped up in yellow cheese."

"You know your mom didn't want to be sick, Tyrone."

He wound the chain up tighter, rising off the ground, and Cora stared across the schoolyard. A teacher near the soccer goal was blowing a whistle, but Tyrone didn't seem to hear.

"Nobody who's sick wants to be sick," Cora said. "She loved you. And she wanted to take care of you. That's why she came to get you. Even though it was scary when she came — that was just the sickness. She couldn't hold it back. There are things out there, things that sometimes we can't protect ourselves from, things we can't control."

He held himself at the top of his chains facing the other children, who were lining up in four columns at the far side of the yard.

"Maybe I shouldn't tell you that. It's scary. But I think you know from scary. I think we all know from scary now."

"Do you think I'm going to get sick when I grow up?"

Cora shook her head, licked her lip. "If you do, we'll work through it together, okay?"

"Uncle Troy just says no." He let himself down a half turn and looked at her from his high seat. Then, he nodded. "Okay."

Across the playground, a wide woman in a long skirt was stomping towards them while the lines of children began marching indoors. A strong breeze kicked up, and a windfall of golden leaves scattered over the fence and across a map of the United States painted on the basketball court.

"Excuse me," the teacher was shouting. "Excuse me!"

Tyrone let the chains go, spinning down fast, and then went running across the yard to fall in line behind his classmates, but the woman kept coming, all the way up to the fence, so close that Cora had to back away.

"Excuse me!" Her breath smelled like salad dressing. "Who are you?"

"Nobody." Cora turned and stepped down into the grass at the curb.

"Nobody?" She arched a plucked eyebrow. "Are you a relative of the boy's? Are you his mother?"

"I'm just a friend of his uncle's. It's okay — I'm going."

"Oh?" The woman pulled a phone out of her jacket. "We'll see about that. If you're a friend of his father's you'll know there's a restraining order out against the mother, and we can't allow —"

"His mother's dead." Cora stepped into the street. "I killed her."

"What?" the teacher said. "What? Hello!"

Cora kept her back turned.

"What did you just say to me? Ma'am. Ma'am! Hello? Don't you walk away from me."

Cora wrestled the keys out of her pocket, opened the door of her Jeep, got in, started the ignition. The teacher was hollering for security, and a blue uniform moved from the shadow of the school's entrance, down towards her car. Staring into the rearview mirror, Cora put her foot on the gas. The tires spun on a low ridge of ice, regaining purchase just as a Sysco truck barreled around the corner. She didn't have time to hit the brakes.

THURSDAY
OCTOBER 27

In the early morning light, the workshed looked hopeful, fresh-faced — it was clean and smelled sweetly of paint. Joe set his coffee on the workbench, turned the radio on to OZ. They were playing some kind of experimental instrument that synthesized theremin music to the weather satellites, and he thought that was pretty rad, thought he'd like to do something along those lines, since he'd decided it was time to find something to do. He hadn't gone back to the hospital last night but had walked home instead through the rain, battered by heavy drops gathered by what trees remained along the country road. He'd walked with his head down, humming, as though he'd find a yellow light at the end of his driveway and a woman cooking at the stove. Instead, he'd loaded kindling into the empty house and sat awhile by the fire, trying to figure out how to be alone. Del had agreed to come and help today; he'd given himself that, as a gift. And since he had, he'd better do something with it.

He opened his sketchbook, flipped from the back through the white pages. Nothing. Literally nothing since landfall, or less than nothing — he'd written down the names of some roofers, two blank pages after the last sketch he'd done at the breakfast table before they'd started to pack up, some bullshit about entropy, cribbed from Yeats. From the high shelf, the Tess portraits looked down at him in judgment.

He was free of her, though, wasn't he? She was gone, had been gone probably for a long time. If he looked at them right, the sculptures, a yearly record of their marriage, recorded the stages of her departure. The girl aged — her nose thinning, her jowls loosening. Little by little, she lost her joy. Those from the first years of their marriage — Tess recumbent on imagined pillows, head thrown back; Tess with her legs crossed at the ankle and flowers in her hair — looked shy of his touch. How pathetic he was. How pathetic he had been all along. This was the foretold loss of pride he hadn't expected, though they had all warned him it would come.

She's a who? his father had asked him.

An Eshleman.

An Eshleman, like I put wax on her mama's furniture, Eshleman. His father whistled, hot as a factory blowing quitting time. *Son, you are out of your ever-loving mind.*

She had always been going to leave him. You could see it in the portraits from 1981, '89, '92, '93, '97. Her lip puffed out over her teeth. Her hand gripping her hair as she bent over an absent desk. Eyes closed. Mouth open. Cuticles bitten. He would invite her to sit for him: an act of devotion, as one would pay to an archaic god. But she saw it as her doing him a favor, and maybe he had been worshipping her for his own pleasure all along, so that his love for her would overwhelm hers for him, so that she would always remain the desired thing, the unattained, the girl who was always slipping from him, evaporating, so that he was left crouching like a boy in a storybook to peel her shadow off the ground.

He reached for his favorite of her portraits: Cora in her belly, she stood submerged to the waist in a sea of negative space, her hands riding the surface of the water. He had carved her whole and then carved away along the line of the water — a wave that skirted her hip then heaved as high as the undercurve of her breast, the yin of the

535

invisible water running up against the yang of her belly. One part of that belly was hers, one part his, and he had felt unexpectedly triumphant at that, the idea of the bit of himself growing inside her, entwining with that bit of her. And now they were gone. Tess was gone. Cora was gone. Everyone was gone. He weighed the little sculpture in his cupped palm. Tess had stood in the Gulf for hours that day, laughing, the water holding the baby up. That night as they'd lain in the gritty hotel sheets, she had thanked him for the child, thanked him for showing her what she wanted. He supposed she'd decided now that he had been wrong.

One of the striplights began to flicker, and beyond the windows, the fog was burning off the lawn. He ran his thumb along the edge of her belly where the wave broke it. A sharp edge. He should bury them, probably, the way people clipped their exes out of photographs, burned their letters. But the paint can still sat in the middle of a mudflat of congealed paint, six inches of brown left in the can. He dropped her into the paint, and she went under, everything submerged but the top of her head and one ocean-eaten arm.

He was so disgusted he nearly spat, his stomach turning over with the chemical smell of paint. He wasn't free, wasn't in control. Probably never would be. He closed his sketchbook, took his coffee, slammed out the door.

"Sylvia?" Papie dragged a breath in through his mouth, coughed.

Del held out the cup to her grandfather. The skinny psychiatric nurse had come in when she'd first arrived, given her instructions. She was supposed to avoid stressing him. She was supposed to, within reason, find a place within his delusions and play along.

"She's not here right now," Del said. "Had to go out and get a few things."

"Funny, you." He coughed, reached out his lips for the straw, drank. "Funny."

Del turned towards the monitors — beeping a steady rhythm, his bodily functions drawing mountain ranges, his temperature getting closer to normal, 101.9. She'd sung a lullaby to Tina's baby last night, and it was still in her head, images of a cowboy alone under his blanket in the Rockies, the trucker cresting an icy ridge. *His horse and his cattle are his only companions.* Zack had said he would come, but if he didn't, she could roll herself up in her sleeping bag and commune with the stars.

"Sylvia?"

"I'm not Sylvia, Vincent. I'm Adelaide."

"Adelaide. I knew an Adelaide."

She nodded. "I heard you needed some help."

"Oh." Papie knit his brows, his hand floundered on the sheet. "I'm sorry, my mind's somewhere else. I was waiting on my wife to join me. Adelaide, you said?"

She nodded.

"Pretty. I knew someone by that name, I believe." His hand scrabbled again, as if he would have liked to shake her hand.

She wanted to tell him about the first Adelaide — to remind him of the looping signature on the free papers, the lithograph of the severe woman in the tignon and lace who had once been a slave and was now the mother of the richest free man of color in the city — but she had been told not to disturb him, and that would definitely do it, all of that history rotted away. She thought of Phillip, how he'd thought it was funny to call her "Little Vincent," half-implying that that was her value to him and to the auction house, her pedigree the only reason they'd hired her. *How marvelous it must have been,* he'd say, *just to grow up among his things, just to be in that workshop* — never mind that Phillip's image of her grandfather was so antiquated he probably envisioned "that workshop" as something out of a nineteenth-century etching. *I would love to meet him — one of the last practitioners of the fine tradition of African American craftsmanship.* Reverence, but always with a twinge of affirmative action.

"I believe we've met before," she said, instead. "You are Vincent Boisdoré, the master cabinetmaker, correct?"

"Oh." He turned to her. "I'm sorry. After the ship was torpedoed, it's like I lose things."

"That's alright."

"It's like my hull's full of holes."

"It's alright, sir. Truly."

"You've heard about me?"

"Someone told me you were an expert. I'm very interested to learn."

"Well, my dear. I'm happy to tell you anything, you have such beautiful eyes. Amber eyes, like jewels." On the folded-back sheet, he brought his hands together, fingers and then thumbs. "This is for the *Picayune*?"

"Sure."

"You'll have to let me check you over. I'm not interested in having secrets just spread about." The hand went up, as if he was sowing seed.

"Of course. Nothing you're uncomfortable with."

He nodded. "Alright. You want I should take you through from the beginning, then? I'm starting a new project. Conceptualizing. You know about oysters?"

"Oysters?" She smiled forcefully and put her elbows on her knees. "I like them fried."

His eyes crinkled up, the green lights in their hazel sparking, and he laughed, a big guffaw. "Me too, child," he said. "Me too. But that's not what I'm talking about. There's something we cabinetmakers call an oyster, 'cause I suppose it looks like one, but actually it's wood, marquetry. The center of the tree. We tend to use walnut or olive, because they have a nice contrast between the heartwood and the sap. By which I mean, normally, I'd take a hunk of a tree — or one of its branches, usually — into my band saw and slice off little disks, then use a template to cut out their middles, where the wood is hardest and prettiest. This time, though, I'm thinking something else. I want it bigger, just a single patera if I'm going to make a table, or one for each door of an armoire. Not oysters exactly, but something more like," he said, and then lids fluttered over his eyes, and he stopped talking. His left hand still moved, though, his fingers tracing a circle on the bedclothes, pulling the bleached cotton into a rough spiral, like a cloud formation. He traced the shape in the fabric as if he was following the edge's of a tree's rings, following their rhythm as they tightened, moving away from the living bark through sapwood towards the dark, dense heartwood formed in decades past.

Augie sat down at the Dobies' patio table and popped open the lid of the Styrofoam box, letting the smell of hamburger into the green air. Troy had called that morning — Reyna's identity confirmed, arson ruled out as a cause for the fire — but Tess's head was buzzing, the sun pouring mercilessly down. It had slipped from the top of the sky and crept in under the patio umbrella, onto her shins. She stood up and tilted the umbrella's head.

"Did you know," Augie said, watching her, "umbrella's the one word we all say the same — and different from everyone else — we New Orleanians? UMbrella, we say, every last one of us. Yats and Sacred Heart Girls and Creoles, whites and blacks alike. UMbrella. Say it."

She sighed, sat, leaned over her legs towards the box of files Joe had tossed

541

together in the office on Esplanade. "Umbrella."

"Exactly. UMbrella. That's how they'd catch you, the FBI, on their wiretaps or what have you. UMbrella. 'Don't you go telling me you're not from N'awlins.' "

UMbrella, her brain said. umBRELla. UMbrella. "At least they've stopped calling it N'awlins."

"Ain't dat da truth." He took a bite of his burger, held it out to her. "Sure you don't want some?"

"This was all I wanted." She toasted him with her wine, gulped at it.

"You've got to eat, you know."

"Oh, don't start."

Augie's hands shot up in surrender, mayonnaise clinging to the wick of his mouth. She pulled out a pile of books — an old DSM, a monograph on Joseph Cornell. On the cover was one of his *Hotel* boxes, all whitewash and painted wire grill, that looked to her like a prison cell. For some reason, even though Troy had said everything she'd wanted to hear, she was scared worse than she already had been; an image of Cora standing outside a burning house, of Cora with a shotgun at her shoulder, wouldn't leave her alone. She was going stir-crazy, probably, waiting around for something that wouldn't come. She saw it constantly in her patients, the desperate scramble to find alternatives when all roads were closing down. They fought hard not to be trapped with the one truth they could not admit.

"It's just frustrating. Being here," she said. She swept her hand around at the patio. Laura's dying plants she had neglected watering, the windows crammed with all of her and Joe's furniture. "I woke up this morning thinking — *the insurance man is coming today, at least we can get a start.* And then the rest of everything fell on me again like a load of bricks."

"I understand." He put the hamburger back down. "Listen. Why not, after you've done with the bureaucracy, pack a little bag? Just a few nights' clothes, whatever essentials you need. Come take a vacation with me on Felicity Street."

She pushed the hair back off her forehead. "I can't come stay with you. Are you kidding?"

"No."

"What if Cora comes home?" she tried.

"If Cora comes home, then Cora's okay. Then we can relax. Besides, Del is here."

UMbrella, her brain said. *UMbrella UMbrella.* "She hasn't been."

543

"But she could be. Isn't that ostensibly why she came back from New York? To help?"

Tess shook her head, thinking of the one short text she'd gotten in response to the five voice mails she'd left: *taking care of Papie today. see you soon.* Del saw the prison cell too, and she was climbing as fast as she could towards that tiny square of blue sky. "She's helping her father, Augie."

Augie shrugged his shoulders, picked up his hamburger again. She pulled out the insurance file and put it to one side with the files on the mortgage. To the other side went the files on the girls' colleges, the file of vital documents.

Her phone rang, and she scrambled for it. Del.

"Speak of the devil," Augie said.

"Hey, Mom!" She sounded so sunny, so pleased with herself, Tess wanted to hit her in the mouth.

"Where have you been?"

"I was at Tina's, as you know. And now I'm across the lake, as you also know. Anyway, I ——"

"Del, I want you to tell me something," Tess interrupted. "Why would you leave me here when you knew the police were coming? When I needed you, to answer questions about your sister. About the fire. Why would you run away like a fucking criminal?"

"What?"

"They confirmed Reyna's identity this morning. Troy called to tell me. And there's no evidence of arson. So, I'm confused about why you implied there was." Too long a pause intervened before Del responded, and Tess imagined her rolling her eyes. "Did you see her do it? Did you help?"

"Help?"

"Adelaide Boisdoré, tell me the truth!"

Augie threw away his sandwich box, and the kitchen garbage can shut with a bang.

"What the fuck was that?" Del said.

"Please." Tess took a deep breath. "Do you know what happened to your sister? That's all I'm asking. There's no danger now in telling."

"Danger?" Del's voice caught in her throat. *Relieved,* Tess would have written in her notes. *Lying, for some reason relieved.*

Augie thumped in from the kitchen, put his hands on Tess's shoulders. She wrenched away. "Just tell me: did you and your sister burn down that man's home?"

"And what if I had?" Del was trying sarcasm now. If she had been in the room, Tess was sure she'd make that ugly moue with her mouth. "What in hell difference would it make? If something's sick, kill it, right? If something's dead, bury it. Only way to move on — isn't that right, Mom? Isn't that how you do things?"

And then Del hung up the phone.

"Arson?" Augie lifted his eyebrows at her. Behind his head was the one thing of Laura and Dan's Tess liked, a photograph of a house at night overhung by an old cypress, the word *Annunciation* scrawled in the corner. "That's pretty unlikely, don't you think? Didn't Troy say the police have ruled it out?"

She stormed out into the heat again, letting the screen door clap shut in his face, but he was right behind her, and he opened it again, calmly as a priest.

"I know you're still worried about Cora. You wouldn't be much of a mother if you weren't."

She shrugged and let him put his hands on her. She wasn't much of a mother, then. She had no business being here, in somebody else's house, with her lover and a gigantic Mardi Gras cup of wine. If she was a good mother, she would be looking for her daughter in diners, motels, truck stops from here to Canada. The problem was, she had given up on Cora just as Del had accused her of doing, and despite all this "sleuthing" as Alice called it, despite these conspiracy theories, what she really expected was that they would find her, if they found her, at the bottom of the lake.

"Let me help you feel better. However I can," Augie said, reaching out to rub her back. "There's a party tonight at Leslie Bain's house. Would you like to go?"

Umbrella, she thought. *Umbrella, umbrella, umbrella.* "Finding my daughter would make me feel better."

"Troy hasn't heard a peep?"

"I'm pretty sure he thinks she's dead." She shook her head. " 'It was over for me a good while ago,' he says. He's done. Done mourning his sister. Not even worried about his house. Says he's just going to let the city tear it down."

Augie cleared his throat, then looked at her the way she imagined Alice looked at her child-patients when they needed the facts of life explained. "Do you know how many fires there have been since the storm?"

She pinched the plastic cup of wine and drank, then fell on her knees on the slate, and put her hands in the files. She pulled out the one on the inheritance her mother had left her, marked CORNELIA M. ESHLE-

MAN SUCCESSION and opened it on the ground.

"Well, I don't know either, exactly, but it's a lot. All the fuse boxes were damaged, the water shifted the wires around. Do you know what knob and tube looks like? When Madge and I renovated Felicity, the wires were just in there — no insulation, just bare wires that crumbled when you touched them, and I'd been sleeping with this stuff behind my head my entire life."

"I know what knob and tube is." She flipped past photographs of her mother's house on Upperline, her Philadelphia sofa on its Persian rug, the caned chairs in the solarium, the tester bed with the marquetry M on the headboard — M for Marleybone, her mother's maiden name, under which she had been Queen of Comus. The Marleybones had vanished in a plague of daughters, and soon so would the Eshlemans, she the only child of an only child in this Catholic place where she knew people with upwards of fifty first cousins.

"Now, imagine what happens when a house hasn't been cared for by people such as ourselves. Say you can barely cover the telephone bill, and now water rises in the walls. The power's off, but then it comes back on and —" He made a zapping sound like a child reading aloud from a comic book, then opened up his hamburger box again. "There's your fire."

"I know," she said. And she knew too that soon there would be no one to care for these houses at all. Already they were gone, and many would not come back. And those that would were not guaranteed to know how to restore any of it to the way things had been. "I know," she repeated.

Augie peeled the aluminum foil back from around his potato with a cringe-making squeak. "Then why are you giving Del such a hard time?"

Under a few more stapled sheaves of paper, she found the appraisal she'd been looking for of all the antiques in their house. She flipped to the back page to remind herself of the exact number — 2.25 million dollars — a figure that had been comforting before they'd had to leave it at the mercy of the heat and the water and the thieves. There was no one left who even knew how to repair any of it anymore.

"Not anymore," she said.

"Because she hung up on you. I'm no shrink, my dear, but I think you're transferring."

"No, I mean, this stuff —" She threw her hand at the windows, the back of an étagère, a Victorian chaise. "— it's not worth shit anymore."

"Hardly. That's not just stuff," Augie said. "Never has been. Anyway, you're insured."

The doorbell rang.

"Speak of the devil." Augie said again. "Listen. I'll go let him in. Give him some ice tea. You compose yourself. Pack a bag. Think about if you feel like going to Leslie's tonight."

"Alright."

"Good. Alright."

Bright bodies of flame sprang from the torn garbage bags and into the small branches of the templed pines. Joe stood leeward of the brush pile, mesmerized — how the broad-winged fire flared up, shaking its feathers, only to vanish and rematerialize in a different form.

He remembered creeping to his bedroom window one St. Joseph's Night when he was a very small child, awakened by the sound of bells. Looking down into the street he saw a masker coming, alone, dressed in deep orange plumes like a magnificent bird of God. The man's suit rustled in the night air, picking up flecks of light from the houses and the streetlamp that flickered at the end of the block, and Joe had held his breath against the power of it. There had been no singing, only the bells shaking at his ankles, the tambourine rustling at his hip as the man walked home, but Joe's feet began to move now in the grass, tapping to the old Indian song in his head, a music to set fires by. *Shallow water, oh mama. Shallow water, oh mama!* He blew out a long breath, listening to the steam hiss from the branches.

When you go outside, my son.
Said you might have to go out in the rain.
— I know.

But don't you bow down.
— No no no no.
On that dirty ground.

He tapped his foot as something clattered inside the brush pile, something made of glass.

He'd set the fire to windward so that the breeze, gusting now from the south, would become a blowtorch, gathering the intense heat from the center of the bags he'd filled with his sculptures of Tess and drenching the tree trunks in it, so that even soaked from last night's rain they wouldn't fail to go. And they were going. Crackling and spitting as the bark rolled back and the branches split and the smoke turned black and dense with sap.

The fire was so loud, he didn't hear Del until she was at his side — come as she'd said she would so that he could spell her at the hospital, her body incurved and ill with sitting among the nurses — and then he didn't turn to her. He only extended his hand from his side, which she took, silently, and held for a moment before dropping it, dropping her head.

She stepped forward, and he saw then what she saw: the garbage bag melted away around the sculptures of her mother, its black residue clinging to their scorched faces, the bag's red tie lying wilted across them like a second-prize ribbon. *Shallow water, oh mama. Shallow water, oh mama!*

The high, crossed poles of the pines were going gray and brittle as they burned, and Joe thought to hold Del back as she moved toward the fire, but he knew he couldn't bear it if she wrenched her arm away. Her face turned from the flames, she reached out her hand and, one by one, took the sculptures that had tumbled away to the ashy edge of the blaze and stood them in the grass — her mother sitting rigid in her desk chair, her mother lying on pillows, her mother bending over and reaching her hand out to an absent child. Side by side, their extremities singed, the sculptures looked like ruins — which was, of course, what they were.

"I'm sorry, Del," he said. "I couldn't look at them anymore."

Del nodded her head at him, but her face was turned to the sculptures in the grass, her hands pressed against her knees.

"All along I was hoping for better, you know," he said. "I thought — I suppose I thought we were getting somewhere."

When you go outside, whispered the silent chief in his head. *I said you might have to go out in the rain.*

"I knew —" he said, "I mean I thought that if we kept our heads down, kept moving, we'd find ourselves in some kind of Promised Land, laughing as we cut our steaks with your mother's silver, as we drank the good wine."

Del was shaking her head. She'd picked up one of the sculptures — her mother looking over her shoulder at him in the doorway to their bedroom, as if his being there was a surprise. *Shallow water, oh mama. Shallow water, oh mama!*

Around the fire stood the remainder of the stand of trees that was supposed to be his daughters' heritage, their branches riffling upward in the heat, as if frightened, and he wondered if they weren't already setting seed in silent evolutionary panic so that the land would come again to be covered in longleaf pine or if what came next would be different, some invading forest of foreign trees.

"That's your mama's world, maybe, baby," he said. *Shallow water, oh mama. Shallow water, oh mama!* "But it ain't ours."

"No, Daddy," she said, her brow creased at him as if he'd suddenly lost his mind. "It's not hers either. It's not any of ours."

Don't you bow down.
— No no no no.
I said I won't bow down.

Leslie Bain's house looked just as it had the last time Tess had been there for some birthday party back when Del and Leslie's daughter Courtney were girls. The oak tree in the side yard hadn't been touched by the storm, and the earthy smell of its leaves merged with the gathering dusk as Augie and Tess mounted the steps. The front porch had always needed a new coat of paint.

Augie pressed the bell. Beyond the leaded glass, men and women in silk and wool stood holding their drinks in the amber light, and the sound of their talking thrummed through the door. Tess shifted the bottle of wine to her other arm and tried to look comfortable. After all, these were "her people" as her father would have said, and she had been raised to know how to act among them, even as a woman separated from a colored sculptor, showing up to a party on the arm of her best friend's widower. As Leslie came through her foyer, Tess smiled brightly, raising her fingers in a little wave.

"Tess, lovely." Leslie embraced her. "You haven't aged a single day!"

"And you've gotten younger." Tess grinned at her — face-lift, hair dye, a good green dress.

As Leslie pinched her on the arm, she knew she would be taken back. Maybe her father had been right after all. *My people?* She heard herself screaming in that first argument over Joe. *My people? That would include you, I take it? Well, that's not a club I want membership in anymore.* But here she was standing in Leslie Bain's foyer on Augie Randsell's arm. It was an old feeling, fitting in — like a ball gown unearthed from a cedar chest that zips up easily over your aged body, whispering, silk on silk, to the girl you had once been. The Boisdorés had never quite accepted her. Her mother, after her father died, welcomed Joe with open arms, but the Boisdorés saw her as yet another manifestation of whatever defect had driven Joe away from cabinetmaking to art and from New Orleans to New York. Tess had never been sure of herself in their home, never known what she'd said to make Sylvia turn sideways in her chair and lift her eyes to God. Tess knew that Sylvia believed Joe guilty of "climbing." No matter what she wore to their house, no matter what present Tess brought — flowers or cheese straws or spiced pecans — Sylvia had treated her with a sort of condescending deference. She was not allowed to help with the cooking. Only after many years was she allowed to clear.

Now, Leslie had her by the elbow, and she heard herself laughing, politely, automatically, at whatever pleasantries were exchanged. A few other couples came towards them, hands outstretched, big grins on. This was easy, and wasn't that a sign of its rightness? It was like lying down in a cast made off your own body, like coming home.

"So good to see you!"

"My gosh, how are you? It was so funny to run into each other out in Houston!"

She smiled back, shook their hands — Mel Bock and his wife Sinny, John and Linda Zimpel.

"So funny!"

"Linda, you wouldn't believe. Ruth's Chris, six days after the storm, and everyone you knew was there, wearing the one nice outfit they'd packed."

"Three shirts, three skirts, six pairs of underwear, one pair of heels."

"And all the jewelry."

"And all the jewelry."

"So funny, how we all thought it was just going to be a long weekend away."

"An evacuation vacation."

Tess closed her eyes. *An evacuation vacation.* She had spent the day after Joe had gone off to New Orleans without her at the subdivision pool with a cup full of the strawberry daiquiri Zizi and Vin kept in old three gallon ice cream tubs in their deep freeze. Then she had shaved her legs, lay in bed with a cold washcloth over her eyes until the puffiness went down. That night at that office-tower Ruth's Chris, among all the laughing refugees, a cold rush of dread had cascaded down her back as Augie poured her wine. *I can't drink this,* she'd thought as he went on about how well Syrah went with steak. *It's wrong to drink this.* But it made no difference whether she drank it or not, it changed nothing, and so she raised the glass to her lips.

"Gin and tonic, lots of lime?" Augie asked, squeezing her shoulder.

She nodded and watched him go.

"When Augie said he was bringing you, I was just over the moon." Leslie's voice was a few decibels louder than necessary, but that was usually the case. "It has been such a long time."

"I know!" she heard herself drawl the words. "My goodness, when was it they graduated? Seven years ago now?"

"I think eight?"

"My God, that long?" Sinny exclaimed. "That ages us, doesn't it? I remember when Allie was just this high." She waggled her hand near her knee. "Did I tell you? She's living in Atlanta, running her own design shop. We should all be retired by now, if the world was just."

"Oh, don't expect a just world," Leslie laughed. "We haven't seen Augie, either, in ages."

They all looked across the crowd towards where Augie stood, with his head bent, talking to the uniformed bartender. Dr. Grunnel, passing behind him, slapped him twice, solidly, on the back.

"When we saw you two, as we were saying, at Ruth's Chris in Houston," Mel said, "I thought for a second I was dreaming. I hadn't seen Augie, except at the Club, in years. Just dropped off the earth. You couldn't drag him out of Felicity Street with a grappling hook."

"He seems so much better," Linda nodded. "Healthier."

"Madge's death was hard on all of us." Tess looked at her toes. "Mourning takes time."

"Yes, Dr. Eshleman," Leslie said. "But five years?"

"We haven't even seen him at the Rex luncheon," John said.

"Honestly, I think it was the storm did it," Leslie said. "The change in scene, even his mother's passing. I think it liberated him."

"Mrs. Randsell never did stop wearing black for August Senior," Mel said.

Sinny was nodding heartily. "I myself feel — I don't want to say better — but more energetic, I don't know, less *ennuieux*, since the storm. There's work to do now. Don't you feel it?"

"And of course, he must be taking great comfort in you." Leslie gave Tess a toothy smile.

"We're propping each other up. We've

been friends a very long time."

Tess looked for Augie again, but he was saying hello to Chris Walsh, who took Augie's hand in one hand and his forearm in the other and shook violently, his madras jacket swinging open. The last time she'd seen Chris, whom she'd known since they were twelve, was at an estate sale by the park. He had been holding a Famille Rose lamp, and, when Joe said hello, he only nodded, didn't even put the lamp down. Now, Chris's eyes scanned the crowd, and he saluted her.

"I hear you had a tree," Leslie said.

Tess swiveled her head back towards the conversation. "Oh, the tree. Yes."

"I'm sorry." Leslie, with furrowed brow, reached out to put a hand upon her arm.

"About the tree?" Tess said, though she would have liked to add *Or do you mean my marriage? Or my daughter?* Augie, suddenly out of his shell, must have explained it all.

"Where are you again?" John Zimpel saved her, and she felt herself smile the sickening smile she'd developed when Cora had started at Buckner and she'd been thrown in with "her" people again, a smile that said *I know you mean well, but let's not pretend.*

"Esplanade and Royal."

560

"Oh?" Sinny knit her brows, as if the Marigny were another country.

"Mmm. Which one?"

Tess smiled. John taught architectural history.

"Not the Gauche House, obviously," he said. "That's Matilda."

"No, just across."

"Royal?"

"No, Esplanade."

"Oh, beautiful building. Gorgeous, gorgeous building. I've always wanted a peek inside."

"If there's anything left by the time we get it patched up again, I'd be glad to have you over."

"If you need any help on the restoration —" He reached into his back pocket for a card, and Linda swatted him on the arm. "What? Who you gonna call?" He did a little dance.

"She was asking us over socially," Linda said. "She doesn't need you in there telling her her steam shower is historically inaccurate."

"We would love to come by," John said. "I promise I will pass no judgments on your shower."

"Well, that would be so nice."

"Lovely," Linda said.

"Wonderful," John said.

John was describing her house to the others — *double galleries, late classical, a wonderful oculus above a curved stair, dentil molding* — things he must have read about in some book or archive, and Tess tried to picture this little crowd on her sofa, Augie in Joe's armchair, cheese straws in a silver dish and Sazeracs all around. She had taken the *café brûlot* set from her mother's after she died, the silver chafing dishes, the vegetable servers and long table cloths, but most of it had never come out of the sideboard. With Joe, there had been crawfish boils, intimate dinners with loaves of crusty whole wheat bread, evenings when they listened to music in the yard, drinking their beers straight from the bottle. The girls had had birthday parties, of course, with water balloon fights and chocolate doberge cake, and she had hosted small Thanksgivings, just the two girls, she and Joe, Joe's parents, and had had Augie and Madge or Andy and Tim over for dinner, but she had never entertained the way her parents had. No one arrived at her door in cocktail dresses and black tie, ready to trim the tree, there was never dancing or confetti, and now the oculus above the stairs was cracked, and in two days the men would start ripping the plaster down. She imagined the Zimpels and the Bocks and Leslie Bain sitting in the dark on the damp cushions of the sofa, fanning themselves, not speaking as they pressed iced drinks against their cheeks.

"You know, I don't think I've set foot in a single house on Esplanade," Sinny was saying.

"Oh?"

"No! I've kept to the American side." She looked to John for approval. "The Garden District — you can still just see the twitchy Victorian ladies pruning their roses — but there's something so much more romantic about the French section, wouldn't you say? I guess I'm getting it out of Chopin, but Esplanade makes me think of octoroon mistresses in their bustles walking the parlors. Visiting cards, a cone of sugar, the moustachioed colonel coming to call."

The others were quiet, and Leslie glanced at Tess with what looked like pity on her face.

"Oh, I'm sorry," Sinny said. "I didn't mean —"

"Oh, not to worry," Tess laughed, though she wasn't sure whether Sinny even knew what she'd meant. Now, it was Cora and Del in their parlor, sitting awkwardly in bustles, cooling themselves with reticulated ivory fans. "It's an old-fashioned word, but accurate in its way. Mixed-race, we're supposed to say now." She nodded.

"I suppose we're all an eighth something or other," John said.

"One eighth English, a quarter French, half German, one sixteenth Irish, one thirty-second Cherokee, one sixty-fourth Dutch, one one-hundred-twenty-eighth Russian, one one-hundred-twenty-eighth Scots," said Linda, folding down her fingers one by one.

"And all New Orleanian," Sinny said in triumph.

Augie had made his way back across the crowd, holding two lime-choked gin and tonics, and he shouldered across John and gave her her drink.

"All 'Creole' means, after all, is 'homegrown'," Leslie said.

Tess sipped at her drink.

The curtain drawn up around the bed quavered in the cold draft. Left the door open again, damn them, as if they didn't know there were sick men here — men like him who couldn't move their arms under the sandpaper sheets — or didn't care.

Seemed like you couldn't get the sea out of your bones. Its queasy motion and the cold of it. It wasn't the kind of sea he'd grown up on, warm and enveloping like a woman's body, like it was meant to take you in. No different from you, just separate — 98.6 and the soft sand yielding between your toes, the minnows come up to nuzzle. We were all sea creatures once, or so they said, and despite yourself you had to believe that more than a story about a snake and an apple and a flaming sword. Come up from monkeys they said. Well, *hee hee hoo.* He bared his teeth. *So what if we do.*

To disparage the body, though, was to misunderstand it. How your blood slows to keep you ticking while you wait, tied up in a piece of floating something in the gray sea. How it keeps on ticking, patient as a clock. Patient, patient. Better than to sink whole to the bottom of the ocean. Some of them did that too.

A patient patient. That was what he was. Harbor the mind in the ticking body. *Get yourself good and strong first, and then we'll see to your going home,* said that little girl in the starched cap standing straight like a soldier. Didn't mind holding the metal pan for the doctor, didn't mind the ping-pinging of shrapnel on the pan. When she came through the curtains there was never blood on her frock; she was impervious, like the cold accent of England. An island nation and defensible. He had tried telling her about New Orleans, how it was essentially an island too, ringed by the lake and the river and the swamps. How Sylvia was waiting at home for him, patient, patient. He kept dreaming about her tearing out dropped stitches in her knitting. He'd received a letter saying yes. He'd built that chest from cypress so it could sink if it had to, down to the bottom of the sea, and still hold tight, hold water like a contract, like a vow, which must be what they understood, why they pulled the curtain around the bed and talked in whispers. But the draft did rankle.

Del stood at the edge of the cabin steps and watched her father's taillights as he drove to spend the night in the hospital, the rain-washed shells crunching under his tires. With all the lights off, it was dark the way only the country can be dark. Low clouds still veiled the stars, and now that the trees were gone she could see off in the distance the orange fairy lights of the strip malls nestled up against the 190. Someone had lit a wood fire somewhere, but the smell only made her feel colder and more alone.

She slipped the key into the lock and went into the house, pulled the singed sculpture of her mother out of her sweatshirt pouch, pulled the hoodie over her head. A stained mug, half-full of coffee, sat in the middle of the table, and the bread was still out on the board. She wrapped up the bread, loaded the dishwasher with the dirty breakfast dishes her father had left in the sink, called for a pizza, and went to build a fire in the hearth.

As she rearranged the logs piled in the grate, something clattered down into the back of the firebox, and she reached back and withdrew it — a carving of a magnolia cone, made of cypress. She looked over her shoulder. The rag rug under the hope chest was littered with wood shavings, and the patina had a new broad wound gouged in it, the product, she figured, of Papie's delirious episode. Del sighed and turned around on her knees, trying to line up the broken-off carving with the leaves and petals on the chest, but she could not find where it belonged. Papie had not simply hacked into the chest this time as he had done in Houston; he had cut deeply down into the wood and begun roughing out a trinity of flowers: a closed bud, an open blossom, a more delicate seeded cone. Even sketched as they were, she could see that they were better, the work of a mature craftsman, not the apprentice he had been when he built the chest.

Del got up and turned on the lamp. Alone in the room, she started to laugh. All day long he had tossed in the bed, mumbling about nurses and shrapnel, but he had worked down the lines of the carving here, expertly building the new figures into the contours of the old so as not to lose too much wood. She moved around the piece, looking again at the so-called damage he had done with Vin's oyster knife. The cuts were rough, but, her fingers on the carving, she could feel how he'd chipped rhythmically with the inadequate knife, incising a deeper trough along the spine of a pine bough to give it depth. The more violent cuts on one of the roses at the center of the lid had just been a first rough pass to thin out the petals, make them finer.

The chest had always been given a place of honor, first in Papie and Mamie's house and then in theirs, but that was because of its sentimental associations, not its craftsmanship. It was clearly an apprentice work — the lines rigid, the curves inelegant — and she'd bet that it had always bothered Papie, deep down, that it wasn't perfect. Mamie would never have let him touch it, any more than a decent woman would allow her husband to exchange the flawed diamond on her engagement ring for a better one, and so it had taken her dying and then his mind going, his inhibitions falling, for him to do something about it.

She pulled her sweatshirt back on, went out, and crossed the lawn to the workshop. Del had rarely been in there since her father had taken it over from Papie, and it still surprised her to smell paint and turps where she expected wood and varnish. It was too clean, no curls of planed wood on the workbenches, the windows and shelves cleared of their thin film of sawdust. There was hardly any evidence of work at all, no sketches or unsold works lying around, and now too, the high shelf that ran along the perimeter of the shop that had been filled with sculptures of her mother was empty. Uncharacteristically, her father had left his sketchbook lying on a sawhorse at the side of the room. It was wrong of her, she knew, but she opened the book and flipped through it, past the pages covered in pencil drawings and phrases — *degradable matter, renaissant image* — underlined and circled and inscribed in boxes, until she reached a page dated *8.28.05*. There, he'd drawn a picture of the hurricane as a serpent eating its tail. On the next page, undated, were the

569

words *vortex,* then, beneath it *vertex,* crossed out, then, in a double-bordered blue ink box, what she made out as *barometric pressure/ things spin apart/ the center will not hold. There is no center.* He had dated the following page *9.1.05* and written, beside the date *reentry* but there was nothing underneath it, and nothing on the pages that followed but a phone number for someone named Roland written in a different pen.

She closed the book and put it back on the sawhorse, shifting it into the angle at which she thought it had been lying. Out on the road, a car passed, and its headlights lit up the window and the Windex streaks on it, the long dull rectangles where something had been affixed to the glass with Scotch tape.

Papie's lathe, though, was still on one of the workbenches, as was his table saw. His chisels and hammers and vises hung within their Marks-A-Lot outlines on the particle board. There was also wood, she realized. Enormous quantities of newly cut old-growth pine.

FIFTY-EIGHT DAYS
AFTER LANDFALL
OCTOBER 26

Cora sat in the passenger seat of Troy's used Dodge, her head down between her knees, running her thumb up and down the bandage the EMTs had taped over the laceration on her shin. Troy hummed as he drove, and through her eyelids, the blue light of the tow truck strobed as it dragged her Jeep, its front axle broken, ahead of them down the frost-edged road. It was all over now — the cops would have called in the license plate and the NOPD would be at her mother's door before the end of the day. She had cash still — she'd only spent $400 of the ten grand from her stash — but it was in the backseat of the Jeep, and if she didn't want to be dragged back home or, worse, to DePaul, within forty-eight hours, she would have to break loose now and run to the highway, hitchhike to someplace she could spend the night, far enough away from here they couldn't find her. She could find a little cave out in the forest, maybe, fend for herself like the island girl. She tried the door handle. It was locked, but Troy's arm came hard against her.

Troy stopped humming and moved his hand around the back of her neck. "You're safe now, Cora. Leave it be."

She shook her head, and it felt as though her brain was rattling inside her skull. She had hit her temple against the window in the crash. Hadn't put her seatbelt on. Just trying to get away.

"I tell you they had me spooked," Troy was saying, "Mrs. Fuscht saying she thought Reyna was there, talking to Tyrone. I mean I know the cops called me saying they'd identified her remains in the fire, but I'm getting to be like Bea and her paranoias."

She pressed her forehead against the freezing window. "Please stop lying."

"Lying to who? How?"

She shook her head, gently, gently, the skin of her brow stretching on the glass. "I know she's dead. I know I killed her."

"What are you talking about?"

"Stop fucking lying to me!" she shouted, made her head ring.

"You think you killed Reyna?"

"I shot her," Cora said. "She's dead."

"Birdshot in her leg. You got me too.

Wanna see?"

He was rolling up his sleeve, and so she closed her eyes. She should have kept running, but her body had quit on her. She'd just sat in the frozen grass looking at the fence of the schoolyard as if she'd fallen out of the sky. She had let them shine their light in her eyes, tap at the veins on the inside of her elbow. *She's going to be alright,* they said, and for some reason, she hadn't argued, she had just let them help. She'd watched obediently as the point of light moved back and forth across her face, watched the Jeep crawl slowly from the ditch, and she touched her ankles, her shins, her knees, thighs, hips, ran her hands up her abdomen, over her ribs, her breasts, along the bones of her arms, pushed her fingers into her hair and felt where the bones of her skull had fused, and thought *I am all here. I am still here. Where is this that I am?*

She opened her eyes and looked at Troy's arm, the flesh of it pocked pink in six places. Looked at his face — his flat nose in profile, the thin chain gleaming against his neck.

"You have to try, you want to kill somebody with birdshot. You have to at least aim."

573

She shook her head. "I shot her. She's dead."

"You shot the ceiling. I drove her to the medic tent. Learnt a new word: 'Syncope.' They sent her someplace else — I got bills I can show you that they sent me a week and a half ago, thanks — how they pulled the birdshot out of her, filled her up on drugs, and set her loose again."

"She's dead." The heater blew its mildewed breath onto her neck, but cold was leaking through the window and the seams of the door. "She came to the house, looking for them. There were lights. I saw her eyes."

"Ghosts. Right." Troy rolled his eyes, laughed, a little sadly. "You sound like one of those tourist mule drivers, you know that? Ghosts." He pointed to a tree in a nearby yard, its branches decorated with toilet paper streamers and polyester cobwebs. "You want me to tell you what I know happened? She got loose from the medics, and she went straight back to you to get her children, and when she didn't find them, she took your granddaddy's gun instead and carried it to my house, and, when she still didn't find them, she took her life. Your mama told me that gun went missing, and I didn't want to say but I knew where it had gone."

"How do you know that? How could you know?"

"You found the gun, right, Cora?"

"Yes."

"Where did you find the gun?"

"With her."

"Where?"

"At your house."

"And did you go to my house, before I asked you to? After I gave you the gun back to protect yourself with?"

"No."

"So, how did it get there, then, if Reyna — as you say — was dead all along?" Troy shook his head. "Ghosts can't carry guns, baby — not as far as I know." He chuckled once, sadly.

She closed her eyes, saw the gun on the tin floor of the upper gallery. Saw the lights in the house — a flashlight beam ascending.

"She only wanted her boys back, you know, Cora. That's all she wanted. But we didn't understand her, and she didn't understand us." Troy breathed out slowly through his nose. "And you know, I would have welcomed that — her taking them back — if I thought she could. If I thought 'back' meant back to the little house she had for a little while off LaSalle Street, where they used to sit out and watch the Indians go by in their suits. If I thought 'back' meant to the East, to Darryl's house, where he was teaching Willy about the Mississippi, saying he was going to see about adopting him once he and Reyna got married, making him his river-pilot next-in-line. Even if I thought 'back' meant Calliope. But none of us can go back there anymore, can we."

Cora heard the woman wailing in the garden. A living woman with a living grief. But Reyna had not found her children. Instead she found a gun, and she took it with her away from the house where her children were not, to the place where she'd last been with them.

Cora took her head off the cold window, and the pain went back to hammering at her temples. Up ahead, a sign hung above a garage: HARMS AUTO BODY. The Jeep bounced in a clash of chains into the driveway. *Tick-tock, tick-tock*, the blinker said, like a clock. Soon they would sit her down in a brown chair and take her keys away. Soon there would be no way to keep running. She sat back up and buckled the seatbelt.

"You believe me now?" Troy said. "She ended her own life, Cora. She'd been heading that way for years. The blessing is only that she didn't take anybody else with her."

"I'm sorry," she said. "I'm so sorry."

"It's not for you to be sorry."

Cora let herself cry, and Troy reached out and put a hand on her upper arm.

"She was your sister," Cora said. "She was their mother. She was beautiful." Cora saw her again at the wheel of Darryl's car, her face golden in the wash of the traffic lights and high-boned like a goddess's, laughing. "She was so beautiful."

WEDNESDAY
NOVEMBER 2

The ride from the airport seemed to take forever. The interstate was congested, and the cab driver kept stopping and starting abruptly, hitting the gas or the brake hard enough to make the cherry-scented Christmas tree dangling from the rearview swing like a censer. Tess had to dig her fingernails into her thighs to keep from throwing up. She wanted to roll her window down, but outside the day was biting, ice-blue. Frozen grass blanketed the hilled margins of the highways, and the bare, dark-skinned trees dragged their claws across the blanched morning sky.

The taxi driver hadn't said a word since she'd gotten in. He just turned off of one highway and onto the next. Supposedly, he knew where he was going. She kept looking for Rome on the mileage signs without finding it. *Rome, Illinois* — it seemed like a joke, that name.

Once they had turned off the highway, though, the house came up quickly — a dark gray thing huddling behind its garage as if for warmth. Tess paid the driver and let him pull her suitcase from the trunk. After he drove off, she stood for a moment on the empty sidewalk, taking deep breaths of frost into her lungs. The cold penetrated her cloth coat, coming up out of the sidewalk and through the soles of her shoes. In the square windows of the house, the lights were on, and the smell of wood smoke sifted down through the air. She went up the walkway under the naked arms of a maple tree and bumped her suitcase up onto the stoop. Before she could ring the bell, the door swung open. Heat gusted out, and two little boys crowded out around her legs.

"We made you a picture!" said the little one, only thigh high. He looked up at her with eyes that shone like granite, while the older boy clutched a piece of orange construction paper to his chest, not speaking.

"Show her the picture!" The little one elbowed his brother in the chest until he held it up: a crayon drawing of a rectangular building impaled by a sideways tree, captioned *ANT TESS s HOUSE.*

"Tyrone drawed it," said the little one. "She says you're getting it fixed. She says nobody can stay there anymore."

"Don't let all the hot air out, boys!" It was Cora's voice, though there was no one visible in the front rooms, not at the long table or on the flowered couch. Tess reached down and took the drawing, and as the smell of coffee and cinnamon rushed at her, Cora came through into the dining room, drying her hands on a dish towel.

"Mom."

She had stopped on the other side of the doorway. Tess went to her, hugged her — the heavy little boy wrapping himself around her leg like a bear cub at the same time. There was already a little bit of meat on her daughter's bones; she felt solid again.

The older boy had his fingers clenched around Cora's thumb, and she smiled down at him.

"This is Tyrone, Mom, if they didn't introduce themselves. And Willy." She rubbed the little one's head.

She's doing fine now, Troy had told her on the phone, by way of explaining why he'd waited so long to call. Tess had interpreted that in many ways as she'd booked her tickets, packed her bag, waited in the security line, braced herself for landing: Cora fine but still in bed. Cora fine but curled up in a recliner and sucking her hair.

With Cora, "fine" meant trying to function. She never succeeded quite.

But now Cora was smiling down at the pair of children she'd fished up out of the flood, a rose-tinged bloom in her cheeks. She had flour on her pants, and one glossy clavicle jutted from the stretched collar of her sweatshirt. The purple had gone from underneath her eyes, and she stood squarely with her feet sunk in the carpet, holding the bigger boy by the hand.

"You look marvelous." Tess reached out and touched her daughter's cheek. "Are you —You're seeing somebody up here?"

"Tyrone." Cora jiggled the boy's hand. "Why don't you and Willy go up to my room and watch some cartoons?"

Willy released Cora's leg, and he and Tyrone ran off up the stairs.

Cora shook her head. "Alice gave me a number if I need it. But I'm doing all right."

"Cora," Tess started. She had a whole speech planned. She was going to pull up a chair beside the bed, take her daughter's limp hand, and try to revise all of those maternal lectures she'd given her since she was a girl, about death and love and what you could hope for, what you should expect out of life. But Cora was looking at her placidly now — Tess had forgotten that she

581

was so tall — and it seemed that they had traded places, and Tess was at a loss for words.

"Mom." Cora took her wrist and led her to the sofa. "I'm sorry about what I've done to you. I've been selfish —"

Tess swallowed, shook her head. "No, honey. You haven't been selfish. You've been sick."

Cora shook her head.

Tess scrabbled for her hands, held them, and looked hard into Cora's eyes. "Yes, honey. Yes, you have been sick. But it's alright. We can get you help."

Cora took her hands back. "If you want to call it sick — if you want me to say I'll get help if I get that way again — then yes, sure, I'll get help. But it doesn't help me to think of it as a sickness." She turned her face towards the windows, to the curtains open to the day. "It doesn't help me to believe I don't have control, even if I don't. It doesn't help to look away, to pretend that it's all okay, that you can ignore it. That's what got us into this mess, isn't it? Pretending everything was fine. Pretending the levees could protect us, that the storms wouldn't come."

"Oh, honey. I am so sorry," Tess said. She was picking at her nails, she realized — always dirty now that the work on the house had started. She put her hands in her pockets. "We never should have left you. We abandoned you."

"No," Cora said. "I chose to stay. And now I've chosen to leave. What happened there, after —" She paused, looking to the stairs, where the *Looney Tunes* theme song drifted faintly from the upper rooms.

"You don't have to talk about it, honey, if you don't want to. I know about Reyna. I know how sick she was. I know the house burned down."

"I can tell you," Cora said. "If you want to hear."

It almost sounded like a dare. Tess looked at her, trying to read from her face whether she actually wanted to talk, whether she needed to. She didn't think she could stand to hear more than what Troy had told her. A mother off her meds in a disaster. Traumatized children. A shotgun. A silence. She had gone back to the house on Esplanade to look at the pockmarks on the upstairs ceiling where the birdshot had entered the plaster. She had seen the bloody water stain on the floor that Troy said came from a wound in his arm. Troy had said that Reyna was only unconscious when he brought her to the Red Cross. She wanted to believe it. Cora looked at her patiently, her eyes open, her face wide.

"That's alright," Tess said.

Cora nodded. "Okay. But you have to understand that with what I experienced — I need to stay away for a while."

Tess curled her fingers up around Cora's, nodded. "I understand. It's completely normal, actually. But I want you to come back, honey. Where we can get you treated for PTSD, where I can take care of you. I can see that you feel good right now. I know this —" She swept her hand around the room, at the upright piano and the saccharine paintings of dogs and flowers and the fire going in the fireplace. "You're comfortable here. They're taking good care of you. But pretending —"

She stopped herself. She'd been going to say that Cora needed to face reality, that running away solved nothing, but she realized in time that that was exactly what Cora had been saying. Evacuation — wasn't that how all this had started?

"I wish you'd let me look after you. You know — I told you on the phone that I'm staying at Augie's now. You could have the bedroom you slept in when you were there with Mrs. Randsell. Didn't you say yourself that it was like heaven? Imagine how nice it is now, with the air-conditioning on. Fall has come, and it is so beautiful just to sit in the garden."

Cora shook her head.

"At least find someone to talk to, honey. It's hard to work through a trauma alone."

"I'm not alone."

"No, that's right." She listened through the ceiling to the boys rearranging themselves on the second floor. "You enjoy babysitting the children?"

Cora smiled again, narrowed her eyes at her, then put her hands on her thighs and stood up. "I've got cooking to do," she said. "You'll come?"

Joe wished Del had come with him for this. Last time he had had everyone there. Tess had done all the talking while Sister Cecelia tapped her pen against the edge of her old oak desk. Then, it had been inevitable, like stepping onto a moving sidewalk in an airport. Once you'd taken the first step, you weren't getting off until you'd reached the end.

All he could see now were exits. They were clearly marked over each doorway, red glowing signs that jarred in the context of pink upholstery and romantic still lifes. The management tried hard to hide the institutional nature of the place; in the front hall, an old woman sang along with a therapist at the flower-bedecked grand piano, but there was no escaping fire codes, or nurses, for that matter, or the smells of industrially prepared food and urine and bleach.

The receptionist looked at him, kindly, from across the desk. "Sorry it's taking a while. You know how it goes — start the day off on the wrong foot and it's hard to get right again."

He nodded.

"Can I get you something? Water? A Coke?"

He could still taste that morning's eggs in his mouth. "I am a little thirsty, thank you."

She stood and tugged at the miniskirt she was wearing under her sweater set.

"Just a little water would be nice."

The receptionist shuffled down the long tiled hall. The noise of the place seemed to get louder once he was alone. Television voices argued in the long succession of rooms. Wheelchairs squeaked on floorboards. Nurses chattered. A microwave hummed and beeped. Beside the door to the director's office, a grandfather clock swept away the seconds with its long brass pendulum, beat after steady beat. His heart was good. Actually, Mark had teased him about it at his last physical, saying that if

Joe was the only person in the city who didn't need Lipitor, he must be doing something wrong. His father's heart was good too, and his maternal grandmother had lived to be one hundred and three. He had thirty years left in him then, given the state of modern medicine and provided he wasn't broadsided on the bridge and sent over into the drink. Thirty years was a long time, as long as he and Tess had been married, as long as he'd lived before he'd gotten his first show. There was enough time in thirty years to build something, fix something, become something, destroy something. Enough time to do it over again.

And he would have to do it again. This would force his hand. No other reason to be here, sacrifice his father's happiness, pay them money he didn't have. He would exercise his power of attorney and sell the cabin and the trees, he supposed — property that had been in their family for nearly two hundred years. He wouldn't get any trouble from Vin. Vin would be overjoyed to see the land parceled into lots, developed; he would probably buy himself a new truck, pay off the kids' student loans. Meanwhile, with his birthright, Joe could buy a derelict little house somewhere to fix up, in the Marigny maybe, but he'd be willing to go farther out.

Something with slaves' quarters behind it which he could ream out like a juice orange and use for a studio. Driving over, he had felt the ghost of Tess sitting in the passenger seat, nodding her approval. *It's the best thing for all involved.*

The receptionist came back with the water in a Mardi Gras cup incised with a drawing of the Greek Revival plantation home that served as the facility's main building. The eponymous "Belle Maison." He took a sip and watched her bend over to peek through the director's door.

She turned around, nodding. "He's ready for you now."

Joe got up, watching the water in his cup tremble.

The director looked up from a file as Joe walked in, adjusted his tortoiseshell glasses. "Lewy Body, I hear." He extended his hand, and Joe shook it. "Please, take a seat."

Joe sat.

"That's a rough one, isn't it." The director hiked up his slacks and sat down again behind his desk. "Worst of both worlds — Parkinson's and Alzheimer's — and then there are the periods of lucidity that show up just to throw you off your game."

"We treasure them, actually," Joe said,

though he was relieved not to have to explain.

"Certainly. It can be a relief, but I personally find it unsettling, like seeing a ghost."

"He's not dead yet."

"I think we're getting off on the wrong foot, here." The director chortled, his dyed hair shifting on his scalp. "I just meant to reassure you that we do understand your situation — I know it was a concern of yours. But we know this disease. Our staff is fully trained to deal with all of the disorders the elderly face. There'll be no Valium here." He waggled his finger as if Joe had requested a personal dose. "And no restraints, never restraints. We are all about calm understanding and compassion. Those are our bywords. Our job is to give you the peace of mind of knowing that your father is comfortable and cared for somewhere he may come to call home."

"I don't think that's going to happen."

The director shook his head. "I assure you it can happen. I'm not saying the transition is an easy one, but being with peers, having every need met — it can go a long way."

Joe was shaking his head. "He doesn't even feel at home in the house he grew up in, with his family all around him. *I want to go home, I want to go home.* And you can

589

drive him around, make a big show of arriving, show him his room, his dentures, but it's still a big show, isn't it. It's all a trick."

"That's the paranoia," the director said gently. "The search for home, it's very common. And then, for some, there are the hallucinations — of loved ones, sometimes, who appear only to vanish again. It's heartbreaking. But I truly think it's harder for the caregiver than it is for the patient. They forget; it's you who remembers. And sometimes, a separation can be healing. Away from the pain of those who love them, away from the anxiety — you'd be surprised at the improvement."

Joe sighed and shook his head. That was where they seemed to be headed: Divorce. Departure. Separation. Tess flying off to collect their missing daughter, bullheaded and alone. They had all gotten so far from one another, and it filled him with a terror of the same sort he'd felt watching John Glenn being launched into space on the grainy little TV in his parents' den. He'd imagined the tight little box being soldered shut around him, the fast acceleration as the man was flung, flaming, into the sky where no one was and no one could reach him, where, if something failed, even help could not go, where, if something failed, he would remain alone until his food ran out, or his air, from where there was absolutely no chance of coming home.

"Getting them set in new routines can help as well. Your father was a carpenter?"

"A cabinetmaker."

"If he wishes to, he can sign up for crafts classes. Work with his hands."

Friendship bracelets, the man meant. They'd have Vincent Boisdoré making elastic-band pot holders and "stained glass windows" out of Popsicle sticks and paste. Joe saw his father working to thread beads on a string. Saw his hands start to tremble, the beads fly, skittering across the floor.

"This isn't going to work," Joe said, making to stand.

"Now, wait —" The director stood up in a crouch, his hand out, quelling the air. "Please. Let's take a step back. Your instinct to come to us was a good one. You need a respite, you said, and your father needs more care than you can provide. Has this changed?"

Joe sat back down and looked through the window. Out on the lawn, old folks were sitting with their aids around a pond. A reflection of the pink plantation house wavered on the surface of the water, bathing their faces in rose-colored light. Old men were walking out among the beds of red flowers, while one of the therapists played guitar. Joe watched a woman lift her hand to catch a golden leaf as it drifted down from a towering gingko.

"You notice our tree?" the director said. "Being from Tucson, I hadn't encountered one before. Living fossils they call them. Their longevity is phenomenal. Several even survived the A-bomb at Hiroshima. And of course, there is some evidence to support the belief that their seeds support memory and cognitive function. I see it as a kind of mascot for the place."

Joe nodded as the tree tossed its golden mane.

"Obviously it is your choice," the director said. "But I must tell you that I do believe your father would do well here. The best way to honor him is to live your own life."

"That's what everyone says."

The old woman held the leaf in front of her face as if she were reading the veins.

"Alright." Joe sat back down in his chair. "Alright."

Del walked along the wire fence that separated the property from the spread next door, where Sol was driving his four-wheeler between the cattle pastures. The strong wind that had been blowing since morning had pushed drifts of pine straw against the chicken wire, and she kicked at the piles, watching the breeze toy with the twigs and needles. She felt jittery, overcaffeinated, and she kept glancing back at Papie on the screen porch whittling at one of the Tess sculptures she'd rescued from the burn pile. Every so often the breeze brought her the sound of his knife. She felt like she was waiting for something — that there was something she needed to remember or to know.

She was almost to the dead pecan when, for no reason, she decided to run. She sprinted, leapt over a log, caught her foot on something and landed in the sand and pine needles on the other side. Her scraped hands burned. She brought them up to her face and turned over, pillowed her head on her arms and lay there, listening to the blood throb in her veins.

She had come through something, she realized. Her mother hadn't let her go with her to find Cora, but Cora had been found. All the fires had died down. Everything moved on, and no matter how you tried to stop it, the earth kept spinning in the infinite sky. Above her, the pecan towered, its broken trunk stabbing at the clouds like the tip of a shivered lance. Suddenly, the wind began to gust, but rather than being shaken by it, the limbless tree stood steadily while the sky vibrated around it.

She thought of the little figure of Fuji wrapped inside the giant wave, the column of water rigid around the leaping carp. That was the sort of thing she would make when she got down to work, she realized, if she could somehow translate it into furniture. It wouldn't be Art Nouveau or Arts & Crafts, not Majorelle, not Mallard, not Theodule or Homer or Vincent Boisdoré. She would not bend chaos around structure, nor make structure out of chaos. She wouldn't make armoires shaped by symmetrical whiplash vines, nor shape pine boughs around the four posts of a bed. She wasn't sure how she would do it, but there would be more tension, a hint of threat, petrified and polished. Neither nature nor structure, in the end, could win.

She scooted herself up and combed her fingers through her hair. On the other side of the fence, the cattle, lying down, had matted the weeds in the pasture in beautiful, complicated patterns. She took her notebook out of her sweatshirt pocket and began to sketch, and she kept drawing until she heard Papie stand up from the rocking chair. The porch light went on. A flock of birds came tumbling in from the north, fighting for headway, wings folded, wings open, dipping, rising, circling each other. A clutch of them alit on the top of the pecan, then took off again, black darts against the sky.

Tess watched Cora move around the kitchen as she peeled vegetables, tied herbs together with string. On the worn table was her prep list, the menu of celeriac soup, roasted beet and parsnip salad, osso bucco with risotto and parsley root gremolata, broken into its component parts: *chop mise, simmer stock, roast veg, sear off shanks.* Cora kept the fingers of her left hand bunched as her right hand, thumb and fore-knuckle around the blade of her chef's knife, chopped carrot at a blistering pace, and when Troy came back from work, she held out a taste of vinaigrette to him, her hand cupped under the spoon. *She seems inhabited* were the words Tess kept thinking. She had been vacant in New Orleans, but now she had returned to herself, and this time, it wasn't the way summer tenants return, throwing their suitcases on the beds and tracking sand into the floors; her actions were considered, careful, as though she were planning to stay. She bruised the thyme between her fingers and smelled it. She pulled the mitts on before opening the oven, and when she opened the lid of the big earthenware casserole, she leaned back away from the rich, wine-drenched steam.

Troy went into the dining room to set the table, and Tess followed him, took the silverware, and went around behind him as he put down the napkins, the wineglasses.

"Is she taking medication?" she said quietly, as she heard the oven open and a racket resumed in the kitchen.

He looked over his shoulder. "Not that I know about. But I don't pry."

Tess nodded. She placed a fork and a salad fork on top of a folded maroon napkin.

"I didn't expect," Troy continued. "When they called from the school, I thought this was going to be temporary. I was just glad I could help out, but how she'd be —" He put down two wineglasses at once, distracted, off-kilter. "I expected bad, but what she was was just strange, like a shipwrecked Martian, thinks they're never going to see another soul again. Then, just like that —" He snapped his fingers. "— she stopped being strange, stopped being anything. We drive up here, I walk her up to the door, holding her arm so she won't fall down, and the kids rush out to hug her, Bea gives her a glass of milk and a piece of fruit, and all of a sudden, she's back in the land of the living."

Tess nodded. "What do you think changed?"

"You know, when we talked on the phone —" Troy paused, his pink tongue sliding out over his upper lip. "I know you're meaning to take her back to New Orleans with you, but I don't think she's going to want to go. She's looking for work here."

"Yes," Tess said. "She told me she was planning to stay."

"There's the boys to think about too — they take to her. And they need all the people they can get, seeing as how their mama's not coming back."

"Have you told them?"

Troy put down the final two glasses and looked at them, adjusted their placement on the tablecloth. "I think Tyrone knows."

"You do have to tell them, Troy. There is nothing harder. Very little that's harder than that. But they need to know."

"I know."

"Well." Tess sighed. "At least she let me come."

"Yes. I was as surprised as you."

"I already called the airline." She lay down the last knife and straightened herself up.

"I'm going back tonight. I don't think I'm helping here."

"Alright." Troy nodded. Behind him, dusk was drawing closed across the front windows of the house.

"Need and want are two different things." Cora had her elbow on the swinging door and a tart shellacked in rose-colored syrup balanced on her hands. She took another step into the dining room and the door batted closed behind her.

Tess turned to her. "Do you want me to stay?"

Cora bent down to put the tart on the buffet, her small bosom pressing into her blouse.

"Do you want to?" She dropped her hair out of its rubber band, did it up again, reached out and plucked a pomegranate seed from the top of the tart and put it in her mouth, cracked it between her molars. For a second, Tess thought she was looking at her twelve-year-old daughter, before the troubles had descended upon them, before anything like this had seemed like a possibility. And wasn't this what she had wanted for her, even then? A good man. Children. Happiness. But safety wasn't guaranteed anywhere. She would have to remind her of that before she left — that happiness, no matter how permanent it seemed, was not something created once but made every day on a thousand different occasions when its opposite might also come to be.

"I do want to," she said to Cora. "But, now I've seen how well you are, there's so much to take care of. They're just starting on the house, and I've got the claim to do, and we've got to get our things into storage before Laura and Dan come home."

Cora nodded.

"But I'll be back up soon? I can bring you some things. Silver? Would you like the silver? Or furniture? Surely you'll end up finding your own place to live. Del and I could come up in a van."

Cora smiled. In the kitchen, the side door opened, bells clacking against the window-pane, and the boys shouldered in in their boots and puffy jackets.

"It's snowing," they yelled, tromping across the kitchen like a herd of elephants.

"I told you take those boots off before you track mud on my rug," Bea said, brooding after them.

"We don't need a lot, Mom," Cora said. "But I appreciate the offer."

"We do appreciate it," Troy said.

"You heard us? It's snowing!" Willy took

Tess by the hand and pulled her through the dining room, across the foyer, and through the front door.

It was getting dark out, though it was only four in the afternoon. A blue streetlight shone at the end of the driveway, and flakes of snow spun through it. Willy yanked her down onto the front lawn, and the wind bit through her blouse. Willy, in his fat coat and hat, tilted his face up, stuck out his hands, twirling off down the path. Snowflakes landed, heavy and wet, in her hair, and when she'd reached the end of the driveway, she turned around and looked back at the house, where Cora and Tyrone stood watching through the living room windows, the fire flickering behind them.

Hibernation, she thought. The bears had it right. Some seasons, we would be better off spending curled in our subterranean burrows. But we never did. Instead, like wolves, we scratched at the frozen carcass of the earth, wound our gaunt bodies through the maze of ice-hung trees, looking out for anything that moved, the remembered taste of hot blood in our mouths. The sleeping ones, we pulled on their hands, saying *Get up. Get up! Come suffer!*

Tess nodded to herself. She had had it all wrong.

"Is that supposed to be some sort of joke?"

Del, sitting on the newspaper she'd laid out around the hope chest, looked up at her father, silhouetted in the bright doorframe. He was wearing pressed chinos and a striped button-down, and he pointed across the room with a rolled sheaf of papers. She followed the line of his pointing — the Tess Papie had been whittling at was sitting on the side table, wrapped in a toilet-paper wedding gown.

"Papie," she said.

He nodded, his mouth a hard line, and moved across the room, picked up the little sculpture and held her in two hands like something small and helpless, an injured bird or a blind newborn puppy, and laid his thumbs over her eyes.

In the hall bathroom, the toilet flushed.

"Well." Joe held the Lonely Tess out to her, pulling the toilet paper off with one hand. "She is your mother. But I'd rather not have them shoved in my face."

Papie ambled out of the bathroom, his pants still undone, and her father hurried up to him, zipped his fly, buckled his belt.

"I think we've been in England today. The

601

war hospital, I guess?" Del said.

Her grandfather shuffled sideways back to his chair beside the hope chest and picked up the sanding block he'd been using on the new pine bow, not looking at either of them. "But it doesn't matter. He's been working."

"He's not going to get any better, you know, honey. In fact, he's bound to get worse. If the infection comes back, and it might without professional care, he could be dead in the year from sepsis, pneumonia, any number of —"

"I know, but look," She pointed down at the rose they'd finished on the chest's lid, which stood out like a teacher's work hung on the same bulletin board with students'.

"I'm putting him in Belle Maison."

"You know, Dad, I can stay here with you. Long term. I can help you."

He nodded. "I don't want you to do that for us."

"It doesn't have anything to do with you. I want it. Me." She beat her hand on her chest. "I want to see if there's anything he can still teach me. And if there isn't, I'm going to find somebody in the city who will."

"You're staying here?" Her father laughed a little bit and shook his head. "Your life is in New York, all of your friends are in New York."

"No," she said, and it was true. The words *New York* no longer conjured the kitchen table on Sixth Street, the red-lit bars, her friends laughing. New York for her was no longer anything more than the scene from the window at Odessa where she'd watched the coverage of the storm, a park criss-crossed with fences to keep the hobos off the grass, giggling girls in flippy skirts and expensive heels, dripping trees, canvas buildings, an oil-paint sky. Prettiness had seemed valuable, once, and success, but that all seemed so superficial now — a way to survive, not a way to live.

"I thought you were going to be the president of Sotheby's." Her father had turned away from her and was looking down at Papie, who, brow knit, was running the sander rhythmically against the cypress. "Or run the Met. I thought you were going to have an office with Matisses hanging on the wall." He picked up the chisel from the ottoman, and then lay it back down again like a chess piece he'd decided not to move. "Why would you give all that up?"

Del opened her mouth to speak and realized her answer wasn't quite ready. She would have liked it explained, why she was drawn back here, as her father had been in his time, to a place that offered them nothing of practical value, a place that was so actively and so vividly falling apart. Her best answer was that she felt the need to try to fix what was clearly unfixable, to save what was already lost. But it had more to do with the water that hung in the air, the smell of old wood, the rumpus of tubas and drums drifting up from distant avenues.

"I'm going to make furniture," she said. "That's what I'm meant to do."

"Meant." Her father sighed, letting his lips flutter, his hands opening, then closing. "I signed the papers this morning. We're going admit him on Monday."

"We can take care of him here."

He shook his head. "That's not your obligation, baby girl. You're supposed to have your own family first. You're supposed to go forward before you have to go back."

She shrugged. "Back is forward. Forward is back."

"Goddamn." He chuckled. "You've got it bad, don't you. I didn't want this for you, Del. I didn't want you to sacrifice yourself to the ruins." He threw his hand around the room, over his father's head, towards the destroyed woods beyond the windows, then threw his arms into the air. "But alright. I give up."

"It's not a sacrifice," Del said. It wasn't an obligation, either. It was hardly even a choice.

She pulled her notebook out of her sweatshirt pouch and showed her father the sketches she'd made that morning: the cattle-matted grasses in Sol's pasture, the wisteria wrapped around the pecan tree's dead boughs. As he read the thing she'd scribbled about the diminishing swamp, the way the marsh grasses grew up over the water to provide the illusion of solid ground, Papie stood and came over, pushing her father aside.

"Yes, yes," Papie said, scrabbling for a pencil at the other side of the table. "That's fine, fine. We could make this line a little sharper though —" And he rubbed his eraser against the paper, penciled in a new and stronger graphite line.

Joe walked away from the house, towards the workshed, the little sculpture of Tess that Del and his father had saved from the fire in his hands. The tree frogs were chirping in what remained of the trees, and their song and the roar of the cars going by on the road were all that was in his head. You couldn't make a sculpture out of that, and yet he'd promised himself that he would go. He waded out of the moat of light that ringed the house and over the lawn, the flashlight unkindled, and the workshed shrank into the dark grass, as if it didn't want to be a party to this. He could already hear the buzz of the lights over his workbench as the night slipped through his fingers like dry sand.

He had never brought dread to his work before. He had never, as others did, allowed a deadline or a sense of duty to make him work. Fuck his professors. Fuck Quincy. Fuck Copenhagen. Even when he wasn't feeling inspired, he made sure to enter his studio with an open mind, so that, while he polished a finished piece or prepared a block of wood, the muse would be able to come like a little mouse through a crack in the walls. It was important to always have something to distract yourself from the emptiness, if that was your affliction. He was afraid that if he sat down on his stool without anything in front of him, his mind would snap shut like a trap.

The workshed loomed, a deeper darkness in the dark, and he suddenly remembered that night he and Vin had locked the dog inside of it when they were kids. The neighbors had been talking about hunting it

606

down and shooting it — a hulk of a dog that had been prowling the woods for days. They held it responsible for the carnage at a nearby pheasant coop and thought it was probably rabid, and so when he and Vin had seen it lurking in the trees, they had gotten a piece of meat from the icebox and thrown it into the shed and waited, hiding, until the dog had gone in, then locked the door behind it. They were imprisoning it for its own protection, they told their parents at dinner. The next day they would start training it, and soon enough they'd be able to parade it out, shampooed and flea-collared, to apologize for the pheasants. By the look on his father's face, though, Joe knew that wasn't going to happen. If the dog hadn't chewed up his father's tools and the couple of old chairs in the workshed yet, he would soon. Animal control would be called.

That night, lying in bed, Joe had heard the dog crying — a low keening punctuated by the sound of it throwing itself at the door — and so, after Vin had pulled the pillow over his head, he'd gotten up and gone downstairs and out across the lawn and opened the shed. The dog bolted into the trees, a dark smudge in the darkness, and two days later, the neighbor who'd lost the

pheasants came by to let them know he'd
shot it.

Now, standing against the wall of the shed
with the little ruined wooden thing in his
hands, he looked into the cleared forest,
knowing that no yellow eyes looked back.
He opened the door, flipped on the overhead, watching the dark retreat to the
corners of the room. As he put the sculpture
— his departed wife pregnant with his
departed child — on the workbench, the
two pieces of pine sounded their hollowness. How could you make art out of absence? You would not paint black canvasses,
make plaster casts of rumpled sheets or
emptied clothes. You would not make portraits out of window screen. He groped
across the table for his notebook, opened it
with its string. Perhaps you would construct
abandoned cities out of glass so that you
could see inside the beds unmade, the dinners burnt, the houseplants parched in the
unremitting sun. You could make empty
parks, empty jails, empty restaurants, their
empty tables set with hamburgers made of
ash and cups of water that trembled as
though someone had just fallen in, and as a
soundtrack, play over them sound of highways — but it was all too obvious, wasn't it?

Of course it was.

He would have to figure out, then, a way to carve holes in the air, to create a hollow chamber of such utter, intolerable blackness that the viewer would be forced to replace what was gone with whatever he had retained.

The key Augie had given her was shiny, newly cut, and she had to jiggle it a little bit to make it catch the lock. Crickets bowed in the darkness behind her, but inside Duke Ellington was playing from the speakers wired into the walls. Plates clattered in the kitchen. The icebox clapped shut. Tess bumped her suitcase up into the front hall, wheeled it to the bottom of the stairs. The chandelier was back in its place, and plaster acanthus leaves curled around in a gilded medallion.

She toed her shoes off and padded back down the rewaxed hallway and waited for a moment outside the door to the kitchen. Augie was humming to himself, sipping bourbon from a rocks glass as he drizzled sauce across a roast filet, washed his hands, took salad plates out of the Sub-Zero.

"A man after my own heart," Tess said.

Augie turned on his heel towards her, his blue eyes swimming, his cheeks a little flushed. "You may be right, Mrs. Boisdoré."

"Dr. Eshleman to you, Mr. Randsell."

She leaned over the counter and kissed him lightly. "You're too good. How did you know I'd be hungry?"

He looked at his watchless wrist. "Eight o'clock flight? You're not the kind to eat a sweaty airport sandwich for dinner."

"Maybe not. No," she laughed. "Definitely not."

"Well, how does cold roast beef, salad, French bread, and turtle soup from the Club sound?"

"You spoil me."

Augie shrugged. "Do you know how long it's been since a beautiful woman surprised me in my kitchen?"

Tess moved around the counter and plucked a piece of meat from the board, ate it, then sucked the sauce, hot with horseradish, from her fingers.

"How's Cora?"

"Fine." She shook her head. "Really well."

"Then this really is a celebration, isn't it?" He came behind her, and he took her hair, which, since the storm, had grown out almost to her shoulders, in his hands. "I'm so glad you're home."

She should have looked around at him. She should have turned, knocked his hands down, corrected him. Instead, she picked up a sweet potato from the bowl, felt the weight of it. On the narrow end, beads of blackened sugar stood out against the paper-bag skin, and she could hear Lurlee, her mother's housekeeper, saying *See there? You know it's a good one if it cried when it came out the ground.* Lurlee had smelled of sweet perfume and spray starch. She was probably dead now. At Christmas the year after she'd retired, Tess and her mother had tried to bring her a pecan pie, but no one was home at the yellow house in the Upper Ninth — she could still see her mother's white-gloved little hand rapping at Lurlee's door — and they hadn't tried again.

"I've got something else for us," Augie said. "If it's not too late for wine, of course."

"No," she said. "I don't have anywhere to be in the morning, do I?"

She listened to his footsteps retreat into the rec room, his feet leave wood for carpet, then carpet for wood again as he opened the doors to the built-in bar and crouched down in front of the wine fridge. The first time she'd ever laid eyes on Augie Randsell had been in that room; she had wandered back during a Mardi Gras party and found him sitting on the floor in a circle of Jesuit boys and Dominican girls, playing spin the bottle while a Bobby Vee record played.

When Tess looked up at her reflection now in the dark windows, she almost expected to see that shy girl in her party dress with her curled hair. But she was only herself — a thin-lipped white woman holding a sweet potato, a rigid woman, still as a statue while the gilded world streamed past.

Bottles clinked delicately as Augie pulled out the shelves, made his selection, closed the door. She settled on a barstool and swiveled around to watch him coming back through the dark room, a decanter in one hand, the bottle cradled against his chest like a baby.

He went around the island and rummaged for a corkscrew, keeping the label turned to him even as he peeled the foil off the bottle's neck.

"I felt like we deserved something special," he said.

"Something wonderful?" She raised her eyebrows at the bottle.

"Quite possibly."

"French, Italian, or American?" He and Madge had used to rent summer houses in Burgundy, Tuscany, Napa, the Loire, but she and Joe had never quite been able to afford to go along.

"A claret," he said, looking at her as he withdrew the cork, wet as a bloody towel.

Joe had always hated the way Augie insisted on calling Bordeaux "claret," the way he'd hand you a good bottle as if you'd won a prize. Now, Augie took the wine by the neck and turned it towards her — Chateau Léoville-Las-Cases 1982.

"Wow," she said.

"1982 was a beautiful year in Bordeaux." He tilted the bottle gently over the mouth of the decanter, letting the wine trickle slowly out. "The vineyards were heavy with blossom in the spring, and the summer was hot but with just enough rain to keep the vines happy without making it too easy for them. The harvest broke records. And then, when it came down to the business of drinking it —" He raised the bottle into the light to see how the sediment lay, then carefully poured the rest of the wine into the decanter. "It changed the game."

He went to the cabinet and pulled down two glasses with his long patrician hands, and she tried to turn her mind towards whatever this dinner, this bottle meant to him, his ideas on where this all might be leading. It seemed he thought they'd be able to walk, arm in arm, through the lion-surmounted arch on the wine label and onto a blooming vineyard where the weather was always fine.

He poured the Bordeaux into the tulip-shaped glasses and raised his towards her in a toast. "To better years."

"To better years," she repeated.

The wine, though, was thin and flat, almost sour; it had boiled, after the storm, in its bottle. But Augie, blinded by his hopes or his memories of what it should be, was smiling, and so she smiled too, put her nose in it. Hummed. Took another sip.

The dog was in the bed when Vincent awoke, her body curled up inside the bend of his knees, her warm body pressing against him and then easing off. There were others breathing in the room too, a concert of shallow inhalations and exhalations matched to his own, but it was too dark to see who was there. The only light in the room leaked in at the threshold, outlining the mouth of the cave.

Vincent breathed in — a crackling sound of air through water — and the others inhaled. He let his breath out in a long, slow gush, and they exhaled. Sheba, though, kept up her own rhythm, in out, in out, as even as the wash of the sea. He closed his eyes and tried to imagine it — the sea coming up on the shingle, the tide creeping in, creeping out. Beyond the cave, the sun was only just rising, and he should sleep, since there was all the time in the world and no good reason to wake: if Sheba was in bed, that meant Sylvia was gone, out to the Pass to see her sister Pauline in that little wire house that smelled of salt. If Sylvia was gone, that meant he would have spread a towel over the coverlet and lifted the old dog up in his arms to be next to him, even though it wasn't allowed, so that they could both sleep, safe and warm.

Sheba's soft back pressed up against him, then eased away.

The gulf washed up to the cave mouth, retreated.

The sea was rising. It rose every day, but all around the bed the others were standing, ready to lift him over it, to set him in his ship if the water came too high. Sylvia, his mother and father, his shipmates, Pauline, that pale-pretty English nurse. Dressed in their mourning clothes, rings taken from their fingers, handkerchiefs clasped in their hands, they watched over him, and so it would be all right if he went back to sleep. It was hot here — he was sweating — and cold at the same time, here in the rushing sea air. But Sylvia had gone to the Pass, and he had all the time in the world. The tide would come slowly up to the cave mouth, and then it would fall away, and even if it didn't, the watchers would see to it that the water did not enter while he slept. Sometime later, of course, he would wake, having slept his fill, and he and Sheba would move the stone from in front of the window and climb out onto the beach, and they would board the ship that was waiting for them and make the slow, gray passage to the far and unseen shore.

NINETY-THREE DAYS
AFTER LANDFALL
NOVEMBER 30

Cora idled the truck up the long driveway, snowflakes spinning like moths in her headlights. She thumbed a button on the sunshade, and the corrugated garage door rattled up onto the orange-lit cave, cluttered with trashcans, ladders, tools on pegs.

"Here we are," she said to herself as she did every day when she returned from work at the sandwich shop, like a promise, an incantation. "Here we are."

The smell of onions, bacon, green peppers frying filled the truck, and she breathed in and lowered herself onto the ground. Inside the house, she could hear the boys running. Bea was yelling for them to wait, not just swarm out at her like a mess of wasps, and Cora could see them already in their collared shirts and uniform pants, she could smell Tyrone's hair as she held him in her lap in front of the TV, Troy's hand in her hand. But she felt uncertain, suddenly, unsure that it was real. She turned around, looking out through the open garage door at the driveway, at the leaf-strewn yard and the bare branches of the tree, the empty street.

She cast around for a second in the chill air, waiting for it to fill her up with something, some dread, some memory, waiting for it to wind itself around her, but the air was still, light, not weighted down with the smells of far-off bodies dancing in low, close rooms or of swamp plants rising huge out of the fertile soil. At the end of the driveway, the tree held the full moon by the tips of its golden branches; even after fading away to nothing, it was possible to creep back to wholeness by small degrees of illumination. Up in the tree's crotch, a little dun-colored bird with an axe-shaped head and red wing-tips was settling herself down into a nest of leaves, and Cora turned around to see the boys coming down out of the warm house towards her, Willy first.

"You're home, you're home, you're home!" Willy was saying, his breath coming in dense white clouds.

She crouched down to them and opened up her arms, let them rush over her, let herself be pushed under by their kicking legs and little riotous hands.

"Yes," she said. "I'm home."

618

ABOUT THE AUTHOR

C. Morgan Babst studied writing at NOCCA, Yale, and N.Y.U. Her essays and short fiction have appeared in such journals as *The Oxford American, Guernica,* the *Harvard Review, LitHub,* the *New Orleans Review,* and her piece, 'Death Is a Way to Be,' was honored as a Notable Essay in *Best American Essays 2016.* She evacuated New Orleans one day before Hurricane Katrina made landfall. After eleven years in New York, she now lives in New Orleans with her husband and child.

The employees of Thorndike Press hope you have enjoyed this Large Print book. All our Thorndike, Wheeler, and Kennebec Large Print titles are designed for easy reading, and all our books are made to last. Other Thorndike Press Large Print books are available at your library, through selected bookstores, or directly from us.

For information about titles, please call:
(800) 223-1244

or visit our website at:
gale.com/thorndike

To share your comments, please write:
Publisher
Thorndike Press
10 Water St., Suite 310
Waterville, ME 04901